GIRL TROUBLE

GIRL TROUBLE

STORIES

Holly Goddard Jones

HARPER PERENNIAL

NEW YORK • LONDON • TORONTO • SYDNEY • NEW DELHI • AUCKLAND

Jon

HARPER ● PERENNIAL

These stories first appeared in slightly different form in the following publications: *The Southern Review* and *New Madrid* ("Good Girl"), *The Kenyon Review* and *New Stories from the South: The Year's Best, 2007* ("Life Expectancy"), *The Hudson Review* ("Parts"), *Shenandoah* ("Allegory of a Cave"), *Epoch* ("An Upright Man"), *The Gettysburg Review* and *New Stories from the South: The Year's Best, 2008* ("Theory of Realty"), *The Kenyon Review* ("Retrospective"), *Epoch* and *Best American Mystery Stories 2008* ("Proof of God").

FIRST EDITION

Designed by Justin Dodd

Library of Congress Cataloging-in-Publication Data is available upon request.

ISBN 978-0-06-177630-4

09 10 11 12 13 OV/RRD 10 9 8 7 6 5 4 3 2 1

For Brandon and my father:
two good men

Women are never virgins. Purity is a negative state and therefore contrary to nature.

—William Faulkner, *The Sound and the Fury*

• CONTENTS •

GIRL TROUBLE

· GOOD GIRL ·

A year before Jacob's son, Tommy, was arrested for raping a fifteen-year-old girl, the police chief came to his shop about the dog. Tommy's dog—a pit bull bitch. Tommy had brought her home the week he graduated from high school, a pup in an old Nike shoe box, eyes just opened. And Jacob had said, "You're not bringing that dog here," but he soon gave in, letting his son keep her on a blanket in the toolshed; weeks later he said, "You're not bringing that dog in the house," but he gave in on that, too, and the dog started sleeping on the living room couch, the same spot where his wife, Nora, had liked sitting when she was alive.

The one thing he'd held firm on, he thought at the time, was the treatment of the animal. Tommy wanted her mean, wanted to beat her and chain her to weights and mix gunpowder into her dog food. Now Jacob wasn't one of those animal rights nut-jobs, and he'd never really liked dogs, or any kind of pet, for that matter—always had to scrub his hands clean after petting one, and even then he'd go to bed sure that fleas and ticks were crawling all over him, setting up camp in the graying curly hairs of his underarms or groin. But he was softer in his middle age than he'd once been—less casual about life since Nora's passing—and he wouldn't stand back while the poor animal was tortured, made crazy by one of his son's misguided whims. So he'd stood his ground. He started feeding her when he noticed Tommy was forgetting to, scratching her belly when Tommy was gone and she seemed slow and disconsolate, and at some point—maybe the day he got home from work and she met him at the front porch, bouncing on her hind legs, eyes buggy and worshipful—he realized he loved her, he was grateful to have her. Though he never said so to Tommy, he felt a bittersweet certainty that Nora would have loved her, too—good as she'd always been with rough beasts, himself at one time no exception. It was easy, on nights when Tommy slept away and the house felt as open and empty as a tobacco warehouse in January, to imagine the dog as his last connection to Nora, to anything good like Nora. It was a desperate way to feel.

The police chief in Roma, Kentucky, was Perry Whitebridge. He'd been a year behind Jacob in high school, a soft-spoken kid with duct tape holding his boots together, which wasn't so uncommon in the county back then, when Jacob himself sometimes snacked on wild onions from the side of the road to keep his stomach from rumbling. Jacob ran a gun shop now, and he had a contract with the city: they purchased their weapons and ammunition from him at a fair price, and Jacob took care of the cleaning and maintenance of their guns for free. So Jacob had come to know Perry, respected him, and even drank a beer or two with him some nights at the American Legion. Two womanless men: Jacob, a widower, and Perry, just plain unlucky. Or maybe lucky—Jacob knew him, but not well enough to understand how the man felt about those things.

Perry came to the gun shop on a crisp afternoon in early autumn, and Jacob knew from the look on his face that something was up. But he tried to play it normal, thinking Tommy must've gotten himself in some trouble, stuck in a situation that would cost Jacob money or face. "Look what the cat dragged in," he said. He wiped the big glass display counter with some Windex and an old rag, looking at his reflection with the guns crisscrossing below it. Perry was taking off his hat by the brim with one hand and patting his coarse blond hairs over to one side with the other; Jacob could see this reflected too as the man walked up.

"Got to talk to you, Jake," Perry said.

"Talk, then." *He stole something. A car, maybe. Broke in somewhere. Jesus.*

"This is hard, man." Perry grabbed the counter, putting greasy smears on the glass.

Jacob sighed. "Lay it on me."

"Your dog, Jake. Tommy's dog, I mean. She got into some trouble up the road."

Jacob was tempted to feel relieved. He imagined overturned garbage cans, the contents strewn across a neighbor's yard. A dead rabbit lying on someone's front stoop. "What kind of trouble?"

"She bit someone—that little girl about two miles up from your place, across from the Methodist church."

"The Pryor girl?"

Perry nodded.

Jacob's heart started to beat up in his throat. "Oh, Jesus. How bad is it?"

"She's going to be all right," Perry said, and if Jacob had been the crying type, he might have started right then. He knew the girl by sight: she was a frail, wild little thing, ranging the neighborhood in her bare feet when the weather was warm enough, so filthy that she wore a ring of dirt round her neck like a piece of jewelry. Feral and almost unbearably lovely. He knew the dog, too: when they played, and Jacob teased her with a thick hank of rope with a knot tied at the end of it, she just about ripped his arm out of the socket trying to yank it free. His mind was putting these two images together, the child and the animal, the scrawny arms and those square, locked jaws. He felt sick.

"It could've been worse," Perry said. "The dog laid into her leg pretty hard. Mrs. Pryor had to whack her upside the head with a shovel to knock her loose, long enough to get the kid inside. She called me, but the dog was gone by the time I got out there."

"What should I do?"

Perry's face was shiny. "I'm supposed to get the dog warden out to your place, have her put down. That's what I'm supposed to do. And the family could press charges against you."

"Shit," Jacob said.

Perry leaned in. "They're good folks, though, and the little girl's gonna be all right, like I said. You give them some money for their bills and a little bit extra, they'll let it go. And do something about that dog. Pen her up, send her to your cousin's in Timbuktu, whatever. I don't know. I'm willing to let this one slide, Jake. Dogs go funny every now and then. Just don't make me regret it."

Jacob shook his hand. "I'm grateful. I mean it. And you won't regret it."

Perry smiled, the lines in the corners of his eyes folded like a stack of clean towels. "No, I'm sure I won't."

Jacob closed the shop right after Perry left and drove straight home. Tommy was gone, of course; he worked fifteen to twenty hours a week for a construction company down in Springfield, Tennessee, spent the rest of his time either messing around with that girl he was seeing—Leela, who was twenty-six and had three kids already and a loose fold of stretch-marked skin that hung over the top of her low-slung jeans, but at least had her tubes tied—or getting wasted with his work buddies, pot or beer, whatever they could get cheaper that day. Jacob was lucky to get a meal in with the kid once a week, and even then he often had to tempt him with something nice, like dinner out at Ponderosa. He realized that he should probably put Tommy out of the house, make him scrape up a living on his own—he was nineteen now, and Jacob was making it too easy for him to waste what little he made on cigarettes and alcohol—but he couldn't do it. Just couldn't. The living was lonely since Nora passed, and Jacob walked around with the dread, the looming possibility of a life by himself in his little house in the country: watching re-runs of *Bonanza* every night on television, eating pork and beans straight out of the can, not bothering to heat them up. Seeing Nora's shadow in her garden in the backyard, now two seasons overgrown. The skeletons of tomato plants—he'd once, because of her, known the names of them all, the Better Boys and Early Girls and Brandywines—still clung to the cages she'd staked them with, like starved prisoners.

Tommy was gone already, mostly, but Jacob would miss the

smell of the boy's cologne, his white athletic socks balled in dirty wads on the living room floor. Even his tired eyes—hungover, yes, but dark brown like his mother's—glancing up from the plate of sausage and toast Jacob cooked up for him on Sunday mornings.

The dog was waiting for him on the front porch, wagging her tail. "Good girl," Jacob whispered, bending down on his bad knee to scratch behind her ears, under her chin. She was an ugly animal: face broad and stupid, fur rust-colored and mottled, like granite. Tommy had gotten her ears clipped when she was still small, and they stood up on top of her head, two triangles of flesh, pink-lined like seashells. But her body was long and smooth, sculpted, and Jacob traced the line of muscle that defined her back haunches, marveling as always at such wild, stealthy beauty it frightened him. She licked the palm of his hand.

"Good lady," he said.

He went into his house, to his bedroom, and opened the closet door. There was a safe at the bottom, under a pile of clothes and shoes that Jacob swept unceremoniously to the side. He turned the dial right, left, right again. What he had, the little he had, was inside: a stack of E series savings bonds, maybe twenty thousand dollars' worth; his grandmother's collection of silver dollars; the deed on the house; and the gun. He'd saved for years to buy it, even before he knew if he'd find the right one: a Colt .45 pistol, still in its original box, with an authentic screwdriver for disassembling. Issued by the Army in 1911, carried by a soldier in World War I, a fellow named Hughbert Waltham—he had all the papers. Jacob had paid nearly four thousand dollars for it at a gun show in Nashville, a bargain he'd considered too good to be believed. He could get at least six thousand for it now, probably more. He thought about the Pryor girl. He would need every penny.

The bullets were in a cardboard box in the back of the safe. Jacob took a seat on his bed near the window, where he could see better, and pulled one out. His .38 was in the drawer by his bedside table, loaded, but that wasn't the gun for this job. You always had to know the right gun for the job. The clip for the Colt was empty. He thumbed the safety, pulled back the slide with his left hand, holding the walnut grip with his right; then he shifted hands and inserted the bullet into the chamber. The gun gleamed in the afternoon light. Jacob looked forward to cleaning it, using the tiny screwdriver, handling the parts with a soft cloth on the velvet-covered surface of his workbench. He took the magazine in his right hand again, grasping the slide with his left, and depressed the trigger halfway, easing the slide into place. He would do this outside, normally, but the dog would hear and know. He didn't want her to know anything.

She sat on the porch with her back to the door, facing the road. She turned when Jacob came outside, storm door clanging behind him, and his hidden hand would have set her on alert with any other human, but she trusted him. He patted her hide and lowered his voice to an excited whisper. "Ball?" he said. Her tail thumped rhythmically. "All right, then," he said, and she leapt off the porch, sprang around to face him in anticipation, then scurried around the corner of the house into the backyard, moving as if she worried he'd change his mind. He followed.

This was the shame: a dog was a dog, Jacob knew, and they weren't born to hurt little girls, only raised to be that way. He'd turned his face away too many times when Tommy played rough, smacking the dog across the jaw with an empty two-liter bottle, shoving her off the front porch with a steel-toed work boot. It wasn't this one's fault. It was his, for being too weak to stand up to his own son and tell him right from wrong. She'd been a good dog to Jacob, a sweet girl, a protector. She'd stopped in the weeds just past the line where Jacob ran his riding mower, waiting for him, quivering in her eagerness but motionless otherwise, understanding that this too was part of their ritual. "Wait," Jacob said: a promise as much as a command. He bent over and stroked her back, the short, bristly hairs there, and she cocked her head, alert, watching the woods behind his property with her intelligent and predatory gaze. He thumbed the safety off the gun, lifted it up to the back of her head, and pulled the trigger.

She fell over, a dark heap in high grass.

Jacob buried her in Nora's garden and waited up until almost four in the morning for Tommy to get back. He explained about the girl and what the dog had done to her, how a bullet was cheaper than a lawsuit. "And once a dog gets human blood in her mouth, she'll never lose the taste for it," he finished. "That's what my own daddy said, anyway." He watched Tommy's face, hoping for a sign that his son understood his own stake in what happened without Jacob spelling it out for him. He was a good-looking boy, short—barely five foot seven—but wiry, with the dark eyes and skin and hair of a Mexican, almost. After a few moments he got up and stretched, his "Hank 3" shirt pulling out of his gray jogging pants, and patted Jacob's shoulder.

"No biggie, Pop," he said. The "Pop" thing was new, something he'd heard from a friend or on TV. "I had my eye out for something different anyhow." He gave Jacob a final patronizing squeeze on the shoulder and shuffled toward his bedroom.

Jacob heard the door snick shut, the lock turn. The air smelled of smoke and that smelly cologne Tommy liked to wear.

Jacob stayed up another hour, working Fill 'Em In's at the kitchen table—"the soulless crossword," Nora had called them whenever Jacob picked up a new copy from the magazine rack at the Piggly Wiggly. He liked the mindlessness of finding an intersection for random words and numbers, all the information you needed in front of you, no clues or guesswork required. He finished one, his eyes weak in the low light, back burning from hunching over so long without moving. He traced his fingers over the surface of the page, feeling the indentations of his ballpoint pen. He reached down to touch the dog, where she would normally have been sleeping beside him, and the emptiness of his life registered in full and aching force. "Nora," he said, looking at her shadow figure on the old living room couch—head bent over one of the mysteries she loved reading, Agatha Christie or Sue Grafton, dark, shoulder-length hair glinting in the lamplight. She lifted her head at the sound of his voice, took off her glasses, smiled. Her face, the face she wore before the cancer and her death: gentle, intelligent, elegantly lined, like crackled pottery.

Three months before Jacob's son was arrested for raping the Winterson girl, Jacob saw Helen for the first time. He was eating lunch alone at Gary's Pit Barbecue on the bypass and thinking about how strange it was to see two nicely dressed women—one quite young, early twenties maybe, the other closer to his own age—eating thick-piled pork barbecue sandwiches between spurts of typing on their laptops. He liked it. He wasn't a man

who adapted well to change, and he probably couldn't even figure out how to turn one of those things on, but there was something reassuring about this picture, nonetheless: the mix of old
and new, the idea that his hometown could move on in some
ways and stay the same where it counted. He squeezed some hot
sauce on his sandwich and took a big bite, still watching them,
and the older woman looked up and caught his eye. His mouth
was full of spicy meat and the sour tang of sauce, but he swallowed fast and smiled.

She smiled back, then turned her gaze down to the screen.

She was a handsome woman—that's how Jacob's mother would
have put it—with gray hair, shortly cropped, styled. Nice hair:
not yellow-gray like Jacob's was turning, but striking and pure,
as if she'd been born with it that way. He couldn't tell her eye
color from here, but it was something light, blue or hazel, and
she had a fine, thin nose with the slightest upturn at the tip. She
was a professional of some kind, he figured—an administrator at
the hospital, maybe a lawyer. He guessed it said something else
about the way the town was changing that he didn't know who
she was, what she did for a living. He liked that, too.

He finished his meal and left a ten-dollar bill on the table, held
down by a shaker of Lawry's. He caught his waitress's eye across
the restaurant—Rita; her boy had gone to school with Tommy—
and pointed at the table. She nodded and lifted a hand.

The air outside was always a surprise after the smells of the
restaurant: the fried batters, the fragrant burn of wood smoke.
From the entrance Jacob could see the bypass: a newly black-
topped slash through what had once been the Brindle farm,
wooded on this side, lined with trailers on the other. He reflected
on another smell in the restaurant, one he'd breathed in as he

crossed the dining room to the door, past the portraits of UK basketball coaches Adolph Rupp and Rick Pitino, and the photos of the Roma High School state championship football team from 1987: women's perfume, an unnameable sweetness, freshening the other scents but not drowning them. The memory of the smell excited him, made the closely clipped hairs at the base of his neck rise. He hadn't felt this way in a long time. He'd dated since Nora's death—two or three times, all setups that ended comfortably but without event—and he'd seen women on TV who struck him as sexy, arousing him so abruptly that he felt almost hijacked. Six months ago he drove to the adult bookstore on 65 and purchased a porn video that he pulled out from under his bed sometimes when Tommy was gone to Leela's. Watching it left him stirred but empty.

When he met Nora—that was over thirty years ago, hard as it was to believe—he'd been twenty-five and reckless as hell, more interested in where the next shot of Jack was coming from than whether or not he'd be alive the next day to feel hungover. And the sex then was like the drinking: powerful but singular, a disorienting night trip that left him wrung out and slimy-feeling, so that the only thing he hated worse than himself the next day was the girl who gave it up to him so easily and thoughtlessly. Then he met Nora—sweet Nora, who'd only been with one man, one time, and regretted it deeply—and it didn't take him long to realize he loved her. Before they slept together for the first time, he told her about the other girls—"whores," he called them, "cheap whores." And she hadn't disagreed.

He pulled out his keys, ready to cross the parking lot to his Chevy diesel and drive back to work. But the smell of perfume was still in his nose, making him light-headed. He turned, went back through the door, and crossed the dining room to her table. There was a deer head mounted to a plaque on the opposite wall, and he felt it staring at him through the dark-tinted sunglasses someone had balanced on its nose as a joke. The young girl noticed him first, drawing her eyebrows together—wary, as if he might be trying to sell her something. The older woman stopped typing on her computer and merely looked up, smiling. It was the kind of smile, Jacob thought, that the loan officer had given him the first time he came in about opening the gun shop. He felt now much like he had felt then: inadequate, ridiculous for dreaming. He almost fled.

"Yes?" the older woman asked.

"You're new," he said, neck hot. "I mean, you seem new. To town."

"I *am* new," she said. Were her cheeks a little pink? He thought so. "I moved down here about a month ago."

"What brought you?" Jacob asked. It wasn't just the deer's eyes that he felt on him now: Rita, the waitress, was watching him over the pitcher of sweet tea she was carrying to a booth. Smirking, Jacob was sure. And the old men at the next table were certainly slowing down their conversation, casting amused looks back and forth between Jacob and each other. As if Jacob were a teenager and not a grown man, a widower.

The woman grabbed her briefcase from an adjacent chair and dug around, pulling out a business card tweezed between two lacquered fingers. Her picture was in the corner, her name beneath it: "Helen Shively, CRS, GRI." To the left was a logo he recognized: "Campbell L. Baldwin & Sons Real Estate and Auctioneers, serving Logan County since 1929."

"You're an agent?"

"Yep," she said. "Just getting started. So if you know anybody shopping around for a house . . ." She shrugged a little and laughed. A nice laugh.

"Maybe I do," Jacob lied. "I'll ask around."

"That would be great," Helen said.

Jacob looked from Helen to her friend and angled his body toward Helen. He lowered his voice. "If you'd like someone to show you around, I have a shop in town. You could stop by. Not that there's much to show. Hell, you've been here a month. You've probably seen it all."

Helen laughed again. "Probably have," she said. "But we could have a coffee sometime anyway."

"A coffee," Jacob said. "Sure. Sure."

She nodded toward his hand. "You have my card."

"Yeah," Jacob said. "I do." He smiled, and feeling his face that way he was suddenly aware of how rarely he smiled anymore. "Thanks for that."

"You're welcome," Helen said as he walked away, and though it was hardly in his nature, Jacob thought he'd call her. He thought she wanted him to.

Outside, letting the wind cool his flushed cheeks, he rubbed his thumb across the raised lettering of her card. Helen—he remembered that name from the baby books he'd looked at with Nora, one of the times she was pregnant. It hadn't made their final list of girls' names, but he'd liked it because the book had told a story about a face that launched a thousand ships, a woman so beautiful that men lost their heads. "If you want to set your expectations so high," Nora had said, "let's call her Athena. I'd rather have smart than pretty." Jacob had agreed.

Now that the fear was behind him, the excitement returned—a

warm fist in his belly, clenching, releasing. He climbed into his truck and tucked Helen's card into the visor, where he wouldn't lose it. He closed his eyes and saw her face, memorizing it, not wanting to lose that, either. Helen. He started the car and pulled out of the parking lot, heading back to his shop.

Later he'd recall how it felt to love a woman again. It seemed to Jacob that a life only had room for so many beautiful things, even if you were lucky: a true love, a healthy child, a job that you could wake up to each day with even faint anticipation. That Helen could see something in him—perhaps the same thing Nora had known lay beneath his bourbon-scented sweat in those reckless days of his youth—struck him as somehow miraculous. A miracle. The miracle of a good woman.

On a Saturday morning in early November, Perry's cruiser pulled into Jacob's driveway. Jacob was on the front porch having a swing, thinking about meeting Helen in town for ice cream and a drive; right now the days were still brisk and eye-wateringly sunny, but the air was already getting that bitter smell. In another week or so he'd need to take down the swing for the winter and stow it in the garage, under a tarp, so that the boards wouldn't warp with cold and moisture.

Tommy hadn't made it home last night. Jacob didn't let Tommy's absences keep him up anymore; he gave himself over to thin, uneasy sleep instead, dreaming with such frantic energy that he usually awoke feeling jittery and out of touch. He financed a cellular phone that his son had never used once to call home. Twice he'd determined to let the bill slip and the service disconnect; twice he'd paid the bill by phone on the day it was due, picking up a five-dollar surcharge for his trouble. He was in awe of his own weakness; he hardly recognized himself anymore.

Jacob had the sense, watching Perry Whitebridge exit his car and begin a slow stride up the front walk, of reliving a nightmare; it reminded him of the way he had felt on waking each morning in the first few months after Nora's death, sure that she was still in the bed beside him, or in the kitchen starting coffee, the sureness contradicted by a depression more physical than remembered. That moment before the two things—the sureness and the depression—came together to make sense of one another was almost worse than the despair that inevitably followed, and the glimmer of hope in the drawer of his bedside table: the .38 that he would surely have used if there hadn't been Tommy to think on and love and worry about, Tommy to hear the gunshot from his bed in the next room.

Car accident. Drinking and driving. He killed someone. He's dead. Please God, someone else, not Tommy. Please God, not Tommy.

Perry stopped at the front step, hesitant. "Need to have a talk with you, Jake," he said.

"Talk, then," Jacob told him.

The day Tommy had started kindergarten—his small arms dangling out of the short sleeves of his new plaid button-down shirt, both hands clutching the handle of his plastic Teenage Mutant Ninja Turtles lunch box—Nora had returned to her job at the nursing home. Jacob had warned her against taking on too many big changes all at once, but she'd been adamant. "I can't stand sitting around that house all day by myself," she told him. "I'd have the house cleaned by lunchtime, then I'd spend the rest of the day watching TV or taking naps."

It hadn't just been that, though, and Jacob knew it. She missed the work. Tommy was late for a first child—Nora had miscarried four times before his birth, and she was thirty-eight when she delivered him—so she had adjusted to motherhood with difficulty as well as joy. When he was crawling age, she started making trips to the home to visit the residents, not worried like Jacob was about what germs the baby might pick up. The old people had loved touching the boy, planting dry, shaky kisses on his bald head. He never got sick, though. Not from them, not even a cold.

Now in the car the day after Perry's visit, driving Tommy home from his night in lockup, Jacob remembered what it was like to have a small, happy son. Random memories: he, Nora, and Tommy picnicking at Lake Malone, Jacob sipping on a Keystone and watching Tommy in the water, buoyant in his Mickey Mouse arm floaties; Tommy graduating from kindergarten, chewing on the tassel dangling from his white cap instead of singing "The Bear Went Over the Mountain" with his classmates; Tommy asleep in the middle of the living room floor wearing only a diaper, the ceiling fan creaking above him and cooling his round cheeks, red-flushed from hard play. Pain raced along Jacob's arm and he grabbed it, sucking air through his teeth.

"Dad, you okay?"

"Fine," Jacob said.

"Don't be a hero, man. Let's get you to the doctor if you're going to have a heart attack or something."

Jacob pulled the car over onto the shoulder, unlatched his seat belt, and backhanded Tommy with his good arm. Tommy's head knocked against the passenger-side window, hard, but he had the good sense not to say anything in return, only to sit there, slack-jawed and wide-eyed, pawing at his red-and-white-blotched cheek.

"You've had that coming for a while," Jacob said. He closed his eyes and kneaded the tight spot in his chest. There was a moment when the pain seemed ready to cross over from bad to serious, and Jacob could even hear that *wonk! wonk!* sound in his head that always announced DANGER in the movies. Then it started to subside. He took deep breaths, massaged the loosening knot, and opened his eyes. A few seconds later, he noticed the road ahead of him, where Les Clemmons's row of neatly kept board fencing ran out into Paul Brown's scraggly old barbed wire contraption; the Presbyterian church up on the hill to the left, where one of his uncles was buried.

"Dad?" Tommy whispered.

Jacob looked at the church, wondered whether he could see the boneyard from here if he strained hard enough. In his line of sight was a big tree, a spot of white under it.

"Daddy, you've got me scared."

Jacob reached across Tommy and opened the glove box. The bottle of aspirin was stuffed behind the owner's manual, and Jacob shook two out; he chewed them dry, the bitter taste drawing him out of his fog.

"I'm okay." He meant it—he felt better. As with the two previous times this had happened—once at work, once just after Nora's funeral—he felt almost silly after the pain passed, as if he'd been imagining the whole thing, or exaggerating it. He wanted to believe this was true; his middle age, these hints at coming infirmity, embarrassed him. There had been a moment when Jacob was just about Tommy's age, when he looked in the mirror, hardened the big muscles in his chest and arms, and thought, *My Lord, I'm iron.* Two seconds of clarity and beauty, nothing more, but he never forgot them. How awful to know that kind of sureness in your life, only to lose it.

He started the car, refastened his seat belt.

"I can pay you back the bond money," Tommy was saying. "I'll sell the truck if I have to."

"A lawyer's gonna cost a lot more than a thousand dollars," Jacob said.

"I'll figure it out." Tommy lit a cigarette and cracked a window, letting the wind catch the ashes and pull them out of the car. "They can set you up on payments. I know a guy."

"I'm sure you do."

"Got Chad off a DUI. He only charged five hundred."

"This is a hell of a lot more serious than a goddamned DUI," Jacob said. "Christ almighty, Tommy, I thought you had more sense. I thought your mother had raised you better."

"So that's it? Somebody says I did something, you right off believe them? Real nice, Dad. Not that I'd expect any different."

They pulled into the driveway and Jacob shut off the car.

"Well, you tell me, then," Jacob said. "Did you hurt that girl?"

"No," Tommy said, not looking at him. His hand, the one grabbing for the door handle, was shaking. "Of course I didn't."

"You going to call this lawyer, or do I have to do that, too? The arraignment's on Monday."

"I'll call him, Dad. Jesus."

Jacob rubbed his mouth, his dry lips, and thought about Helen for the first time since yesterday, when Perry came. He hadn't even remembered to call her. "I wonder about you, Tom," he said. He looked at his son, who was staring off in the direction of Nora's overrun garden and playing with the flip top on the car door ashtray. "I just wonder."

"Don't," Tommy said.

Jacob left it at that.

Tommy was gone the night before the arraignment—Springfield again, spending the weekend with Leela; Jacob hadn't had the energy to argue—so Helen came over Sunday night, bringing with her some cobbler and a bottle of Maker's. While Jacob gave her the details about Tommy's arrest, she searched his cabinets for food, then started cooking grilled cheese sandwiches and chicken noodle soup, her movements fluid and efficient— the way she could butter the bread without tearing it, or flip the sandwiches in the pan with one fast motion that didn't shift the corners. He hadn't had a woman cook for him—for him and only him—in almost three years. He'd missed too many other things about Nora, important things, to allow himself to grieve for something as selfish as this, but he grieved for it now: the gift of a meal you didn't make yourself.

"I wasn't much older than Tommy when Nora and me got married," Jacob told Helen, watching her work. She knew this—she knew most of what there was worth knowing about him, he was sure—but he needed to say it again. To make sense of it.

"Me, too," Helen said. "It was a different time." She had, Jacob learned in the two and a half months of their careful courtship, married when she was twenty, divorced twenty years later.

It wasn't something she often talked about, but his name was Harry, she'd told him, he drove trucks for Overnite, and *he* left *her*—not for a twenty-five-year-old "slip of ass," which she could just about have understood, but for a lawyer seven years his senior down in San Antonio.

"He and this girl he's with just spend the night together like it's nothing," Jacob said. "He lets her kids call him Daddy, then comes here and eats my groceries. Don't think nothing of it." He poured another shot of bourbon into his coffee mug, grateful for the warmth. Nora had never fussed when Jacob drank but didn't like being around him when he did, and she would've died before going out and purchasing a bottle of whiskey herself. "Marrying settled me somehow. These kids don't ever figure that out. I sure wasn't born a good man."

"But you are one," Helen said.

"If I am, it's because Nora made me that way."

Helen stopped stirring the soup and sighed. "Goddamn, Jacob, you sure give a girl a lot to live up to."

She'd said things like this before, and hearing her jealousy—there wasn't a better word for it—always surprised him. Nora was as much a part of his life as his son. He could stop talking about her, thinking about her, no better than he could stop breathing.

"Don't mean anything by it," he said into his drink. And though he didn't feel his comment had warranted an apology, he offered one: "Sorry. I'm sorry, hon."

"No need," Helen said. She sighed again—he didn't even think she was aware of doing it—and stirred the soup more vigorously.

He hadn't eaten much of anything since Perry came by

with his news—drank coffee, nibbled on a bear claw he got out of a vending machine at the police station—so he indulged himself now, putting away two sandwiches and two helpings of soup, plus a slab of blackberry cobbler drenched in some of the vanilla ice cream Helen had found in the back of his freezer. He washed the dishes while Helen read a magazine, and then they made love—not for the first time, of course, but it was still new, and Jacob had never felt so satisfied, so frankly grateful to another human being. He didn't love Helen like he'd loved his wife, but he did love her, and he told her so.

He was close to sleep when she rolled over and worked her way between his arm and side, resting her head on his chest. "There's a house," she said, her own voice soft and sleepy. "Right outside of Auburn. It's going on the market in a few weeks."

"Yeah?" he said, moving his feet into a cooler pocket of sheet.

"Yeah." Her breath hit his nipple, sending a chill down his back. "It's a nice place, Jake, part of an estate. The kids are in a hurry to close and split the sale money."

He was awake now. "So what are you saying?"

"I'm buying it, Jake." Her finger traced the line of his rib cage. "I want you to live with me there. I want us to get it together."

He didn't say anything; he couldn't. What about Tommy? Tommy wasn't part of this plan, he was sure.

"Don't worry about it now," Helen said. She stretched and rolled away, because they'd both figured out that they didn't sleep well in each other's arms. "It was a bad time to mention it. But the offer's there."

"I'll think on it," Jacob said.

"That's all I'm asking."

But it wasn't all she was asking, he knew. And when she fell asleep beside him, the same place his wife had slept when she was alive, he went to Tommy's room, sat on his son's bed, and wondered if Helen wasn't trying to strip him of the little he had left of Nora—killing her again with softness and warmth and the possibility of something new and alive.

Perry Whitebridge called Jacob on the evening following the arraignment, asked him if they could meet somewhere. Tommy, for the first time since Jacob had picked him up from the county lockup, was quiet and morose. He sat in front of the television after dinner, not bothering to flip the channel, and ate from a bag of Reese's peanut butter cups left over from Halloween. A pile of brown paper wrappers spilled off the edge of the end table and littered the carpet, crinkled and twisted like dead leaves.

"Well, I guess you're scared now," Jacob had told him, driving home from court. A mean thing to say, he knew, and ironic, considering: Jacob himself had found the arraignment much less intimidating than he'd worried it would be, schooled as he was in episodes of *Law & Order*. Tommy hadn't had to say anything; he just sat there while the judge outlined the charges, and it was his lawyer who called out "not guilty." The Winterson girl—the victim, they'd called her—wasn't even there. That was what had worried Jacob more than anything: seeing this girl his son was supposed to have hurt.

"Of course I'm scared," Tommy had said. Then he started to cry, high-pitched hitches that shocked Jacob so badly he almost ran the car into the shoulder. He went ahead and slowed to a stop, unlatching his seat belt. Tommy shrank back when he put his arms out, no doubt remembering their last car ride, but Jacob grabbed him roughly anyway, pulling him to his chest, and Tommy shook in his arms while he thrummed an awkward, consoling rhythm on Tommy's back. And just as he was reminded of how much he loved this boy, this piece of himself—more fiercely than he'd ever loved anyone, even Nora—he understood that Tommy really had done something to that girl, and that the hurting was maybe only just starting.

"Well, I'm here," Jacob had said, patting, feeling both comforted and repulsed by the warmth of his son's back. "There's that."

Jacob and Perry arranged to meet at a truck stop in Bowling Green—a thirty-minute ride from home, but Perry had insisted on getting out of town, and Jacob hadn't wanted to question him. He was hunched over a mug of coffee when Jacob arrived, blowing the liquid between quick sips. He stood when Jacob approached the booth, and they shook hands, strangely formal in a way that Jacob didn't understand.

"Have a seat," Perry said, and he did.

"I haven't been here before," Jacob told him. "Cozy."

"Yeah, it's all right." Perry tapped a beat on the scratched laminate of the tabletop—"Shave and a Haircut," it sounded like. "I come here now and then."

They looked at each other. An eighteen-wheeler roared to life outside, and they both jumped a little.

"Well, Christ," Perry said. "I'll get right to it."

"What?"

"It's one of those good-news-and-bad-news things. I'll give you the bad first, okay?"

"Okay," Jacob said.

Perry leaned in. "There's a couple of witnesses, say they saw Tommy picking the girl up in his truck down by Sonic the night she says it happened."

Jacob nodded, rubbing his face.

"I talked to this one kid, off the cuff, so to speak. He told me this girl, this Winterson girl, she worked at Sonic Thursdays and Fridays, and Tommy had an eye on her. Always parked in her section."

Jacob waited.

"Well, you see where I'm going with this."

"Yeah," Jacob said. "Yeah, I do."

"I'm sorry, man," Perry whispered.

Jacob put his hand over his eyes, noticing how the bright fluorescents in the diner made the edges of his fingers glow orange, like a jack-o'-lantern.

"There's good news, remember."

"Let's hear it," Jacob said hoarsely.

"There's a process for all this, you know," Perry said. "The grand jury's the next step. That date got set, right?"

"January," Jacob told him.

"All right, then. Well, the commonwealth attorney has to prove to the jury that there's sufficient evidence to try the case. If he can't—or if he doesn't—they'll throw it out."

Jacob's heart started to beat so hard that he was sure Perry could hear it. "What's this mean?"

"Where do you think the attorney gets his evidence from, Jake?"

Jacob exhaled in a rush, his face hot, peppery-feeling. "You wouldn't be willing to. You wouldn't—"

Perry raised his hand. "Hold up just a second. Let's be straight. I'm not going to lie about anything. I have the mayor to answer to."

Jacob made a fist under the table, trying to push all of his anger into it. Just as soon as he'd allowed himself to feel hopeful he understood that this was Perry's game, and the little divide between them—the things he hadn't known, hadn't wanted to know—was deep, and much darker than he'd figured. But how little had he known his own son? And what kind of man could he himself be, letting things turn out this way? Nora, even in that last, difficult year of her dying, had been able to reach Tommy, to make him do right. Jacob couldn't do it without her.

"What I'm willing to do is talk to the commonwealth attorney," Perry said. "He takes my word on things. If I say back off, he probably will. Can't guarantee it, but I'd bet on it."

"Why would you do that?" Jacob asked.

"Hell, Jake, we go back."

"Still."

Perry shrugged and pulled away from the table. "These girls. I don't know. They're different nowadays. Time was, a girl knew what she should and shouldn't do. You know what I'm saying?"

Jacob, not sure if he did, nodded.

"She got in the truck with him, that's what I mean. And I heard things about her from that kid, the one who told me about Tommy. He said that she hangs out at the Sonic after her shift ends, smoking and drinking and all that shit. Fifteen, I mean, Christ."

"Fifteen," Jacob echoed.

"A good girl just don't do that. Good girls know better. Maybe it was mutual and maybe it wasn't. Either way it's tough to prove. How old is Tommy again?"

"He's twenty," Jacob said.

"Well, you see, that's already something. Another year and

they could've got him on third-degree rape, and that's as much as a five-year sentence."

Too many ages, numbers. Jacob couldn't think.

"This one wouldn't fly, Jakey. Not likely, anyway. It's her word against his, and like I said, her word ain't so respectable from what I've heard."

"I don't know," Jacob said. *Jakey.* His father had called him Jakey.

"What don't you know?" Perry pulled a pack of Camels from his shirt pocket and lit one. "All I'll do is push the common-wealth attorney a little. Make sure he does what he'd probably do anyway. Tommy's learned his lesson, I bet. There's no sense in his life getting ruined over this."

Jacob wondered what Nora would say. But if Nora were still alive, this wouldn't ever have happened.

"You're a good man, Perry," Jacob said, feeling like a liar.

"Hell, buddy. So are you."

Katie. That was her name, Tommy had told him. Katie Winterson.

Jacob watched, truck parked in the back of the lot, away from the drive-up order intercoms. There looked to be three wait-resses on duty: one older, late thirties probably, and two teen-agers. He felt, for no reason in particular, that she must be the smaller of the two—one of those too-tiny types in clunky shoes, breasts like dumplings, dishwater blonde hair in pigtails that bobbed against her thin shoulders. She carried a tray full of white fast food bags out to a minivan, balanced it on her hip, counted out change from a metal dispenser belted around her waist. She didn't look beaten or traumatized. She didn't look happy, either.

A half hour before closing, he pulled into a slot and ordered something called an Arctic Slush. The older waitress brought it out. It looked like Windex, tasted like watery toothpaste. He got out of his truck and pitched it into a wastebasket.

At eleven the lights around the intercoms dimmed, and the Sonic sign shut off. A few teenagers hung out in the parking lot playing music that blared from souped-up speaker systems, their cars seeming to hover over the neon light effects custom-installed along their bottoms, a sight that struck Jacob as somehow mystical and horrifying. A sedan pulled up to the back door at eleven-thirty, and the girl—Katie, he was even more sure of it—exited the restaurant moments later, climbing into the passenger front seat. There was a moment, when her door was open and the dome light flared, when Jacob could see everything: the middle-aged woman behind the wheel, a dog—some kind of Lab mix—putting his nose into the front seat, Katie turning to put her face into his, rubbing the scruff behind his ears. Then her door slammed, and the car was dark again. He watched it pull out and drive away.

A week after Tommy's arrest, Jacob drove out past Auburn, following the instructions Helen had written for him in her old-fashioned script: *Two miles after crossroads, turn left at the red barn. Drive out five more miles. House down gravel drive on R, just past Presb. church. Red brick w/ brown shingles.* She would meet him there, she'd said. She'd had a busy week, houses to show in Auburn and Lewisburg, plus a trip to Bowling Green that afternoon to sign papers. He hadn't seen her in a few days, and he already missed her.

Her car was parked in the drive when he arrived, and Jacob pulled in beside it. The house was larger than he'd imagined it would be, nicer. It was a full two stories, cottage-style, with a wood door and shutters and a roof that looked like it needed some repair, but not much. Shade trees lined the drive, and the backyard sloped down into a thicket of evergreens and brush, the kind of dense growth Tommy would have called a jungle when he was younger. Most of the leaves had fallen from the trees, and they made a thick carpet around the house. As he walked the grounds, looking for Helen, he was reminded of a trip he and Nora had taken to the Biltmore estate in North Carolina. This would have been about ten years ago. Nora had remarked that the forest looked like a fairy tale forest: tall trees making a canopy high overhead; neat, unlittered ground surrounding them. No weeds, no snarls of kudzu or scrawny saplings. That forest had been carefully pruned and manicured by a whole team of day laborers, but this little grove was merely quiet, untouched.

"So what do you think?" Helen called from behind him.

"Not too bad," he said, crossing the yard to hug her. Her gray hair was tucked behind her ear on one side, and he kissed the silky bit of skin just south of her earlobe, breathing in where she'd dotted her perfume—White Shoulders, he knew now, an old bottle she'd made last. There was something about the smell that made his heart ache irrationally, as though Helen were gone like Nora instead of pressed against him, nuzzling her smooth face into his neck. He clung to her more tightly.

"Do you want to see the inside?" she asked.

He didn't know. Did he want to see this kitchen he and Helen would eat dinner together in, or the living room where they'd watch television, the sound getting louder as the two of them got deafer? Did he want to see the bathroom where he'd hang the antique shaving mirror Nora had bought him for their fifth anniversary? Or the toolshed he'd putter around in after he sold the gun shop and retired? Did he want to see the master suite, this bedroom he and Helen would share for the next twenty years, maybe more, first making love, then simply sleeping, and maybe, finally, Helen tucking pillows behind his head so he could eat the soup she was spoon-feeding him, catching dribbles with a napkin before they fell off his chin and landed on his flannel pajama top? Could he imagine a life where Nora was just another memory?

"Maybe we should just sit here for a minute," he said, motioning to the front stoop.

"It's kind of cold," Helen said.

"I'll keep you warm."

They sat side by side, Helen leaning into his chest, and Jacob took the left side of his big quilted coat and pulled it around her, shielding her face from the wind.

"Sixty-five thousand," she said, her voice muffled. "I mean, I just couldn't believe it at first. The twenty acres alone are worth that."

"Kind of late for starting over, don't you think?"

"I have some money left from selling the house with Harry," Helen said. She wrapped her arm around his waist and her hand brushed the bare skin between his shirttail and work pants, chilling him. "I could mortgage the rest easy, get it paid down in five years or less. Or you could put up the other half."

"I have a house," Jacob said. Her touch was so cold it seared.

"But there're so many memories attached to that place."

"Maybe I want my memories," he said.

"I never said you had to give up your memories."

They watched a gust of wind pick up a pile of leaves, swirling them.

"What about Tommy?"

"You don't have to give him up, either." She exhaled, her breath frosting a current of air. "But he's a big boy, Jacob. He has to move on with his life at some point. And so do you."

"You're saying he wouldn't have a place here, then," Jacob said.

"I'm saying he shouldn't."

When Jacob was young—high school age—this woman down the street from him had stroked. She was young, too, he knew now—early forties, probably, an age that had seemed impossible to him at the time. Still, watching what the stroke had done to her—twisting her face ("handsome," his mother had said; "she was a handsome woman"), turning her into something witchlike—was terrifying. This woman's husband had stayed with her, but a few years after the stroke he was seeing other women, and before too much time had passed one of these women was living in the house, too. Quite the scandal. Jacob's mother was up in arms, but his father, in his quiet way, had only said, "There's lots of ways to love, son," and that had made more sense to him back then than his mother's yelling and flapping of dish towels. There *were* lots of ways to love, he thought now—ways that made you a better person than you were, maybe, and ways that got you through lonely times, and also ways that could destroy you if you let them. So many ways to love a woman, but only one way to love a child, and that was the single thing he felt sure about anymore.

"I guess I won't be coming in," he told Helen, holding his coat tight around them both, wanting to keep her under his arm for as long as possible. She didn't say anything. He could feel her warm breath through his shirt, and he held her tighter.

A little over two months after Jacob's son raped Katie Winterson, Jacob and Tommy ate dinner together at Ponderosa. He had a coupon he'd clipped from the newspaper—sirloin tip dinner with salad bar for $6.99, limit four persons. The grand jury had met two weeks earlier and dismissed the charges, just as Perry had told Jacob they would. He hadn't seen much of Tommy since, between work and the time Tommy was spending with that woman in Springfield.

"I'm starving," Tommy said, grabbing a plastic plate from a stack at the end of the buffet. While Jacob put a salad together, Tommy made two trips back and forth to the table, salad on the first plate, chicken wings, mashed potatoes, a slice of pizza, and two dinner rolls on the other. There'd been a time when Jacob could eat like that, never gain a pound. Like so many things in his life, that time had passed.

They ate silently, Jacob working through his salad, wincing at the metallic taste of the processed bacon bits, then his sirloin tips, dipped in a puddle of A1. Tommy's chicken wings, stripped free of meat and breading and even cartilage, piled up on a saucer in the middle of the table. A waitress refilled their glasses of sweet tea a few times, and Tommy finished with a saucerful of soft serve ice cream, the kind with the chocolate and vanilla swirled together. He still put sprinkles on the top. Tommy had always liked his sprinkles.

"So I'm thinking," Tommy said, eating his ice cream, "that I might try school again next year, after I have some money saved up. Like, maybe vocational school. But the tattooing thing could also still work out. Did I show you . . ."

He unbuttoned his left shirt cuff and rolled up the sleeve, revealing his forearm. There was a Celtic cross tattooed on the inside in black, not badly drawn, a little wobbly where it crossed a tendon. The skin around the design was blotchy and hot-looking, and tiny red dots made a trail across the length of his arm, all the way up to the bend in his elbow.

"Mikey let me use his gun, and I hear the guy at the Purple Dragon in Bowling Green is looking for an apprentice. That's good money. I mean, that would be awesome. . . ."

Jacob stopped hearing him. He watched Tommy's mouth—the lips so much like his mother's—forming words, empty things Nora would never have said, or believed. He wondered about Helen, whom he'd last seen on Christmas Eve by accident. This was at Wal-Mart. She was standing over by a display in the holiday aisle—a big table with a Christmas village built on it, fiberfill snow and ceramic houses lit from within by tiny bulbs, miniature cedar trees, a train. The train circled the village, making an electronic whistle every time it rounded a corner. Helen watched the train. Jacob watched Helen. She never saw him.

• LIFE EXPECTANCY •

Coach Theo Burke was standing outside his classroom during morning break when he noticed Josie across the hall, pinned up against a locker. One of the varsity basketball players, Jatarius, was doing the pinning—his near seven feet making Josie seem short in comparison, big hands straddling her shoulders, too-handsome black face leaned in to kissing distance. The worst thing—the thing that felt like a punch in the gut—was the look on Josie's face, a look Theo knew well. Her head was tilted, and she was smiling, but just a little: that smart smile, that sexy half-smile with the bottom lip barely caught under her front teeth, an expression that Theo recognized as the smallest bit calculated but mostly genuine. Mostly the only way Josie knew how to be.

He strode over, hands shoved so deep in his khakis that his watch got caught on one side. He cleared his throat.

"Jatarius," Theo said.

"Yeah." A slow breath, dusky, directed on Josie and not at him.

"Move it along."

Jatarius pulled to a slow stand, languid, his skin gleaming as if oiled. "Just talking, Coach," he said, and Josie giggled. Theo turned to her, and she looked away.

"You're supposed to be swapping books now, not talking," he said, realizing as he said it how ridiculous—how *old*—he sounded. Josie was losing interest in him, and all he had to cling to was his authority as her teacher and her coach. Her better. And how false that felt, watching her now, knowing what her breasts looked like beneath that T-shirt and hooded sweatshirt: small, spread apart—a tall girl's breasts.

Jatarius pulled his book bag up over his shoulder. "See ya," he told Josie, and she fluttered her fingers at him as he sauntered off.

"What are you doing?" Theo whispered, looking around to make sure nobody was watching them.

She tried to laugh again, but her voice caught a little, and she stopped. Her eyes were overbright, her shoulders stiff, but she smiled—for him, for the group of girls crossing behind him. "I'm pregnant, Coach," she said. She opened her mouth, then closed it again. She shrugged.

The bell rang, and Theo turned to walk back into his classroom, where twenty-six sophomores were waiting to learn about the Fertile Crescent, the first bloom of civilization.

•　　　•　　　•

Abortion, she told him. Soon, now, so I don't have to miss any game time. Right away. Yesterday.

"All right," Theo said, patting the air with his palms, a gesture implying *Calm down* that he used when students freaked out about a bad test score or got into fights. He and Josie were in his coach's office. He'd let practice out early that day, after only an hour. Josie had seemed normal—made her warm-up sprints at top speed, missed only a single basket as they ran figure eights— but *he* could barely concentrate enough to follow the action or to guide the girls to the next drill. They looked the same out there in their practice jerseys and white high-tops: lanky girls with brown ponytails and acne. Only Josie stood out, her gold hair alight under the gym's fluorescents. Only Josie seemed real. "All right, slow down. Give me a minute."

She looked at her hands, as if she were counting off the sec-onds. "Antibiotics," she said finally. "I was sick over Christmas break. That's what did it."

Theo was thinking: *baby.* He had a baby, and a wife. His baby was eleven months old, and they called her Sissy, short for Cecily. Five months ago they found out that her breathing problems were caused by cystic fibrosis, which turned the name—their affection— into a lousy pun, a cruel joke. "Wait," he said. "What? Did what?"

"The antibiotics affected the Pill," she said. "I looked it up on the Internet. At least I'll know better from now on."

"From now on?"

"Jesus," she said. "I'm eighteen. I'm not going to stop having sex."

"I'm just saying," Theo said. He wondered, despite himself, if she would still want to have sex with him.

She pulled a package of gum out of her purse and unwrapped a piece. "I'm just ready to get this over with," she said, now chewing. "I've got a lot to worry about. School and all."

"Of course," Theo said. She was going to Western Kentucky University in the fall, a full ride. He had helped her get it. He had posed with her, her mother, and Western's basketball coach three months ago when they signed the letter of intent, and the photo ran in the *News Leader*. "Cute girl," his wife had said when she saw it. And Theo—who was already meeting Josie for fast screws in his office and his car and a few times at her house, when her mother was pulling seconds at the sewing factory— had only nodded.

Now Josie sat in the chair opposite Theo's, the desk between them, and played with the end of her thick, yellow braid, wanting, he saw, to put it into her mouth. He'd done his best to tease her out of that habit, seeing it as the one solid piece of evidence between them—other than the obvious fact of their positions as teacher and student, of course—that being together was scuzzy and wrong, an embarrassment to them both. Because in so many other ways, it hardly seemed like a problem at all. She'd turned eighteen in December, and she was about to graduate. She was mature. She had a good future ahead of her. There was the infidelity, but Theo tried, with some success, to keep his home life and school life separate, and it seemed to him that he was okay—getting by, at least—as long as he was able to do what had to be done in both lives. He was an average teacher, but better than most coaches: he liked his World Civ classes and tolerated Kentucky Studies. At least he wasn't just popping a movie in the VCR every day like Mathias, the boys' basketball coach, who famously screened *Quigley Down Under* for his freshman geography students during their Australia unit. He thought that he was a better-than-average father, at least most of the time. He'd hoped for a son, sure—pictured a boy all those years he and Mia were trying and failing to conceive, a boy to play basketball with and to fish with, all of the clichés. But he'd been happy with his girl, and if her delicacy dismayed him a little—how could it not?—in so many ways, it only made him love her more.

Some days, driving home from work, he thought, *I have a house,* and was instantly filled with pride. House, yes—he was a man, all right. *I have a wife. I have a child.* Before coming in the front door, he would picture all three—house, wife, daughter— as they ought to be: clean, happy, healthy. *This is my life,* he'd think, and then he'd open the door.

"My mom probably wouldn't be too upset if she knew," Josie said. "She likes you. She doesn't get hung up on stuff like you being a teacher. She'd take care of it if she had the money to, but she doesn't."

"How much?" Theo asked.

Josie shook her head. "I don't know yet."

How much was an abortion? Two hundred dollars? A thousand? He tried to imagine withdrawing that much money from the checking account without Mia noticing. Mia was in her own world a lot of the time these days, but she could surprise him with her sudden sharpness.

"But you'll take care of this, right?" Josie said. She was going to cry, he was sure. *Put the braid in your mouth,* he thought. *Do it if that'll shut you up.* "Right?" she said.

No less than five hundred, he bet. But he could scrounge it up. Mathias might loan it to him out of his pot fund. Theo could pay it back slowly that way—twenty this week, fifty the next. There wasn't any question, though: it had to be done. His job paid for shit—and he'd have to pick up something part-time this summer, probably, just to make ends meet—but it was all he had, and the insurance was good. He couldn't lose that. Not with Sissy to worry about.

"Okay," Theo told her. "You get the information and set it up, and I'll pay for it."

"And drive me," Josie said. "I can't ask Mama to do that."

"Okay, I'll drive you," Theo said.

She pulled the rubber band off the end of her braid and raked her fingers through the thick weave of her hair, setting it loose. It ran over her shoulders, halfway down her back, wavy and almost iridescent. Rapunzel hair, he'd always thought. Her nose and cheeks were freckled, and she had that balance between strength and delicacy that most of his girl athletes lacked. Miraculous.

"We could have sex," she said, almost with resignation.

He nodded.

When Sissy's cystic fibrosis was confirmed, the doctors threw a lot of numbers at Theo and Mia, too many to make sense of. Life expectancy. Percentage of cases in the U.S. Chances of this, chances of that. But the fact that stayed with Theo—the data that confirmed for him everything wrong with his marriage and his life—was this: a child could only get the disease if both parents carried a defective gene. *Defective*: the doctor's word. Dr. Travis—the first of several—told them this in his wood-paneled office with dark green carpeting, and Theo could remember thinking that he, Mia, and Sissy, who was too small at six months but still porcelain-pretty, were now lost in the woods together. He and Mia, two unknowing defectives, had somehow found each other, beaten the odds, and brought forth a child who was drowning in her own chest because the two of them should never have been together in the first place.

When he came home that night after making arrangements with Josie, Mia was in the old recliner, Sissy in her lap, and they were rocking, watching TV. Mia's bare foot bobbed above the floor, keeping time. The house was filthy, and Theo was made nauseous by the smells that assaulted him as soon as he walked in the door: soured food stuck to the dishes that were piled up on the kitchen countertops; the heavy metallic tang of piss, where the toilet hadn't been flushed; and shit, too, he was sure of it. Maybe the baby's, but probably the dog's. Mia took care of Sissy to the point of obsession, but she seemed to forget that they had a dog—a beagle mix they'd gotten free from an unplanned litter—though bringing him home had been her idea. She'd read in some magazine that dog owners had longer life expectancies, and cancer patients with dogs more often went into remission or had spontaneous recoveries. He didn't ask her how the cancer thing was supposed to apply to their daughter.

"Smells like crap in here," Theo told her, setting his briefcase and duffel bag down by the front door.

"I hadn't noticed," Mia said. "Baby-girl's clean." As if in support, Sissy erupted into one of her chants: *ma ma ma ma ma MAAAA!* Theo picked Sissy up and kissed her clean neck, trying to fill his nose with her scent. She hooked her small hand and paper-thin fingernails into his ear and twisted. "Ma," she said again.

"Daddy," Theo told her. She hadn't said it once, ever.

"Might be the dog," Mia said. She kept watching TV, and Theo knew what she was thinking just as clearly as if she'd spoken out loud: *You'll take care of this, right?*

Theo put Sissy down, his stomach already starting to churn. "I'd say that's the most likely option." He whistled and walked around, trying to find the source of the smell. "Joe!" he yelled, whistling again. The odor—thick, sickly—seemed to be everywhere at first; then he rounded a corner, and it hit him like an arrow, coming from the bedroom. He got down on his knees and looked under the bed.

"Christ," he said. "Fuck."

Joe was in the corner, as far from the bed as he could get, and Theo could see the fast rise and fall of the dog's stomach. "Hey, boy." The dog cowered at first—his eyes, so eerily human, rolled up at him warily—then let Theo lift him and carry him into the living room like a baby.

"Dog's sick," Theo told Mia.

She nodded.

"Did he get into something?"

"I don't know. He was out back for a few hours. Maybe he got into the garbage." She was still watching the TV. "Poor boy," she said without interest. "Should we take him to the vet?"

"Probably just needs to finish his business," Theo said, and he went to put the dog out. In the low light, he could see Joe make a slow circle in the backyard, then lie down. Theo went back inside and tried his best to clean up the mess, using every chemical he could find under the kitchen sink, moving the bed and pulling up the corner of the carpet so he could get to the pad and subfloor, too. The smell lingered, and he opened a window.

In the living room, Mia hadn't moved. He sat on the couch and watched what she was watching: a cooking show. Not a regular show, though, like his own mom had watched on PBS when he was in high school—*The Frugal Gourmet* or the one with the old Cajun guy, Justin Wilson, shows where somebody stood behind a counter and cooked the food regular-style. This show had a fattish woman with brown hair, and she looked to be in her own house, because the sunlight seemed real and not put on. As she cracked an egg into a mixing bowl, the camera zoomed in, which you didn't see happen on Justin Wilson.

"What is this?" he asked her.

"My favorite show," Mia said. Her voice was dreamy. "This woman owns a restaurant in New England. She cooks very simple foods. She doesn't use margarine, only butter."

"Margarine's better for you," Theo said.

"Not true," Mia told him. They watched as the woman dipped a fancy silver measuring cup into a bowl of sugar. "This dish is fragrant and delicious," the woman was saying. "Margarine is a trans fat," Mia continued, "which doesn't break down in your system. Natural foods are better."

"Why do you like this so much?" Theo asked. The woman was now grating lemon peel.

Mia stroked Sissy's arm as she talked. "Her hands. She has such clean hands and fingernails. And her sugar, it doesn't just look like sugar."

Her medication. She'd been a mess since Sissy's birth—postpartum depression, her doctor had said—and she had just started to come back, to be herself again, when Sissy was diagnosed. Her meds were a square dance at this point: Prozac helped for a while, then made her worse than ever. Paxil worked, but they couldn't get the dosage regulated, and the doctor warned them that taking her off it early would result in a major crash. They'd gone on a date a few weeks ago—left Sissy with Mia's mother, tried to dress up and make a night of it—and at the movie, *Million Dollar Baby,* Mia had stared, emotionless, through all the parts that would have had her sobbing a couple of years before. Theo had asked her what she thought of the story on their drive home, and she seemed surprised by her own answer—or not even surprised, exactly. Perplexed. Like the changes in her were cause for a scientific kind of curiosity and nothing else. *I don't know what I thought of it,* she'd said. *I could see that it was sad, but I didn't feel sad. It was intellectual. Is this what being a man is like?*

"Looks like sugar to me," Theo said now.

"Figures."

"You could try making that," Theo told her. "Doesn't look hard. I bet it's real good."

Mia kept rocking. "No, I couldn't do that," she said.

Theo left her and went to the kitchen, unbuttoning his shirt cuffs and rolling up the sleeves to his elbow. He started organizing the dishes and cleaning the counters, pitching empty Lean Cuisine boxes and a Tropicana carton and ramen noodle bags into a Hefty sack. He couldn't get Josie out of his head, not even for a second. Too easy to think of her, to feel her warm hips between his hands even as he plunged them now into scalding dishwater. He pictured her in the hallway that morning, with Jatarius, and tried to remember the exact look on her face. *You'll take care of this, right?*

He noticed the wet circle in the driveway as he was taking out the trash, but the detail didn't click into place until he was closing the lid of the garbage can and he realized that Joe wasn't there to meet him. It occurred to him that there wasn't any strewn garbage out back, no sign of disturbance at all, and he remembered the wet spot then—not oil, not water, but antifreeze, probably leaked out while his car was warming up that morning. He peered into the dark shadows of the far corner of the yard, where the security light didn't hit. "Joe," he said. "Joe, old boy."

There was a tire propped up against the toolshed—Theo had been meaning to take it to the rubber yard behind Kip's Garage for months now—and he found Joe curled up in the space between it and the concrete wall, the thin scrim of green foam on his jowls barely visible in a sliver of moonlight. "Joe," Theo said. He looked at the still body. "Joe," he said again.

The first time he kissed Josie was in August, two weeks before Sissy's diagnosis. Someday, he might be able to blame the whole affair on his difficult home life, on the fear of losing his baby girl before she could have a home and family of her own. Someday, he might be able to forget that those two weeks existed.

When it happened, though, he wasn't thinking of Sissy, or of Mia. He'd known Josie for four years by then, pulling her from JV when she was still in eighth grade—she was that talented—and letting her start power forward in her first game as a high school student. He had recognized in her the quality that would later attract him: the blend of rawness and refinement, power and grace. In the beginning, though, she'd only seemed a grand kind of experiment. What could he turn her into?

The girls came in for mandatory weight lifting in the summer and through September, before real practice started, and the kiss came after one of these late-afternoon sessions. She was telling him about her father—how he left her mother in June to move to Nashville with his new girlfriend, a thirty-year-old wannabe country singer. How her mother had been struggling since then to make ends meet. She wasn't crying, but Theo could tell she wanted to, and the desire he felt for her—until this moment hypothetical and even harmless, like a childhood crush—was overwhelming. So he kissed her. He did it because she looked like she needed it. He did it because he knew he could get away with it.

Now, two days after the dog's death, Theo was determined to make it through a full practice without stopping early or fading out mid-speech, which had been his habit since Josie dropped her news. Some of the girls were beginning to look at him strangely, though he actually wondered more about the ones who weren't. He wondered if Josie had told a friend about the two of them, and if that friend had told a friend. She had always promised him complete secrecy, but he'd worked with young girls long enough to understand how unlikely that was, especially among teammates. Before the news of her pregnancy, he and Josie had fallen into a strange sort of complacency with each other, an ease that he was now terrified to remember. How careless they had been—with the sex, of course, but also with too-long looks, knowing smiles, risky, ridiculous moments between classes when they passed in the hall and let their fingers brush. They should have been caught already, he knew. They would get caught.

On the court, the girls were running a pass drill. Josie caught the ball, made it around Lisa in three easy strides, and pistoned upward, sinking a two-pointer. She landed hard, and Theo felt his heart wallop. "Josie?" he said.

Her expression was bewildered. "What?"

"Are you okay?"

"Yes," she said testily, already dribbling again.

He'd buried Joe in the backyard, not far from the spot where he died. Mia cried, which was more emotion than Theo could remember seeing from her in a while. He'd dug the grave; then, still sweaty and dirt-streaked, he'd hosed the greasy patch in the driveway, watching the liquid blur, blend, then run off into the grass, indistinguishable from a light rain. *I couldn't have known he'd gotten into that,* Mia had said, and Theo had stripped off his old University of Kentucky sweatshirt and blue jeans without a word, wadding them into a ball and throwing them in the hamper. His muscles, once long and powerful, ached now. *Sissy was coughing again, and I had my hands full. You know how it is.* He'd nodded and started the shower running. *It was your car, for fuck's sake.*

The girls thundered down the court, mechanized, rehearsing a series of dribbles and passes: Sasha to Rebecca, Rebecca to Carrie, Carrie to Josie. Josie was in top form, her gold braid snapping behind her with each lunge and jump. Her breasts quivered under her jersey and spandex sports bra, and each time she landed—each time the ball connected with her hands, rattling her—Theo felt his chest tighten. If he and Mia ever had another child—as if they'd want another child together—there was a 25 percent chance that it would have CF like Sissy. *Chance, chances.* A gamble. Josie was a gamble, too, or maybe just a stupid risk, but she was carrying their child, and Theo felt—no, he *knew*—that their baby wouldn't be sick. Their baby would be okay.

Josie caught the ball and Lisa slid into her, knocking them both out of bounds. Theo ran over and Josie quickly jumped to a stand. "I'm okay," she said. She still had the ball.

"I think you should take a break," he told her. The gym was suddenly very quiet.

"I'm fine," she said, tapping a nervous rhythm on the orange skin. She started to dribble it and put a hand out to block Lisa. "Come on, babe. Let's do this."

Theo leaned forward and knocked the ball out of the way, mid-bounce. "I told you to take a break," he said. The ball rolled across the floor, and he imagined that every eye in the gym was following its path. "So take one, unless you'd rather be running laps."

Josie stared at him, face bright with sweat, then bounced on her toes. "All right," she said. She started to jog, and the rest of the girls looked at one another, then at Theo, and he knew he had to go on with practice or lose them all completely. He clapped his hands two times. "Back to the court," he said. He pointed to Amanda, who was on the bench. "Take her spot."

The girls resumed their drill, and Josie ran laps. Theo lifted his eyes every time she rounded the corner and passed in front of him, and her speed actually seemed to be increasing instead of slowing. Her braid trailed behind her.

"Pace yourself, Jo," Theo yelled.

She didn't look at him.

They started a new drill, and while he tried to focus as the players ran layups, he watched for Josie in the periphery of his vision, sure that she would lose steam and stop at any moment. But she kept going. Forty minutes passed this way, and though the practice shouldn't have been over yet—they had a big home game coming up against Franklin-Simpson—he called it to a halt. The girls, who normally would've been happy to have a long evening ahead of them, hovered mid-court, looking at him. "Hit the showers," he told them.

"I'd like to get a little more time in, Coach," Carrie said. "I don't feel ready for Saturday yet."

"Practice at home," he said, and pointed to the locker room. "Go on, now."

The girls jogged off the court, and Josie continued to run. Her face was dripping, her hair dark now with sweat, and her pace was finally beginning to flag. Her big leg muscles trembled with every jolt against the polished wood floors.

"Stop now," Theo yelled to her. "Practice is over."

She shook her head.

"Do it, goddammit!" he said. "Unless you want to ride the bench Saturday."

That did it, as he knew it would. She lunged off a final three or four steps, then hunched over, grasping her knees. She coughed, the sound seeming to rise from the bottom of her stomach, scraping her insides raw. Theo ran over and put a hand on her neck.

"Get the fuck off me," she gasped, knocking his hand away. Her freckled face was scarlet across the nose and cheeks, her forehead and chin still ivory. Her neck was red-streaked, too, welts that could have been made by a claw.

"You happy now?" Theo asked. He could hear a couple of the girls sneak out of the locker room behind him, could feel their eyes on his back and on Josie, who had since lain on her side and was pulling her knees to her chest. "You're going to kill that baby," he said, keeping his voice low and steady, more steady than he felt. "You're going to bleed him out right here on this gym floor you love so much, if you aren't careful."

"Good." Her eyes darted to his and then away, childlike.

"You stupid bitch," he said, thinking, absurdly, of Joe. He hadn't wanted a dog—hadn't seen the sense in committing to another responsibility—but Mia had insisted, and he'd gone along. And the dog was all right. Not man's best friend, exactly, but good enough. Joe didn't get walked much, but when the walking got done, he was always full steam ahead. Didn't matter where they were going, or coming to, he wanted to dig into the ground with his toenails and drag—*mush*—himself forward. Joe didn't care about the destination, so long as he was moving. "Maybe you don't know what's good for you," he told Josie.

She looked up at him, her cooling face now bleached, the freckles like tiny bullet holes in her fair skin. "What do you mean?"

"Have you made an appointment yet?" he whispered.

She stood up and brushed off her shorts. "I was going to tell you after practice."

"Come to my office," he said, leading them off the court.

He could still hear showers running in the locker room as they walked to his office, so he closed and locked the door behind them, hoping anyone remaining would assume he and Josie had both gone home. Unlikely, given the public nature of their weird argument, but he couldn't think about that right now. "What did you find out?" he asked her.

"It'll be four hundred," she said.

He nodded, relieved but detached. This wasn't as bad as it could be.

"I found out about this clinic in Louisville online," Josie said. "So I called them, and they told me I'd have to come in for counseling and then wait twenty-four hours, because of some law. The closest day I could get was next Friday for the counseling, then Saturday for the other."

"Saturday's the Todd County game," Theo said.

"We'll just have to miss it."

He rubbed his forehead and laughed. "You can miss it, maybe. But I can't, hon. What would people think, both of us gone? It wouldn't look right."

She was very still. "It would look a lot worse if I started to show."

She was right, of course. But part of him was inexplicably picturing his future, *their* future, and how quickly a thing like this—her one remaining semester of high school, the fifteen years between them—would blow over in Roma, Kentucky. People would probably be more upset if they found out about Mathias's little stash in the head coaches' lounge. They would understand that there's a difference between taking drugs and falling in love with the wrong person. Because he *did* love Josie, he was sure of it. He wanted to do right by her, and he wanted to hold on to her. People here would understand that, too. And if they didn't, so what? There was always Bowling Green or Lexington or somewhere else.

"No, it wouldn't look right at all," he said, mostly to himself.

Her face crumpled—that was the only word for it—but she still didn't understand him, still didn't realize what he was proposing. She drew an invisible line on his desk with her finger, trembling, and then the action turned loopy, and her face drew into her old sexy look that Theo knew so well, and he was fascinated by how he could follow her thought process through that one nervous finger, like she was a planchette, divining messages from a supernatural power.

"We could make a whole weekend out of it," she said. "We could go early, you know? Maybe go to Kentucky Kingdom—"

"They'll be closed," Theo said. "For winter."

"Aw, that doesn't matter. Not there, then. We'll have dinner somewhere nice. And I can wear something for you. Real special."

"What would you wear?" Theo asked. He sensed his cruelty, but he was also following her, imagining with her. Honeymoon: the word seemed silly, ridiculous even, but he thought it anyway.

She tilted her head. "You know," she said, blushing, "like a nightie or something. The night before won't matter. We can really live, you know? It'll be the best time."

"And that sounds like living to you," Theo said. "Dinner and a movie and then we get this baby taken care of. Might as well make a big weekend out of it, right? You want to tour the Slugger Museum while we're there?"

She stopped tracing with her finger. "You're screwing with me, aren't you?"

"No way," he said.

"You're not going to take care of this."

"I'm going to take care of you," he told her. "I just don't know that this is the way to do it."

She started to cry, the first time he had ever seen her do it. "You bastard. You selfish asshole. I'll tell. I'll tell the principal."

"Tell her," Theo said. She wouldn't, he felt sure. She had as much at stake as he did. He thought about Sissy, his insurance. *I don't care,* he told himself. *None of that has to matter anymore.* There were other schools, other jobs—positions at factories, right in this very county, that paid better than teaching did. He saw it all suddenly: an apartment like the kind he'd had in college—a house was too much; why had he and Mia been so dead set on mortgaging one?—Josie in the bed beside him, Sissy on the weekends. He could be a better father to his child on the weekends. And she'd have a brother or sister to play with and love, maybe a boy who could help look out for her. Was it wrong for him to imagine this life? Was he crazy for thinking that he could save himself by saving this baby?

Josie picked his cup of pencils up off his desk and threw it against the wall, but the sound was small, lightweight, and Theo could tell that the gesture embarrassed her. "I'll tell my mom!" she yelled.

"Calm down," he said, waving his hands at her, open palms patting air.

"My scholarship," she whispered.

"Honey," he said, "you can still use it. We could do this."

She ran out of his office. He didn't follow her, but he felt certain she would come around. He wasn't being reasonable, exactly, but this was the right thing to do. His adrenaline was high—he hadn't felt this way since college, when his own feet pounded the court, matching his heartbeat.

When he came home from that night's practice, Mia was in the kitchen, scrubbing the counters, and Sissy was sleeping in her playpen across the room. Much as he'd been disgusted by the state of the house for the last several months—and the dog; the dog had been the most senseless, irresponsible kind of loss—it hurt him to see his wife like this: so ardently domestic, so desperately sorry. She raised a finger to her lips when he walked into the kitchen, and he wondered if he was supposed to play a part in this sweet little Moment: tiptoe across the linoleum in his sneakers, silently plant a kiss on her forehead, then her mouth.

She had an apron on, for Christ's sake; should he untie the neat bow, unbutton her clean blouse? He remembered her as she'd been before the burden of Sissy's birth and disease had landed so heavily on them both: not his soulmate, maybe, but a woman to feel proud of. A woman to feel good about coming home to. Mathias had called her "eleven different kinds of fine" just after Theo came to Roma High School, and that was maybe the best compliment he'd ever been paid. She'd been dark-haired and lively and lovely. She'd been a thing worth beholding.

Her eyes now, though, were just as empty to him as they'd been the night Joe died. She smiled and turned back to the counter, yellow rubber gloves brushing the bends of her elbows as she scrubbed hard water stains out of the grooves around the faucet, SOS pad rasping against the stainless steel. Maddeningly single-minded. He went to the playpen, leaned over his daughter, and brushed his thumb against the satiny skin of her temple. She was gorgeous, tiny, doll-like. Mia took good care of her. Theo worried for them both—and already, the thrill of deciding to be with Josie and raising their child was ebbing, becoming entangled and complex. Sissy sighed in her sleep: a luxurious sound that made Theo ache. He wished he could have done better by her. He'd spent the first few months of her life resenting her, despite himself; he'd expected hard work and lost sleep, but he hadn't been prepared for the sudden changes in Mia, who cried so often that her face always shined and who told Theo one night, with a calm that chilled him, that she was thinking about swallowing a bottle of pills. He suddenly understood that what he and Mia had was fine in the good times, when they could rent movies and eat out and shop for a new car together, but that hard times were another matter. Then Sissy started getting sick, and he realized at some point that he wasn't thinking of her as a child anymore, or as his daughter: she was a hypothetical, a baby who might or might not live to see thirty, and if he expected too much, or loved her too much, he'd be disappointed. Her weakness dismayed him, but he was weaker. "Night, baby," he whispered, and Sissy sighed again. He went straight to bed.

Mia slipped in beside him an hour later, skin still faintly redolent of Windex and Lysol. "I do the best I can," she whispered against his back, and the sensation stirred him, surprised him. She ran her fingers lightly across his ribs, tickling.

"I know you do," Theo said. He rolled over and kissed her, slipped his hand into the open neck of her gown, touching the familiar slope of her breast—the first time in a long time, and maybe, he thought, the last. He traced the line of her collarbone, making a chart in his head, two-columned: *Mia, Josie*. One bigger in the chest, one taller. One with lines at the corners of her eyes, one with acne clustered around her temples. He thought about songs they liked—songs he thought they liked—and the way they wanted to be touched. One of them liked him to flick his tongue lightly across the nape of her neck, where her real hair turned into the fuzzy baby-down of soft skin. One liked him to breathe into the cup of her ear, not words, just heat. He couldn't remember which was which right now. Sissy slept, and as he pushed the gown up around his wife's hips, raking his boxers down at the same time with his knees and then his feet, he imagined the wet gurgle of her chest as she drew in air, mobile of stars suspended above her, the moon a smiling crescent in neon.

•   •   •

They won the game against Franklin-Simpson. He and Josie had never been so in synch. It seemed he merely had to *think* an instruction and Josie reacted: cut quickly to the left, passed the ball to Lisa, who was open, took the chance at the three-pointer and made it, sealing the victory. At some point in the game, he looked up at the bleachers, and in a throng of black and gold sweatshirts and flags, he thought he saw Mia. She used to come to his games, unannounced, before Sissy was born, when she was still teaching special ed at the elementary school. She'd sit closer down, though, just behind his row of benched players. He often thought that some of the best moments in their marriage had happened then, unspoken, when the Panthers would score, the crowd would erupt, and the band would kick into "Land of a Thousand Dances," all the sounds punctuated by the occasional slide-whoop of one of those noisemakers the Band Boosters were always selling in the lobby. Amid all of this—his favorite kind of chaos—he'd turn around, savoring his moment, and see Mia just a few paces away; they'd smile at each other, and he'd know that she understood him. That she was feeling the same way he was.

This woman he thought was Mia, though, was up pretty high, just short of the second tier of bleachers that only got full at the boys' games, and she didn't smile or wave when she saw him, and why would Mia be at the game anyway? She'd no sooner bring Sissy than she'd don sequins and dance to "Tricky" with the cheerleaders at halftime. He turned away from the woman in time to see the other team score, and when he looked back, she wasn't there anymore. A guilt hallucination, he was sure. He wasn't made of stone, after all.

The game ended, and Theo felt someone sidle up beside him, shoulder hitting his shoulder.

"Theo, man," Mathias said.

Theo glanced at him, then back at the court. The girls were filing out, and Josie was already gone. He scanned the crowd for her.

Mathias stuck his hand out and Theo shook it, hesitantly. Mathias wasn't in the habit of coming to the girls' games, even when his boys played the occasional Friday night game and the schedules didn't conflict. Theo had always been sore about that, but now he wanted Mathias to leave—to hightail it back to his bachelor's pad and his dope and his easy life.

"Good game," Mathias said.

"Yeah." Theo looked over his shoulder, where the Mia look-alike had been. "Yeah, the girls did good."

Mathias crossed his arms. He was almost a foot taller than Theo, broad through the chest, and he had a presence—as a player so many years back, now as a coach—that Theo deeply envied: the reason, he knew, that Mathias was coaching the boys, though they'd joked a few times that the boys' team didn't have Josie-style perks. Uncomfortable joking.

"You're out, friend," Mathias said. He didn't lower his voice at all, but parents and teenagers were a churning mass around them, and the words felt muted, unreal. Theo understood them, though.

"Out," Mathias repeated. Then he looked at the court. "I guess things got around. You know—some parent, then a teacher got involved. Then Rita Beasley."

"Well, don't draw it out, for Christ's sake," Theo said. "What's going on?"

"They're having an emergency school board meeting tonight, and I expect that you'll get a call by tomorrow. That's what Noel

Price told me." He sighed, and Theo could smell Listerine.
"They'll let you resign. They won't want a big stir."

Sissy. Theo couldn't breathe.

"You okay?" Mathias said.

Theo laughed out loud. "She's pregnant, Matt."

"Mia?"

Theo shook his head.

"Goddamn," Mathias said.

"She's going to leave me," Theo said—out loud, but to himself.
Saying it, he realized that she probably already had: *Things got
around.* Mia had been in the bleachers, watching him, and now
she was gone: to her mother's, with Sissy. He would come home
tonight to an empty house, to the lingering smells of Joe's sickness and Sissy's baby lotion, and the rest of his life would begin.
He didn't know what kind of life that could be.

"I'm sorry," Mathias told him.

Theo went to the locker room, where the girls were gathered
for his wrap-up talk, Josie nowhere to be seen, and he said the
nonsense things he always said—"Good game, good teamwork,
let's focus on defense at practice this week"—watching the girls'
faces, wondering who among them knew. All of them, of course,
but they made their expressions innocent and blank, and he appreciated them for it. He said a prayer with the girls and called it
a night, and he could hear, as he left, their talk shift from *amens*
to discussions of parties—Chad's house or Tresten's?—prom
dates, and *Man, we were so fucked up!* It occurred to him that
Josie had a second life too. On game nights, when Theo went
home to Mia, changed a token diaper, and made himself watch
Sissy sleep, she was over at some kid's house, nursing a bottle
of Boone's Farm that somebody's older brother had charged

her eight bucks for. She studied for tests, asked her mother for money. In another month or two she'd start shopping for prom dresses, and whatever she'd find would look awkward and hopeful, and on prom night she'd stand out in the middle of this very gymnasium wearing too much eye shadow and lipstick, unsure for once, graceless.

He saw her as he was walking to his car, the February night air like novocaine to his bare arms. She was with Jatarius in the parking lot and the light from a security lamp fell over them softly, the scene picturesque, staged. She was still in her jersey—she'd never showered—and Jatarius was working his big hands up and down her bare arms, warming them, and in a moment Theo knew that they would kiss, that Josie was just waiting for him to see it. He could get in his car and follow them—she'd let him, she'd make sure Jatarius slowed down, using any excuse that came to mind; and he'd do it, do whatever she asked, spurred on by the promise of her. He'd do it, because Josie was a girl—a woman—who would, Theo was understanding, have her way, with his help or without it. Now, no more than thirty feet away, she lifted her chin, and Jatarius lowered his, and they were a single dark shadow outlined in a hazy yellow nimbus—gone already, she was telling him, and he was a fool to think otherwise.

Later, he could turn off on whatever country road they turned off on, drive a little past the thick of trees where they'd park, and pull his own vehicle over to the shoulder, quieting the engine, shutting off the headlights. His overcoat was in the passenger seat. He'd put it on, creep back down the road, take a spot behind the trunk of a leafless water maple. And they'd watch each other through the rear windshield of Jatarius's car: Josie's slow undress, her mount, her gentle rocking, baby between them.

• PARTS •

I had a daughter. When she was eleven, my husband and I took her to Spring Acres, the local pool park, for swimming lessons. She wore a purple bathing suit, the bikini I allowed over Art's grumbled protests, and she bounced on the diving board a little, and leaped, and cannonballed right into the deep end. The splash of blue-tinted water made a fragile shell around her, gorgeous, and then she went under. She was fearless. There was that moment a mother feels when the heart pauses and the throat goes dry, that fear of—or desire for, maybe—the moment of crisis, when everything changes and you have to change, too, to make sense of it all. That's a strange word: *desire*. But it's there. When your wheels catch water on a rainy day and your brakes are suddenly useless, the pedal under your foot mush; when you're a few swats away from spanking your child too hard, and the coldness in your heart both terrifies and delights you. It's unexplainable, that desire, and perhaps it should also go unacknowledged, but I've decided that the desire is useful, not shameful. Because it keeps you sane when the worst happens. And the worst does happen.

I felt that moment, and then she broke the surface of the water, and we caught our breaths together. Art, beside me, never looked up from his medical journal—the luxury of fatherhood.

I like to keep her here: young and alive, so many years away from the horror of that night in the dorm room. Her innocence and mine. She caught her breath that humid July afternoon, and I swear, it was just like the moment of her birth: the intake of air, the shriek of delight and fear. She waved to me from across the water, and I waved back, and we were laughing together. Felicia.

She was murdered eight years later, in the fall semester of her sophomore year of college. The boy who killed her, who got away with it, was named Simon Wells, and they'd met a few days earlier at a keg party on State Street. He'd made a pass at her, but she went home that night with his friend instead. The story came out at trial, and the boy she went home with, Marty, was the one who did most of the telling. The police put the rest together. It went something like this: The boys went to Felicia's dorm room—"to see if she wanted to party," Marty said. They smoked pot together, talked for a while, and then Felicia and Marty fooled around some, kissing and "second-base stuff," not wanting to make Simon uncomfortable. "He's a lonely guy," Marty had testified. "I felt sorry for him." After that, Marty claims that Simon "got crazy jealous," pushing him out of the way and forcing himself on Felicia. When she started to scream, Simon covered her mouth for a moment with a pillow—a novelty pillow, rainbow-striped, fish-shaped, that I'd bought for her myself—and when she screamed again, he covered her face again, and she was dead when he removed it the second time. Or at least seemed to be, Marty had amended. She wasn't moving. Didn't seem to be breathing. It had happened so fast—he hadn't known that Simon could hurt her that way, or he would have done something, he would have risked his own life to save her. It had happened so fast.

"Then Simon sent me to get the car started," Marty said on the stand. "I didn't know what he was going to do. I wasn't thinking too straight by then."

So many holes in that. So much to doubt. But I want to believe that Marty told the truth because Felicia had deemed him good, or at least good enough to sleep with. I've spent the five years since Felicia's death trying to reconcile the girl I knew, the daughter I'd made it my life's business to love, with the secrets that reveal themselves in death. You either make allowances or you lose the person a second time, and that's just the way of things.

When Marty left the dorm room, Simon set about covering up his crime. He sprayed Felicia down with a can of air freshener, wove a comforter around the room's two sprinklers, closed the windows, and locked them. He tossed the emptied can on the bed, good as a bomb, and then he lit a match, set her on fire, and ran out of the room, pulling the door shut behind him. The doors at Keough Hall are solid oak, and they lock automatically. The first campus police officer to arrive after the fire alarm sounded secured the perimeter but didn't open Felicia's door. He waited for the fire department to arrive, and by the time they were able to break in, the room was a black and steaming husk, and Felicia, who shouldn't have still been breathing, was.

In another lifetime—the life before my marriage and even my courtship, the life before motherhood, when I still had interests and ambitions and hopes that existed outside of my daughter—I was an English major at a good university. And as every English major must, I took a survey on Shakespeare, whom I regarded with a kind of automatic, passionless appreciation. It was all too big for me, too grand, the fall of kings and death of lovers and old men raising their fists against thunderstorms and God. I believed in Shakespeare's goodness the way I believed in God's goodness: hypothetically, trusting the opinions of the majority over my own disinterest. I hadn't known any tragedy in those days. I had no real reasons for faith or for doubt.

The play I liked that semester was the one I wasn't supposed to like, *Titus Andronicus.* The professor presented it to us as a curiosity and sometimes as a joke. "Shakespeare does *Texas Chainsaw Massacre*," he'd said, affecting seriousness. He would read passages aloud with a melodramatic warble, working us like a stand-up comic, sounding, I would think later, almost desperate, as if the only way to excuse the play, to restore Shakespeare for us, was to shout the disdain that he'd rather have kept private. What bothered me was that the play affected me more deeply than I could admit during final examinations, when I dutifully penned into my bluebook that it was "easily dismissible, though noteworthy as a testing ground for themes Shakespeare would later put to better use." Here is the sketch of things: There is a great Roman general, Titus, who gets on the wrong side of a powerful woman named Tamora, who becomes empress. Titus has many sons, and most of them die during the play, but the important thing for you to know is that he has a daughter, Lavinia. Lavinia is raped by Tamora's sons, who then cut out her tongue and cut off her hands so that she can't tell anyone who's committed the crime. Lavinia doesn't die, but she spends the rest of the play miming and weeping silently, and then Titus himself slays her at the end, along with a stageful of others.

That was the image I couldn't shake: Lavinia, led onstage by her torturers, robbed of her tongue and her hands. The outrageousness of it. The cruelty.

I hadn't thought about that play in my daughter's lifetime, all those good years of health and plenty. I'd had no reason to. We were, as families go, successful. When Felicia chose the local state college over Vanderbilt, Art's and my alma mater, Art had groused—but he wrote the tuition and housing checks without so much as a blink, and he drove the half hour to campus at least once a week for a surprise visit, which she nearly always welcomed. She was a good girl. She'd loved her father. And Felicia, the mere fact of her existence, had continually fixed anything that threatened to break between Art and me. We were better together, united in loving her, than we could have been apart. It wasn't a perfect life, but I can look back on it now and know that it was as close to one as Art and I had deserved.

Then it was gone. Suddenly I was sitting at her bedside, listening to the hitch and hiss of the respirator, backing away every few moments to allow the doctors and nurses to change the bedding, which she frequently wet—the fluids poured out of her as quickly as they were pumped in by IV—and her dressings, which served as her skin. She was so swollen and bandaged that she was unknowable, her dark blonde hair burned almost completely away, the wisps clinging to her forehead as brittle and dark as curlicues of graphite. The room's heat was cranked up as high as it would go, almost 100 degrees, because—an irony, one of so many—her scorched skin couldn't retain any heat. The doctors and nurses wore hand towels around their necks. Art was stripped down to his sleeveless undershirt.

I passed out at one point, came to in a room down the hall, and vowed that I would never be so weak again, that I wouldn't leave her. I returned to find Art pacing the hallway outside her door, rubbing his face briskly with both hands. He'd been crying. Of course, we both had. But I could tell he was upset about something new.

"They're going to amputate her hands," he said. He wouldn't have known how to soften his words. "She isn't stable enough to go to the operating room, so they're trying to sterilize her room. They're going to work on her right here."

I had stared at him, still light-headed. It didn't make any sense.

"She can't live like this," he said, his voice high and choked. "It isn't possible. It isn't right."

I didn't know then what Felicia had suffered before the fire. It was six in the morning, about five hours since we'd gotten the call, and we didn't know that she was the victim of anything but an awful accident; it hadn't even occurred to me to wonder. Later that day Marty Stevenson would walk into his eleven-thirty section of American History fifteen minutes late, stumble on his way to a desk at the back of the room, and erupt into a fit of hysterics, scaring some of his classmates so badly that a handful fled the room, dialing 911 on their cells. That's when the truth, however distorted and partial, started to emerge. By the time the campus police chief came to the hospital to tell me and Art about Marty's confession, Felicia's hands and one of her ears were gone. It had come off into the doctor's hand like overripe fruit.

It was then that I thought of Lavinia. My daughter lay mute in her hospital bed, unaware of what she'd lost during her unconsciousness. She was swollen all over, bandaged into anonymity, her arms lopped and wrapped and strangely dear, resting on her stomach like paws. "You should touch her," a nurse told me, folding back the thermal blanket at the bottom of the bed. I watched her carefully peel down a stocking, revealing a foot that was peach and smooth and barely blemished, the toenails painted bright blue. Can you see it? That perfect small foot, the round, almost chubby toes, the cheerful, bright nail polish. I took it in my hands, pressed my cheek against it. I kissed each toe, the way I'd done when she was a baby. I whispered into the delicate arch.

Art couldn't do it. Here he was: a man, a father, a doctor. He'd given Felicia his high forehead and his hands. He'd given her his name. But when I backed away from her foot and beckoned him, he pinched his lips together almost prudishly and shook his head: a hard snap, left-right. The way a child refuses vegetables. Disgusted. Frightened. Absolutely determined. And that was when I began to understand that our marriage wouldn't survive this, even if Felicia could. He was already pulling away from her, wishing her dead, wanting to stop her agony and start his grieving. He didn't want to be father to a creature as destroyed and defeated as this one was, but I, in my selfishness, was determined to hang on to every last bit of her, even if she turned to ashes in my embrace. Titus had killed Lavinia because he couldn't bear to see her live with her shame. To me, Art's turning away from his daughter's foot was the harsher act, because it was rooted not in love, or in selfishness, but in weakness.

Felicia died three days later.

You know more than any mother should know, Art told me in the weeks after her death.

And he was right. I worked part-time at the library, a job I'd picked up after Felicia went to college, and now I was spending slow mornings on the public computer doing searches on the Internet, reading articles in the newspaper, scanning the blogs. *Simon is creepy, I know him from class, he totally did it,* I read on one page, and felt the bitter thrill of absolute surety. *Its so sad but she fucked them both and this is the kind of shit that happens,* I read on another, and the thrill turned to fury and shame, and I don't think it's an exaggeration to say that I, too, could have been a murderer if I'd known who so thoughtlessly and cowardly posted that. I was breaking down, my sleeping hours only distinguishable from the waking hours by my dreams, which made my grief somehow more articulate. Over and over again, Felicia jumped into the swimming pool at Spring Acres. Over and over again, she failed to resurface. And the dream-me would think, looking at the still water, that it would be wrong to jump in after her because water puts out fires. That's when I'd usually wake up.

This is the kind of shit that happens. I started searching her bedroom, going through the items she'd left behind after moving into the dorms: the cheap jewelry box with the little spinning ballerina inside it, her Cabbage Patch doll with the yarn hair, the band posters she'd put up during high school. I looked under her mattress. I pushed aside clean underwear and balled-up socks, finding only a lavender sachet and a cracked plastic egg, the kind pantyhose used to come in, with a single stocking inside, twisted like a dead thing. She'd taken her secret self to college, and the artifacts of that life went up in flames with her. I was left with dolls and old yearbooks and the clothes I'd purchased for her, the life I'd allowed her while she lived under my roof, the remnants of a Felicia I had known and understood.

I'm good at finding that dark matter in the white space, and I'm maybe too good at living there, wallowing in it. I think things I shouldn't think: that Felicia awakened after the fire started and screamed for me; that Simon and Marty laughed when they reunited at the car, high-fived and lit cigarettes with the same lighter, or book of matches, that had started the fire. I wonder about the times Art was with her alone, when she was a child. Had he hit her? Had he touched her? Art is a decent man, and he wouldn't have done either of those things, but some nights— when the last of the wine is gone and I can feel Felicia all around me, through me, even, like my pulse—everything I should know for sure doesn't seem so certain anymore, and I think about calling Art, at his new house across town, where he sleeps next to his new wife: Did you love her? Did you love me?

He just wanted to move on, Art told me as I was packing my suitcases on the day I left; he wanted to remember what happiness felt like. I wasn't thinking then: where I'd go, how I'd pay for it. And I should have felt *something* when he handed me that

stack of crisp twenties—everything in his wallet—with assur-
ances that I could also go on using the credit card for as long as I
needed. Something other than embarrassment, or gratefulness;
it was my money, too. But I took what he gave me and tucked it
into my purse, and I murmured something like *Thanks* in a voice
I didn't recognize.

"Don't mention it," he said, leaning over to pick up my bags
for me. The bigger person, the big man. Our daughter had been
dead for five months, and the trial hadn't started yet. "Where
will you go?"

I didn't know. My parents were both dead, and my sister lived
in Ohio. I had friends in town—women who resembled friends,
at least—but most were also hospital wives, and few were good
for more than the occasional light lunch at the country club.
When Felicia died, none of them called me, but they all sent
flower arrangements: gigantic bouquets that collectively cost
more than my first car had. "A hotel, I guess."

"Take a room at the Washington House," he said. "I'd feel
more at ease."

I nodded.

He put the bags back down and came forward, then put his
arms around me. I let him. I tried to hold myself stiff at first, but
I needed his touch—Christ, I always had—and he melted me,
that silly old phrase I hate, the stuff of Hallmark cards and easy-
listening love songs.

"You don't have to leave," he said.

I inhaled the good smell of his neck, the Old Spice he still
wore because his father always had. There were reasons for loving him, I know that even now.

"I'll call tomorrow," I said.

He backed away and picked up my bags again. Gentlemanly to the last, but I should have recognized how easy my leaving was—too easy. *Twenty-two-year marriages don't end like this,* I thought as he loaded the car and kissed me, as I turned over the engine and pulled out of our drive. They don't simply flatline. Not if there was life in them to start with.

He's a gynecologist, one of only two who still practice in Roma, which has a history of attracting the doctors fleeing malpractice suits and driving away the ones with real skill. But Art, who could have had a more glittery life than the one he chose, is good. Very good. His clients are loyal, all ages, and even now, the divorce four years done, one will approach me occasionally, recognizing me from the old family portrait he still keeps in his office. Crazy, but true. And she'll say, "What a good, good man he is. So understanding." I usually nod and agree and leave it at that. There are all kinds of understanding, I could tell her—all kinds of goodness—but what would it matter?

We both agreed, from the start of the marriage, that I'd be better off seeing another doctor, when the need arose. Another decision that came perhaps too easily, but it worked for us. When Felicia was sixteen, and she approached me about birth control, I took her to my doctor in Bowling Green—quietly—to get her examination and prescription. Art and I could function like that when she was still around, with these compact lives that were separate and whole and in no way intersecting. In mine: Felicia's sex life, which I considered myself with it enough to understand and even support a bit; my housekeeping and little trivial errands; and my books, devoured more often than not with a glass or two of wine. In his: the monthly trips to Nashville with Beau Markham and Robert Zipes, the anesthesiologist and the surgeon—business trips, he called them, though we both knew that I knew better. I'd accepted that they probably played golf and drank to drunkenness; and perhaps they'd gone to strip clubs, too, but I never considered, or allowed myself to consider, the degrees of betrayal beyond that.

His work was in that life too. One evening at dinner, when Felicia was an eight-year-old playing over at a neighbor's house, a question—perhaps the most obvious question—occurred to me for the first time, and I put down my salad fork, the look on my face apparently bizarre enough that Art paused mid-sentence. "Do you ever get aroused at work?" I said.

"No," he told me, mildly enough that I believed him. In bed that night, though—at least an hour or more after I had slipped off into sleep—he shook my shoulder. "Every now and then," he whispered, and I knew what he was talking about right away. "Once in a blue moon. And it shocks me."

"When does it happen?"

I turned around but couldn't see his face because his back was to the window, casting him in shadow.

"Sometimes during a breast exam. Most of the time just before the exam starts, and I can see a slice of her skin where the paper jacket gapes open."

"What about when you—" I couldn't finish.

"Do a pelvic?" His shadow shook. "Never. I may as well be kneading bread dough."

My stomach lurched. "Jesus."

"You think I'm some kind of pervert, don't you?" he said.

"No," I told him. I think that I meant it.

"Because it's common enough." He rolled onto his back and sighed. "It's a big joke in med school. But it happens less and less with time, anyway."

"You get used to it," I said.

"Something like that."

I pulled the covers tighter around me. "Do you worry about my doctor?" I asked him.

He was yawning. "Huh?"

"Dr. Nickell," I said. "Do you worry he's getting a boner when he touches my boob?"

"No," Art said, laughing. "It's real rare, hon. Ninety-nine percent of the time they're just parts to us."

"Parts," I said.

He patted my arm. "Yeah. Like Picasso: a breast here, a leg there. When you get hard, it usually doesn't even make sense. It doesn't have to be a beautiful woman or even a young one, just someone who hits your senses the right way."

"Thanks a lot," I said.

"I like your parts," he told me, pulling the waistband of my pajama bottoms down so that he could slip his hand between my legs. He moved against me. "This," he said lowly. "This is what does it for me."

Bread dough, I kept thinking. But we had sex anyway.

I knew when Art called three weeks ago that he had news for me. He only calls to hurt me with his happiness, and he always prefaces his announcements with, "I wanted you to know first." Like it's a gift he's offering me, a neat little package of despair: *Dana, I'm selling the house. Dana, I met a woman. Dana, we're getting married.*

"Dana, Stephanie's pregnant," he said. "We're having a baby."

All I could make clear was this: Felicia would be twenty-four. While Art blathered on, that thought cycled in my head, first in words, then in images: the graduation she never attended, the boyfriend—the *one*—she never met, never had a chance to bring home. Some days I wonder if my life would be different—how my life would be different—if Felicia had been in a car accident, or had cancer, if she'd gone some way that wasn't so goddamned grotesque. Can you quantify grief?

"She's about midway through her second trimester," Art said, and that snapped me back in a hurry. Stephanie. She works at the Chamber of Commerce, and I always see her picture in the local paper: cutting a ribbon at some new business nobody wants to see in this town—Blockbuster or Burger King, nonsense like that—hosting a Rotary luncheon, "kicking up her heels" (the *News Leader*'s words) at the Tobacco Festival Street Dance and Tamale Hour. She's thirty-five, and though those twelve years between us burn sometimes, I'm thankful that he didn't choose someone Felicia's age. He could have, too. He's more attractive now than he ever was: tan, fit, the kind of man who wears his middle age like a Rolex, a sign of his good breeding and achievement. I carry my middle age around like an ulcer. "Twenty weeks or so," he finished.

"Pretty far along," was all I said.

"Well, she's starting to show." I could hear the television behind his words, and a sound like cabinets opening and closing, dishes being removed and stacked. I pictured Stephanie, apron tied neatly around her cute little pregnant bump, starting supper, giving Art concerned looks, marital shorthand: *Is she okay? Is she flipping out? Do you want one pork chop or two?* "But we wanted to keep it quiet for a while, make sure everything looks good. We're not in our twenties."

"You had an amnio," I said, knowing as I said it I was right. No Down's baby for Art.

"Well, sure." He cleared his throat.

"Congratulations," I said.

"I'd like her to know you," he said. "And so would Stephanie. We'd like you to be involved, I mean."

"A girl, then." I pinched the bridge of my nose, willing my tear ducts to behave. I thought about the Art in Felicia's face: her blue, wide-set eyes, her high forehead. And Art's hands, too: long, graceful fingers that she'd applied toward no particular talent or vocation, surgery or piano-playing or any of the old clichés. When she was a little girl, and my hair was still long—down to my waist, almost—she'd loved brushing it with my big wooden paddle brush, long strokes that lulled her toward nap-time better than rocking or warm milk ever had. With Art gone to work, we'd lie in the big master bed together, drowsing, and sometimes she'd reach over and pat my face with her still-chubby little fingers: *Mama*, she'd say. Like a blessing.

"Yep, a little girl," Art told me.

"Why do you think I'd want to know your child, Art?" I said. "I mean, did it cross your mind that the situation might be a little awkward for all of us?"

"Because she's Felicia's sister," he said.

That's the thing about Art right there: how on the one hand he can be so *good*—so damned noble, even—and on the other, a monster. Who would I be to this child? Aunt Dana? The babysitter?

"I don't think it's a good idea," I said.

In the background on his end of the line, a hot cooking sizzle—supper almost done. My own stomach, unbelievably, growled; I decided that I'd drive down to Hardee's for a burger, bring it home, and eat it with a glass—or two or three—of the good red wine that I bring back from my occasional trips to Nashville. I've gained about twenty pounds since Felicia's death, and when I saw my sister last Christmas, she had the audacity to tell me that I was "hiding from men"—as though my greatest trouble after the death of my daughter was figuring out how to date again. As if a man were any sort of solution.

"It's an open offer," Art said. "Indefinitely, okay?"

We said our goodbyes and hung up. *Indefinitely*: the word almost made me smile. This offer of his—made to assuage his guilt about an old wife, an old *life*—would be forgotten in a few weeks, dead as Felicia. There would be baby showers and first kicks, a nursery to decorate, cigars—the good Cubans—to ship in and pass out among his friends. I would see his child only by accident, and probably more often than I'd like: Roma's a small town. In a few years she would start coming to the library, and when I'd lead Story Hour or one of the Summer Reading Program sessions, maybe she would be one of the small faces looking up at me. Maybe? Christ, it was likely. There was only one library, and if he was as demanding a father as he used to be—he'd wanted Felicia to be every bit as driven and successful as himself, though he'd regarded my own modest smarts, my own lack of worldly ambition, as natural—Art would have her there. Come hell or high water.

I dug my car keys out of the basket I keep by the back door, pulled my light jacket off a hook, and checked my purse for cash: eight dollars. I wouldn't be gone long. At Art's house, they would be sitting down to eat dinner, the relief palpable between them, perhaps even confessed out loud: "Thank God we have each other."

I will never have another child. This is a truth I settled with long ago, because I was forty-two when Felicia died, and by the time the idea of a new baby presented itself as a kind of solution—*Yes, I could just have another*—Art was gone, and my own body was changing, going bad on me the way a woman's body will inevitably do. I'm not a modern woman the way my daughter was: Felicia, whose confident sexuality had fascinated and even impressed me a little, naive as I had been at her age; who saw college as a step in a logical progression; who'd taken for granted that she could choose her own path in life, go slowly, treat dating as recreation and not husband-hunting. I'm not a modern woman, but I can't help raging a little at the unfairness of the situation—Art's ability to simply move on, to replace our daughter with a new child as easily as he'd replaced our old Toyota Camry with a Cadillac Escalade. Upgrading. I find myself thinking more and more of that day when I left him: I'd thought that I was leaving him, that I'd taken decisive action, but I see now that Art ushered me out of the marriage just as he ushered me out of the house that afternoon.

Some nights, all of the things I know for sure—should be able to count on, like gravity and oxygen and sunrise—lose their power over me. I know who killed Felicia. I caught his eye a half-dozen times in the courtroom and simply understood, felt the guilt baking off him like a fever, settling on me sick and damp and poisoned. I know that much. But some nights, it's Art I want to see destroyed, see broken. I want him to feel at least as bad as I do now, to know loneliness—a woman's loneliness, the way it feels to be childless and manless with nothing else to define you or drive you.

We met when we were in college at Vanderbilt. I was a sophomore, Art just starting med school. And the first time we had sex—my first time ever—was in my dorm room, when my roommate was gone for the weekend, visiting family. We locked the outer door, turned the radio up loud so no one in the hallway could hear. I don't remember what was playing, but I remember the scratchiness of the sound, and of my blankets; the coolness of the concrete block wall that my left arm kept brushing as we kissed, the bed was so small. There was the usual pain and blood, and when he finished I cried, because I felt trashy, because I wondered what my daddy would think. My daddy, who'd sold off twenty acres of good farmland to make up the costs that my scholarship didn't cover.

Sex is always violent. Even consensual sex, or *lovemaking* as the hospital wives would always put it, prudish and vulgar all at once. I'm not saying that I hated sex—I didn't—or that Art was somehow rougher than other men, because he wasn't really rough at all. That night in my dorm, when I started to cry, he held me close, patted my hair, whispered in my ear that we never had to do it again if I didn't want. What happened to Felicia, the way our marriage disintegrated: none of that takes away from his essential decency, as much as I sometimes want it to. I don't know if Art is a good man, but sometimes a decent one is all you can hope for.

•   •   •

Two days after Art's phone call, I got in my car to drive to Felicia's grave and ended up in Bowling Green instead, sitting in front of the Wells Brothers Furniture Company. Simon's car—a newer black Corvette than the one I'd seen him enter and exit a half-dozen times during Felicia's trial—was parked on the store's side lot, angled across two spaces so that the doors wouldn't get dinged. He'd done that at the courthouse, too, and on the hottest days—this would have been late July—he'd prop a metallic visor up in the windshield. I could often see it in the lot from the courtroom: a wink of light in the distance, like a faraway ocean or a mirage.

His trial lasted two weeks, and the jury deliberations lasted two and a half hours: acquittal on all nine counts. No physical evidence linked him to Felicia's room, which was scorched, then flooded when the sprinkler system finally engaged—no sperm, no fingerprints, no sign of him on the Keough Hall security tapes, though the girl helming the front desk admitted that it wouldn't be hard to sneak by her—and the investigation got botched by a team of campus investigators who'd never handled anything more complex than noise violations, DUIs, and the occasional stolen bike or book bag. Simon cried alibi as soon as the police dragged him off, but the campus detective began interrogating him without investigating it, a point the defense hammered over and over again at trial. He was at his mother and father's house, his father said on the stand—definitely home at three a.m., when the dorm's fire alarm went off. Everyone was awake, his father insisted: a happy family sitting at the table, having a middle-of-the-night heart-to-heart about Simon's career anxieties. He was, after all, a twenty-three-year-old college sophomore positioned to inherit a regional furniture chain of more than thirty stores.

His friend, Marty, is in prison. He pleaded guilty to voluntary manslaughter a year before the trial in exchange for a recommended sentence of twenty-to-life. His testimony was supposed to cinch Simon's conviction, but he ended up doing more harm than good: Simon's slick defense attorneys pinned Marty on a handful of piddling inconsistencies in his testimony, confused him on the stand, made him look like a fool and a liar. I don't feel sorry for him. But the hate, which has become so much a presence in my life that I may as well call it a part of myself, like my eyes or my hands, is for Simon. It's a useless sort of hate, though, one that I haven't the courage or even ambition to hone into a weapon. But I like the idea of revenge—big revenge, the kind Shakespeare wrote about. In *Titus Andronicus*, Titus kills his daughter's rapists and serves them to their mother in a meat pie. Crude, silly—that's what my professor had told us, anyway. But satisfying, too. We live, I've heard, in a civilized country, in a civilized time. Our movies are violent but our laws are just. The system will serve us. And I put faith in that, because I'm a middle-aged woman, most of my life a homemaker, and I couldn't even bring myself to give Felicia spankings when she deserved them. What was I supposed to do when the system failed me? What, if not destroy what was left of my own life instead of my daughter's murderers'?

I knew that Simon worked the flagship store most evenings. He was on Bowling Green's local news less than a year ago, red "Wells Brothers" polo tucked into neatly pressed khakis, hair streaked blond but still trimmed short: a solid, all-American male. The segment showed clips of him unloading stock next to his dad, muscles well-defined as he lifted plastic-wrapped couches and recliners from the back of a semi; in another shot, he counted out change for a customer, and said, in a lull in the reporter's voice-over, "You have a nice day now." The interview was sympathetic. The reporter mentioned that Simon's car had been vandalized, that he was accosted one night outside a bar. "I'm just trying to lead a good life and put this behind me," Simon had said. "I don't bear any grudges." The goddamn nerve.

I'd never gone inside Wells Brothers, even before Felicia's death. They didn't carry the kind of furniture I would have put in my home—not then, at least, when I was still a doctor's wife. I'd driven by once before Felicia started college, thinking that I might find a cheap bookshelf small enough to fit in her dorm room. They were closed, though, and I ended up buying one at Target instead.

I went inside. The showroom smelled cool and plastic, not rich with the earthiness of hardwoods and leather. Theirs was the cheap stuff, just short of disposable: pressboard entertainment cabinets and laminated kitchen tables, overstuffed vinyl recliners in burgundy, green, and brown. Ceramic vases and lamps cluttered glass-topped end tables, the vases filled with dusty stalks of eucalyptus, that medicinal scent I've always hated, like cut grass and anise. It was early evening on a Wednesday and quiet; a couple was at the far end of the showroom looking at the dining room tables, but the store was empty otherwise. The furniture was arranged into little areas meant to mimic rooms in a house: couches with chairs and coffee tables, kitchen tables set for dinner with place mats and plates. I wondered if Simon had designed some of these arrangements and knew that he must have. It was fitting: this man who understood nothing about the fragile construction of a family, piecing together bad fictions out of bad furniture.

The double doors between the stockroom and showroom swung open, and Simon came out. He saw me, started toward me.

I stood where I was and waited for the step that would bring him close enough to feel suspicion, then the step that would make him certain: I waited for him to understand that the mother of the girl he killed was finally confronting him, doing the thing she'd been too scared and weak to do during the trial. So many days I'd sat in that courtroom, Art next to me but careful not to let his arm or leg brush mine, watching this young man pass in his crisp, navy blue suit. So many times I'd caught his gaze, seen something inside him that I knew his own parents had been able to deny, or ignore: the combination of weakness and meanness, self-hatred and vanity. I'd known better than even Simon what a dangerous mixture those traits were, how they could—in the wrong circumstances—drive an otherwise average boy to commit the act of a psychotic. I knew all of that, but I couldn't do anything about it.

He stopped, less than a yard away. "Can I help you, ma'am?"

We made eye contact. I waited. In a moment, I was sure, he'd react: his body would become tense or his hand would start trembling; he'd say something like, "Why are you here?" or "I swear, I didn't do it." I had envisioned this meeting a thousand different times and ways—considered the dialogue that would follow—but this was the part I had always accepted as a given: he'd see me and he'd *know*.

"Ma'am?" he said. He rubbed the back of his neck, and I noticed for the first time how much fuller his face was now, three years after the trial—a detail that hadn't come through over the television. I could see that he was anxious, but only because he was confronted with a situation he didn't immediately know how to handle. Humor the crazy woman? Call the guys in the little white coats?

I looked at the floor. "I'm browsing," I said.

"Oh, okay." He nodded. "Make yourself at home; just holler if you need anything. We'll be running a special on Leatherlook through Memorial Day, so keep that in mind."

"I will," I said.

He backed away, smiling carefully. Before he turned—before he struck out across the showroom floor toward the couple in the dining area—I thought I saw something in his face. I went back to my car knowing that I was probably kidding myself, that *my* face meant no more to him than Felicia's life had. He'd moved on, like everyone else. Everyone but me.

I think that there are moments in a life when you have to leave a part of yourself behind to function—like molting. Felicia's birth was the first such moment for me: in the weeks after my labor I understood that my body wasn't the only thing that would always be different, that my soul had changed, too. Some loss there, but the gains were greater. When she died, I had to molt again, but I did it badly and never really finished the job, because I get up mornings feeling like a mother, still, and I go to bed nights mourning my daughter all over again. If the anger is a part of me, Felicia's loss is a kind of amputation, and I haven't yet figured out how to function without her.

I left Simon's store that night understanding what a small thing a life is—how quickly it comes and goes, how even the bereaved, like my ex-husband, can evolve and adapt and find new ways to get by. I drove home thinking about Art's baby. Intoxicating to imagine this new child, this sister of Felicia's. She is a miracle and a curse: half of Art and none of me.

• • •

The library is never a loud place, but its energy changes. During the spring, before the middle school lets out and all of the buses begin their afternoon run, the light falls through the windows differently and the books almost seem to sigh, scattering dust particles around in swirls. I sit at the front desk reading a novel or magazine, and the big grandfather clock in the front entrance—the one the city purchased the year of Roma's bicentennial—counts off the new hour with low, springlike thrums, a brassy, ancient sound. We don't have the world's oldest or most charming building. They made a lot of "improvements" in the '80s: dropped the ceiling, installed cold fluorescent lighting. Five years ago they covered the hardwood floors with wall-to-wall blue Berber carpeting—to minimize noise and retain the heat, the head librarian said, but now the children's sneakers smack against the nubby plastic runners that crisscross the floor at all angles, and I get tripped up at least once a day. A graying woman in cardigan sweaters and khaki skirts and neat leather loafers: the stereotypical old maid librarian, or getting there.

Yesterday, Stephanie arrived in that silent hour before the afternoon rush. Soon, the girls and boys would tear in, and as oddly respectful as they are in this place—the only place besides church, perhaps, that holds such sway over a child—the very walls vibrate when they're here. Until they start to drift off to home for dinner, I'm captivated, and that short period of my day is when I can leave Felicia behind me for a little while. I love watching them sit at the tables, kicking their heels against the chair rungs, chins tucked into palms. They turn the pages of books so carefully, the little ones.

That silence right before is when I'm at my most vulnerable. It's physical—the emptiness around me, and within me, a kind of husked-out, cried-out place that's almost a pleasure because it's numb. And that's how Stephanie found me: sitting in my familiar chair with the worn-in seat cushion, printing a pile of overdue slips for mailing, sleeping with my eyes open.

"I hoped you'd be here," she said.

What do you say about a woman like Stephanie? She's attractive, but I was more attractive at thirty-five; smart—that much is obvious by speaking to her—but not especially deep or sensitive, not *soulful,* which is what Art used to say he loved about me: *How much you care about everything. How you feel so much, all the time.* Polite, not necessarily kind. She is the woman who marries men like Art, who is able to understand, with a savviness that borders on calculation, that her modest charms have more value because she's the new model.

But she's also one of those women who seem more real in pregnancy. And it hurt me to see her that way—brown, nicely trimmed hair a bit more mussed than usual; the way her badly cut sailor blouse pulled tight around her middle but sagged under her arms, making her both sad and kind of lovely, too. I could glimpse, for a moment, what a person might love about her.

"Good to see you," I said, the lie so obvious and empty that I think we were both embarrassed by it.

"You, too." She gripped the edge of the front desk before me. Her fingernails were painted a smooth, even coral. "I've been wanting to talk to you for a while."

The library was so quiet. The only patron was an older man—one of those retirees who comes by daily and stays for hours—and he was off in the back corner, tucked away with the paperback mysteries and true-crime books. One afternoon, this old man, Jimmy, his name is, stood right where Stephanie was standing, for hours, it seemed like, telling me about one of the books he was reading: *The Red Light Murders*. I let him. The victims were young women, he explained, wannabe starlets and prostitutes living in the bad part of Los Angeles, circa 1925. Killer filleted them like fish, took their eyes for trophies. And the author had proven, through new DNA technologies and old documents found on his family's country estate, that his own grandfather was the likely murderer. "Helluva thing," Jimmy had said, tapping the book's cover. "Just goes to show." He said that a few times as he talked—*Just goes to show*—but he never finished the sentence, never told me *what* it showed, what kind of sense you can find in ugly death.

"How are you?" I said to Stephanie. I found myself motioning toward her stomach and felt ridiculous.

"Good," she said. I was glad that she didn't lay her hands on each side of her belly and smile serenely, like women on TV always do—like I had even done on a few occasions during my pregnancy, as if I were carrying around the secrets to the universe: me, the Goddess Mother, the first woman to ever create life. "I'm comfortable right now. My mother keeps telling me that I'll be suffering come July. And the humidity's always so bad midsummer."

"I wouldn't worry so much," I said. "I enjoyed my pregnancy, right up until those last couple of days."

"Oh, I'm enjoying it," Stephanie said quickly. "I'm just dreading the heat."

The grandfather clock chimed the half hour, and my arms broke out in chill bumps. I wasn't ready for a sermon from Stephanie, who appeared so full of good intentions that she might've been hauling them around instead of Art's baby. I knew what she was going to say to me, could've scripted it out for her on the back of the checkout cards we don't use anymore but keep around for scrap paper: *This means a lot to Art. Think it over, okay?*

"Stephanie," I said. "Why are you here?"

"I wanted to let you know that I'm with you," she said. "You know, thinking that you and the baby getting close would be a bad idea. Or weird, at least."

"Yeah, weird," I said, nodding. I wasn't quite processing what she was saying. I looked down at her round middle, how the red bow on the front of her blouse drooped, one length of ribbon hanging much lower than the other.

"Art cares a lot. He can't see too far ahead sometimes, though."

I nodded again, but only because that's what she expected. The whole time we were married, Art was *always* looking ahead: to the next car, the next promotion, the next big vacation.

"He's not thinking of this baby as a person yet." She touched her stomach then. "He's just seeing her as this way of getting a little bit of Felicia back. You can't put that kind of burden on a child. She has her own life to live out."

"If you're lucky," I said. Unfair, probably, but I felt justified when I saw the look on her face: pitying, that look, and so certain. *Not me. Not my baby.* As if reason governs these things, or desire.

"I guess that's in God's hands," she said. I could see that she believed it—believed in this God of hers, his big hands in the sky. Fitting, really. Reduce God to his hands, his parts—big male hands that could hit or hurt on whim: like Simon's, like

Marty's. Like Art's, for Christ's sake, those long, lovely fingers that he gave our daughter, that had touched me on too many nights to count, that had handed me those crisp twenties on a day that now felt like a million years ago. I pictured God as a pair of hands.

"I understand what you're saying," I told her.

She adjusted her purse strap and smiled. "He still loves you, Dana. Just like he still loves Felicia. That's okay, you know? I knew what I was getting into with him. I knew that he came with . . ." She hesitated.

"What?" I said, waiting for her to say "baggage." Stephanie looked like the kind of woman who'd spout pop psychology of the Dr. Phil variety.

She shook her head, all that nicely trimmed hair. "Ghosts."

I didn't want to cry—not in front of her, not at all. So I kept my face still.

She came around the desk, took my hand, and pressed it to the side of her stomach, where the curve started to recede into the sharp angle of her hip bone. The skin there was tight, dense but yielding, and the intimacy of the touch was infuriating and unfair: a shameful miscalculation, and I think she knew it as soon as she took my hand. I could smell her perfume—something light and floral—and beneath it, a sour note of perspiration. There was a flutter beneath my fingers, so familiar that for a second I couldn't breathe. "I'm sorry," she whispered. Outside, the air brakes of a school bus whistled, then hissed. I drew my hand away.

Two years ago, a couple of months after marrying Stephanie, Art showed up at my house with a box of Felicia's things, scavenged from his basement, and a bottle of Jim Beam. *I couldn't do this alone,* he told me, and so we went through the items together, trying to decide what to keep and what to give away, realizing that we had to hold on to all of it. We sat side by side on my sofa, and we flipped through the pages of yellowing photo albums, laughing over pictures of ourselves—young, thin, tan before tanning was taboo—crying over pictures of our daughter, taking swigs from the bottle and beginning the business of sleeping together before either of us would have acknowledged the possibility. There was that moment before we decided to go to the bedroom when we both knew that everything could change again, and probably for the worse—but desire's a funny thing, the only way you can cope sometimes, and we didn't pause long.

We collided in the dark, clumsy, out of practice; it had been years since we'd touched, and I was conscious of the ways my body had changed since the last time we'd had sex. And when was that? I have no clear memory of a *last time,* just a vague sense that it happened before we got the call about Felicia— days, a couple or a dozen—and that it didn't happen after her death, despite a few halfhearted, disastrous attempts. Art was careful, even reverent. And though I never once harbored hope that he'd come back to me, there was a moment—when he placed his ear to my heart and listened, and I felt it quicken beneath his warmth, traitorous as always—that I believed, despite everything, if I gave enough of myself I could have them back again. That wanting it badly enough could make a difference.

• ALLEGORY OF A CAVE •

Ben's father was a truck driver. He was gone as often as he was home, so Ben's mother conducted herself for most of the days in the week like a single parent, suffering no foolishness. She worked in the cafeteria at the middle school, where Ben was in the sixth grade. She'd rise at five a.m., bathe and dress in about fifteen minutes, drink a couple of cups of coffee, black and sugarless, and kiss Ben on the forehead at exactly five-thirty, breath sour. "Up and Adam," she'd say, or that's what Ben heard, anyhow, and by the time he'd fumbled for his glasses and pressed his bare feet against the cold hardwood floor, she was gone. She didn't have a car or even a driver's license, and so she had to walk the two miles between their home and school, getting there in plenty of time to start the breakfast line for the poor kids. Ben took the school bus.

There were plenty of reasons why he loved his mother, but this was one of them: At lunch, on the days when she was put on the register, standing at the end of the buffet with her apron and her hairnet and her white pantyhose, she didn't so much as acknowledge him. She would collect the forty cents she'd left that morning on his nightstand, glance at his lunch card, and instruct him to "keep it down" like everybody else. She saved her razzing for the end of the day, back at home. "Who's that girl you were sitting with at lunch, lady-killer?" Or, "If I see you walk through that line again with nothing but French fries, you'll be sorry, buddy." She didn't cook during the week, when Ben's father was away—she said she did enough of that at the school—and so they feasted together most nights on frozen pizzas and peanut butter sandwiches, or they'd walk to McDonald's on quarter-hamburger day, eat as much as they could stuff in, and take home an extra bagful to freeze for later. They were both tall and rail-thin; they could eat whatever they wanted and not gain a pound. She also smoked. Ben knew this; his father supposedly did not. When his father called from Nashville to announce that he was on his way back to Roma, his mother would wink at Ben, stash her carton of Camels in Ben's closet, and clean out every ashtray in the house. Ben liked that she trusted him.

His father was, as fathers tend to be, another case. Ben loved him, of course. But it wasn't an easy or effortless love, and Ben felt a guilty relief whenever his father's Buick Regal backed out of the gravel drive on Sunday afternoons, Nashville-bound. The man had four modes: absent—and this Ben could depend upon, at least four or five days out of seven—asleep, jolly, or grumpy. And even his jolliness was kind of ironic and grumpy and begrudging, as though he were playacting, making fun of happiness. He got along with Ben's mother mostly by sparring with her, both of them frowning, then smirking, then frowning again, and eventually they'd all go to bed and Ben would suffer through the sound of jouncing bedsprings for twenty or thirty minutes. The food wasn't as good when his father was around. He wanted home cooking, the same bacon-and-egg breakfast and the same two or three suppers, which he called "dinner" and ate at two or three in the afternoon, throwing Ben off his regular routine. His father liked the stuff he called "peasant food": pinto beans and stewed cabbage, anything that smelled awful and could be spooned onto a chunk of buttered corn bread. He liked to tell Ben about the days when he'd been poverty-stricken enough to eat "jam sandwiches": "two pieces of bread jammed together," he'd quip, pointing at Ben with his fork. "You're spoiled," he'd say. "You don't know how good you've got it."

His father was, despite his attempts to hide the fact, really, really smart—the smartest person Ben knew, schoolteachers included. He could multiply triple digits in his head, could tell you the stats on any Kentucky Wildcat basketball player from as far back as Adolph Rupp's days. He had a confident eye and hand for drawing, and Ben would happen upon his father's little sketches all week, all over the house. On the cover of *TV Guide*, he'd doodled a pterodactyl sitting atop Ted Danson's shoulder. On the pad in the kitchen where Ben's mother kept her shopping lists, he'd drawn Ben, glasses exaggerated and gleaming, mouth mournful. Ben had stared at that image for a long time, heartsick at the thought that this was the way his father saw him: a sad kid with giant glasses, eyes magnified and stupid behind thick lenses.

His father was an avid reader—there wasn't much else to do in the lag times on the road, he'd told Ben—and, in the right mood, a talker, a storyteller. This was the version of his father that Ben liked best, and the times with his father when he felt most at ease were the ones when they seemed to accidentally find themselves in conversation: when his father would say, "Hey, buddy, want to drive to the bank with me to cash my check?" or "Ben, help me get these leaves raked before it's too dark to see." Then, lulled by the task, the two would stumble into a kind of intimacy. Driving, Ben's father might say, "They've changed the length of this traffic light," and Ben, thrilled by some unconsidered possibility—*they* can change traffic lights?—would ask a question, would ask, "Who are *they*?" And his father would talk, and Ben would learn. His mother talked, too, and she was smart in her own way, but her stories were somehow less honest than his father's, more conventional. She told him about Jesus—she was an on-and-off churchgoer—about dead relatives, about her high school prom. Ben's father, if properly coaxed, would explain what it meant to live.

"Imagine," his father said one Saturday afternoon, "a cave." It was summer, the summer of Ben's twelfth year, and the October when everything changed for him was still a full season away, the difference, as his father could tell him, between a solstice and an equinox. They were on the porch swing, watching lightning bugs start to flicker. His father was sipping a beer.

"There are some prisoners tied up inside it, so that they face the back wall," his father continued. "They've always been in the cave. They've never known anything else."

"Why?" Ben asked.

His father shrugged. "Don't know. That part doesn't matter."

"But that's stupid," Ben said. "How can you be a prisoner unless you've done something wrong?"

His father had a mustache, bright red though the hair on his head was brown, and it bristled as he pursed his lips. "Do you want to hear the rest of this story or not?"

Ben nodded.

"There's a fire behind the prisoners, and a walkway between the prisoners and the fire, and so whoever passes on that walkway—a man, say, or a woman, or a dog, maybe a wagon; whatever passes—casts a shadow on the wall of the cave." His father motioned with his hands, sketching on air: the fire, the walkway, the left-to-right motion of passing travelers. "And the prisoners, they've never looked behind them. They don't know about the fire, they don't know what a dog is or a woman is. All they see are the shadows that those people and things cast on the wall of the cave. So to them, those shadows are real. They watch the shadows and that's what they live for: waiting to see what shape will pass in front of them next."

"Like TV?"

"Sure," his father said. "I reckon."

Ben was sitting next to his father, watching a few seedpods from the water maples pinwheel down onto the sidewalk, but in his head he was tied up in that cave, feeling the heat of the fire on his neck and back, watching the play of shadows on the wall. "Wait," he said. "Who's feeding them?

His father shrugged again, making the swing rock. "Don't know that, either. You can't be so literal about everything."

Ben went to bed that night flushed with some emotion that was too complicated for him to label, like anger and embarrassment and frustration all mixed up together, and something else, too:

the sense that his brain, like his eyes, was only good enough to grasp the shapes of things but not the color or texture or nuance. Sometimes, around his dad, he felt that he was squinting with his mind but still not seeing what his father wanted him to see. How could you be a prisoner if you hadn't done anything wrong? How could you stay alive if nobody was feeding you?

He'd been considered a late child in those days. His father, the family legend went, had been a ladies' man, a confirmed bachelor, and his mother, at twenty-four, was eight years his junior when they married. It took them over a decade to have Ben, a period of time he'd never thought to question until his mother let slip one day, discussing another matter entirely, "Oh, that would've been around the time I lost the second baby." They'd rolled the dice once, twice, three times. Fourth was the charm. And then Ben, their late baby, was born with cataracts, a condition so rare in children that it must have seemed to them the punch line of some cosmic, unfunny joke. Or to Ben's father, anyway. He had a way of smirking at bad news, shrugging at misfortune. "Shit happens," he'd say. "And usually to me." It irritated Ben that *his* cataracts had been turned into his *father's* problem, his *father's* burden to bear.

The irony for Ben was that he didn't quite know what he was missing, what all of the fuss was about. Since he'd been born with the cataracts and they'd been surgically removed before he was even a couple months old—there were photographs of him, heavy baby-head lolling on his neck, eyes covered with bandages and gauze—Ben regarded the problems with his eyes as simply another part of his being. His lenses weren't corrective so much as an extension of his eyes, to replace the cloudy ones that the doctors had removed. This didn't mean that he liked his eyeglasses, that he didn't often resent them. They were thick-framed, blue plastic, designed more for function than for style. They had to be able to support the considerable weight of those two half-inch-thick chunks of glass: Coke bottle glasses, the kids in elementary school had called them. Ben himself they'd called "Hoot Owl," and his first-grade teacher had dubbed him The Professor, a nickname he'd pretended to like but was actually mortified by. He was no whiz kid. A set of ugly eyeglasses didn't make him a genius.

Without his glasses, the world was a blur of light, shadow, and color, like the view through a rain-spattered window. Sometimes it was a comfort to him. Sometimes, on the rare morning when he awoke before the dry press of his mother's lips on his forehead, he would open his eyes, notice the fuzzy impression of light where he knew the window was and the brighter, more defined bar of yellow where he knew the bottom of his bedroom door was, and he'd listen. He could hear the groan of his mother's bare feet against the hardwood floors, could almost make out the rasp of each board shifting against the one beside it. He could tell by the sound, somehow, when his mother's running bathwater had gone from cold to warm, knew when she'd stop the drain, when the low thrum of suction would echo through the pipes all over their cheap house. He could smell which soap she was using, knew that the Ivory was for most days and the Caress ("Before you dress, Caress," the commercials went) was for days when his father would be home.

He pretended that he was a superhero on these early mornings. He liked comics, and his favorite was of course *Daredevil*, which made blindness seem almost cool. Not that Ben was blind, thank goodness. He counted on his glasses for the power of vision. After tiring of his made-up powers, he'd press his glasses to his face, blink, and see his way to his door, to the bathroom, to the bus stop. If he squinted, he could read a book, could distinguish the small form of an 8 from a 6. It was a secret thrill to know the difference between the sound of hot and cold water, but it was also useless. He would always choose a life with his glasses. He took for granted that he'd always be able to.

That changed in October, when his eye doctor told him and his parents that he might be going blind. The doctor was out of Nashville, the same surgeon who'd performed the cataract removal when Ben was a baby, and Ben saw him only once a year—a routine checkup, fast and painless; the worst part of the whole thing was the machine that puffed a quick jet of air into each eye, but even that was easy-breezy, as his mother would say. No big deal. When he went to see Dr. Schwartz, he, his mother, and his father would get the appointment out of the way early, eat a late breakfast at the Cracker Barrel, then drive around downtown to look at stuff. One year they toured the Country Music Hall of Fame, and once, when Ben's appointment fell in the middle of summer, they went to Opryland for the day, and Ben rode all of the roller coasters, even the Wabash Cannonball, which made an upside-down loop; he'd had to press his glasses to his face with both hands. Until that October, Ben hadn't known that there was anything to dread, hadn't questioned the reason for the visits. Like the glasses, he accepted them as a part of what it meant to be Ben.

The doctor hadn't said "going blind," exactly. He'd said that the surgery to remove the cataracts, especially when performed in infancy, sometimes had side effects—that this was the reason they'd insisted on the annual eye appointments. He'd said that there was sometimes damage to the developing eyes, and that the damage could lead to a gradual increase of ocular pressure, which appeared to be the case now that Ben was in the early stages of puberty. If the pressure was allowed to climb unabated, Ben would develop glaucoma.

Ben looked at his father. "What's that mean?"

"Means you could go blind," his father said in a thick voice. Ben's mother was already crying.

"That's not what I'm saying," Dr. Schwartz said quickly. He tapped Ben's knee. "No, son. You're not even close to that. But it means that we've got to start you on medicine that will regulate the pressure. We can control this with the right medications."

"What kind of medicine?" Ben's mother said.

"Eyedrops," Dr. Schwartz told her. "I'll start him on two kinds. He'll have to take one in the morning and both at night."

"For how long?" His father's voice was wary.

Dr. Schwartz sighed. "Well. This isn't treatment, Mr. Thompson. It's maintenance."

"So you mean forever," Ben's father said.

Dr. Schwartz smiled reassuringly at Ben. Ben had known him all his life, had revered the man a little as a savior, the savior of his sight. He'd always liked him: his big, sunny office on Vanderbilt's campus, his glasses—like Ben's, thick-framed and styleless—his bad, sweet jokes when he ran the usual eye exams: *Look up, look down, look all around.* Then, tapping Ben on his nose: *You're a clown.* From as far back as Ben could remember (and read), a photograph of Albert Einstein had hung behind the examination table, with this legend brandished across it: *If the facts don't fit the theory, change the facts.* Ben had always liked that, too.

"Children are extraordinarily adaptable," Dr. Schwartz said. "And the technology is constantly developing. By the time Ben's an adult, there may be options that we can't even imagine." He turned on his roller stool and scooted to his desk. "But for now," he said, writing, back to Ben and his parents, "yes, the medicine will have to become a new routine."

Their late breakfast was somber. Ben ordered blueberry pancakes and a side of the potato casserole, both of his favorites, and his father didn't even make noises as he usually did about the price—though he'd muttered plenty at the clinic pharmacy, where the two small bottles of medicine had rung up for $150, just in copays. But Ben didn't have much appetite, and the food sat thick and gummy on his dry tongue. He pushed around the pancake on his plate until his mother finally put her hand over his. "That's enough now," she said, but her own breakfast, a cheese omelet, was also mostly untouched. Ben's father ate methodically and thoroughly, whipping together margarine and maple syrup with his fork and loading a healthy dollop of the mix onto each bite of his biscuit. He patted his mustache with a napkin unconsciously, took loud slurps of his coffee. "Expect the worst," he said finally, making eye contact with the waitress and raising his mug. "Expect the worst and hope for the best. That's what they say."

Ben's mother let her fork drop with a clatter. "For God's sake, Will." She composed herself while the waitress topped off the mug of coffee.

"Who are *they*?" Ben asked dully.

"Damned if I know," his father said. "Bunch of idiots, probably."

His mother's neck had gone blotchy red. "You're a one to talk."

His father shrugged amiably. "Maybe so." He was dumping sugar and cream into his coffee, stirring with gusto. His spoon made a cheerful ringing on the sides of the mug. "Put not your trust in princes, my dear. Schwartz told us that Ben had to have the surgery. Had to have it, he said. Tragedy if you don't. So we did. And here we are."

His mother looked at Ben almost pleadingly. "We did the best we knew to do at the time."

"So I didn't have to get it?" Ben asked. He hadn't considered this before.

"They can't force you to do anything," his father said. "But they didn't give us any other options, either."

Ben pushed his glasses to his forehead and closed his eyes, pressing his fingers into the lids. They were burning, and his sinuses ached. His pulse throbbed in his ears.

"You've upset him," he heard his mother say, but she was faraway-sounding, unimportant. There was country music playing through the restaurant speakers, the soft roar of a hundred different conversations, a clatter of plates. The air was thick with grease and sugar; it was a veil settling on top of Ben, nauseating, making it impossible to breathe. He hated it here. He hated his mother and father: she with her scared look and her secret cigarette smoking and her sour breath—her quick morning baths, sometimes so fast that Ben could still smell the previous day's lunch on her hair when she gave him her goodbye kiss. And his father! His smirking, know-it-all father. When Ben was first learning to ride his bike and fell off, skinning his knee, he'd run to his father for a hug, tears streaming down his face, and his father had said, matter-of-factly, "Cry me a handful," putting his cupped palms out teasingly until Ben, screaming with rage, had kicked his bike and run inside the house. His father was never enraged or heartbroken or full of joy; he was an edifice of calm, occasionally shadowed by irritation. And Ben couldn't stand it any longer. He pushed back from the table, making the silverware rattle, and shoved his glasses down on his nose. The tears were still blurring his vision, but he made it through the restaurant's general store and to the front porch easily enough, and then he was standing there, watching the interstate, feeling the cool air and realizing he'd left his jacket inside on the back of his chair.

He had been sitting on one of the rocking chairs out front for a full fifteen minutes, shivering between his crossed arms, before his parents emerged, his father clutching a couple of plastic containers of leftovers. His mother handed him his jacket without comment. No one spoke until they were barreling up I–65 toward home.

"Don't do any good to have a temper tantrum about it," his father finally said. He looked from his rearview mirror, catching Ben's eyes, to his wife beside him, and Ben could tell by something in his manner, the combination of carefulness and defensiveness, that they'd spent their time alone arguing about him. "Don't do either one of you any good."

"Just shut up," his mother said. She was slumped against her door, her head pressed on the window glass, her back rigid.

They were home in another forty, silent minutes, and Ben spent the rest of the day in his room, pretending to watch his 10-inch black-and-white TV but really just opening and closing his eyes. Now you see it. Now you don't. He woke briefly that night to the sound of his parents' quaking bedsprings and thought, for the first time with some humor, that it would be better if he were going deaf instead of blind.

•   •   •

The medicine became his routine in the following weeks. His mother now slipped into his room as soon as her alarm went off at five, turned on the lamp beside his bed, and quickly administered the first set of drops. It got to where she was so efficient, and Ben himself so used to the process, that the whole transaction could take place without Ben's even properly waking. At night, just before bedtime, they repeated the ritual; and this time Ben got the second dose of drops too, from the bottle of medicine that had to be stored in the refrigerator. The drops were cold, at first shockingly so, but he got used to that as well, and he came to almost enjoy these moments spent reclined, his mother hovering above him, her clear gray eyes close enough that he could just make them out before the drops hit. The gentle weight of her elbows against his chest. The smooth assuredness as she pressed her finger against his eyebrow and her thumb against his cheekbone, the musky salt smell of her dimpled palm. She was hardly ever this close to him now that he was in middle school, now that their days converged for half an hour in the lunchroom. There'd been a time when, his father on the road, she'd let Ben rest his head in her lap while she watched TV, or she'd kiss him on the lips instead of the forehead when she left for work in the mornings. And then those things had stopped, so gradually that Ben could mark the change only in retrospect. He had a vague memory of seeing his mother in nothing but a bra and half-slip, hair twisted up in a towel, crossing from the bathroom to her bedroom, calmly and unhurried. Now she didn't even like him to see her in her bathrobe. Her shame had made him ashamed, sometimes awkward, and the good thing about the medicine was that it briefly dissolved the awkwardness between them—they now had a ritual for being close to each other.

It was the only good thing about the medicine. Glaucoma was
a cloud that hung over everything in his life now, the drops a
twice-daily reminder in case Ben was able to briefly forget. If he
read a great comic book and had that excited feeling in his gut,
the one that made him want to flip back to page one and read the
whole thing through again, he'd stop, panicked, and think, *What
if I can't read them anymore?* He knew that it was silly for him
to mourn the sight he hadn't even lost yet, especially when Dr.
Schwartz had gone out of his way to assure Ben that there was
no reason for it. But he couldn't help himself.

All of this angst was made worse by Ben's suspicion, rendered
more tender and urgent by the threat of blindness, that he was
in love. He had admired the girl, Rose, for most of his school career, thinking her pretty with her long, smooth strawberry blonde
hair and her freckles and her naturally straight teeth, never in
braces. She was smart, too, consistently on the straight-A Honor
Roll, and soft-spoken. Nice. She'd never joined in the choruses
of "Hoot Owl." Also, and perhaps most important, she'd seemed
possible: a pretty girl, a smart girl, but not so pretty that Ben
couldn't aspire to one day be her boyfriend. Ben was just a little
bit too skinny, and Rose was just a little bit too chubby. Ben had
his glasses, and Rose had her ugly hand-me-down sweaters and
long Wal-Mart denim or corduroy skirts. She always wore skirts,
and she wore them with off-brand sneakers, kept blindingly white
with shoe polish, and athletic socks instead of the Eastlands that
were the rage now. She, like Ben, was one of the poor kids in
their class; she, like Ben, discreetly slipped the reduced lunch
fee of forty cents to the cafeteria lady instead of the dollar-and-a-
quarter that the rest of the kids paid. Ben had dreamed, on and
off over the years, that he'd one day be able to get his eyes fixed

through some fancy new surgical technique—and he'd dreamed that, like Clark Kent, he'd be a new man when he was finally rid of those huge Coke bottle lenses; that, when his eyes were no longer magnified and almost distended-looking, he'd be handsome, and that's when he'd ask Rose to be his girlfriend. That day wasn't going to come now, he knew; he was as good as he was ever going to be. The thought threatened to depress him at first, but there was something exhilarating, something freeing about it, too.

He woke up the Monday before Thanksgiving early, before his mother's alarm had gone off, and felt a ball of nervousness in his stomach, imagined that it was pumping adrenaline through his veins the way his heart pumped blood, for his whole body was suddenly charged and tingling, and he was happier than he'd been in a month. He'd had an idea—a plan. The kids at school were calling it "going together." Ben, who was mostly a loner, even knew the couplings: Janet Matthews was going with Scott White. They were the queen and king of the seventh grade; you could see in their faces the attractive teenagers they would become. But the popular kids weren't the only ones pairing off. Darren Stone, whose ugliness was legendary, had a girlfriend, even if she was a fat fifth grader. The guy had warts all over his left hand, and the doctor had frozen them off one time, only for them to come back doubled in size. Ben got the heebie-jeebies just looking at them.

Going together, from what Ben could tell, was a delicate transaction, usually negotiated by friend or expertly folded note, though, as he understood it, sometimes it was okay, too, to look up a person's number in the local phone book, hope you were guessing correctly about the father's first name, and call. There wasn't a lot of precedent for just going up to a person and saying, "Hey, want to go together?" but that's exactly what Ben decided he'd do. He didn't have friends he trusted; he didn't want to risk putting the request in print. He'd just go up to her directly, put his feelings out there, and hope for the best. They went to lunch in the same period, immediately following Social Studies with Mr. Kennedy, so that would have to be his moment.

He rushed after class to get behind her in line, bumping Jonah Simpson on the way and muttering a fast "Sorry" as he went. Jonah looked too surprised to retort. But he accomplished his mission, sliding in behind Rose just before the line narrowed to single file as they passed through the door to the lunch line. He was close enough to smell her hair, to admire its glossy sheen. It had always looked this way: long, spaghetti-straight, falling evenly just past the middle of her back. It had never been shorter, never much longer, and though she occasionally pulled it up into a ponytail or pinned it half up with a barrette, she usually wore it as she did today: pushed off her face with a plastic headband, bangs curled under and sprayed to hold their shape. When Ben was a grown-up, he'd think of Rose Smucker and suspect for the first time that her hair had been as much a reflection of her mother's preferences as her own—that it was the kind of hair only a mother would have the energy to shampoo and condition into daily perfection, and of course only a mother would insist on that carefully sculpted curl of bangs, so round and uniform that they made a tunnel across Rose's forehead. But these were a grown man's thoughts. Twelve-year-old Ben thought that long, brilliant head of hair the very essence of femininity, and the most overtly erotic thought in his life so far had been of plunging his hands into the satiny curtain, combing his fingers through the length of it. Behind her now in line, he could detect the scent of strawberry shampoo even over the constant, cabbagelike stink of the cafeteria, the scent his mother carried home in her own hair.

His mother. He looked around guiltily.

"Kid. Hamburger or chicken patty?" It was a cafeteria worker he knew by sight but couldn't name. Throat dry, he motioned to the chicken patty, which she slapped onto a bun, then onto his tray. Rose was down to the green beans by now.

He took a paper sleeve of French fries, a sugar cookie. All of the food on his tray was the same color as his hamburger bun. He felt sick to his stomach. He looked over at Rose. She hadn't put her lunch money on the tray the way the kids with a dollar bill did. She had her coins palmed; she held her tray awkwardly because of it. So did Ben.

"Rose," he said. Mrs. Tipton was taking money at the register. His mother was nowhere in sight.

She turned with a start. "Huh?"

The line inched forward.

"Where you sitting?" he stuttered.

She flushed. Her cheeks were as pink now as her plastic head-band. "Um. Why?"

Ben hadn't expected this question. He hadn't known what to expect, but this? This wasn't answerable. He motioned toward Mrs. Tipton, who had her hand out. Rose quickly paid and walked into the dining hall. Ben handed over his own forty cents.

She was already sitting down when he emerged. Alone, by the windows—was this an invitation? His tray rattled in his hands. He walked her way, noticing her trying not to notice him. She had squeezed her hamburger bun until it was almost flat. *Do you want*

to go together? His mind shaped the words. He didn't think she'd
say yes. He didn't think she'd say no. He felt the eyes of his peers on
them both as he put his tray down across from Rose's, as he tried
to arrange his long legs over the bench and under the table. It occurred to him then, once seated, that he could take off his glasses.
So he did, and he feigned wiping them on the hem of his flannel
shirt, wondering if she was looking at him now or still examining
her tray and her deflated hamburger. He couldn't see her. She was
a soft blur of peach skin and yellow hair with a nimbus of sunlight
behind her. His left eye twitched as it sometimes did, and the vision in that eye suddenly *swished*—that was the only word for it,
this sense that everything had turned a quarter of the way and
then bounced back, like a radio dial pushed all the way to the right.
It occurred to him, horrified, that his eye had probably wandered,
that he was sitting here with his glasses off and his unfocused eye
circling in its socket like a frog's or a lizard's would, and he shoved
the lenses back on his nose in time to see Rose's expression of fear
and disgust, the look Ben figured he had on his face whenever he
saw Darren Stone's warty left hand. "Want to go together?" he
said before he could stop his tongue, the words jammed together
and not so much spoken as expelled—*wannagotogether?*—but
his meaning seemed clear enough, for Rose shook her head, eyes
back on her tray, and said, softly, "I can't."

He couldn't help himself. "Why?"

"My mama wouldn't let me," she said.

It had taken only a minute, beginning to end. The first heartbreak in a lifetime full of them. The first bubble burst. In a couple
years' time, he'd consider that Rose might have been telling the
truth that day. She was Pentecostal—he hadn't realized that
then—and when the other girls in their grade started shaving

their legs, Rose would take to wearing pantyhose or knee socks, even in gym class, and the light teasing she'd gotten over the years would crescendo into outright mocking. In eleventh grade, Ben would notice in the hall one day that Rose was looking heavier than usual, and by the end of another week it had gotten around that she was pregnant, kicked out of her parents' house, and living with some cousins. She didn't come back to school once the baby was born. Ben never saw her after that.

He couldn't have even guessed any of this that day in the cafeteria. He stood, stumbling as he pulled his long legs back out from under the table and very nearly falling, and he heard a sharp, bright "Ha!" from someone nearby, but he didn't turn to look. Had he thought that there was nothing left to lose? Because there was, Ben knew now. There was self-respect. There was hope. He left his tray at the table and walked as quickly as he could toward the door, away from the giggles and catcalls he imagined were mounting behind him, and when Mr. Evans, the assistant principal, called out, "Benjamin Thompson! Where do you think you're going?" he ran. His sneakers slapped the tiles. He collided with his mother on the way out—she'd emerged from the kitchen, hair netted, hands wringing a dish towel— and she shrieked, "Ben!" but that didn't stop him, either. He rounded the corner and hesitated, his hands pressed against the double doors that would lead him out of the middle school and onto the street. He was out of breath already. He could hear the squeak of shoes behind him.

There was nowhere to go. He put his forehead to one of the door's windows and squeezed his eyes shut against tears, wishing he had the courage to push through and keep running. He knew that the hands settling on his shoulders now were his mother's.

"Ben," she said. "Ben, what was that about?"

He shrugged under the weight of her hands.

"Ben," she whispered. "You know you can talk to me."

This was the worst moment, he'd think later. Not the morning at Dr. Schwartz's office; not later, after what happened with his father. It was here, now, standing at the double doors of Roma Middle School, eyes shut against a world he didn't have the courage to venture into, back to the mother he was no longer sure could understand him.

He spent the rest of the short week in the Alternative Learning Center, a trailer behind the school with three cubbyholes and a desk where one bored coach or another read magazines. He had to silently do his schoolwork all day, eat lunch alone at one, after all of the other students had gone back to classes, and write an extra thousand-word essay on the importance of listening to authority figures. It was the best possible thing that could have happened to him. His mother hadn't punished him, but she'd worked on him both Monday and Tuesday night to explain what had happened and why. "It's not like you," she kept saying. "Was someone mean to you? Are you getting picked on?" She came out of the kitchen to take his lunch money the rest of the week, had obviously volunteered, and Ben bristled under her frank but silent appraisal of him as he paid for his greasy rectangle of pizza on Tuesday, his turkey and dressing on Wednesday.

"Are you fighting with your friends?" she asked Tuesday night. They were watching *Roseanne*, his mother's favorite show, and she didn't even wait for a commercial break to start in on him again. "Is that it? Is that why you stormed out like that?"

"I don't have any friends," Ben muttered.

She looked miserable, shocked. She took a drag from her ciga-rette. "Ben, honey. That's not so, is it?"

"God, Mom, what do you think?"

The cigarette was tweezed between the first and middle fin-gers of her right hand, and she pulled it back long enough to rub her lips with her ring finger, as though she were smoothing on gloss: a nervous tic that Ben knew well. He had never been able to decide if his mother was pretty. She wasn't fat, had no ugly features; her hair was a noncolor between blonde and brown, and she wore it all in one length at her shoulders. There were moments, when she was happy, when she lit up so much that Ben didn't know if his heart could take it; and then there were others, like now, when her face seemed deflated and loose, as though the cigarette had been pulling air out of her instead of the other way around.

"You're always sitting with somebody at lunch," she said.

"Everybody has to sit with somebody."

"I've seen you talking to people, Ben. I've seen you laughing with your friends."

He looked at Roseanne on the TV. She was sitting on her ratty living room couch with the crocheted blanket slung across the back, and it could have been Ben's couch, his house. He wasn't sure if his mother had deliberately lied just then or if she'd only convinced herself that what she'd said was true. He tried to imag-ine a world in which he had friends to sit with and laugh with at lunch. What would that feel like? Even when he found himself among the other losers in his grade—Darren Stone with his bar-nacled left hand or Toby Gunderson, who stuttered—there was no ease, no kinship. If anything, they all repelled each other, recognizing that their faults would only seemed heightened if collected, that to take up with one another would be to reject, for once and all, the company of everyone else. No, there were no friends. There were no lunches spent laughing.

All of a sudden she looked sly. "It's a girl," she said, mouth trembling at the corners as though she wanted to smile but was afraid of embarrassing him. "Are you just having some girl trouble?"

He felt tears, and he stoked his sorrow and depression into rage, because rage seemed more useful, more dignified. "Stop it!" he shouted, so miserable that he felt sick. "I'm ugly, and nobody likes me, and I hate you and Dad for making me like this." Then he ran into his room, slamming the door behind him so hard that the house shuddered. He could almost track its echo. He could hear the sofa creak and he braced himself to face her—but then there was a sigh, the exhalation of old cushions, and the volume on *Roseanne* went up a notch or two.

She didn't come at bedtime to give him his eyedrops, and Ben didn't rouse himself to remind her. It was a standoff. One night of missing his medicine wouldn't hurt him, he knew, but he lay under his covers ramrod-straight, trembling with the knowledge that he'd been cruelly treated. That he had a terrible mother. He thought, too, that he would have told her everything if she'd only followed him into his room, if she'd only leaned over him, pressed his eyes open with her cool fingertips, given him his medicine as she was supposed to do. If she'd only said to him, *You're not going to go blind, Ben.* She hadn't said that yet. Neither had his father. And what was their silence, if not confirmation?

His mother, he'd learned, had two ways of punishing him. The first was to act immediately, taking only her own counsel on the matter. When Ben sassed her, she'd swat his leg, send him to his room. Then she considered the issue final, done; she didn't mention it to his father, she didn't subject him to double jeopardy. The other punishment, though, was to hold off, to stay silent, and by that silence to let him know that her plan was to save the evidence against him for his father, to let his father act as judge, jury, and executioner whenever he returned from his latest run. This was clearly worse for Ben, and rarer; it happened only when he'd hurt her personally, Ben suspected, when she didn't trust herself to raise a hand against him. So when she let him go to sleep without his medicine—when she woke him the next morning with his eyedrops but didn't rouse him again with a kiss—he knew that she was going to have A TALK with his father. And how that would go, Ben didn't even want to guess.

The man's spankings weren't any worse than hers, and if anything he took Ben's transgressions less seriously than she did, having never cared much, he'd always said, for "Old Granny rules" such as "no cussing." He was angriest, he said, when it seemed to him that Ben didn't act with "a little goddamn common sense": the time when Ben ruined the DustBuster, which his father used to clean the car, vacuuming up some paint he'd spilled on the carport; the time when Ben broke a pair of glasses trying to jump a ramp with his bicycle. The DustBuster fiasco had earned him the worst spanking of his life. The broken glasses were a close second, his father's fury perhaps tempered by the sight of Ben's skinned knees, palms, and chin. Ben wasn't sure if this incident was the kind of wrongdoing that would earn a spanking, but he'd take the spanking over one of his dad's sarcastic, humiliating lectures: "Cry me a handful" all over again.

Wednesday night arrived, and so did his father. Thanksgiving passed as it always did. They watched *Home Alone* on TV after his mother had put foil on the leftovers and cleared the plates, and still no one mentioned the incident at school; Ben didn't know if this was a holiday reprieve or a genuine stroke of good fortune. When his mother gave him his drops before bedtime, she told him she'd be gone early the next morning to hit the sales with Aunt Sheila, and Ben thought, *Here it comes.* A whole day alone with his father. A punishment all by itself.

He awoke to a flood of light, sudden and awful. "Wakey, wakey," he heard his father say dryly. Ben blinked, groaning, as a dark shadow blotted out some of the violent brilliance. "Can't put in the drops if your eyes are squeezed shut," he said, so Ben forced his eyes back open, irritated that his father, whose hand wasn't as steady as his mother's, managed to send most of the medicine running down the side of his face, into the cups of his ears.

"Did that go in?" his father asked.

"Yeah," Ben lied. His eyes were shut again. He always slept in on holidays from school.

He felt a sharp push on his arm. "Giddyup, son. Daylight's wasting."

Ben rolled over and put the pillow over his head. "Leave me alone."

"Get up," his father repeated, less cheerfully, so Ben did.

The light in the kitchen was the color of dishwater. His father was at the stove. This was a novelty, a sight to goggle at: his father scrambling eggs in the old aluminum pan with his mother's stained wooden spoon, whisking together flour and grease in the cast-iron skillet. Slices of sausage sat draining on paper towels. His father dumped milk in on top of the flour, whisked a little, then dumped in some more. He shook in salt, lots of black pepper.

"What are you doing?" Ben asked.

His father grabbed a dishcloth and pulled a pan of biscuits out of the oven. "Knitting a sweater," he said. "Jesus, kid. Ask a stupid question, why don't you."

Ben took his seat at the table. There was already a plate, a paper towel folded in half, a fork. His father had poured him a glass of orange juice.

"You can cook?"

"Every now and then," his father said. He turned the pan of biscuits onto a dish towel, then put two, wincing at the heat, onto Ben's plate.

As punishments went, this was an odd one. In the past, when Ben's mother had decided to go shopping after Thanksgiving, he and his father had napped on and off all day, grazed on leftovers, watched a little TV. Ben's father sometimes liked to go to the local Wal-Mart to look at electronics, but they never bought anything. It was dull and excruciating. They would both run like puppies to Ben's mother when she walked in that night.

His father pulled up to the table, dumped some eggs on his plate, and passed the bowl to Ben. They looked different than his mother's.

"I put cheese in them," his father said. "And crumbled-up Ritz crackers."

Ben took a tentative bite. "Good." They were.

His father stabbed at his eggs, ate half of a sausage in a bite. "I'd thought," he said, looking at his plate, "that we might take a little road trip today."

Ben thought instantly of Opryland, which would be closed for cold weather, and then that made him think of Nashville. Dr. Schwartz. His eyes. Was this why he hadn't been punished yet?

Did his parents know something that Ben didn't? He remembered Tuesday night, his mother's casual, even cruel dismissal
of him and their nightly ritual. She hadn't bothered because it
hadn't mattered. The doctor was going to tell him that he was
going blind.

"I don't want to go to Nashville," he said in a rush.

His father gave him that look: the one where his eyebrows
drew up in the middle and his mustache bristled. "Who said
anything about Nashville?"

Ben flushed. "I thought you were taking me back to the doctor," he muttered.

"Well, you'll have to go back eventually," his dad said. "April or
May, probably. But that's not how we're spending today."

Now Ben felt a grudging excitement. Theirs wasn't a trip-
taking family. They'd been to the Smoky Mountains twice, and
in the summer they sometimes packed a picnic lunch and drove
thirty minutes to Lake Malone. Just as Ben's mother hated to
cook when she wasn't on the job, his father generally hated to
drive. He came back grouching about places that Ben didn't
know if he'd ever get to see: Chicago ("worst traffic in the
world"), Texas ("nothing but rednecks and Mexicans"), even
California ("can't get a damn hamburger for less than five dollars"). Sometimes Ben sensed that his father was being that way
to protect him and his mother. When his mother said things
like, "I reckon I'll die without ever seeing the ocean," Ben's
father would wave in a dismissive way and huff. "Water's water.
I tried to go to the beach last time I made a run to Florida, and
you couldn't see it for all the tourists. Bunch of pollution. It'd
just depress you."

"So where're we going, then?" Ben said now.

"Mammoth Cave," his father said. "You shouldn't go your whole life without seeing Mammoth Cave."

Ben was confused. "We're going to Mammoth Cave?" It was about an hour and a half from Roma, and it was the biggest cave system in the world. He knew that because he always tried to take some pride in little positive facts about Kentucky, like Mammoth Cave and the Derby and the Judds, and the fact that Abraham Lincoln, his favorite president, had been born here. He was supposed to go to Mammoth Cave on a school trip back in third grade, but he came down with chicken pox just before, had to sit out of school a whole week. That was just his luck—always had been.

"That's what I said, isn't it?" His father shook his head in an exasperated way. "I tell you what."

"Is it open?"

"It's always open."

"Even in the cold?

"It's a cave, son. Once you're in there it don't matter."

Ben thought. "Does Mom know?"

His father threw his hands up in the air. "Do you want to go or not?"

"Okay," Ben said, nodding. "Okay, thanks, Dad."

They were on the interstate outside of Bowling Green within the hour. His father had a lead foot. "My rig has a governor on it," he told Ben as they passed the Park City exit. The scenery passed mildly on either side of them, everything gray: trees, road, sky, houses. "Makes me crazy. I can't take it over seventy. And the traffic's just faster south of here. The rigs all go at least seventy-five or eighty in Tennessee, and you can add another ten mile an hour to that in Alabama. It's just the way things are. Even the

cops know it, or at least most of them." Ben liked the way his father steered, using all of his arms in big motions, as if he were at
the prow of a ship; then sometimes just pushing the wheel side to
side with his left palm, straddling the other on Ben's headrest.

"Do you like your job?" Ben asked. It wasn't a question that
had occurred to him before.

His father was silent a moment. "I almost told you no just now,"
he said, watching the road and his mirrors. "That's what I'm supposed to say. But that would be a lie. Yes, I like my job quite a bit."

"Why are you supposed to say you don't?"

He shrugged. "Because of you and your mother. Most of the
drivers I know go one way or the other. There's the guys that
hang pictures of their kids in the cab and call home every night
and act like their hearts are always breaking. Some of them mean
it. They're the ones that need the money so bad they ain't got a
choice but to keep driving."

The Cave City exit was ahead. His father slowed a bit and
turned on his signal.

"The drivers who love it wouldn't know how to live any other
way. And I guess I'm one of them. I love you and your mother,
but I like having my time to myself, too. I hope it don't hurt your
feelings to hear that."

Ben thought about his secret, guilty relief at watching his father drive off on Sundays. He thought about his mother, who had
the first cigarette between her lips before the Buick was even
down the road all the way. *One of these days I really will quit,*
she'd say sometimes, the expression on her face blissful. *But this
ain't the day.*

"I guess not," Ben said finally. They were driving in the opposite direction of the sign that read "Mammoth Cave, 8 miles."

Ben figured that they were stopping for a snack, or to top off the gas tank.

His father looked at him. "I love your mother," he said.

"I know that," Ben said instantly. But in the next moment he wondered.

They were pulling into the parking lot of a low metal, windowless building, then stopping. His father put the gearshift into park and shut off the ignition. Ben looked out. It wasn't a gas station. It wasn't a restaurant. He leaned forward and craned his neck, and then he saw it. Above the door, in bright red letters a couple feet tall, the kind that would be lit at night: ADULT. He would have seen the sign as they'd approached if he'd been paying attention, but he hadn't. He'd been focusing on his father, on this strange moment rising up between them in the car.

"Your mother told me what happened at school," his father said.

Ben sensed that he wasn't in trouble, so he just nodded.

"And she told me how you talked to her. How you sassed her."

"I'm sorry," he muttered.

His father released his seat belt and leaned back a little. "I didn't know if I'd have the nerve to drive you here or not. I thought we just might go to the cave after all."

Ben looked at that cryptic sign again: ADULT. There were two other cars in the lot. He didn't know what any of this meant. Now that the car wasn't running, the cold outside had started to creep in, and the windows were fogging. In another two minutes he'd have to wipe the glass to see out.

"This is—" His father cleared his throat. "It's a kind of gentlemen's club, Ben. It's a place I go to sometimes when I have to make a run to Louisville or Cincinnati."

Gentlemen's club. Ben imagined men playing chess, throwing darts. Secret handshakes. But he knew that none of that was inside this ugly metal building with the red letters above the door.

"It's not a nice place," his father said, as though reading his mind. "But it's not a bad place, either. It's just a way station, a place to look."

"Look at what?" Ben whispered.

"At women," his father said.

Ben swallowed.

His father was pretending to adjust the rearview mirror. "I remember how hard it was to be your age. And you have it harder than most boys. Your mother and I know that. I reckon it's worse with me gone half the time."

Ben wasn't sure that last part was true, but he didn't interrupt.

His father's breath plumed as he spoke. "I worry about your eyes, son. I think you'll be all right, and that's the truth. You know by now that I've never been able to lie to you. But the truth is that I still worry, and I think there are things you ought to be able to see in a lifetime."

"Like Mammoth Cave?" He meant it as a joke, sort of, but his father nodded seriously.

"Well, yeah, and we could still go do that. It really is open today."

"Okay."

"Or we could go in there," his father said, motioning past the windshield. ADULT, the sign blared.

"And look at women?"

"At one woman," his father said. "They're not open yet. But this one lady's a friend of mine. She said she'd do me a favor."

Ben was embarrassed to ask, but he did: "Will I like it?"

His father laughed, not in a mean way. "I honestly don't know," he said. "You're young yet. But I'm sure you'll find it interesting."

Ben took off his glasses, wiped the lenses with his gloved fingers. He thought that his father would regret today, that perhaps he already did. There was something between them that was like static electricity, a thing that could spark painfully if either of them moved. He wondered what it meant that his father knew this place, that he knew a particular woman here. He wondered what it meant that his father was the kind of man who'd show this to his son, if all those days away—half of Ben's lifetime, at least—had made them strangers.

He wondered most of all what his mother was doing at this moment. He could see her at Wal-Mart with Aunt Sheila, the two of them laughing too loud the way they always did when they were together, pulling pure strangers into their conversations. He felt angry at this image. Ashamed of it. What would she think about him sitting here with his father, making a pact that excluded her? When she'd asked him what he wanted for Christmas last month, he'd told her a Hot Wheels car wash set, even though he knew that he was probably too old for it. He'd said so as much for her, for the love of her, as he had for himself.

ADULT, the sign screamed. A few snow flurries landed on the windshield of the car, then melted.

They went to Mammoth Cave, they'd tell her that afternoon. They got home only an hour before she did, and she walked in noisily and red-faced, smelling like the cold, still vibrating a little from her good time with Aunt Sheila. Greenwood Mall was "full to bursting," she told them, and Sheila had bought her a good lunch at Rafferty's. She unwound her scarf from her neck, pulled the fingertips on her gloves before removing them, like women in old movies did. Then she put her hands against Ben's cheeks, first the back of her fingers, then the open palms, and Ben jerked away from her before he could stop himself.

"What's with you?" she said.

"Cold," Ben muttered.

Her eyes were very bright, her lips chapped. "Let's not be mad anymore, Ben. It's almost Christmastime." She put her arms out, flapping her hands at him. He let her pull him close, but he couldn't bring himself to hug her back, to put his hands on her. His father, sitting at the kitchen table, observed them mildly.

"Let the kid breathe, Abby. Stop babying him."

"He's still my baby." He felt her lips press against the top of his head. "Aren't you?"

He nodded a little, swallowing against something sour and knotted.

"He'll always be my baby," she said.

When Ben was a grown man, he'd tell the story of that day to his wife. He liked to make a joke out of it. "I saw a Mammoth Cave, all right," he'd say, and Ellen would slap his arm and pretend to be angry with him. He knew every centimeter of her, down to the gold flecks in her green eyes, the mole inside her right thigh. He took his drops, morning and night. He made love without his glasses on.

The woman at the strip club had been young, Ben knew now, though at twelve he'd seen her as that indeterminate age of "grown"—older than himself, younger than his mother. She was wearing a sweater and blue jeans. She'd shaken Ben's hand when they entered the club, elbowed his father in a familiar way, a way Ben hadn't liked. A man waved from an open office in the back.

"Will," he said.

"Lance," Ben's father said back.

"It's very nice to meet you, Ben," the woman said, talking to him like a babysitter would before the parents left for the night: wanting to win him over, wanting to impress. He caught a look exchanged between her and his father, a flash of understanding. He pulled his hand away.

It was dark, but the stage was lit. The woman reemerged a few minutes later in a short black dress, and music played too loudly through the overhead speakers. Her hair was brown, cropped to the chin—nothing like Rose's—and so Ben tried to picture that curtain of red-gold shimmering against her shoulders, but he couldn't, and the attempt made him feel stupid. His father sat beside him, hands folded politely in his lap, as though they were at a church service. The woman started unbuttoning the dress. Her hips swayed. The music thumped along with Ben's heartbeat.

He found himself staring, not at her, but at her shadow. There was a beauty to it: the way the legs stretched, impossibly long, to the seam between floor and wall, and the body emerged from the floor as though half-buried, first solid, as the arms folded in, then segmented, a shadow-arm arcing above a shadow-head. Ben knew well enough what his father wanted him to see, and he snatched a glance at a pale breast, a rosy nipple, then flushed, shamed, and averted his gaze back to the shadow-woman, the puppet's dance of light and dark. He pushed his glasses back on his forehead, not caring what his father thought, and let her finish the dance that way, a pale shimmer, a mystery. When they emerged from the club fifteen minutes later, Ben was so sunblind that he at first didn't see the fresh fall of snow, the last good one of his childhood.

"Don't tell your mother," his father had said as they walked to the car, and Ben just shoved his bare hands into his pockets and hunched his shoulders up to keep his neck warm. There had been a silence in the parking lot that day, the kind that settles in the first moments of a certain kind of snowfall, when the flakes are large and damp and the air seems almost strangely warm. Ben could tell without touching it that the snow was the sticking kind, good for snowballs.

That night, when his mother came to his bedside—when she pressed her forearm against his chest and started to unscrew the cap to the bottle of drops—Ben shrugged her off, roughly. "Do it myself," he said, and she only nodded, leaving the medicine with him. It would be his responsibility from here on out. He knew it, and he was sorry. But he didn't know what truth she'd recognize in his eyes at so little distance—what he'd give away about his father, about himself. Ben didn't want to go blind, but he was starting to understand that there were things in life that you had to turn your face away from, that you had to shut your eyes against.

• AN UPRIGHT MAN •

1.

I met Robbie McCaslin the summer after we graduated from high school, me from city, Robbie from county. I say *met*, though I'd known of Robbie for a while. How could I not? He was six-six and he probably weighed close to two-eighty, had a mass of auburn hair and a full red beard that made him look like a lumberjack. He was known throughout Logan County as two things: a hell of a nice guy if you were on good terms with him—a big softy, really, who might clap your back too hard if he'd been drinking but was harmless otherwise; or a monster, a senseless idiot who turned mean on a dime and would thrash anyone who looked at him funny. I was never sure which was true—or if both were true—so all through school I kept my distance.

Roma, Kentucky, was one of those towns that was so small and useless that its teenagers had to make up phony rivalries just to have something to do. During the school year county kids would hang out at the Hardee's on Friday and Saturday nights, while city kids (though calling Roma a city always struck me as a bit optimistic) set up house at the McDonald's across the road. There was some fraternizing, of course, but maintaining an appearance of separation was important. They'd call us snobs and queers and wiggers, and in turn we'd call them rednecks and hillbillies and retards. None of which made any sense, considering some of the richest kids in the area went to county and had daddies who farmed tobacco, while a lot of us city kids—me included—were shouting distance from the housing projects. Also, city girls were the world's worst about getting knocked up, then giving their kids names like Kennedy or Madison or Jefferson, as if those babies were destined to live in a fancy house in Dellview and not in the projects or one of those tumbledown rentals out by the sewing factory.

What happened is this: Robbie and I ended up out at Spector Plastics on the same paint crew, a temporary summer gig that paid well—six-fifty an hour—and was pretty miserable. We'd put in nine-hour days painting all of the interior walls of the plant a flat, ugly gray, sweating buckets in 100-degree heat, and I would go home every night nauseous from the fumes and aching, really sore, for the first time in my life. There were seven people on the crew, and just like high school, there was a pretty clear divide between us. Three of us were going to college in the fall. I had a full ride to Western Kentucky University, which was the default for any RHS student with no money or no special aspirations, but still a lot better than rotting away in Roma for the rest of my life. The rest of the painters, including Robbie, were hoping to transition at the end of the summer from temp crew to permanent positions. Every day I looked down from the scaffolding Robbie and I shared and watched as dull-eyed men and women filled molds, popped parts out of trays, counted and sorted. My dad worked down the road at another factory, Price Electrics, and I knew what this kind of work did to you after a while. I knew what Robbie didn't seem to: that nine dollars an hour sounds like a lot when you first get on, but you're not making much more than that when you retire forty years later, when you leave with a broken-down body and a broken-down spirit and a broken-down version of the Chevy truck you bought when you were still young and wifeless and flush with cash. My dad left Price a few days before my graduation ceremony, but not voluntarily; he had a heart attack and collapsed, and they carried him out on a stretcher.

Robbie didn't get it. He was saving everything he made on paint crew—hoping to trade his truck in for a Harley-Davidson that a guy he knew was selling cheap—and he couldn't see much beyond that, couldn't imagine a life like my dad was now leading: sitting at home alone, broke, putting together puzzles and taking walks and waiting for the doctor's okay to return to the job that had crippled him in the first place. Me, though—I wanted out of Roma more than I'd ever wanted anything. I thought that I was better than guys like Robbie, better than my own father. I was eighteen years old. I was a fool.

No, Robbie and I shouldn't have gotten along, much less become friends. Robbie was large and muscular and handsome. His favorite activity outside of drinking was working out, and he had his routine down to such a pattern, such a science, that I couldn't help being impressed and a little surprised. The LCHS football coach had begged him to play all through school, Robbie told me, but Robbie was never interested. He was committed to the human body, though. He knew his muscles and the exercises necessary to build and tone them. He knew nutrition, which foods to eat when he was training, which ones to eat when he needed to lose a few pounds. He drank protein shakes in the morning and alcohol at night, and he filled the middle hours with chicken breasts and green salads. He was more disciplined than most athletes, but training for nothing.

And me? I was small, sure—anyone looked small next to Robbie—and about as average as a teenage guy can be. Brown hair and eyes. Fairly straight teeth, which was a good thing, because my dad couldn't have afforded braces. Not fat or skinny, just *there*. I was pretty smart, too, I guess. Hard to think of myself that way, considering what a fuckup I could be most of the time, but I'd known for a while that Roma wouldn't be able to keep me, that I'd roll out of town one day just like I'd ridden my bike, on the sly, out of my subdivision as a kid. Back then my father had set boundaries—the rock quarry south of our house, Harper Hill and the town watchtower on the north side—and warned me never to go beyond them. Out of Dad's sight, I'd pedal until my thighs burned, top Harper Hill, and go coasting down the other side at the kind of speed that would have killed me had I been old enough or smart enough to know any better. And still now I couldn't get out fast enough; I had bigger things ahead than factory work and Wal-Mart and the yearly Battle of the Cats. I was majoring in anthropology, because I could limit my program focus to forensic anthropology and maybe get a detective job someday.

"I know all I need to know about you," Robbie told me when I confessed this dream. "Just don't even say another word. Been good knowing you."

I was pretty sure he was joking. It was Friday, the first full week of work behind us, and we were rolling primer together on the factory's north wall. Burt, the supervisor, had paired us on the first day—"You take tops and you take bottoms," he'd said to us, and can you guess which took which?—and I think Robbie and I were both surprised that we got on so well.

"I'll be crooked," I told him.

"Christ, Matt, that's a given," Robbie said. "All of those fuckers are crooked." But he thumped me on the back. "All right. Just remember your old buddy Rob when you're flying your helicopter over some suspicious-looking plant life, out Olmstead way."

"Don't you worry," I said. "You'll be the first person I think of."

Robbie laughed—a rich, older man's laugh. "You're all right," he said. "You and me, we should have some beers tonight. I'll even pay."

I wasn't much on beer—not then, not yet—but I knew better than to say no. "Sounds good," I told him.

"I'll get my girl to meet us," he said. "You know Tina?"

"Know of her," I told him. Tina Sanford was another county kid. She was hard to miss: tall, blonde-haired, and built, as my father would say, like a brick shithouse. The kind of girl who'd turn you on if she wasn't so damned intimidating.

"Yeah, she'll get a kick out of you. Her mouth is about as smart as yours is."

My stomach was starting to churn. I didn't know how to relate to a guy like Robbie. Would I have to be funny all night? What would he do if I wasn't?

"You should bring a girl," Robbie said.

I almost laughed. The way he said *a girl*—so easy and casual, as if getting one were no more trouble than ordering a pizza. "I don't have one," I said.

"Sure you do." He jerked his head over to the next set of scaffolding, never slowing the motion of his paint roller. I looked. Jason, a guy I'd graduated with, was leaned over on the railing, smoking a cigarette and watching people do actual work. Behind him, April Franklin was rolling paint on the wall like her life depended on it, bony arms folding and unfolding. April had gone to county with Robbie, but she was one of the college-bound paint crew kids—heading to Western, like me. She was thin and fair-skinned, with a dusting of freckles across her nose and cheeks that made her look like the girl on the Little Debbie boxes. I hadn't actually thought much about her, outside of finding her boring and nice.

"April?"

"She's real sweet," Robbie said, wiping his brow with a forearm that looked like a lamb shank. "Cute as hell, too. You'll like her."

"I don't know," I said.

Robbie winked. I hadn't gotten used to his face. He had these normal, even refined features—straight, narrow nose, wide-set eyes, high cheekbones—on a body designed for tackles and heavy lifting and bare-knuckled fighting. He was sort of spectacular and freakish all at once, like a centaur; he looked like he ought to have a lightning bolt in his hand instead of a paint roller. "Don't you worry," he said. "I'll set it all up."

Between his afternoon break and a cell phone call, he did.

• • •

Robbie knew a place where we'd all get served, no IDs needed. Guys like him have to, right? It was a dump called Trudy's on the outskirts of Bowling Green, and it looked like the set of some low-budget action movie—one where the hero comes in, and a redneck biker dude threatens him, and the hero proceeds to kick the biker's ass and everyone else's, too. This place had it all: pool tables, sawdust, a jukebox that played nothing but country and Lynyrd Skynyrd. April looked terrified. We took a corner booth and Robbie ordered a pitcher. Then he slung his arm around Tina, his girl, who shook her streaked bangs out of her eyes and drummed her fingertips on the table. "Let me out, babe," she said. "I want to play something."

"Got any quarters?" Robbie said.

"Yep." She squeezed around him and went to the jukebox, and I watched her, discreetly, wondering where she had room to store coins in such tight jeans. She was a thick girl, broad through the hips and soft all over, with lovely, large breasts. A touch chubby, I guess, but her proportions were good, and she carried the weight, those breasts and hips, with a kind of confident strut that was sensual but not outright slutty. It took my breath away. For the first time that summer, but not the last, I looked at her, and I looked at the frail, sweet-faced girl beside me, and I knew the kind of woman I was destined for, the kind of sex I would have when I finally got to have it: nice and safe, because girls like April weren't designed for anything else. Simple engineering.

A waitress brought over our pitcher, and "Ring of Fire" started to play over the rattletrap sound system. Tina came back in time for Robbie to fill her stein.

"This is a great song," she said. "I just about cried when I heard Johnny died. Broke my heart."

"She was a mess," Robbie said. He was rubbing her neck, making small circles with his knuckles. "You'd have thought it was Elvis."

"He was better than Elvis."

I noticed her eyelids were streaked with some kind of sparkly makeup, a purple color that made her blue eyes almost violet. She, like Robbie, had a face so pretty that it didn't seem to fit with the rest of her. I wondered what she looked like with her shirt off. I'd only seen breasts—real and warm and right in front of me—one time, at a party three months earlier. Kimberly Coker, a sophomore, let me touch hers, and we made out some, and then she didn't want another thing to do with me. Hers were small and droopy, with nipples that pointed up. Like wooden shoes. Tina's would be round and heavy with broad pale nipples, like the models in my dad's old-school copies of *Playboy*—the ones before women started getting implants. I began to sweat. Then, all at once, I remembered Robbie, and I was sure that he could read my mind—or at least the expression on my face—and that a beating was forthcoming.

But he was looking at Tina, and I saw in *his* face love: plain, simple, silly love. I couldn't help but be moved by it. And jealous of it at the same time.

"What are you doing this summer?" I asked Tina.

"Helping out a vet," she said.

"She's being modest," Robbie said. "She's got an internship. She's going to UK in the fall."

"I wanted to be a vet when I was little," April said. "I thought I'd get to play with puppies and kittens all day."

"I'm planning to concentrate on large animals." Tina pulled a soft pack of Camels out of her purse and tapped it against the palm of her hand. "I'm mostly interested in horses. The Center for Equine Studies there is a big deal. I don't know if I want to do the medical end or the research end. The research part's cool, though. That spring a few years back when all the foals were dying? They're the ones who figured out what was killing them."

"Lot of money in that," I said.

"She don't care about the money," Robbie told me. He pulled her to him, big hand wrapped around her shoulder, and kissed her temple. "Nobody has to worry about money."

"I just love horses," Tina said. I could tell from her voice that she was simplifying things, and I wondered how often she had to do that for Robbie. Not because he was stupid—I'd already learned better than that—but because that's probably how he'd want things between them.

"We're gonna have us a horse farm someday," he said. "Thoroughbreds and a bunch of acres. I swear to God, we're going to put a horse in the Derby. We've got the name picked out already."

"Like a baby name," April said.

"You got it."

"What is it?" I asked. I watched Tina's face. She was pulling on her cigarette and looking away.

"A secret," Robbie said. "For now, anyway. Right, Tina?"

She nodded.

"I wouldn't want to jinx it," he said. He pulled his fingers through his beard, whiskers so bright in the dim room that they seemed almost metallic. He was careful with that beard; he had a little comb and fold-up mirror that he carried with him wherever he went, and he never ate something—a full meal or even just a package of saltines—without pulling the comb and mirror out and regrooming. I was struck by the combination: his masculinity and his vanity. "That's for me and Tina right now. It's our little pact."

"How sweet," April said.

Robbie laughed. "Aw," he said, exaggerating his drawl. He looked at Tina. "Ain't it?"

"If you say so." She was smiling.

"Why don't you dance with me, pretty lady."

They got up together and walked over to a cleared-out spot in front of the juke, the only couple out there. They could do that— do whatever they damn well pleased—and who would stop them? Who would try to tell Robbie no? I thought about one of my father's favorite sayings: *If wishes were horses then beggars would ride.* He had a million of them, all just as cynical and irritating. *Life's hard, then you die. Half past the crack in my ass. Done bun can't be undone.* When my mother died ten years earlier—hit by a car on one of her early-morning walks—he'd pulled out another chestnut: *She was too good for this world.*

"They're something else, huh?" April said.

"Yeah." I sipped my beer and grimaced.

"I like Robbie, though." She picked at a fingernail, and I noticed that she kept them chewed down to the quick. "We didn't run in the same circles in school, but he was always nice to me. He let me interview him for yearbook."

"What about Tina?"

She looked out on the floor, where Robbie and Tina danced: Robbie a good foot taller than Tina, Tina's face pressed against Robbie's wide chest. "We went to Auburn Middle School together, and she was sort of a bitch then. You know, a bully. We were in the same English class in seventh grade, and she sat behind me every day and pulled my hair. I hated her. But she and Robbie hooked up in high school, and I guess that changed her a little."

"She seems smart," I said.

"She is," April said. "She graduated salutatorian. She didn't even have to work for it."

"Who was valedictorian?" I asked. I already knew the answer.

"I was." Her smile was wry. "But I *did* have to work for it."

"So why are you going to Western of all fucking places?"

"I was going to have to go to state school one way or the other," she said. "I qualified for all kinds of scholarships, but places like Centre or Cumberland were only going to finance part. Like they'd pay for tuition but not housing, that kind of thing. Anyway, Western has one of the best journalism schools in the country. Did you know that?"

I shook my head.

"The school paper there's won all kinds of awards."

"I had no idea," I said.

The song ended, and out on the floor, Robbie and Tina kissed: slow and heavy, like there wasn't anyone around to see them do it. I couldn't decide if I thought they were a perfect match or a perfect disaster. I wondered what Robbie was going to do when Tina went to school in the fall; I knew he didn't have plans to pick up and go to Lexington himself.

I looked back at April. She *was* a sweet girl; Robbie had pegged it. I think that I knew even then that I was going to hurt her, but I liked her—more important, I could see she liked me—and that seemed enough at the time. What did I know about girls? About love?

"I'm glad you'll be at Western," I told her.

She blushed—I'd never made a girl blush, not once—and looked at her hands, her chewed nails. "Thanks," she said.

That night I drove April home. I had my dad's car temporarily—he didn't need it much while he was still on leave from work—and I was saving that summer for something cheap and gas-efficient to get me back and forth from Bowling Green once school started. Dad's heart attack made breaking away from Roma difficult. I would still be living in the dorms—I had free housing, so I figured I might as well—but I'd have to drive home more often than I'd planned to help around the house, keep the yard mowed, that kind of thing. I was willing to do that for my dad, of course, because I loved him; but I was frustrated, too. With my mother gone, we were more like roommates than father and son: we took turns cooking crappy food out of cans and boxes, then ate it watching TV; we got into arguments over pure nonsense, like who left the wet washrag on the floor. The morning after his heart attack, just before the doctors performed a heart cath, I sat at his bedside and listened as he planned for his death. He had two savings accounts, he said—one at Citizens and one at Southern Deposit—and a fireproof box in his sock drawer filled with savings bonds, "about ten thousand dollars' worth. Maybe enough to keep the car gassed up, way things are going these days." He told me that the house was mine and the car was mine. He told me that he kept a Polaroid of my mother, naked, in an envelope in the drawer of his bedside table, and he asked me to burn it, to please not look at it. I wrote everything down on a sheet of notebook paper, except for the stuff about the picture. That I tried to forget.

The cath took two hours. I sat in the downstairs waiting room of St. Thomas Hospital in Nashville, watching TV, watching people. There were air mattresses and sleeping bags scattered across the floor, with families—groups of five or more some-times—nestled like campers or picnickers, sharing sandwiches and Coca-Colas out of tote bags, laughing together or crying to-gether, but together. I was alone. I had aunts and uncles—two on my mother's side, one on my father's—and Dad's brother, Ricky, had stopped by the night before, but he'd left before midnight and no one else came. I waited, and at some point I cried, knees pulled to my chest, face hidden in the neck of my T-shirt. Dad got better, of course—got off lucky, the doctors said, because they were able to repair the blockages with stents instead of surgery—but I couldn't just rebound to that life we'd been sharing. We only had each other, and we were settling for so little.

I told April some of this on the half-hour ride home from Trudy's.

"I'm sorry," she said. That was it: not *That's tough*, or *My grandpa had a heart attack*. None of the usual bullshit. Just sorry.

"Thanks," I said.

We were sitting at the curb in front of her house. She had a nice place, nothing fancy: a medium-sized brick ranch in Chapman subdivision, purely middle-class but still intimidating enough to make me feel small. Dad was good with the money he made, but he made a pittance, and our house—he called it "the cracker box"—pretty well reflected that.

"I guess I'll see you Monday," April said.

"Yeah."

She was a cute girl, like Robbie said—not quite pretty, but she looked better than pretty that night in my dad's car, with a streetlight shining in and making her eyes sparkle. She was flushed, too, and that was maybe the most attractive thing. I could see that she wanted me to kiss her, that the possibility of me kissing her made her nervous and excited. She wet her lips quickly, like she didn't want me to see her do it, and I leaned in, put mine against hers. I wasn't very experienced, but I could tell that she was even greener. We managed.

I drove home with the car windows rolled down, thinking about Tina. She and Robbie were having sex—you could see it between them, solid and familiar—and I tried to imagine a time in my life when sex would be commonplace, something I could rely on and not worry about too much. Seemed like a dream, like hoping to be president or a movie star.

Dad was watching Jay Leno when I got home. That was another thing we argued about: Leno or Letterman.

"You should get some rest," I told him. Dad was supposed to be on a low-fat, low-sodium diet—and alcohol was a big no-no—but he had a beer in one hand and the other wrist-deep in a bag of Munchos.

"You don't get any more relaxed than this," he said, motioning to the footrest of his recliner. His slippered feet were propped up, spread far enough apart so that he could see the TV between them.

"You're not supposed to be eating that shit."

"Look who's talking," he said. "Anyway, I'm on Lipitor."

"That's not a—" I stopped. *Free ride* is how I meant to finish, but having this conversation with him—again—was stupid. Useless. I went to the kitchen and scrounged around in the freezer for something to eat, finding a box of Banquet fried chicken in the back under some pot pies. I dumped a few pieces out on a baking sheet and stuck them in the oven.

"Can't break what's already broken," Dad called from the living room, and I didn't bother to tell him that he'd gotten the saying screwed up.

I ate in the living room, plate propped on the couch's armrest, and watched Leno with Dad. He had this habit of laughing too hard at the funny stuff, then looking at me and smiling, wanting to see me laugh too. Some days, when I felt like giving him what he needed, I'd smile and nod and try to say with my eyes, *Yes, that's funny. You're right.* That night, when I sensed Dad looking at me, I pretended not to notice and just stared at my food or the TV screen. That was my summer to be selfish. When Dad had his heart attack, I went back and forth between worrying for him and worrying about my graduation ceremony, whether I'd be forced to miss it. Now I worried about the next heart attack— I was sure there would be one—and what I'd do if it happened after I left for college. If Dad ended up in worse shape than he was in now.

Leno ended, and I realized that Dad was asleep, bag of chips still in his lap. I felt a sudden, desperate need to wake him, to put in one of the movies he loved—*Caddyshack* or *Fletch*, which we'd copied from video rentals—and stay up late watching with him, laughing with him. He snored a little and shifted in his chair, a man of average height with a big, round belly: hard fat that he carried up high, close to his heart. He had changed since my mother's death. Of all the things I remembered about the life we had before we lost her—my mother's smell and her laugh, her exercises in front of the cabinet TV, our Friday night dinners out at Pizza Hut—what I remembered most was Dad, the differences in him between then and now. I had in my head an eight-year-old's image of a father: a man two miles high with big arms and a broad chest and a deep, echoing voice; a man who could toss me up over his shoulder like a bag of feed, who smelled like coffee and engine grease, who kissed my mother when he came home from work and looked strong and satisfied, like a king.

Now his head was rolled over to the side, so that his chin rested on his shoulder. He had a few droplets of beer in his mustache. I took the chips out of his lap and folded the opening over, so they wouldn't get stale. Then I turned off the lamp and went to bed.

2.

Summers last forever when you're a teenager, and that summer—the last before college and work and life as I would come to know it—was no exception. A month passed at the factory, and I felt like I'd never been anywhere else. I guess it was easy to lose touch: I wasn't good at making friends, and the few I'd managed during high school had scattered—my best friend Jim off to college early, getting a jump on his composition and algebra requirements; the third guy we sometimes palled around with, Kevin, in Honduras for a church missionary thing. I had nothing else going on outside of work and the people I worked with for those stretched-out weeks. Robbie, Tina, and April became my life.

I felt about Robbie and Tina the way I knew I should feel about April; I was nervous around them, excited, and when I wasn't hanging out with them I wanted to be. Robbie wasn't like Jim or Kevin; he was loud and confident, and he was fun. Hilarious, sometimes. When we were working, and the factory wall stretched off to our right unpainted and seemingly never-ending, he'd tell me stories about the crazy shit he'd done—most began, "This one time when I was drunk"—and he always had an idea about somewhere to go, something to get into. That's how he'd put it: "Let's get into something tonight." I liked that about him too. We didn't just *do* stuff; we *got into* it, and that may seem a fine distinction, but it was everything. *Getting into* was the difference between Friday night computer games and all-night drunks down at Lake Malone, which was a lot of excitement for a quiet do-gooder like me.

I wasn't sure how I felt about April. I liked her, of course: she was intelligent and gentle, but she also had a sense of humor that surprised in its occasional fierceness. A couple of weeks after that first kiss, she asked me—cheeks so red that she let her hair hang over her face, trying to hide—if we were boyfriend and girlfriend. *I just want to know how to think of us,* she said. *I don't like not being able to give something a name.*

Just like a reporter, I told her.

You're hedging.

Okay, then, I said. *Yes. You're my girlfriend, if you want to be. I'm your boyfriend. If you'll have me.*

I'll have you, she said, and she kissed me.

I knew that April had plans for us—that she pictured us at WKU together, signing up for the same classes and hanging out in each other's dorm room. I knew, too, that she didn't want to go to college alone, and of course I didn't either, which was one of the reasons I smiled through moments like the girlfriend conversation without letting her know how I really felt—desperate and trapped. I'll admit it: being with April had taught me that I *could* be with a girl, and not far behind that understanding was a desire for something better. Someone better. April's hand was the one I held when our little group went out after work—to Trudy's, or down to Gary's Pit Barbecue for dinner—and April was the girl I made out with when I'd had too many drinks on a Saturday night. But Tina was the girl I went to bed thinking about, fantasizing about, and Tina was the girl who could make my heart hurt just by brushing my arm on accident or smiling at me in that way she had: one corner of her mouth higher than the other, one eyebrow raised slightly, making her appear sly. I had a crush, I had it bad, and my friendship with Robbie—or my commitment to April—did nothing to temper it.

Fourth of July landed on a Monday that year, and we all got the day off. I figured we'd go and watch fireworks somewhere. Nashville was supposed to have a really great show, because you could spread a blanket out on the riverfront and see the lights reflect on the water, but Robbie said that he wasn't in the mood to fight the crowds. "It's overrated," he told me at work the Friday before. "Besides, I got something better in mind."

"Like what?"

"You'll see," he said. "Bring April to my house Monday afternoon, and we'll all go in my truck."

We ended up down in Todd County, at Pilot Rock—a big plateau right off the highway, popular among the Fort Campbell set because it offered an accessible rock face for rappelling. My dad had taken me there once when I was in middle school, but I'd almost forgotten it existed until we topped a hill in Robbie's truck and it appeared ahead, raised and craggy like a wart.

"Hiking," April said miserably. "I'm wearing sandals."

"It's not that bad," Tina said, and beneath her tone of reassurance I could detect the slightest sharpness: evidence of the bully

April told me about that night at Trudy's. "We're just going up the main vein, and there's stairs most of the way."

We weren't the only people celebrating the Fourth at Pilot Rock, but it wasn't crowded, either, and we found a quiet spot on the north side of the plateau with no trouble. Pilot Rock wasn't a mountain, but the height was impressive enough, and the elevation continued to drop, gradually, as the land sloped away on all sides. You could see a lot from up there: western Kentucky's gentle hills, Highway 507 winding off back toward Allegre and finally disappearing into a heat-hazy horizon. Tina spread a stadium blanket out on a bare patch of ground a few feet from the edge of the precipice, and we all just sat for a while, silently. April was stiff at first—she didn't want to be here and was making no secret of it—but after a few minutes she tucked her shoulder into the crook of my arm and sighed, a tired sound that was also content and apologetic. I kissed the top of her head. We hadn't had sex, but we were building toward it; every date I was pushing the physical stuff a bit further, nudging her to take another step, and another. I think she would have complained about hanging out with Robbie and Tina so much if she didn't feel that our time with them was a reprieve from all that pressure. I knew, though, that sex was inevitable, that the question now was a matter of when and not if. Because she wanted to make me happy.

We had sandwiches and potato chips, drank beer. Robbie put away six cans in the span of an hour, crushing each new empty under his boot heel, then dropping the disk into the cooler. At the end of our meal he pulled a watermelon out from the bottom of the grocery sack, the one Tina had carried, and I realized, humiliated, how much heavier her load had been than my own.

"Keep clear," he said. "And grab a fork."

He walked away a few feet, then brought the watermelon down with one short, swift motion, cracking it in half on the squared-off edge of a boulder. He came back to our blanket with a wet, ragged piece of watermelon in each hand, passing the smaller of the two to April and me before we could refuse it. "Dig in," he said.

The rind was smeared with sticky juice, and Robbie hadn't brought napkins. We ate without talking, almost solemnly, and after a few minutes Robbie walked off to find a dark corner he could take a leak in. April stopped eating after a few bites and I finished what was left of our half, then wiped my hands on the sides of my blue jeans. I hated getting my hands dirty; my dad had taken the liberty of pointing that out to me a number of times.

"Sorry," Tina said flatly. "He doesn't think ahead sometimes."

I shrugged. "It was good. Hit the spot."

"I can see why he likes you," Tina told me. She looked pissed off, and I couldn't figure out why. "You wouldn't say shit if you had a mouthful."

"Hold up just a minute," April said. "What's your problem?"

Tina looked like she was going to give April an answer—and then some—but Robbie came back, grinning, and she closed her mouth.

"Get up, guys," Robbie said. "Come check this out."

We followed him to the far side of the plateau, where a group of men were rappelling down the rock's south face—this side sheer and almost smooth, where the opposite had been thick with small trees and shrubbery, spikes of sandstone. The men were clearly Army; a few were wearing worn-out issue—the lace-up boots and cargo pants—but they also had the buzzed-off haircuts, the air of swagger and maybe even meanness.

"This is my girl," Robbie told one of them, apparently picking up on an earlier conversation. "Tina. And these here are a couple of work buddies, Matt and April."

"Good deal," the guy said. "Happy Fourth, folks."

"You, too," April said, voice high.

"Chad," the guy said, holding his hand out to each of us, oddly formal. He was sawed off but solid, barrel-chested, and his head—bald on the top, shaved to the pore everywhere else—looked shiny and hard, like mica. "Who's first?"

"What are you talking about?" Tina said, looking at Robbie instead of Chad.

"These guys do this shit every day," Robbie said. "I'm gonna go for it."

"Don't be stupid." Her whisper was harsher, louder, than her regular speaking voice. "We don't even know them."

April's hand locked onto mine—a death grip—and the touch repulsed me: the neediness of it. I pulled free and stepped forward, thinking—I don't know—that a trip down the side of Pilot Rock was better than the touch of a good girl.

"I'll go," I said, and Robbie slapped me on the back a couple of times, laughing. Tina seemed merely curious, like the thought of me falling and going *splat* was strange but not actually scary or tragic.

"Matt," April said, voice higher than ever.

"You can stay up here," I told her. "Somebody should watch the cooler and stuff anyway."

She looked like she might cry.

"Me, too," Tina said suddenly. "I'm going down too."

"We just have the one extra harness," Chad said. "So you'll have to take turns."

I was buzzing a little from the three beers I'd had with dinner. No great drinker. And I was also sure—positive—that I was going to die, that something would go wrong on accident, like the rope would snap, or that these guys were psychos who preyed on dull people with uncharacteristic desires to thrill-seek. That they would let me fall. But I allowed Chad and one of his buddies to help me into the spare harness, a little weirded out by the proximity of their bodies—Chad yanking the leg holes into place like my mother had once yanked up my underpants, his friend tightening the waistband until I had to suck my stomach in.

"Yeah, that's a little uncomfortable," the friend said, still adjusting. "Can't go down loose, though." He held up a metal latch-like thing. "This is your carabiner." He snapped the carabiner onto a metal loop at my waist and pulled two times, roughly. "How's your crotch?"

"Fine," I said. I glanced over, saw Tina and April—Tina's expression a smirk, April's near-devastated. "I mean, I'm okay."

The rope was tied off on a tree about twelve feet from the drop-off—it looked sturdy enough—and Chad waved me over to it. "Put these on," he said, handing me some gloves. He took another metal device and hooked the rope through it, then to my harness, a series of knots and pulls that I couldn't follow. "Figure-eight," he said, pointing to one spot, "autoblocking knot. Left hand here." He put my hand on the knot. "Right hand holds the rope. Figure eight controls the speed of your descent."

He hunched down, miming the rappel posture. "Right hand's your brake hand. You brake by pulling the rope right into your lower back, just north of the butt crack. Follow me? When you want to rappel, pull your hand out of the position and let the rope slide through your hand. Take it slow at first. Let's see you practice that."

I practiced a few yards from the edge, dropping into a sit to test my brake hand, trying to get a feel for the release. I knew they were all watching me, wondering if I'd have the nerve to go through with it, and I looked over my shoulder at that sheer edge, chest tightening so quickly that I thought, *Heart attack.* I thought about my father. *Foolish,* he'd say. *Son, you're asking for trouble.*

"There's a guy at the bottom holding the other end of the rope," Chad's friend said. "If you slip, he pulls. You won't go anywhere."

"Promise?" I tried to sound like I was joking.

"We guarantee it," Chad said. "Now get over that edge before we lose daylight."

I looked at April again. She was sitting away from the group now, staring out at the scenery.

I went down.

It wasn't such a big deal, I know that now. But going over that edge—well, I've never been so terrified. One minute you're on good, solid ground; then, all at once, you've lost it, you've shifted from one plane to another, and all the things you think you know about the world don't matter anymore. The rules, the science.

Then I adjusted, found my center, and began to descend, hesitant at first—barely lifting my brake hand, baby-stepping—then bouncing off the wall, feeling, if only for the space of a few feet at a time, free fall. I didn't look up or down, and when I hit ground, I was surprised at first, uncertain, like I wasn't a man built to walk upright. My legs shook, and some guy I didn't know clapped my back, then started unhooking the carabiner and the harness. He put everything into a grocery sack and knotted the handles to the rope, yanking it. "Harness!" he yelled up. I followed its ascent and saw my friends—Robbie, Tina, April too—looking down at me, waving. I waved back.

Three more important things happened that night.

The second thing came at nightfall, when the four of us were all back at our picnic site, stretched out on the blanket. We'd drunk a lot of beers by that time, and Robbie was setting off the fireworks I'd hauled up: cheap bottle rockets that made beautiful whistling sounds, fancier stuff that sprayed sparkle patterns—gold, red—across a night sky that was ebony this far out of town. A nice breeze had picked up and the air was cooling; I felt strong and alive and fearless, like I was the kind of person who belonged among the Robbies of the world, like we were equals.

When the fireworks were all fired, the beer gone, and we were packing up our mess of cans and food wrappers, Robbie grabbed my hand, clapping it between the two of his: a hard gesture, emphatic, the pressure of his fingers a promise I didn't yet understand. Before that summer was over, I'd see those hands put to their rumored purpose—all of Robbie's anger balled into a weapon, anger as big as the man—and I'd know for the first time in my life what real fear felt like. For now, though, I just felt accepted and grateful. "You're a good friend," he told me, and that word, *friend,* touched me in a way that April's devotion couldn't. "You're a good man."

The third thing happened after we returned to town. I was sobering up after the drive back from Todd County, but sleepy, so April took my keys. She didn't drive me to my house, though; I woke up from a doze in time to see that she'd driven me to hers. I thought that she was out of it, maybe—operating on autopilot—but she turned the motor off and sat for a while, looking at the security light over her front door, then faced me.

"My folks are gone for the night," she said. "They're camping out at Kentucky Lake."

"You didn't tell me that."

"I'm telling you now."

I waited. I knew what she was trying to decide, and I tried to decide too: Was I strong enough to do the right thing by this girl? Was I good enough?

"You can come in if you want," she said.

I barely paused: I leaned in and kissed her, smelling my beer breath as I exhaled, and nodded, my lips still against hers.

First, though, was Tina.

She was the next to rappel down. I knew that I should start back to the top of the rock and get back to April—she'd be scared and upset if Robbie left her alone with those Army guys, and of course she'd blame me—but I couldn't help watching as Tina navigated that square edge, adjusted, and started down slowly, just like I had. She was so high up. I couldn't believe that I'd been there myself, just minutes before.

"Damn," the rope-holder said, laughing. "That girl's got junk in the trunk."

"You better not talk that way around the big dude up there," I said. "He'd mess you up."

"Are you kidding me?" He wiped his brow, letting go of the rope end temporarily. "I saw that hoss earlier. I'm not an idiot."

"Maybe you should just hold the rope," I told him, wishing I could say more—that the little threat I posed, if any, didn't come from my connection to Robbie. The guy grabbed the rope again, and he didn't say anything else.

Tina was getting more confident: she pushed off of the wall, descending a few feet at a time, then a few yards, the rope making little twirls, lasso-style, where it was running through her hand. She reached bottom in just a couple of minutes, face pink, exhilarated.

"That was awesome," she told the rope guy.

"Glad you enjoyed it, hon," he said, helping her out of her gear, mannered as a butler. It was fascinating to me how quickly a man could shift from his real self to something made-up, a Good Guy face. Did women realize? I thought about the women, the girls, I'd known in my life: my mother, so long ago; neighbors; classmates. I thought about Miss Wilkinson, my eleventh-grade science teacher—a young woman, mid-twenties, with full cheeks and very white teeth, and thick, muscled calves and arms that belonged to a softball player—and how the guys had all talked under their breaths about her during class, even the nobodies like me: Miss W's tits, Miss W's ass, how we'd like to get Miss W bent over that big old school desk of hers, teach *her* a thing or two about biology. I thought about the time I stayed after class to do some makeup work—I'd been home sick for a week with strep throat—and Miss Wilkinson told me, in her soft young voice, about her bout with pneumonia the year before, how sick she'd been, how good it felt to come out on the other side of it. She left for a few minutes to go to the teachers' lounge and came back with sodas: a Diet Coke for her, a Coke for me. When I'd completed the work and packed up my things to leave, she smiled at me and said, *You feel better, Matt,* and I could tell she meant it, that she wasn't just giving me lip service.

Tina came over and stood beside me. We looked up together.

"I'm glad I did it," she said.

"Yeah."

She put her hand on her chest. "My heart. It's still beating so fast."

I looked at that hand, then looked quickly away. Rope Guy was sending the harness up again.

"I'm sorry I was such a bitch before," she said.

"You were okay."

She leaned to the side and bumped shoulders with me, playful and maybe a little embarrassed. "You don't have to handle me, Matt," she said. "I'm not that delicate."

I grinned. I couldn't help it. "You think I don't know that?"

"It's just been hard lately," Tina said. "I guess you wouldn't understand."

"What wouldn't I understand?"

"Robbie and me."

"I might," I said.

The sun was setting, huge and red off to our left. It cast a pink-ish glow, the play of light and shadow making Tina's face soft in some places, hard-lined in others.

"When I was a kid," Tina said, "I had this Cabbage Patch doll. I loved that thing. I'd had it so long I didn't even remember getting it. Slept with it every night. So when I was ten, I got invited to my first slumber party. I'd never been to one before. I was so excited."

She'd planned out this story, I knew. Worked it out in her head—maybe on her way down that rock face, maybe weeks ago.

"Nobody told me this—I mean, my mom or my dad didn't—but I knew I couldn't take the doll with me to the slumber party. I was too old for that. And I felt so upset once I'd decided, but not because I wanted her with me and couldn't have her. I was upset because I didn't want her with me. I knew that I'd get to that party and I'd have so much fun that I wouldn't miss her at all." She paused and looked up, where Robbie was just coming over the edge. "Do you get what I'm saying?"

I nodded.

"What about April?" she said. "I mean, do you think you two are serious?"

"I don't know. It's complicated."

"We went to middle school together," Tina said.

"Yeah, she told me."

"I guess she told you that I was shitty to her, too."

"She said you pulled her hair a few times," I said.

Robbie was halfway down now, moving more slowly than I would have expected: careful, deliberate. He didn't seem timid—just unconcerned. Like he knew the ground was down below him somewhere, and he had no good reason to get there any sooner than necessary.

"I feel bad about that," Tina said. "But April's one of those people who just takes shit. You know? I knew that I could hurt her and get away with it, so I kept doing it."

She was right, of course. The world wasn't just divided between bad men and good women, but between weak people and strong people.

"I guess you don't think much of me," Tina said.

Robbie had reached the ground, and I must have blurted out what I did because I knew there wouldn't be another opportunity, that Robbie would always, one way or another, be hanging over our heads.

"I do, though," I told Tina. "I think of you all the time."

Then Robbie was coming toward us, laughing, and Tina was hugging him; I started back up Pilot Rock, to my girlfriend, my words trailing me like a stench. I didn't know what Tina would have said back to me, but I was glad—relieved, for now—that I didn't have to.

3.

I didn't see Tina for a while after that. My dad went back to work on the fifth of July, and the car—I had already started thinking of it as *my car*—became his again, and I was all at once back to high school: hitching rides with him to and from my own job each day, begging him at night for the keys. Dad was in a lousy mood most of the time. Kentucky becomes a sauna in July, and the typical 90-degree day felt more like 110 or higher in Dad's part of the factory. There was a single fan back there, he told me, and all it managed to do was circulate the stale, electric air. "So you just feel hot quicker," he said.

Instead of rolling out of bed at six forty-five and barely making my seven a.m. punch-in time, as was usually my habit, Dad had me up at six so I could get my shower in while he was making breakfast. He insisted on breakfast every day, and not just cereal: a fried egg and buttered toast, black coffee. For me, too, whether I wanted to eat or not. Then I'd stretch out in the easy chair and doze while Dad showered, my stomach too sleep-sluggish to digest properly. We didn't talk much during our drive to town, and I'd sit in the passenger seat, drowsing, thinking of all of the questions that I knew I should ask him just in case the worst happened. Questions about his childhood and his beliefs. Questions about Mom. And I could have told him stuff too: about April, for instance, of whom he'd received only the most scant detail, and maybe even about Tina. All of my girl trouble. We had opportunity, on those drives, to catch up, to try to make the best of what my mother had left us. But it just seemed so damned tiring. And to start that conversation—to try bonding with my father, seeking his advice after so many years of tuning him out—felt as obvious and futile as the bottle of nitroglycerin tablets he now carried each day in his breast pocket.

I let the car situation be an excuse to see less of April, which I knew confused and disturbed her, especially after she'd gone against her better judgment and had sex with me. What can I say about the person I was then? I'm older now—better, I hope—and I realize that sex is always awkward for the inexperienced, often regretful. Once a week or so April would call me at home—voice edgy and hesitant, as though she'd had to talk herself into dialing—and ask me if I wanted to come by her house, have some pizza, watch a video. This meant her parents were gone, and I always took her up on it, which seemed to make her happy at first—we'd eat and flip channels, and she'd stretch out beside me on the couch, head in my lap. We'd make sarcastic comments about whatever we were watching, have a few laughs, and I'd realize at some point that I was stroking her hair, a show of tenderness that I was normally hesitant to offer. Later, when we'd had sex—fast and quiet in her bedroom or on the couch in the den, always aware that her parents could abandon their night out and return home early—she'd get quiet and morose, and a few times she cried. *You don't want to be with me,* she'd say. *You're just using me until school starts.* I'd deny it, but not with a lot of heart; and she'd accept my denial, though she never looked convinced. What I remember best about those weeks is an image of April's bare, freckled shoulders: how they drew in when we were having sex—that delicacy I'd predicted, somehow more arousing than I'd imagined it—how they slumped after, when April drew her cast-off shirt to her chest and started dressing, looking at me like I'd disappointed her, the disappointment deeper than anything so trivial as my performance.

The factory was almost painted by late July, the walls fresh with a coat of the most dismal gray sludge I'd ever seen—a color meant to disguise smoke and grease stains, not to brighten a room or energize workers. In another couple of weeks, we'd finish the trim work and the inner offices, collect our final paychecks, and some of us would walk out of that place for good, summer officially over. Robbie, who had secured a floor job, would just change to a different set of work clothes—old T-shirt and jeans swapped for Wal-Mart Dickies and steel-toed boots—and start a swing shift, the typical rite of passage for new guys. He wasn't saving for that Harley anymore, he told me one Friday afternoon, yelling as usual over the constant racket of machinery.

"I'm too old for that shit," he said. He used the neck of his shirt to wipe sweat off the bridge of his nose, then readjusted his baseball cap.

"You're just eighteen," I said. And though I'd considered the Harley plan a pretty dumb one from the start—the kind of meat-headed logic that tied guys like Robbie to Logan County from time immemorial—this declaration of his scared me. Maybe a part of me sensed what was coming next, or maybe I just felt safer knowing that the Robbies of the world would go on hanging out at the bowling alley bar and getting their cars repossessed and having to fill out credit applications in their mothers' names. I don't know, but I remember feeling invested, all at once, in Robbie's decision—as though his choices defined *me* somehow. "You have plenty of time to get serious."

"I'm not gonna start walking the straight path, if that's what you mean," Robbie said. He laughed. "I've got too much partying left in me. But I don't have to be a dumb-ass either. I'm trying to get my priorities straightened out."

"What are your priorities, then?"

"Well, Tina," he said. "Tina is."

"You're going to ask her to marry you," I said.

He laughed again. "Jesus, buddy, you make it sound like can-cer." He waved me over, and I drew closer. "But yeah," he said, hand on my shoulder, voice lower. "I am, Matt. I'm going to get a ring with the Harley money and ask her."

"Oh."

"I think you're supposed to say 'Congratulations.'"

"I'm just confused," I said. "I thought she was going to Lexing-ton this fall."

"I'm not stopping her from going to college. Hell, I want her to go. I'm proud of her." He started rolling paint again, and I backed up to my own spot, where I was trimming out a window. The windows had bars, and I wondered who would want to break into this place, what could possibly be stolen. "I mean, we're too young to get married yet anyhow. I just want her to know I'm serious, and I'm still going to be here when she gets back."

"You think she doesn't know that?"

He shrugged. "It takes a gesture sometimes. Didn't your mama teach you that?"

"My mom's dead," I said, just because I knew that would stop the conversation. Cheap, but I didn't really care at that point.

So when Tina called me that weekend, on Sunday morning—the first time she'd ever called, ever made any sort of extra effort with me—I figured that she'd caught on to Robbie's plans, though she wouldn't give me any specifics. "Just come over," she said, and she gave me directions to where she lived—outside of Auburn, "in Siberia"—and added that her parents would be at church until late afternoon, because they were having a big potluck for the Vacation Bible School kids.

"All right," I said, once I had the directions written down. "My dad might be weird about the car, though."

"Just—" She didn't finish. I heard a sigh, then the hiccuping breaths of heavy crying—sounds that I associated with weakness, with April. I didn't know what to say.

"Just do your best," she told me, and hung up.

Dad was taking a nap—his Sunday specialty—so I grabbed the keys and slipped out, not even bothering to write a note; I'd take the heat if necessary. The drive was about a half-hour long once you factored in the half-dozen or so turnoffs, each new road more narrow and snakelike than the last. At least they were paved; some of the county roads were still gravel this far out, and Dad would have a shit-fit if I brought his car back dusty, even if it was just a Chevy Nova working on its second hundred thousand miles.

Tina's house was a surprise after so much backwoods traveling. I guess now that I'd have to call it a Southern Colonial, though it was one of those bastardized versions you often see in Kentucky, where the major plantations were fewer and not so *Gone with the Wind*–grand. It was still pretty impressive, though—situated on a small hilltop and set back from the road several hundred yards, with what looked like three full stories, or perhaps two with a half-floor. On the north side of the lawn were hundreds of cedar saplings, marked here and there with a yellow tie; a horse barn, freshly painted in the traditional red and white, was behind the house but still visible from the road. I remembered the first time I'd driven April home—how nice her house had seemed—and felt ridiculous.

Tina came up the drive to meet me, on horseback. I braked and rolled my window down.

"Are you okay?" I said, having to crane my neck to see her. She looked okay, but her face was scrubbed clean of her usual heavy eye makeup, and her hair was pulled back into a messy knot. I liked her even better this way, actually; she seemed less severe somehow, more vulnerable.

She nodded, and patted the horse's neck. "I always feel better after I ride."

"Where should I park?"

"There's plenty of room up by the house," she said. "I'll put Hank up and meet you on the porch." She turned her heel into the horse's flank—a tiny nudge, barely noticeable—and they took off for the barn at a fast clip, Tina's back straight and steady. I could tell that she'd been riding all her life, and I wanted to be caught in the romance of that moment: the horse's smooth gallop, Tina's hair running out behind her in slow motion. I wanted to, but I felt almost nothing. Only some jealousy—bitter and use-less, and a touch self-righteous, as most jealousy is—and some fatigue. Because I knew she'd planned this scene for me just like she'd planned the slumber party story, not because she was vain or manipulative—though she could have been both of those things, for all I knew—but because she couldn't just *be* and let a person take her or leave her, though that's the face she put on for the world. She needed more control.

I parked and waited for her on the porch, as she'd instructed. There was a swing. I leaned into it and enjoyed the breeze, which was cool and constant on this little hilltop. The swing chain creaked above me, echoing across the wood planks of the floor, and I felt sleepy and sad. It was warm out, still—into the 80s, at least—but I could smell the end of summer coming on, and for the first time since childhood, I truly mourned it. In a few weeks my life would be different. No coming back.

"I like it out here," Tina said, coming up and sitting beside me. "I'd invite you in, but there's not much to see."

"You have a great place," I told her. "I didn't even realize."

"It's okay." She pulled a bare foot up on the swing and pushed off the floor with the other. "We don't take good enough care of it, though. My mom has a dog, and I have a dog, and now my kid brother has one. They pretty much have the run of the place."

"What about your dad?"

"He has his trees." She motioned to the cedars I'd noticed coming in. "They're his hobby. 'Some hobby,' my mom says. But he gets a kick out of it. He tends them all year, and then he sells them at Christmastime."

"I like Christmas," I said. Normally I would have felt silly, say-ing something like that. Like a kid.

"Yeah, me too. It's nice. Before Dad opens the lot to every-body, he'll have our family over for the day—all the aunts and uncles on his side and Mom's, too, all their kids and grandkids. He gives whoever wants one a tree, and we do a hayride, and we drink cider and eat cookies and all that good shit. It was my favorite day of the year when I was a kid." Her voice sounded hoarse, full—like she was just registering a fresh loss. I waited.

"Matt, I'm pregnant," she said.

My throat swelled, metallic-tasting and hurtful, and I tried to catch my breath. I was flattened. Devastated. Those words were final to me in a way that *I'm not interested in you, Matt* or even *Leave me alone* could have been.

"Pregnant?"

She started to cry, and I let her put her face into my shoulder. I patted her arm, keeping my own face still.

"My parents would be humiliated," she said. "They'd want me to marry Robbie, and so would Robbie. Goddammit, Robbie would be over the fucking moon. He doesn't want me to go to Lexington anyway."

"He's never said that to me," I said.

She wasn't crying anymore, but she kept her head against my chest. "There's more to him than you get, Matt. Okay? He doesn't say it to me, either, at least not in an obvious way. But he lets me know."

"How?"

"His voice gets loud when he talks about it. He smiles too hard."

I knew what she was talking about, but I didn't want to agree with her. My heart was beating so fast, and her ear was right next to it. "You could be reading into that. Especially if you've got it in your head that he doesn't want you going."

"I know what he's planning," she said dully. "The ring. I can read him like a book."

I didn't have any answer to that.

"I love him. I'm sure you think I'm some kind of heartless bitch, but I do. That's the problem. If I didn't love him, I could do what I had to do and just fucking be done with it. No regrets."

"You mean, get rid of it," I said.

"What the hell else could I mean?"

"I'm sorry."

I felt her nod. "But that's not all of it. I can't go to Lexington and do everything I want to do and still hold on to Robbie. Baby or no baby. You can love somebody like crazy and still know that you're meant for something else."

I knew what she was really saying, because I'd looked at April too many times to count and thought the very same: not something else, but something better. *Someone* better.

"What do you want me to do?" I said. "Drive you somewhere?"

"Probably. At some point."

She was warm and soft in my arms. I thought about what I'd do if she was having my baby and not Robbie's.

"I'll drive you," I told her.

"What do you think of me?" she said. "You tell the truth, now. I'll know if you're bullshitting me."

"I think you're great," I said. "I think you're brilliant. And beautiful." I thought a second. "Fearless."

"Not nice, though."

"No," I agreed, and I think that pleased her more than she let on. "Not nice. But nice is overrated."

"You're nice," she said.

"Yeah." Admitting it felt like defeat. "Most of the time."

"I'm going to make you an offer, Matt. You just listen, and I'll talk. Here it is." She shifted, leaning her body in closer to mine. Her breath was suddenly on my neck. "You have sex with me. Just this one time. And then when I get my appointment set up, you drive me to it, and that's that."

I flushed, head to toe. I was going to set us both on fire. But I kept my voice steady. "You don't have to do that, for Christ's sake. I said I'd drive you."

"This is for me. I need to do something I can't take back. And then I can do the rest of it."

I pulled my arms off Tina and rested them on the back of the swing, afraid that she'd sense something in my touch—the eagerness or revulsion or nervousness, maybe some combination of the three—and change her mind before I could make up my own. "You're not thinking straight," I said.

She touched my knee—the most gentle gesture I'd ever seen from her, and I think she meant for it to be, though there was the suggestion of a reprimand, too. "I'm thinking just fine," she said. She put her fingertips just under the lip of my shorts, and my skin knotted into goose bumps. "I want to do this. I want to do it with *you*."

I can't remember if April crossed my mind between then and later, when I was driving my father's car back to Roma, so shaky that I kept letting the right tires travel over to the shoulder. I don't think she did.

I thought about Robbie, though. I pulled Tina's chin up—she was still leaning against my chest—and I saw him in her eyes as surely as I saw my own doubled, distorted reflection. I remembered him grabbing my hand a few weeks ago at the top of Pilot Rock: *You're a good friend. You're a good man.* I could have stopped then and not even felt any regret. Lord knows, I'd been dreaming about a moment like this all summer, but not this way: not as an arrangement, a pact, and not with that baby to make the whole thing seem even tawdrier. In fact, as I kissed her, as I put my hand on one of those full, heavy breasts, it seemed to me that the baby was a witness or even a spy, and to touch Tina this way wasn't just a betrayal of Robbie but also unholy somehow. Unnatural.

I thought all of that, but I kissed her anyway—only because I could. Because she'd allowed it. I was eighteen years old and confronted with the object of my desires, my fantasies, and I assumed, feeling that breast, that sensation would overwhelm thought at some point, and none of the rest of it would matter. And for a time, however brief, I was right. We went upstairs and had sex in her bedroom, her dogs scratching a backbeat on the other side of the closed door, demanding to be let in. And an hour after pulling into the driveway, I left.

My father was sitting up in his recliner when I came home, wide awake but oddly blank. The TV was off. The lights were off. He was rocking, though, and I lay back on the couch, noticing that his chair was squeaking almost perfectly in time with my heartbeat.

"I took the car," I said. "Sorry."

He kept rocking. "I don't care about the car."

"Are you okay? Are you hurting?"

"No more than usual," he said, and he kneaded his chest with the middle and ring fingers of one hand. I don't think he even realized he was doing it. "I'm just tired. Figured I'd rest my eyes."

It sounded like a good idea. I closed my eyes and thought about Tina—how soft she was, soft all over, and how what came out of her mouth and what you saw in her face were the total opposite of each other: sharp, sometimes too sharp. I figured that I must be in love with her—whatever that meant—but as quickly as I acknowledged this fact I understood that the two of us didn't have a chance in hell of getting together. I was another thing she'd try to forget once she'd moved to Lexington. If she thought about me—and really, I wasn't convinced she ever would—she'd associate me with betraying someone she cared for, and with the day of her abortion: the person who was seated behind the steering wheel, the person who was there in the waiting room to receive her once the irrevocable had been done.

"I want you to know about your mother," Dad said.

He *was* tired, I realized. I'd never seen him looking so tired. His lips were almost the same color as his skin—I could make that out even in the dim light—and the wrinkles around his eyes and mouth were much deeper than I'd realized. The more I looked at him, the less familiar he seemed, and I found myself squinting, searching for the details I knew, like the eye that was slightly smaller than the other, which I'd inherited, and the eyebrow with a faint scar running through its center. A bicycle accident, now over forty years past. The old markers were there, but they were situated in a face that seemed almost alien, a face that, for all the sense it made, might have been a stranger's.

"What about her?" I said hoarsely.

He sighed. "I don't know. What she was like."

"I remember what she was like," I said, but that was a lie. I had some memories, sure: Mom slicing potatoes into a bowl while she watched her afternoon soaps, Mom mashing her thumb down on the end of my shoe to make sure I had "growing room," Mom cussing because she got burned by a splash of grease, Mom stopping a run in a pair of pantyhose by dabbing it with clear nail polish. The smell of the polish: chemical and nauseating. I remembered what Mom looked like, but only because Dad had hung pictures of her all over the house, and even in my memories she seemed to have that picture-face on, so that I didn't even know for sure what was real, authentically mine, and what was Kodak.

"I haven't done so good without her," Dad said. "I tried my best. But there are times when a kid needs his mama, and I couldn't give you that."

"We've done okay."

"I should tell you all about her," he said. "She was a good woman. She loved you to pieces. She held you so much when you were a baby I told her you'd be spoiled, you'd come out a mama's boy." He stopped rocking. "I don't know why stuff like that matters so much when you're younger. I wish I had it to do over."

"What would you change?" I asked him.

"That's the trouble. I don't know. Maybe I would have spanked you less than I did, and I'm sure I would have hugged your mother more and told her how much I appreciated her. It doesn't do a bit of good for me to worry myself to death about all that, but I do. I worry about you, Matty. I think about you going and I feel like crying. You're all I got."

What do you say to that? There's nothing to say. I stayed on the couch a bit longer, just so he wouldn't think I was angry, and then I slipped into the kitchen and poured myself a Coke. The lights were bright in there, casting the den in deeper shadow; from where I sat, my father was a slumped dark space and nothing more—I couldn't even see the whites of his eyes. I couldn't tell if he was looking back at me.

4.

We finished painting on a Monday afternoon in early August, four days ahead of schedule. Burt, the supervisor, had tried to stretch the work out—he was a good guy, and he knew most of us would miss that extra two hundred bucks or so, and sorely—but there wasn't anything else left to do. The factory walls were all painted, the trim, the offices. The weather took a cool turn that week—temporary, I knew, but still a preview of the coming fall. Summer, at least in my own head, was over.

Robbie clapped me on the back as we walked outside together for the last time. I wasn't sorry to be going—to escape that heat and the constant racket and those god-awful paint fumes. But I felt worn out and empty. April hovered at my side, knuckles barely brushing mine.

"Don't forget about Friday," Robbie said, pointing a big, dirt-creased finger at me, grinning. "Nashville. You and me, friend. We're gonna get sauced."

"Wouldn't miss it," I said, trying a laugh. I couldn't even look at him.

April stood on tiptoe to hug Robbie—he could have pitched her like a javelin—and kissed his cheek. It was a tender gesture, and final. "You take care," she told him.

"Hell, girl, we'll see each other." He still had the grin on his face, but I saw, for the first time, uncertainty. Fear of being left behind.

April just nodded.

•   •   •

I drove her home—for the last time, as things turned out. It had been just over a week since my afternoon with Tina, and April and I hadn't had sex since then. We'd tried. She'd invited me over to her place on Saturday, and we went through our usual song and dance: takeout, making out, and we'd even made it as far as her bed—her shirt off, my pants unzipped—when I knew for sure that I couldn't go through with it. I wanted to, and it seemed to me that sex with April would somehow be the right thing—the noble thing, even. If I could sleep with April again, I'd be bound to her, and I'd never have to tell her about Tina. If I could sleep with her again, I could erase the terrible thing I'd done, and we'd go to Western together, and everything would be all right. But I couldn't. I mumbled some excuse about my stomach bothering me and hightailed it out of there as soon as I had an opening.

Now, in the car, she was pushed up against the door with her arms wrapped tightly across her chest. She had a flannel shirt on—much too large and probably her father's—and it accentuated her frailness, making her seem tender and precious. Her hair had the faintest reddish cast; I hadn't noticed it before.

"You look pretty," I told her, and meant it. I couldn't have said it before.

Her mouth twitched a little. She didn't believe it. Or else she didn't believe that the compliment came without some price. "Thanks," she said.

I glanced back and forth between her and the road. "You look like a college girl. I mean, I can really picture you there—holding your books to your chest and walking across campus with the leaves falling around you." I steered with my left hand and touched her hair with my right, tracing the line it made down her back. "With a pencil stuck behind your ear," I said, fingering her earlobe.

"What about you," she said. "How do you see yourself?"

I took the turn into April's subdivision, trying to decide how to answer her. I didn't know, and maybe that was the problem. April would flee Roma like a refugee, and she'd look back on her time there with pride and a little horror, thinking, *I survived that. I paid my dues, and now I never have to go back.* Robbie, on the other hand, would never leave. He was built for that town, and he could thrive there, but anywhere else he was a nobody. Anywhere else he was just another oversized redneck.

"I think I'll go to classes and get decent grades," I told her. "And I'm pretty sure I'll graduate. But I'll probably hate the dorms and spend a lot of time by myself, and I probably won't join any clubs or activities, and when I leave nobody will remember I was there in the first place." As I said it, I realized it was true.

"That's depressing," she said.

I shrugged.

By this time we were parked in her driveway. I could see someone in the kitchen window, pushing the curtain aside for a better look at us.

"No, I think that's a cop-out," she said. "I think that's your spineless way of telling me you want to break up."

I sat very still, waiting for the curtain to close again. If April cried, I didn't want an audience.

"Is that what you're telling me, Matt? Because I'm tired of not knowing where I stand with you. You act quiet and pissed off half the time and I can't figure out what I did to deserve it."

"You don't deserve it," I said.

"Then why am I putting up with it?" She sighed, a trembling sound that seemed to catch in the middle of her chest. "This is what guys do, isn't it? Act like a dick until the girl breaks it off with them. You're not even man enough to say that you're tired of me. God forbid you feel a little bit guilty later on."

"I had sex with Tina," I said then. Bald as that.

Her face, until that moment red with her anger or embarrassment, went white. "You what?"

I didn't repeat it.

She rubbed her face. She reached for her tote bag with a trembling hand, missing it at first grab, and then reached for the door handle. She waited, as if trying to decide what to say to me—what note to leave on. *Make it a good one*, I thought. She deserved it. *I* deserved it.

In the end, though, she got out of the car without saying anything at all, and she tripped at her front step, landing awkwardly on her hip and elbow. I wanted to help her, but I didn't want that figure in the window—her mother or her father—to see April this way, then to look at me and know that I was the cause. I put the car into reverse and backed out, tires squealing a little in my hurry. I can't imagine how that sounded to April. Most days, I don't try.

There would be nights, that fall, when I'd think of April and know that she was somewhere nearby on Western's campus—at the student center, having Chick-fil-A with some friends, studying in her room or taking a night class in Cherry Hall—and I'd wonder when our paths would collide again. It seemed inevitable.

In my head, she was always that college girl I'd described on our final car ride, a picture that somehow became more detailed with time. She would have her hair combed back into a neat ponytail, and the end would swing between her shoulder blades with the motion of her hips; she'd be wearing something tailored and grown-up, but still flattering—fitted blue jeans and a sweater, maybe—and her cheeks would be a little fuller, pink-tinted from the chill of an October night. She'd have the brisk walk of a college girl, the air of confidence, and those autumn leaves would be swirling around her, making little dive-bombs into the sidewalk, fetching up in gutters, blackening in the damp of a previous rain. There were nights that fall when my roommate was gone and the dorm room, with its cinderblock walls and bunk beds, seemed too much like a prison; and I'd leave the homework undone and step out into the night, roaming campus, hoping to find the girl I'd constructed in my fantasies. Maybe she wasn't even April anymore. Maybe her face, like my mother's, had transformed with time into something that no longer belonged to me.

5.

An hour before Robbie was supposed to pick me up for our trip to Nashville—the last hurrah, we'd been calling it—Tina called. I figured that she had scheduled an appointment for the abortion and was phoning to tell me when. Already I wished that I hadn't agreed to be her chauffeur. School started in two weeks, and that seemed like worry enough; the thought of holding her hand through this—being her coconspirator in yet another betrayal of Robbie—made me sick to my stomach. It also made me wonder about her motives on that afternoon, whether I was right in my first reaction: that Tina had just been paying me in advance for services rendered.

"This is a bad time," I told her. "Robbie'll be here any minute."

"I know he'll be there," she said. "That's why I'm calling."

My dad was watching TV across the room, sound blaring because he was losing his hearing—another company bonus. For years now he hadn't been able to hear certain frequencies: the beep of the microwave, the smoke detector. I picked up the phone and carried it to the kitchen, as far as the cord would stretch. "Okay," I said. "What's up?"

"He knows I cheated," Tina said, and I immediately felt faint, short of breath. Then: "He doesn't know it was you, though."

My heart slowed slightly. "Are you sure?"

"Yeah." She was quiet for a few seconds, and I could hear her dogs barking in the background, high-pitched and far away. "I told him that I wanted to break up, and he went nuts. He punched a hole in my living room wall. I thought he was going to hit me, Matt. His face was as red as his beard, I swear to God. Then all at once he calmed down."

I pictured it, glad that Tina was on the phone with me and apparently okay. I imagined his calm—sudden, predatory—and it chilled me worse than the vision of that hole in the wall did.

"Then what happened?"

"He asked me if I'd cheated on him. If there was someone else. And I was so caught off guard that I didn't say anything at first, and I guess it was all over my face. I told him no, but he already knew better. He just left after that."

"When was this?"

"Just a few minutes ago."

I pulled a kitchen chair out from the table and sat down. *Someone else*. Was that really me?

"Hold up a minute," I said. "How can you know for sure that he doesn't suspect me? Christ, Tina, he's on his way over here. We're supposed to fucking hang out. You sure picked out a great time to drop a bomb on him."

"Trust me, Matt," she said. "You're the last person he'd think of."

"What's that supposed to mean?"

"Nothing," she said. "He thinks you're a good kid. He doesn't even think I like you."

Not *someone else*. Just a kid. A good kid. I thought about having sex with Tina, how fumbling and ridiculous I must have seemed to a woman who'd been with Robbie, who wasn't just a man, but a god. I never regretted giving in to her more than I did at this moment.

"Do you?"

"Do I what?" Tina said.

"Like me."

She laughed in a distracted way. "Sure I like you," she said. "I'm not in the habit of sleeping with guys I don't like."

I looked around the door frame at my father, who appeared to be working the *TV Guide* crossword. "Where do we go from here, then?"

"Just take care tonight," she said. "Don't let Robbie drink too much, and sure as hell don't let him drive. I can't tell you what to expect. He's never been mad at me before."

"That's hard to believe."

"Never," she said. "He loved me. He loved me no matter what."

• • •

A little over two hours later, Robbie and I were sitting down to our first round of shots. We were at a place called Gibb's on Broadway—a dark, dirty pocket in a strip of Planet Hollywoods and Hard Rock Cafes and Hooters, all those joints that had seemed so cool to me just a few years back but now appeared babyish and fake, like Chuck E. Cheese. Robbie seemed to know the bartender; as soon as we were on stools he tapped the bar and put up two fingers. "Jack," he yelled over the racket around us and a blasting jukebox not too different from the one back at Trudy's in Bowling Green.

I realized, a half-second before opening my mouth and embarrassing myself, that he was requesting the whiskey and not calling for the guy by name. After a few minutes, the bartender came over with shot glasses, filling them in front of us. Robbie lifted his.

"To you, man," he said, and I saw that his hand was shaking a little. "A person needs friends when the shit hits the fan. When a woman fucks you over. I hope things go good for you. I hope you're the biggest poon-hound at Western." He tossed the shot back and I followed, coughing a little. The flavor coated my tongue, burnt and sugary.

"That's not likely," I said.

"Hell, you're better off." He motioned for more shots, and I decided that Tina's warning, however wise and well-intended, was pretty much irrelevant at this point. I could stop Robbie from getting drunk tonight no sooner than I could wrestle him to the ground. "Girls have a way, Matt. My mistake was hooking up with a girl who's smarter than me. I'll admit it, hell. I never gave a shit about school. But the smart ones get in your head and fuck with the works, and then they turn it around on you and make it your fault somehow. Tina should win an award."

I thought about April, how she'd stumbled on those steps leading to her door. "Me and April are through," I said, and I sipped the second shot instead of swallowing it whole, hoping I would stand a better chance of keeping it down. Someone would have to drive us home, and I had a feeling that Robbie wasn't going to be that person. In fact, getting him *really* drunk was starting to seem like my best option; if he was anything less than passed out, I probably wouldn't be able to wrangle the truck keys from him. I ordered a beer before he could put another shot in front of me.

"Like I said, it's the best thing, really." Robbie pulled a credit card out of his wallet and waved the bartender over. "Buddy, tell you what. Switch to that bottle of Old Crow over there and just keep lining up the shots." He handed him the card.

"You got it," the bartender said. He put three shot glasses out and filled them all.

"I'm gonna have to roll you out of here," I told Robbie.

The whiskey disappeared and he sat for a moment with his head bowed, breathing heavily. I thought he might want to puke—surprising enough—but then it seemed to me that he was crying, or choked up at least, and that shocked me. I looked away.

"Fucking bitch," Robbie said. He lifted his head and wasn't crying after all. At least his face wasn't wet.

"I'm sorry," I told him.

"Do you have any idea who she could have screwed around with? I mean, have you ever seen her with anyone?"

I shook my head, maybe too hard.

He stared at me. His eyes were a pale blue, like a Siberian

husky's. Eerie. He tugged his beard a little. "So why'd you and April break it off?" he said. He was rolling an empty shot glass around between his fingers, dexterous as a magician. I had the sudden, absurd notion that he could hear my heart beating over the noise of the place, and I put my hand over it.

"Just seemed smart to," I said. "College and all. We would've grown apart anyway."

"Did you ever fuck her?"

I shrugged.

"What, you don't know?" He laughed, too loud and too hard. The laugh Tina had talked about.

"Well, yeah," I said, shrugging in what I hoped was a modest, *aw-shucks* sort of way.

He clapped me on the back. "Good for you, man," he said. I smiled and pretended to be studying the lettering on my beer stein. Something was happening. I tried to remember things about fighting that my dad had told me in fifth grade, when Toby Mercer was cornering me every afternoon on the walk between the band building and the gymnasium. Out of nowhere this had started: me heading for sixth-period P.E., swinging my grocery bag of shorts and sneakers at my side, letting it bump against my knee as I walked; then, all at once, Toby shoving me into a narrow crevice between two building walls, his body filling my only escape route. Every day for a week he did this, sometimes just standing there and staring—like he couldn't think of what he wanted to do with me once he had me—sometimes kicking or spitting or saying he'd tell people I'd pissed my pants if I didn't lick the lichen-caked brick wall. What had Dad said? Something about always landing the first punch and making it count; about aiming for the nose or chin;

about how there was no shame in crotch-kicking if you didn't have any other options. Only as a last resort, though, even if the guy was nothing but a piece of scum like Toby Mercer. I never got to try any of Dad's advice out, though, much to my relief. I didn't know if he'd found another kid to pick on or if he'd simply gotten bored, but as quickly as he'd started on me, Toby backed off. He even smiled at me in P.E. class, as though we'd had ourselves a little tussle but were now A-OK. Right as rain. As though my week of sleepless nights and mornings of puking up breakfast hadn't happened.

There was a difference between Robbie and Toby, though, a big one: I'd hurt Robbie. I'd hurt April, too, and I deserved whatever I had coming to me. But that didn't resign me to it, didn't make me content to suffer through the broken nose—or anything else—that Robbie could give me. I didn't want to land on my ass.

"April's a good girl," Robbie said. "I hope you treated her okay."

I finished my beer a little too quickly and burped. "I can't say I did," I said, almost glad that I could be honest about something. "Not as well as she deserved."

The bartender lined up three more shots. Robbie downed one.

"Hard to tell the good ones from the bad ones," he said, running his finger around the rim of the second shot. "You know that, Matt?"

I looked into my beer.

"I've gotta go piss," Robbie said. He rose, steady, and walked to the bathroom, not getting in any hurry. I thought seriously for a moment about grabbing Robbie's keys on the bar and cutting out without him. Calling a cab to take him back to Roma. Paying the fare and counting my lucky stars that I hadn't had to pay some other way—with my face or with my kidneys. In the end, I stayed, and Robbie came back looking a little pale but okay otherwise. He drank the last two shots. "Ready for the check," he told the bartender. I started to pull my wallet out, and Robbie roughly knocked my hand away. "It's on me," he said. I didn't argue.

We walked out together, up a short flight of steps and into the sudden glare of neon and headlights. There were two Nashvilles—one below the street and one way above it, one that sounded old and rough like a Merle Haggard song and another that was New Country mixed with a dance track, so that the under-twenty-ones could groove to it down at Outer Bass. A Ford Explorer drove by and some dumb-looking frat boy type stuck his head out the window. "Nice hair, retard!" he yelled at Robbie, flipping us off with both hands. The Ford pulled ahead and made a quick shift to the middle lane, blowing through a light just as it turned red. How different their lives would have been if they'd been forced by traffic to stop. Robbie was already red-faced and tense; his hands were shoved into his blue jeans, but you could see the shape of fists, grapefruit-sized, through the denim.

"What now," I said. It wasn't a question, exactly.

"Who the fuck knows," Robbie said. "Home, I guess."

I didn't want to go to the parking garage with him, to leave the lights and relative safety of the street. "It's only ten-thirty."

"Yeah, well, I'm not feeling real festive right now. You hear me?"

I hesitated, then nodded.

"Let's walk," Robbie said.

We crossed a block over to the garage and climbed three flights up to our level. The lights were low and piss-colored—naked bulbs protected by metal gratings—and our footfalls echoed in a way that only emphasized how isolated we were, sandwiched between layers of concrete. The city was a bright strip of night on either side of us.

Robbie stopped. "You tell me," he said. "You tell me what you know about Tina right now."

"I don't know what you're talking about," I said.

"The fuck you don't!" Robbie screamed. I thought for sure he would hit me then, but he turned and swung at air instead, then covered his face with both hands, slumping. His back was to me, so broad it was surreal.

"You think you're smart?" he said, voice muffled. "You think you have a poker face? You're just a fool. I don't know what you saw or what you did, but if you think it means you got anything on me, you want to get over that notion in a hurry. I've got your goddamn number, Matt."

I was shaking, almost crying—yeah, like that long-ago fifth grader—when a car door slammed behind us. The man who emerged from it was almost as tall as Robbie but not quite so muscular; he was scary enough in his own right, though: had long hair pulled into a low ponytail, tattoos down the length of both arms and creeping up from the neck of his T-shirt. His jeans were faded and tight but almost pressed-looking, and a dressy pair of cowboy boots poked out from under their length. Even in my fear, and even from a distance of five or six feet, I could smell the guy's cologne: something syrupy and almost citrus, like the oils my mother would rub into our wood furniture once a week. I'd seen men like him back in

Roma: middle-aged types with a divorce or two under their big-buckled belts, nice guys but shifty—the type who trolled places like the Black Horse Saloon, hunting for single mothers. My dad worked with a bunch of them. This guy, I'd think later, was probably on his way to one of the line-dancing clubs on the strip; probably he knew all the numbers, could croon along to Randy Travis and kick his heels and make eyes at a woman all at once, never missing a beat. He didn't make it, though. At least not that night.

"There any trouble here?" he said, and I'll bet now that he saw me before he did Robbie and assumed it was a situation he had a handle on—just a couple of high school punks, no sweat.

Robbie turned around and pulled himself up to full height and breadth—a terrifying sight all on its own, worse still because his face was almost lavender in his anger, and a vein pulsed across his forehead like a tendon. Like his head, too, was nothing but muscle. Someone was going to end up in the hospital tonight; I understood that and felt a calm settle on me. It was, I imagined, how a fugitive must feel when he's finally caught and shackled and headed for lockup: not happy, of course, but at least no longer afraid of what he can't see.

"Stay out of this," Robbie told the man. "Keep walking."

I thought at first that the man would take Robbie's advice. He started for the stairwell, but then he looked back at me, and I don't know what was on my face. Maybe nothing. Maybe he just saw me as pathetic and innocent and undeserving of such punishment, and his good nature outweighed his good judgment. He came back toward us.

"Look, buddy," the man said, putting a hand on Robbie's bicep. "You just calm down and leave this little guy alone. What kind of fight would that be, anyway? You might as well hit a woman."

When Robbie punched him then—sent him staggering across that concrete floor and onto the hood of a nearby Buick—I was almost glad.

You couldn't call it a fight; I don't think the guy got a single blow in, only lay there and took and took and took. It didn't last long: just enough time for Robbie to lay down punches that were sometimes doughy-sounding and sometimes wet-sounding and that at least once sounded like bone exploding. The man screamed and begged Robbie to stop, and at one point he looked at me—his face red-drenched and terrifying, one eye swollen shut but the other locked tight on my two good ones—and managed to stutter out *Get help* before Robbie finished off his mouth, too. After that I think he passed out; his body went limp and Robbie backed away, holding his right hand up to his chest.

"I think I broke it," Robbie said, and it took me a few seconds to realize that he meant his hand and not the unconscious heap on the floor in front of him.

"Yeah," I whispered.

He reached into his pocket with his good hand, having to cross to the opposite hip awkwardly to snag his keys. He held them out and didn't look at me. "You drive," he said. "We're gonna have to move fast."

I glanced at the floor once more before following Robbie to his truck. That was me down there; that man had taken my beating. I opened my wallet and pulled out the wad of money I'd cashed out at the bank earlier that afternoon—my last Spector Plastics check, about three hundred dollars with the short week added. I shoved it into the man's jean pocket as far as it would go, getting close enough to his body to hear his slow, ragged breathing. The air was full of his stench: his sour fear-sweat, the brassy tang of blood, and that Pine Sol–smelling cologne, like the punch line to a bad joke. I didn't want to look at his face, but I couldn't help myself. Not twenty minutes ago he'd been a pleasant-looking guy with lines around his eyes and the ruddy tan of a farmer; now his face was alien—frightening—with swollen, puffed skin where his eyes were supposed to be and a weird slump at the jawline. I prayed that the damage wasn't as bad as it looked, that the swelling would go down and the bruising would fade and the blood would get cleaned off and his old face would be there beneath the trauma of this night and his hapless act of goodwill.

"Let's go," Robbie called from the truck.

We left. I navigated the narrow spiral drive out of the garage, sure that I'd wreck, I was shaking so badly; in a few moments we were barreling down I-65 and out of Nashville, the skyline growing distant behind us and finally disappearing around a turn. Robbie groped through the glove box and pulled out a bottle of aspirin, swallowing at least four or five with a grimace. By the time we reached Springfield he was out cold, broken right hand resting on his chest.

When I was sure he was asleep, I steered with my left hand and felt for Robbie's cell phone with my right, finding it after a breathless two or three minutes on the floorboard. I'd planned to call my dad, but when I flipped the mouthpiece open Tina's face appeared in the picture window. She was looking at me and laughing, her face loving and genuine, and I knew that hers would be the first number on speed dial.

I hit Call.

·   ·   ·

It was after midnight by the time I reached Roma, and the parking lot of Logan Memorial Hospital was close to empty. I found Tina easily. She was parked a few rows away from the emergency room entrance, out of her car before I had the chance to maneuver Robbie's big pickup into a space and ease the gearshift into neutral. Robbie stirred beside me, and I rolled down my window, high enough from where I sat to have to look down at Tina. Like that day at her house, her face was scrubbed clean, her eyes red and overbright in the glow of a nearby security lamp. She was wearing a sweatshirt—University of Kentucky, I remember, with a decorative wildcat clawmark slashed across the lettering—and ratty blue jeans, sneakers.

I wanted to say something to her before Robbie finished waking and remembered, but "I'll help you get him inside" was the only thing I could think of. She just nodded. I got out of the truck and opened Robbie's door, then shook his knee a little.

"Robbie," I said. "Get up, man, let's go."

His eyes were completely sober, but he allowed me to tug him out of the cab, and he didn't argue when I threw my neck and shoulders under the considerable weight of his left arm. Tina took the other arm, careful not to brush his hurt hand, and we started toward the red neon lettering of EMERGENCY. The night air was cool and smelled of ozone, like the coming of a heavy rain.

I didn't say another word to either of them. I went to the receptionist and signed Robbie in, then I tucked Robbie's truck keys into Tina's hand and left. When I got outside and knew they couldn't see me, I looked back. They were barely visible through the two sets of doors: the back of his head and hers, that mane of red-gold hair and her blonde hair, touching, tilted together in a way that told me more about love—about its holiness and desperation and utter lack of hope—than anything in my life up to that point, or since.

I walked home. I'd given all of my cash to that poor man back in Nashville, but I was pretty sure that the cabs didn't run this late in Roma anyway. It took me an hour: down Nashville Road to West 9th, around the town square—a few cruisers were still making sluggish circles, not yet chased off by cops or invited to a party somewhere—and up Harper Hill, toward the ratty old subdivision Dad and I called home. I wasn't in any hurry. The rain started spattering down just as I'd nearly topped the hill, close to the abandoned watchtower that my dad had told me never to ride my bike beyond and never, ever to scale. Harper Hill was the highest point in town, and as late as the '70s the tower had housed an air horn, hand-cranked, that some miserable bastard had to sound at noon every day and whenever a tornado was spotted. Now the horn—the noon whistle, Dad called it—was electronic and located downtown, in the courthouse. The watchtower was empty, the steps leading to the top mushy as wet cardboard. I knew because I'd climbed the thing at least a dozen times as a child, not because I wanted to so much—I was scared out of my mind, actually, and the fear never lessened—or because I wanted to cross my father: I didn't. I climbed it because so often, then, doing the thing I wasn't supposed to do seemed better and braver, seemed necessary, even.

The rain was cold, and for a moment I thought about climbing the fifty or so feet of weeds and tangle to the top of the hill, ascending the tower, and waiting out the worst of the storm with a view of town spread out beneath me. In the end, I didn't. I picked up my pace and made it home in a few more minutes, before the bottom fell out. When I crawled into bed that night, it seemed to me that I'd missed an important moment: a rite of passage between one part of my life and another. I don't fault myself now for thinking that way; if there's one thing I miss about my teen-aged self, it's the knack I had for orchestrating drama out of the smallest, most worthless moment: smoking a cigarette for the first time, seeing a sun-burnished cloud on a summer evening and thinking I'd found God. But I did the smart thing that night and went home, went to sleep. In the morning I started packing for college.

6.

My dad looked more out of place in a dorm room than anywhere else I'd seen him: on the beach at Lake Malone, wearing swim-ming trunks and picking his pale feet up delicately, like the tex-ture of sand was just too much to be tolerated; eating dinner at a nice steakhouse with one of his old high school buddies—a rare social excursion—and ordering meals for us that I knew he couldn't afford, insisting that he foot our bill and his friend's, too. The room was too small for him. He paced the strip of floor between the twin beds, flipped the lamp beside my desk on and off a few times, opened the minifridge and tested it for coolness. It was a Sunday, so he was wearing what I remember as Dad's Good Clothes: a plaid button-down shirt with short sleeves, green dress slacks, a creased pair of leather loafers. He had his class ring on, too: a big gold piece with an onyx setting, which he'd put aside money for all through high school, skimming a few dollars here and there off the top of his paychecks. The ring, he told me once, had taught him a couple of things. First, he said, you shouldn't work when you're a kid unless you have to. Dad had worked construction after school for a few hours every day and on weekends, because his folks told him he'd better contribute to the household in some way or "quit and get"—as in *quit school and get a job*. The other thing he'd learned was that a good thing's worth saving for, and he thought that his class ring was something special. He bought me one my junior year—insisted on it, even though I told him that I'd never wear the damned thing—because he said I'd want it later on.

"Not the most comfortable bed," Dad said that day in my dorm, sitting on the bare mattress and bouncing a little. "You've got to sleep good if you're gonna make the grades."

"It'll be okay," I said.

"I don't mind driving up here to pick you up until you get the car business sorted out," he said. "You can use the Nova when you're home. I don't mind."

I sat down beside him, loving him so much then that my chest ached. I remember his smell—the minty scent of shaving cream—and the way the low summer sun hit the curly hairs on his freckled forearms. The mattress *was* hard. The tile floors were hard, the fluorescent light coming from the cracked casing overhead was hard. I looked at my dad's hands. He had big knuckles and joints from a lifetime of work and at least a few fights, but his fingernails were broad and smooth. I thought about Robbie then, just as I'd think about Robbie—and Tina, and of course April—on a pretty regular basis for the next month or two, and then less often as my life in Bowling Green started to become . . . well, my life. I don't know how you move past a night like that one in Nashville, how you stomach the guilt of hurting somebody and get up the next day to pack. But I did, and a week later I was at Western on a sleepy, golden sort of Sunday afternoon, my father beside me.

"You'll have laundry to do anyway," Dad said. "No sense wasting your money on washers if you don't have to."

I nodded. "We'll see. Maybe I'll have to do some work this weekend, but maybe not. I'll call and let you know."

"Call me anyway," Dad said. "You can call tonight if you want, tell me how you settled in. And if your roommate showed. You might have to get in touch with somebody if he don't get here soon."

I just nodded.

We didn't hug. He patted me on the back, then squeezed my neck a little. "All right, then," he said, and he opened his wallet and pulled out a hundred-dollar bill. He put it on my dresser and set a bottle of my cologne on top of it.

"Don't lose that."

"I won't."

"And don't spend it on a bunch of crap, either."

"I won't."

He left. I went to my window and looked down at the parking lot. In a few minutes he came out into view, a medium-sized man with a thin spot on top—I could see it from the third floor—and a bottle of pills making his shirt pocket jut out, always. When he died three years after that day, struck by a second heart attack at home, he was clutching the bottle of nitroglycerin tabs in his hands, apparently unable to pop the top off once the pain hit.

I saw Robbie and Tina one other time, a little over a year after starting college. I'd driven home for the weekend to attend the Tobacco Festival with Dad. He thought the parade was a wash—got worse every year, all the floats replaced by pickup trucks full of Girl Scouts or flag football teams and nonsense like that—but the food was always worth the trip to the square, and we were packing it in that afternoon: pork chop sandwiches and Italian sausages, corn dogs, a funnel cake. Robbie and Tina were together, standing on the front steps of Southern Deposit bank and waiting for the parade to start. Tina had a baby on her chest, strapped in with a harness. She'd gotten heavier. So had Robbie, that brilliant beard no mask for the fullness in his face. Robbie spotted me and waved.

"You know him, right?" Dad said, dipping his corn dog in a paper tray full of swirled-together ketchup and mustard. "Weren't you guys buddies?"

"Yeah," I said.

"You should go over there," he told me.

I had imagined seeing those two again a thousand times. Sometimes it was a nice meeting—hugs and hand-shaking and forgiveness—and sometimes I simply wanted them to bear witness to the older, better, more filled-out version of me: the Matt that a year in college had produced, the Matt that Tina couldn't have played games with and Robbie couldn't have lorded his strength over. In that version, they looked at me, and then they looked at each other, and they understood the consequences of their choices.

"Go on," Dad said. "Don't worry about me. I'll wait over here for you."

I was starting across the street when the first siren sounded, so loud and close that the air vibrated. The parade had begun. The fire trucks, which I'd clapped for as a young boy sitting atop my father's shoulders, rounded the corner, gleaming damp from fresh washes. I tried to slip through in the space between the trucks and the Roma High School Marching Panthers, who followed with the official festival banner in tow, but I knew that getting back to Dad would be harder, and I wasn't going to leave him to watch the parade alone, no matter what he said. It was an easy choice, made easier by the fact that I wasn't sure if I wanted to see Robbie and Tina or their baby—wasn't sure what the point would be. It was October in Kentucky: the leaves had turned, and the air was crisp. I stepped back and stood next to my father, and the band, passing between me and my old friend, was blasting out a rickety rendition of the theme from *Superman*. They were something to depend upon: the band, then the Shriners in their funny go-karts, the flatbed trucks stacked with hay bales and cheerleaders, and finally the horses, whose steaming piles of shit would have to be navigated by festivalgoers for the rest of the afternoon. There would be crafts and folk art to wander past on the courthouse lawn, local bands wailing out lousy covers of lousy songs by Garth Brooks and Jimmy Buffett. In a few hours, Dad would want to go see the yearly reenactment of Jesse James robbing the Old Bank, and the horses would get spooked by the blasts of popguns like always, making them skittery and distracted, even more entertaining to watch than the terrible acting. It was a small town and perhaps a small way of life, but on days like this one I felt at peace with it.

Dad had forgotten about Robbie. He was finishing his corn dog, stripping the wooden stick clean with his teeth and watching the parade he claimed to hate. A man, walking alongside one of the floats and wearing a clown costume, tossed a spray of candy into the crowd. My dad put his hand up—an easy gesture, so instinctive it was graceful—and made a fist. He turned to me, opening it, and two pieces of Double Bubble lay on his palm.

"Hey-hey," he said with a laugh. "One for you and one for me."

I took the gum and looked back over at the bank. Robbie waved again, as if he thought I hadn't seen him before. He might have beckoned. Tina, baby sleeping against her belly, did nothing, and when I turned and pretended to have missed them I was sure that we understood each other.

• THEORY OF REALTY •

I.

When Ellen was a girl, she spent her summers down at the Hoffmans', paddling around three or four hours a day in their in-ground swimming pool and frying her skin with baby oil. The Hoffmans were, it seemed to Ellen then, grown-up but not old—maybe her mother's age—and they had a big, fancy house and sad eyes. All the neighborhood kids who swam at the Hoffmans' place, and that was most of them, knew the story about Caleb Hoffman, Mr. and Mrs. Hoffman's little boy. A while back, some teenagers had used scrap wood and aluminum to piece together a couple of bike ramps on either side of Town Creek. If you got a good, fast start up on Poppy Street and aimed your wheels right, the rumor went, you could fly over that creek *Dukes of*

Hazzard–style, though you risked screwing your bike up in the process. All of the boys tried it, and Caleb was practicing by himself one summer evening when the first ramp collapsed, sending him headfirst into the ditch. The creek was barely a trickle in August, but the fall knocked him unconscious, and he drowned in about four inches of water. He was eleven years old. Ellen had been six when it happened, and from then until the time when she was more interested in talking on the phone than roaming the neighborhood on foot or bike, the name Caleb was her mother's near-daily refrain: "You stay away from that creek, now. Remember what happened to Caleb," or "I don't want to lose you the way poor Greta lost Caleb."

Ellen didn't remember much about him, but he became a constant, invisible companion whenever she, her brother Andy, and the other kids played at the Hoffmans'. There were pictures of him in the house: on the kitchen counter where Mrs. Hoffman served them sweet tea and lemon cookies, on a shelf in the bathroom where Ellen went to pee. He'd looked like every other boy in the neighborhood, like Ellen's own older brother: brown-haired and skinny with crooked teeth and freckles. When Mr. and Mrs. Hoffman were together, smiling but faraway-looking, Ellen thought that the space between them appeared about as wide as Caleb would have been.

Later, Ellen would consider the irony of those days at the pool. Caleb Hoffman died in four inches of water and Town Creek became a death-place, but that backyard rectangle of blue water, the sound of children cannonballing and belly-flopping, was somehow holy and necessary, even to the other parents. *Go to the Hoffmans*, they'd say if the late-afternoon doldrums set in. *They'll appreciate the company.* And they did. Even as a girl

Ellen knew the look of loneliness, and her heart was of the tender sort; she was the kind of kid who felt guilty when she saw
a man eating by himself at Dairy Queen, and the sight of her
own mother laughing too hard—eyes squinting behind cheap
plastic-framed glasses, cigarette stains prominent on her two
front teeth—made Ellen's stomach knot with pity and shame.
Mrs. Hoffman was a tiny woman, thinner and prettier than Ellen's mother, and she was always offering to braid Ellen's hair or
paint her fingernails. One time, she invited Ellen into her dressing room—such a big, lovely place, with pink-tinted lightbulbs
and a makeup table cluttered with delicate, pastel glass bottles—
and showed her how to put on eyeliner.

"Just a smidge on the lower lid," she'd said over Ellen's shoulder with her soft voice, demonstrating. "Right here in the corner. Not too much, or you'll look cheap. Now here"—she guided
Ellen's hand—"just past the edge. It widens the eye. Oh, that's
lovely. Now look at me."

Ellen did.

Mrs. Hoffman riffled through a makeup bag and pulled out
a tube of mascara. She held up the wand. "Big eyes," she said,
showing Ellen, making her own eyes pop out. Left eye, then the
right: a few strokes on each side. "Okay, take a look," Mrs. Hoffman said.

Ellen turned and faced the mirror, then caught her breath.
Her eyes looked bluer and brighter, almost glittery. She blinked,
pleased with the new heaviness of her eyelashes. She felt like her
old baby doll, the one she'd named Kissy Kay, whose eyes fluttered shut if you laid her on her back. The doll that she still allowed herself once every couple of weeks or so, when she felt sad
or bored or overwhelmed by school, and when she was sure no

one—not her mother, especially not her brother—was around to see her play with it. Looking at herself in the mirror, Ellen had an insight that was almost grown-up: *This is the person I'm giving up the dolls for.*

"You're such a darling girl," Mrs. Hoffman said. "I always wanted a daughter."

And then there was Mr. Hoffman. Ellen saw less of him, which usually suited her fine. He was a nice enough man, but she'd grown up watching TV movies with her mother, the kind with titles like *Sleeping with Danger* or *No Means No,* and she knew that some middle-aged men—not a lot or even most, but some— were rapists or girl-touchers or the kind who slapped their wives if the casserole didn't come out right. For all she knew, Ellen's own father could be any of these things; he'd left her mother when Ellen was three and now lived down in Miami with his new wife and their eight-year-old twin daughters. Once a month he sent a child support check, which Ellen's mother split evenly between her checking account and Ellen and Andy's savings account, and he always mailed fifty dollars for birthdays, one hundred for Christmas. Ellen sometimes thought this was a better bargain than an actual dad. Two years earlier, when Ellen was eleven, he'd invited her and Andy down to Florida to hang out for two weeks and meet their half-sisters, and the whole thing was a disappointment. He lived in an apartment—not even a real house—that was so far away from the beach that you had to take a cab to get there, and the twins just wanted to stay inside and play Nintendo all day. They didn't even have tans. Also, Janet, her stepmom, cooked everything in weird ways: spaghetti with butter and green flecks but no tomato sauce, hamburgers with onion soup mix and red peppers, stuff like that. She also served buttered toast with every meal, which was a good thing, because that was all Ellen could bring herself to eat the whole time she was down there. "Bread and water," her father kept saying at mealtime. "I'm not running a prison here. What'll your mama think if I send you back to Kentucky ten pounds lighter?"

Fathers, she decided, were probably overrated.

She had to admit, though, that Mr. Hoffman was a lot of things that her dad wasn't. Handsome, for starters. He was tall and sandy-haired—her own father's hair was mostly gone—and he wore the kind of clothes Ellen usually only saw on TV: suits when he was coming home from work, khaki shorts and white button-down shirts with the sleeves rolled up for sitting around the pool or in the kitchen. The sight of that white cloth on his tanned forearms fascinated Ellen. He was an engineer at Spector Plastics, Ellen's mother had told her, and everybody knew that Spector was the best factory in town. He had a nice voice, too: proper, like a TV anchorman's, and not punctuated with the *ain'ts* and *fixin' tos* that her teachers had deemed ungrammatical and just plain ignorant-sounding. The way her mother talked, for starters. Ellen asked him why one day, and he laughed. "Greta and I aren't from here originally," he said.

"Where are you from?"

"Ohio," he told her. "Columbus, Ohio."

They were sitting by the pool during this conversation, and Ellen felt okay about talking to him because Mrs. Hoffman was a few feet away spreading a towel out on a lounge chair and Andy was in the water with his best friend, Kev Brewster, doing clumsy flips off the diving board. Also, Mr. Hoffman had his shirt on. When Mr. Hoffman stripped down to his trunks for a swim, Ellen was usually so embarrassed that she made up an

excuse to dry off and go to the bathroom. Or home. She knew
that the sight of Mr. Hoffman in his trunks was nothing to feel
anxious about, but she did all the same. She thought about all the
times she'd accidentally walked in on her mother changing, or
how they sometimes collided in the hallway between the bathroom and their bedrooms, towels wrapped around their middles.
She tried to picture her dad in swimming trunks—or in just a
towel—and shuddered. Grown-ups didn't seem to worry that
much about what they exposed you to: private, ugly, or otherwise. She didn't want to know about her mother's stretch marks.
She didn't want to know about the strip of wiry hairs between
Mr. Hoffman's belly button and shorts.

"Is that a big city?" she said.

"I didn't think so when I was there." He laughed again. "But
moving to Kentucky has a way of putting things in perspective
for you, no offense."

Ellen liked the fact that he said that: *no offense*. Casual and not
sarcastic at all, like they were equals.

"That doesn't bother me," she said. "I hate Roma. I bet Columbus is a whole lot better."

Mr. Hoffman shrugged. "Ah, it's not so bad here. The weather's
better. And you can have a whole lot more house for the money.
This place cost me ninety thousand. Two-story house with a pool
and an acre, and I'm a five-minute drive to work. I've been here
almost ten years and I still can't believe it. Now when you live in a
city, houses get a lot more complicated. It's all about location. Have
you heard that saying before? 'Location, location, location'?"

Ellen wasn't really sure what he was talking about. She
shrugged and nodded at the same time so that she could seem
knowledgeable without actually being deceptive.

Mr. Hoffman adjusted his lounge chair and lay flat. "I'm probably boring you silly. How old are you? Ten? Eleven?"

"Thirteen," she said.

He lifted his sunglasses and looked at her. "Huh. How about that. Well anyway, here's the best advice I know to give a little girl like you. When you go to college, get as far away from here as you can. Go somewhere totally different from Kentucky, like New Mexico or Oregon or, hell, Europe. It's only four years of your life, and you can always come back." He took a sip of something: a short glass with ice cubes and amber-colored liquid.

"What's that you're drinking?" Ellen said, sensing that the question was inappropriate but unable to help herself.

"That's a straightforward question," Mr. Hoffman said. "So I'm going to give you a straightforward answer. This is an alcoholic beverage called bourbon. The brand name is Maker's Mark. Come to think of it, this is another reason why Kentucky isn't necessarily so bad. Did you know that all of the world's bourbon comes out of Kentucky? There's a fact for you to take some pride in."

"Adam," Mrs. Hoffman said sharply. "For God's sake."

He winked at Ellen. "Don't mind her."

"Can I try it?" Ellen said.

Mr. Hoffman looked like he was thinking it over. "I guess not," he said finally. "The thing about bourbon is that you can't mistake the scent, and you can't really cover it up, either. Lean in."

Ellen did, and he exhaled into her face: a burnt, tangy smell that made her eyes water. His lips were only a few inches away from hers. "Uck," she said.

"You see what I mean, then," he said. "That's basically how it tastes, anyway. Did you know that ninety percent of taste is smell? That's why food doesn't seem as good when you have a cold."

"I don't think I'd like it," Ellen said.

"That's probably for the best," Mr. Hoffman told her. He pulled his sunglasses back down and reclined again. In another couple of minutes he was snoring.

"You shouldn't mention the bourbon to your mother," Mrs. Hoffman said after a moment. She looked at Mr. Hoffman's sleeping figure and sighed—the sound Ellen's mother made when she was frustrated with Andy, when she said things like, *I'm at the absolute end of my rope here.* It was odd, seeing that kind of frustration directed at an adult; odd that she was allowed to share in it. "Come over here, dear," Mrs. Hoffman said finally. "You need some sunblock on your nose."

Ellen let her apply it, enjoying the coolness of Mrs. Hoffman's fingertips. Everything about her was more delicate than Ellen's mother. Her touch, her voice, her smell: sweet but not overpowering, not like the apple-scented body spray Ellen's mother used, the tang of her work-sweat still evident beneath it. Ellen loved her mother—too much, it seemed some days, when the love felt like something that could wrap itself around her heart and crush it—but she was certain then that she'd do whatever Mrs. Hoffman told her to, that the Hoffmans' pool was a place with its own secrets and rules, a place that had to be protected. A haunted place. If she looked out at where Andy and Kev were in the water, now playing volleyball—if she half-closed her eyelids and let her vision blur—she could almost make out a third Caleb-shaped figure. Turning toward her. Smiling.

•   •   •

Two weeks after the bourbon conversation, Ellen ended up at the Hoffmans' pool alone. Andy had gotten an air pellet rifle for his fifteenth birthday—their mother's compromise, because his heart had been set on a real rifle, a .22—and all he felt like doing anymore was setting up Shasta cans in the backyard and practicing his aim. He wouldn't even let Ellen try it.

"Mama'd be pissed if you shot a window out," he said.

"I wouldn't aim at a window, dummy. Anyway, those stupid pellets probably couldn't shoot through a slice of bread. It's just a baby gun, anyhow."

He shrugged and took aim, not bothering to look at her. "Then what's your problem?" He missed the can. "Shit. Anyway, you're one to talk about baby stuff. I saw you playing with that doll the other day."

Ellen felt her face go hot. "You're a liar. I don't play with dolls anymore."

Now he looked at her, and he was grinning. She wanted to smack him. "Sure you do. I saw you through the window when I was weed-eating." He let his voice go soft and girly: "You was brushing her pretty blonde hair wis your itty-bitty brush—"

"I hate you," she said, kicking a clump of dirt his way. He just laughed.

"Go swim or something," he said. "I've got to practice. Kev's dad said he'd let me use his rifle the next time they go deer hunting."

"I hope you shoot yourself in the foot," she told him, running to the back door. She slammed it behind her, and her mother yelled from the living room—that bellow Ellen couldn't stand— "Don't slam the goddamn door!" She couldn't win.

She went to the bathroom, where her bathing suit was hanging, and stripped down, tugging the spandex over her hips and
shoulders with angry jerks. She pulled on a pair of cutoffs, then
grabbed a towel and the baby oil. She looked at her reflection in
the mirror, trying out different faces and angles, searching for
the combination that would age her, that would show Andy just
how invincible she was. But the grown-up she'd spied in Mrs.
Hoffman's dressing room was gone. She was round-faced and
red-blotched, with tears trembling on her eyeliner-less lids. She
was a child.

She usually approached the Hoffmans' backyard slowly, at an
angle; if no other kids were there, she'd slip back toward home
before anyone could see her. She knew it had something to do
with that space between her and adults who weren't her mother.
The sense of formality she felt around them, and also unease.
Though kids were sometimes just as bad. If Kev Brewster was at
the pool and feeling bored, he'd grab Ellen and force her underwater, not letting her surface until she was thrashing with panic.
A couple of weeks ago, he'd shoved her down with Andy's help—
Andy, who was usually just a laughing bystander—and straddled
her shoulders, tightening his thighs around her ears until Ellen's
world was nothing but a distant sense of wetness (she'd remember later on, more than anything else, the grotesque push of his
groin on the back of her neck) and a high-pitched, alarmlike tone.
She couldn't hear anything else. Then the pressure disappeared.
She surfaced, light-headed, and struggled to get to the ladder,
snorting water, sinuses aching—and then there was yelling, and
a pair of hands grasping her under the armpits and pulling her
over the rough lip of the pool. "You go straight home and don't
come back until you can behave yourself," a voice said, and it was

then that she realized that Mr. Hoffman was the one pulling her to a stand and leading her to a deck chair, putting a beach towel around her shoulders. Mr. Hoffman's hands had been the ones under her arms, brushing against the sides of her small breasts, and the embarrassment she felt at this realization was almost worse than the threat of drowning had been.

It wasn't that she believed Mr. Hoffman meant her harm. If he hadn't come outside when he did, there was no telling what Kev might have done, accidentally or on purpose—Ellen had known him long enough to count on his stupidity and even his cruelty. *He*, at least, was predictable. But with grown-ups, you couldn't predict anything. They cried at the moments when they were supposed to be laughing, laughed when Ellen couldn't grasp what was funny. There were grown-ups who were determined to hide the big scary world from you and grown-ups who were determined to make you see it, and Ellen thought that Mr. Hoffman was one of the latter.

So was Gloria, the mother of Ellen's best friend, Ray. Gloria was small and flat-chested, and she dressed a lot like her daughter; she wore short-shorts and T-shirts with sayings like "Flirt" or "Call Me" written across the front in sparkly cursive, and on Saturday nights when she didn't have a date or a party, she'd take Ellen and Ray cruising through Roma and buy them all Diet Cokes and Tater Tots at Sonic. She'd play songs by Roxette ("It Must Have Been Love") and Michael Bolton ("How Am I Supposed to Live Without You") loud out of her car's sound system and explain why the lyrics were special to her. Usually her stories were about old boyfriends from high school, like Toby Taylor, who had "long hair and a hot Trans Am." On other nights, she'd leave Ray and Ellen home alone while she drove to the

Executive Inn in Bowling Green with some girlfriends. Sometimes she returned laughing and in high spirits; she'd wake Ray
and Ellen up so that she could show them the cherry stem the
bartender had tied with his tongue, or she'd tell them about the
"nice man" she'd met and how he promised to take her to dinner
at 440 Main as soon as he got paid the next week. Sometimes
she came home with her eye makeup smeared, mouth tense and
almost old-looking, and on those nights she wouldn't talk to Ray
and Ellen at all; instead she stormed through the house and ran
water in the bathroom for long, uninterrupted spans, smoking
and having intense conversations on the cordless phone. Ellen
never knew which version of Ray's mother to expect, but she
feared them both.

The adults of the world gave permission and took it away,
stocked the refrigerator, punished you, drove you to soccer practice. But you still couldn't trust them.

She didn't mean to stumble upon the Hoffmans' pool that afternoon the way she did. She was almost there—head down,
every stomp of her foot a release of the anger she felt at Andy—
when she realized that no other kids were around, and no Mrs.
Hoffman either. Just Mr. Hoffman, kicked back in a lounge chair
with a book folded open over his face, and he didn't even have
his shirt on. His nipples looked like wads of bubble gum. She
stopped all at once and thought about backing away slowly—
she'd seen this in a movie, when a guy who was camping didn't
realize that a bear was a few feet away until he'd unzipped his
pants to take a whiz—but Mr. Hoffman must have heard her.
He took the book off of his face and sat up, squinting. "Ellie?"
he said.

"Ellen," she said. "My name's Ellen."

"I was close, though." He waved her over. "Don't mind me. I was just snoozing."

"I was looking to see if my brother's here," Ellen said, the lie coming to her lips so quickly that it stunned her. "I guess I better go find him."

"Aw, hell," Mr. Hoffman said. "You have your suit on. Go on and swim. I won't bother you. Probably don't want to get stuck in another conversation about real estate, huh?"

Ellen shrugged.

"Go on and swim," he said.

She went to the edge of the pool and sat, sketching the surface with her toe. The water was sun-warm and pleasant—and Mr. Hoffman had already reclined again, book back on his face—so she wriggled out of her cutoffs and slid into the pool, quiet as possible. As always, she made herself open her eyes underwater, grimacing through the sting of chlorine, and touch bottom. It was her lucky charm, one of many. If you could force yourself to do something scary or hard, Ellen believed, then good things would happen. She had a few other habits along those lines— at school recess as a little kid, for instance, she'd always make herself jump out of the swing at the height of its arc. And she often made up charms on the spot. One time, she'd wrapped thread around her pointy finger until the tip turned blue and cold, promising herself that if she could keep it that way for sixty seconds, she'd make an A on her fractions quiz. Another time, she decided that Robby Barrow would like her back if she could run around the house twenty times without stopping.

When she resurfaced, Mr. Hoffman was sitting up again, watching her. She felt a flush break out on her face, spreading to her neck and chest like a rash. Wasn't this just like those made-for-TV movies? In another minute, he'd say, *You're growing up so fast, Ellen,* and invite her to sit beside him in the lounge chair. The thought was sickening, but also kind of exciting. How would she escape? Was Mrs. Hoffman inside? If Ellen yelled, would she come running?

"So what do you think?" Mr. Hoffman said. "Want to try some alcohol?"

"I probably shouldn't," Ellen told him.

"Well, that's true," he said. "Greta would have your ass, and mine, too."

Ellen swam to the ladder, sorry that she hadn't left her towel close enough to grab without getting out of the water. She thought about Andy teasing her and wondered if he'd ever had anything to drink. He probably had, over at Kev's house. Maybe Kev's dad had even offered it to him: Andy was always bragging about how cool Mr. Brewster was. And she knew that her friend Ray had snuck tastes from her mother's drinks, that Gloria had even given Ray her own drink once when her girlfriends were over and everybody was cutting up and laughing really loud. The next day, Ray had bragged about how good Kahlúa mixed with rum tasted, and she'd said that sipping it had made her feel "fucking great" and that her mother's friends had all told her what a "trip" she was. Then she had acted cool and sophisticated for a week or so, hinting to Ellen that she'd have to catch up or bug out—that she was hanging with a much better crowd these days. A week later, after her mom had refused to let Ray go cruising with her, Ray gave Ellen a carefully folded note that said "Still BFF?" in purple ink. "Circle Yes or No." Ellen circled "Yes," but she also circled the "No" and then scribbled it out. Just to let Ray know that she was on thin ice.

Ray would be impressed if Ellen drank alcohol, she thought now.

"Maybe I'll try it," she told Mr. Hoffman. She was still in the water, the bottom rung of the ladder hard and bumpy beneath her right foot. She realized how quiet the afternoon was: a distant car, some birds, the occasional hiss of the pool filters—lazy sounds, the kind that just made the silence louder. Mr. Hoffman stood, and Ellen saw that he'd gotten badly sunburned before hiding beneath the shade of his book: bright strips of red across his forehead, nose, and cheeks, the skin on his collarbone almost purple-looking. It occurred to her how early in the day it was—an hour after lunch, maybe—and she wondered why Mr. Hoffman would be home already.

"Now you're talking," he said. "Wait here. I have just the thing."

As soon as he went inside, Ellen climbed out of the pool—heavy with the water, moving slowly—and grabbed her big towel. The air outside was freezing. She was fumbling into her jean shorts, legs sticky with the damp, when Mr. Hoffman returned. He had four bottles in his left hand; he was holding one between each finger, by their necks, and when he lifted his hand to show her he almost lost his grasp on them. "Shit," he said, quickly unloading them onto an end table. He had a glass of the brown stuff—the bourbon, Ellen guessed—in his right hand, and he took a big sip from it as he got in his lounge chair. He looked sweaty and a little sick, like he'd eaten something that wasn't sitting well. He grinned.

"Wine coolers," he said. "They're Greta's. Girls love them."

Ellen examined the bottles. They were small with foil wrappers, wet with condensation. She chose one that said "Tropical

Sensation" because orange was her favorite color and opened it. She put her lips on the rim, a crescent of cold glass on her tongue.

"Go on," Mr. Hoffman said.

It was sweeter than she expected, good-tasting—not as bad as she'd feared, at least—but strange, too. The alcohol hit her tongue right before she swallowed, alien and familiar all at once, with a barely concealed bitterness.

"What do you think?"

Ellen nodded. "I like it."

"I figured. I told Greta—I told Mrs. Hoffman—that I was going to give you your first drink. Told her that I bet somebody on this block knows how to have a good time. She was pretty raw about it, but she never told me 'no' outright." He squinted, like he was thinking. "Mrs. Hoffman doesn't *say* 'no,' you gotta understand. She thinks it and expects you to read her mind."

"Where is she?"

He wiped his forehead with the corner of the towel he was lying on. The skin that hadn't reddened was pale, almost white. He took another sip of his bourbon.

"At her mother's place up in Cincinnati. Visiting." He shrugged. "'Just visiting.' Like it says on Monopoly."

"Cincinnati's pretty far away, huh?" Ellen said. She drank some more of the wine cooler, the sugary citrus taste coating her tongue, the alcohol already starting to hum a little in the bottom of her stomach. The goose bumps were gone, and she was starting to feel the sun again.

"Honey," Mr. Hoffman said, "she may as well be on Mars. You know what I'm saying?"

Ellen took another sip.

"It's all about location," he said. "It's distance. The distance between points A and B. I could write an equation out for you, Ellie. You know that? I could write a proof explaining the distance between Roma and Cincinnati, and the answer would be infinity. We couldn't get there in our lifetimes."

"I don't get it," Ellen told him.

Mr. Hoffman laughed. "You know what I'm going to call it? The Theory of Realty. Hoffman's Theory of Realty. I haven't worked out the particulars yet. But I'm onto something." His hand slipped as he tried to rest his drink back on the end table and the glass fell, cracking on the cement instead of shattering. Ice cubes spilled out in a fan.

"I think I better go," she said.

Mr. Hoffman grabbed one of the wine coolers and held it to his forehead. His eyes were squeezed shut. "You haven't even finished your drink yet," he said. "Christ alive, am I that hard to be around? Do I smell bad?"

"No," Ellen said. She sat back down across from Mr. Hoffman, her face and neck hot—from the alcohol or from nervousness, she wasn't sure. He looked sick, and he looked sad: the kind of sad Ellen remembered from the days—the years, even—after her father left, when her mother would start crying out of nowhere, for no apparent reason. Her mother cried at the grocery once, in front of a stock boy and everybody else, clutching a package of Oreos until the cookies inside started to break. She was wearing lipstick that day, Ellen recalled: a bright color, garish and greasy, that Ellen didn't recognize from before and hadn't seen since.

"You're a good kid," Mr. Hoffman said. He looked at her again, peering as if she were on the other side of a keyhole. "Are you old enough to remember Caleb?"

"I remember a little about him. But maybe I think I remember because I see the pictures of him in your house."

Mr. Hoffman opened the wine cooler. His eyes were red and wet. "Good Lord. Do I know that feeling. And I was his father, saw him every day of his life for eleven years. We were a close family. Greta and Caleb would come with me on business trips, even." He kicked one of the spilled ice cubes into the pool. "But every now and then I forget what he looked like until I take a picture out and examine it. Then I have to focus on a detail, like his ear, and remember in my hand what his earlobe felt like." He rubbed his thumb and forefinger together, looking at Ellen as though she ought to be able to see the piece of flesh between them. "Sometimes it clicks for me and sometimes it doesn't. Sometimes I see a picture of us down at Gulf Shores and I know what's in my memory is the real thing and not made up. Because I can remember how Caleb screamed when a wave went over his head, and I know how the shrimp down there tasted—these big shrimps, hon, like little mini lobsters—and I even remember what Greta looked like in her red bathing suit. She was a knockout. You couldn't tell she had a kid." He stared into his empty glass like he might be trying to conjure up more bourbon. "But there's this one photo that worries the shit out of me. Caleb was maybe four when Greta took it, and he's bopping me in the head with a Nerf bat, and we're both laughing like crazy. I can hear his little giggle in my head, but the only thing I can see when I try to go back there is the photo, so I'm seeing him and me, too, and you know that's not how a person's head works. Right? If I really remembered I'd be seeing him out of my own eyes."

"Maybe it doesn't matter," Ellen said.

"Maybe not," Mr. Hoffman said. "But maybe it's the only thing that matters."

Ellen shifted against the wet pull of her jean shorts. Mr. Hoffman had entrusted her with his grief, and though she wanted to withdraw from it—though she sensed that this confession was as inappropriate as his offer of alcohol had been—she also felt his heartbreak, his desperation. She didn't want to run away like a kid, to pretend that she didn't comprehend his pain. So she did what the women in those TV movies did when they finally found a decent man to confide in: she put her hand on Mr. Hoffman's forearm.

"Mr. Hoffman," she said. "I wish I could help you."

They stayed that way just for a second—long enough for Ellen to register the tremble in Mr. Hoffman's arm muscle, the texture of his thick arm hairs under her fingertips. And then he was shaking her off, roughly, and she stood up so quickly that something in the middle of her forehead throbbed.

"I think there's been a miscommunication here," Mr. Hoffman said loudly, slurring a little. He looked sick still, but also something else: scared, disgusted. Caught? Whatever it was—or the combination—made Ellen so nervous that she grabbed her tennis shoes and backed away.

"I'm going," she said. The taste of the citrus wine cooler was still in her mouth, cloying and almost bitter, and she felt like she'd be sick if she didn't lie down soon.

"That's right," he said. "You take off. And you might watch yourself a little better from now on, Ellen. You're at that age. I wouldn't want to have to call your mother."

She ran the whole way home, stomach sloshing, eyes hot and sore with her sudden tears. She crossed two gravel drives barefoot, the pain almost satisfying, and she didn't make it inside before the little bit she drank came up on her: first in her mouth, thick and hot and almost chemical, and then in the bushes beside the back porch of her house. She stumbled up the steps and pressed her forehead against the glass of the storm door. Her mother had opened the window on the door a bit, so air could circulate, and she could hear home through the screen: *Guiding Light* playing loud on the TV; water running in the kitchen, where Ellen's mother was probably getting ready to mop floors, her Friday afternoon ritual. Ellen would have an excuse, at least, to creep to her bedroom through the den and into the hallway, skipping the kitchen and her mother; she was always catching hell for tromping across wet linoleum.

She yelled, "Home, Mom" from the living room, wiping her face with her beach towel.

"You better rinse that water off quick," her mother called back, as she almost always did. "That chlorine'll turn your hair green."

A shower sounded good: she felt scummy, felt like she wanted to scrub with hot water and brush her teeth two or three times and never drink anything orange-flavored again. She crossed the hall, treading lightly in her bare feet past Andy's bedroom—his Sega was blasting that infernal Sonic the Hedgehog theme song, the one that got stuck in Ellen's head some days until it made her half-crazy—and went to her own room, planning to grab a clean pair of shorts and one of her tank tops. She was already pulling a bathing suit strap over her shoulder when she realized that Kev was there, standing in front of her dresser. Her underwear drawer was open.

"Oh." That was all she could say.

His back was to her, and he stiffened, his neck all at once red and blotchy. But when he turned, his face was casual, teasing: the face he wore right before dunking her in the Hoffmans' pool. He pushed the drawer shut with his bottom. "Later," he said. He walked out with his hands plunged deep in his pockets, and Ellen shut the door behind him. She wished that she had a lock, but her mother wouldn't allow it, even when Ellen had explained that Andy came in sometimes and stole her babysitting money. She went to the drawer, opened it, and looked at the tangle of cloth and straps, wondering what Kev had touched and why. Everything was thin and cotton, some patterned with flowers, most with popped elastic in the leg holes or waistband. A few pairs had faint stains in the crotch, and at least one was smeared with a ghostly red-brown: the imprint of washed-away blood. Seeing this, and knowing that Kev had seen it, made her want to cry again. There wasn't anything private. There wasn't a corner of this world—of her own room, even—that she could stake claim to, that belonged to her and her alone.

II.

The morning after what happened at the Hoffmans', Ray called and asked Ellen to come over for the night. "Mom might stay home this time," she said. "If you come, she said she might. I've almost talked her into taking us cruising with her."

"Yeah?" Ellen knew that she should be excited—Ray sure sounded it—but Gloria seemed like the last person she needed to be around right now. She thought about what Mr. Hoffman had said at the pool, the look on his face as he said it: *You might watch yourself a little better from now on, Ellen. You're at that age.* Hadn't he been right? What did Kev's presence in her room mean, if not that she was doing or saying something—putting out a signal—that she shouldn't be?

"Yeah," Ray said. "The FOP is doing the Summer Carnival thing again out behind Pizza Hut, and she mentioned wanting to go out there. Say you'll come, okay? I always wanted to go, and she'd never do it. She said it was silly. But she's into it for some reason this year. What do you think?"

"Mom might not want me to," Ellen said.

"Oh, bull. Please, just come. If you don't, she'll probably take off somewhere. And there's nothing to do around here."

"Okay," Ellen said. She knew what Ray really meant: *She'll take off somewhere, and I'll be alone.* "I can talk Mom into it."

"Wear something cute," Ray told her, and hung up.

Ray and her mother lived in a duplex on 2nd Street, close to the sewing factory where Ellen's mother worked seconds. When Ellen went there for sleepovers, her mother always made her write the phone number for the factory in pen on her arm—up above the wrist, where she wouldn't wash it off—and promise to call if anything seemed wrong or even unusual. "You call," she'd tell Ellen just before dropping her off, which was pretty often that summer. "Don't worry about bothering me. If you hear anything funny outside, or if Gloria brings a man home—that last, especially. Do what I say now. You promise?"

Ellen would promise.

"All right, then," her mother would say, smoothing Ellen's hair, eyeing the house—Ray and Gloria's half of the house—with suspicion. She'd have her work clothes on: the gray shirt and slacks, the big denim apron. "Make sure you give Ray some money for the pizza. I'm going to drive by when my shift ends and make sure things look quiet over here."

And her mother always did. At midnight, when Gloria was still who-knows-where doing God-knows-what, Ellen would peek through the miniblinds and see her mother's slow drive-by. It was a comfort, especially those times when Ellen and Ray *did* hear strange sounds in the surrounding neighborhood—barking dogs, loud, teenage laughter, and once something they were both sure had to be a gunshot—and the doors seemed like paper, like nothing would stand between them and a person who meant them harm. A house—a half of a house—was nothing.

But Ray wanted her over there, and Ellen wanted, at least a lot of the time, to be there. They had fun together. Gloria would leave them money for pizza, and there were usually movies to watch, because Gloria managed the local video store and got all of the new releases the weekend before they officially went on the shelves. Ray had a real grown-up's room, too. Her mattress and box spring were on the floor—"So we can just crash," was how she put it—and her walls were covered with posters of bands that Ellen had never heard of, all of the members long-haired and greasy-looking with black boots and layers of rings on both hands. She hadn't witnessed Ray listening to their music, ever, but the posters themselves were dark and dangerous and impressive. Best of all, Gloria didn't make Ray pick up after herself—and she sure didn't pick up after Ray, the way Ellen's mother would do some days out of pure frustration—so the carpet was covered in clothes and fashion magazines, a kind of happy mess that hid all kinds of good stuff: the scatter of jewelry on top of Ray's little black-and-white TV; the Caboodles case, stuffed full of Gloria's old, powdery compacts and glittery eye shadows and tubes of lipstick, on the floor next to Ray's pillow. She had a line of her mother's empty beer bottles on her windowsill, too, the labels colorful and each different, like tiny flags: Corona. Budweiser. Miller High Life.

By six that evening, Ellen was wearing the cutest thing she could find in her closet—a denim skirt and a blue silk shirt that she'd splurged for with her birthday money; not great, but the best she could do—and sitting on her front step, overnight bag between her feet. Her mother had already left for her shift, grousing about working on a Saturday but clearly glad for the overtime nonetheless. She'd been feeling Andy out recently about finding a part-time job—just a few hours a week, something to help her cover his equipment costs for baseball in the spring and basketball in the winter, plus the eating out and stuff he liked to do—but he got to complaining about it in typical Andy fashion, and the conversation appeared to be dead, at least for the time being. Ellen wanted to love her brother, and there were times when he was almost all right, like the afternoon a few weeks earlier when he walked with her down to the Bethel Dipper for milk shakes; but most of the time he was nothing but a loud laugh and a bad smell coming from the room across the hall, and she just about hated him. It was no wonder she liked staying at Ray's place, strange sounds and Gloria drama and all. Maybe her mother even understood that.

Gloria's red Firebird pulled into the driveway, and the horn sounded. The windows were tinted dark enough that Ellen couldn't see inside from this distance, but she knew that Ray was probably squeezed up next to the gearshift so that they could share shotgun. She felt a little thrill despite herself. Whatever else you could say about Ray's mom, she was fun:

she spent money easily, not checking tags and agonizing over a two-dollar pair of earrings the way Ellen's mother did; and she talked to Ellen and Ray like they were her own age, like friends. As if she'd read Ellen's mind, the dark window on the driver's side rolled down partway and Gloria stuck her head out. "You going to stand there and show off your outfit some more, or are you going to get in? We've got places to go, sugar-bunch." She was grinning.

"Coming," Ellen said, waving too hard, like a dork, in her giddiness. She tossed her bag into the backseat and squeezed in front next to Ray, who smelled of Aqua Net and watermelon-flavored Bubblicious. Like her room, Ray was scattered and occasionally overwhelming, but full of good if you looked hard enough. Even Ellen's mother had to admit to that.

"You look great," Ray said.

"You sure do," Gloria chimed in, backing into the road too fast so that her tires squealed a little before she braked and shifted. She had to sit on a cushion to see around her own headrest. "Cute as a button."

Both the windows were now down. Warm evening air funneled into the car, blowing Ellen's hair across her mouth, and she put her hand out slightly, letting it ride a current of wind, jumping driveways and mailboxes with her fingertips. She saw a couple of teenage guys skateboarding by the old bank and smiled, feeling powerful and gorgeous, like a movie star. She didn't know if they'd seen her, but she turned to Ray and hugged her suddenly, knowing somewhere deep within her that a night like this was fleeting and too soon forgotten, a fragile thing, a treasure.

"I'm glad I'm here," she said, and Ray hugged her back.

"Me too."

The carnival was visible as soon as they drove out of the thick of buildings around Town Square: a huddle of multicolored lights where there was usually only a dark parking lot, the arc of a Ferris wheel. One of the things Ellen liked about summer was the way things cropped up out of nothing: carnivals, snow cone stands, and the old guy who parked off Stevenson Mill Road every June and July and sold produce out of the bed of his truck. When you drove past him, he always sounded the same call— "Cantaloupes, watermelons"—in a tongue that seemed ancient and a little exotic: *Canna-loop, wadda-meyon.*

They parked behind Pizza Hut, not far from a row of pickups and lowriders—most of them souped up with chrome wheels and metallic detail work, all of them playing music, a mix of rap and country that hurt Ellen's ears and made her heart feel hijacked, forced into a rhythm that wasn't its own. Young men leaned out of windows, watching as Gloria climbed out of the car and made a big show—even Ellen could see it—of bending over to adjust the ankle strap on one of her high-heeled sandals. "Girls," she said loudly, looking their way but not seeming to see them. "Let's get a move on." There was a whistle, and Gloria didn't acknowledge it, only smirked a little and picked up her pace. "Damn rednecks," she said.

Then the parking lot music gave way to carnival music—the waltz of the merry-go-round, last year's New Kids on the Block playing out of speakers above the funnel cake stand, the electronic hisses and beeps of the Bullet and Gravitron—and Ellen felt better. This was familiar; these were the sounds of a lifetime of carnivals, the kind of music meant to blend together and fade out, a backdrop to the lights and the smells and the fun. She couldn't listen to music the way the older kids, the way those guys in the parking lot did: so loud that it wiped out thought. Some teenagers, she'd noticed, gathered around a boom box like it was a fireplace, like it was something that could warm them. Even Andy. He'd lie in his bed and play Nirvana's *Nevermind* album over and over, and he'd get pissed if Ellen came in to ask him a question or tell him that dinner was ready, as if he didn't already know the words to every song.

Gloria stopped them at the ticket stand. "Here's some money," she said, handing Ray a ten. "That should keep you guys busy for a little while, at least."

"Aren't you going to hang out with us?" Ray said.

Gloria craned her neck, searching the crowd. "I'll be around," she said. "You girls have fun and don't run off. If I haven't seen you by ten, I'll meet up with you in this same spot. Okay?"

"But, Mama," Ray said. She tried grabbing Gloria's hand, but her mother pulled away.

"You're so serious all the time. Why are you so serious?" Gloria smiled nervously and smoothed her curly brown hair. "We'll hang out later. We'll get a pizza when we're done here and go home and stay up late. How does that sound? I'll do my tarot cards on you."

Ray crossed her arms and turned away, so Ellen spoke up: "That'll be fun."

"You're a good girl," Gloria said to Ellen. She walked away before Ray had a chance to turn around again.

"Fucking bitch," Ray said.

Ellen nudged a piece of gravel with her toe.

"I know what she's doing. I know why she brought us here. I'm so stupid."

"Why?" Ellen said quietly.

Ray walked to the ticket stand and traded the ten-dollar bill for a strip of tickets. "This won't even last us an hour," she said miserably.

Ellen linked her arm through Ray's. "I have some money. Let's just have fun, okay?"

Ray looked in the direction her mother had walked off, eyes dry. She nodded.

They rode the Ferris wheel first, and when they stopped at the top, waiting as the next bucket was loaded, Ray closed her eyes. "This is where you're supposed to kiss if you're with a guy. Mama told me that. She said that her first kiss was at the top of a Ferris wheel."

Ellen hadn't had her first kiss. She thought about Mr. Hoffman again and wondered if she should mention what happened to Ray. She could be casual, totally blasé about it: "So yeah, I had a wine cooler yesterday." Ray would like that. She'd want details, and for a few moments, Ellen would be the powerful one in their friendship—the one with knowledge and experience, the one with a story worth telling. But she didn't feel blasé about that drink and what Mr. Hoffman had said to her: the way his trust had turned so quickly to disgust. And if power came from this kind of knowledge, she wasn't sure that she wanted it. Could she explain that to Ray? If she revealed the part about the wine cooler, she'd have to spill the rest of it; and she knew that her explanation wouldn't justify the way she felt, the guilt and the emptiness. Ray would say, "It was just one drink," and she'd write Mr. Hoffman off as "an old perv" or even a "dumb fucker," and that would be that. "Nothing happened," she'd say. "What are you so bent out of shape for?" Ray was Ellen's best friend—her BFF, the person she liked most and had liked longest, since they were assigned to be study buddies in fifth-grade Social Studies. Ray was a good person, Ellen knew, but she suddenly wondered if being around her was costing her something.

You might watch yourself a little better from now on, Mr. Hoffman had told her. *You're at that age.*

Ray's eyes were open again. She was leaning over the edge of their Ferris basket, looking down below them. "Mom's doing a cop," she said. "That's why she's here."

"That doesn't seem so bad," Ellen said. "I mean, at least it's a cop."

The Ferris wheel started moving again, fast this time and not stopping. The rush of warm air was pleasant, and the sun was just setting to Ellen's right. The basket they were in creaked with each descent, as though a screw somewhere were working its way free.

"It's RoboCop," Ray said. "Do you know who I'm talking about?"

She sure did. He had white-blond hair and blue, almost clear eyes, and he was investigated a year or two ago for using his nightstick on a fourteen-year-old boy. A lot of people were pissed when he wasn't fired, including Ellen's mom, who told her and Andy that there was a lesson in what happened: "Cops can get away with anything. Not a thing you can do about it."

He also had a wife and some kids, Ellen was pretty sure.

"Wow," she said.

"Yeah. Wow is right." The ride stopped, and they wandered over to the line for the Scrambler. "He's a jerk. He comes over real late on weeknights, and he leaves before I get up in the morning. He parks his cruiser right out front like he doesn't give a shit. My mom is such a slut."

As if summoned, Gloria appeared, grabbing them each by an arm. "I need to borrow you guys a few minutes," she said. "I was looking all over for you."

"What's up?" Ray said, brightening.

"Let's go to the Gravitron," Gloria said. "Everyone's saying how fun it is. You two ought to ride it."

They went to the line, which was pretty long—at least twenty people—and watched as the Gravitron slowed its spin. It was white and cylindrical, like a soup can, and you couldn't see inside it. Just watching its motion made Ellen uneasy, as did Gloria: she looked high-strung and determined, like she was up to something; she kept standing on tiptoe so she could look over the heads of the others in line. "Be damned," she said suddenly. "I see her."

"Who?" Ray said.

Gloria adjusted her blouse, fluffed her curls.

"Who do you see?"

The doors to the Gravitron opened, and people started streaming out, some laughing, some sick-looking. Ellen could guess which category she was going to fall into. The line moved, and Gloria grabbed Ray by the elbow, almost pushing her into the man ahead of them. "Go on," she said in a loud, hard whisper, and for a moment Ellen felt the sudden and irrational fear that Gloria was going to force them into the Gravitron, then abandon them. She looked down at her arm, where the phone number to the factory was usually written, and realized that she'd forgotten it this time. Her mother, in a hurry to get out the door, hadn't reminded her. She could look it up, of course, or she could call Andy and get it, but its absence seemed like a bad omen. Ellen was as conscious of bad omens as she was lucky charms.

She saw RoboCop just before they reached the entrance. He was in uniform, seated at a folding table behind a sign that read "Fraternal Order of Police," and a woman was next to him—his wife, had to be. She was chubby but attractive, and Ellen guessed that she hadn't always looked like somebody's mother. The woman was smiling and bobbing her head as she collected tickets, and in a moment they were in front of her, handing their own tickets over. RoboCop was giving Gloria a look—angry, maybe, or desperate—but his wife didn't notice it.

"I'll wait out here," Gloria said. "You girls go on, you're holding up the line."

"I don't want to ride," Ray said loudly.

RoboCop looked at her and stood, nudging his wife with an elbow. "I need a smoke," he said in a low voice—a cold and emotionless voice that seemed closer to his nickname than did anything physical about him—and he walked off. Gloria laughed, a high-pitched sound, almost hysterical.

"A smoke," she called after him, and now his wife *was* noticing her, and the look on her face was confused but also sort of resigned, too—like she knew enough about trouble to recognize it, but she hadn't figured out the brand yet. "What?" Gloria said, putting her hands on her hips and leaning over, so that her face was just a few inches from the woman's. "Who do you think you're looking at?"

The woman shrugged. "I don't know you," she said, keeping her voice low. "And I don't want to know you."

"Your husband knows me," Gloria said, and that's when Ray broke from the line and ran, sending a swirl of gravel dust up behind her. Ellen started to follow, but Gloria caught the tail of her silk shirt as she turned, yanking her back. The ride hadn't started up yet. Everybody was watching.

"You tell her—" Gloria stopped, mouth drawing up into something ugly and despairing. She covered her face with her hands and pressed, as if she were trying to rub off that ugliness, and it seemed to work—when she pulled her hand away, she looked like herself again. "You tell her to get her ass in the car and not move until I get there." She opened her purse and felt around, then pulled out a ring of keys. "Take these and stay put."

Ellen found Ray in the parking lot, sitting on a curb and scratching her initials onto fresh blacktop with a piece of limestone: RAW, a light gray against a darker gray. Ellen sat beside her.

"Ray Anne Whitaker," Ellen said, rubbing her fingers over the letters. "I hadn't noticed that spelled out a word before."

"Yeah, well, it's stupid," Ray said. "Because my mom's stupid. Didn't even know that Rayanne is one word."

"I like your name."

Ray shrugged against Ellen's shoulder, then leaned into it, resting her forehead on Ellen's neck. Ellen could feel her cheek, cool and dry, and she took Ray's hand in hers. They sat that way for a while, watching the carnival, listening to Mr. Big blasting out of somebody's lowrider: *I'm the one who wants to be with you. . . .* Gloria loved that song. She turned it up when it came on the radio, which was a lot these days, and sang along without embarrassment, like the lyrics touched her somewhere deep and she wasn't going to hide it.

She came out maybe a half hour later, face bright and triumphant, pulling the neck of her shirt out and fanning with her free hand. "Sorry about that. The carnival sucked, right? But the night is young."

"I want to go home," Ray said flatly.

"No pizza?"

Ray shook her head, then glanced at Ellen, checking. Ellen nodded.

"Just home."

They both rode in the backseat this time, and when they got to Ray's house, Gloria went straight to her room and her telephone. Before long the house started to smell like perfume and hairspray and that low burn of a curling iron against hair, and Gloria's high-pitched laugh carried across the house every now and then, bold as an exclamation point. Ellen and Ray watched a video. When the doorbell rang at eleven, Ray didn't budge. "It's for her," she said. "She can get it."

"Is she going out?" Ellen whispered.

"Probably."

Gloria came to the door and paused, hand on the doorknob. "Ray," she said. "I know you're upset. Just don't mess this up for me, okay?" She was wearing a different outfit now: cropped pants and a tank top, no bra. Her brown curls trembled at her shoulders.

Ray stuck out her middle finger, eyes still on the TV screen. Ellen couldn't believe it.

"Let me tell you something," Gloria said. "My life ain't easy. Things didn't turn out how I planned. Maybe someday you'll get a taste of what that's like. It's real easy to be a princess when you're thirteen and somebody else is making the payments. You hear what I'm saying?"

The doorbell rang again, followed by three hard raps. Gloria opened it, and RoboCop came in, still wearing his uniform. "Hey," she said, standing on tiptoe to kiss his cheek. He didn't say anything back, just stared at Ray and Ellen like he was trying to figure out what they were, how they'd gotten into Gloria's living room. Gloria took him by the hand and pulled. "We'll be in my room," she said. "Listening to music." They walked to the back of the house, and in another few minutes the stereo was blaring. When the first song ended, the sound of bedsprings echoed for a couple of seconds, and Ellen focused on the streetlamp outside, aware that her face and neck were reddening. Ray turned up the volume on the television.

"At least she's here," Ray said, sounding like she might cry. "Right? That's something, isn't it?"

"I guess."

Ray jumped to a stand, grinning. "Hey! We can have drinks!" She went to the kitchen, stopping in the doorway when Ellen didn't follow. "Come on, Mom won't care."

"I don't want any," Ellen said.

"Bullshit." Ray disappeared, and Ellen could hear the refrigerator door open and close, then the roar of the freezer. "I'm making you one," she yelled over the bass line of a new song. "This is my own invention. It's just like Cherry Sprite."

Ellen looked at Ray's living room: the big-screen TV with the image that warped on one side; the coffee table littered with ashtrays and an old HBO guide and a half-dozen glasses, different sizes, all crusted with the remains of milk or juice or beer. This wasn't a home; it was a hotel room. And Gloria was no mother. Ellen had loved Ray enough all these years not to see what was right in front of her, but she was too old now to play stupid, to let Ray and Gloria turn her into something she didn't have to be.

Ray came back with two large tumblers. She handed one to Ellen, took a big swig from the other, grimaced, then smiled.

Ellen looked down at her glass and sniffed. The liquid was bubbly with a reddish tint, and the smell was nauseating, like nail polish remover.

"Check this out," Ray said. She took Ellen's hand and flipped it over, pulling her fingers open so that the palm was exposed. "This is your life line," she said, tracing around Ellen's thumb with a sparkly-painted fingernail. "This is your career line. And here on the side"—she showed Ellen a few faint lines marking off the edge of her palm, just below the pinkie—"these are marriage lines. Mama knows all about this stuff. You know what's funny?"

"What?"

"She put our hands side by side one time," Ray said. "And the lines were almost the same. She said that means we're soulmates." She let go of Ellen's hand. "What do you think?"

"I think it's all a load of crap," Ellen said, and it seemed true, even though there were days enough when she felt like her own life hinged on the tiniest thing: how many twists to remove an apple stem, how many laps she could run in P.E. Forgetting to write the number for the factory on her arm had felt like a bad sign—and perhaps it was, given the events of the night—but she knew that her mother would be driving by at a few minutes after twelve, and that kind of certainty had nothing to do with charms or superstition or luck. She looked at the digital clock on the end table: 11:45.

Ray frowned and gulped down more of her drink. "You're just jealous," she said. "I mean, your mom's nice but it's not like she's pretty or fun or anything."

This hit Ellen square in the middle, stealing her breath for a moment. She tried to think of a retort, of evidence to prove Ray wrong. But Ray was right. Her mother was chubby, with dull, graying hair and old acne scars on her face. She wore sweatpants and T-shirts around the house, and her idea of a good time was watching *The Golden Girls* with a bag of Charley Chips in her lap. When she tried to be spontaneous—like the day last year when she took Ellen and Andy to Bowling Green to watch a movie—she always made some kind of miscalculation. That time, the movie had been lame, the popcorn was cold, and they'd argued the whole way to the theater and back. Her mother had said, "Lordy mercy, prices sure have gone up" to the teenager working the ticket booth, and Ellen had wished that a piano would drop from the sky and land on top of her, putting her out of her misery. Her mother's efforts inevitably led to such cataclysmic failures.

She loved her mother, though—scars and bad teeth and everything else—and she felt that she owed it to her to say why now, to put Ray in her place once and for all. But "I'm going outside" was all she could manage.

"Wait," Ray said. "What do you mean, outside? Why would you do that?"

Ellen rose. "To wait for Mom to get here."

Ray ran to the front door, stumbling a little, and stretched her arms out in front of it. "Don't go, okay? I'm sorry. I'm being a bitch because I'm mad. But we can still have a good time." Now she was crying, the first time Ellen had ever seen her do it. Ray held up a hand—*Just hold your horses a sec*—and went to the phone. "You're hungry, right? Let's get a pizza. Anything you want."

Ellen put her hand on the doorknob and shook her head.

"Please, Ellen," Ray said. Pleaded, really. She lowered her

voice. "I'll pour the rest of the drinks out. We can go straight to bed if you want. Just don't leave me here alone with them. If you're my friend, you won't."

Ellen felt the brass of the knob getting hot and wet under her palm. She could stay this night with Ray, she knew, and everything would be fine. RoboCop would leave. Gloria would be in high spirits tomorrow; she'd get up late and make chocolate chip pancakes, and then they'd go to the mall. Tonight wouldn't seem so bad in the morning, because Ray wouldn't let Ellen remember the way things had really gone down. At her mother's side, she'd be too happy—too satisfied—to do anything but pretend and forget.

"I've got to go," Ellen said finally.

"Okay, sure. I understand. But take me, too." Ray came over and grabbed her free hand, then hugged her, not seeming to notice or care that Ellen didn't return the embrace. "I'll go home with you and your mom. Your mom is great. Okay?" She squeezed Ellen tighter, and Ellen felt the hot press of Ray's face against her neck. "Ellen, *please*."

Ellen pushed her away. She knew she was being selfish, but she was also being practical: Ray couldn't stay with her forever. This was, she'd think later—and with more sorrow than she could ever have anticipated—her first real adult decision.

"I'll see you at school," she said, and stepped outside. The door slammed shut behind her, so hard that the living room window rattled in its frame.

"Bitch!" she heard Ray scream, the closed door and the loud stereo making her voice seem puny and distant.

There was a swing on the neighbor's side, but the idea of using it seemed rude, so Ellen sat on the front steps, legs pulled up to her chest. The night was warm and strangely bright—there was a not-quite-full moon out, riding high in the sky—and she waited, sitting up straight when she saw headlights, relaxing when she realized that not enough time had passed, that it was early yet.

Her mother came just after midnight. Ellen didn't know the time, but she knew her mother well enough to be sure of it.

She looked surprised when Ellen came to the car, but she didn't say anything about Gloria as Ellen had worried she would, only stared at the house—the police cruiser, dark and silent in the drive—and touched Ellen's shoulder: "Is Ray all right in there?"

Ellen nodded, feeling like a liar. She wondered what Ray would do now: watch TV, go to bed? Finish what was left of her drink, and Ellen's, too?

"Are you okay?"

"Yeah," she said. And that much seemed true. Her mother put the car in drive, and Ray's house—her half of a house—disappeared around a dark corner.

Ellen marked the changes outside her window. As you drove closer to the Square, the duplexes gave way to older houses, and then the houses east of town, in Dellview, were the nicest, where the doctors and lawyers all lived. Gloria called it Pill Hill, and this one time, when they'd gone cruising, they'd driven through Dellview with their windows rolled down—Ray and Ellen squeezed into the front, like always—screaming the lyrics to "Blueberry Hill," saying, *"I've had my thrills on Pill Hill"* instead. On West 9th you passed Arthur Baldwin's house, which was the biggest and fanciest in town, but just a few streets later you got to the Shell station and the cemetery and Kip's Garage, which always had tires piled in the back so high that you could see them over the roof of the building; and then you got to Ellen's subdivision, which wasn't the worst in town but sure wasn't that great, either. In the dark you could see what a difference a mile—what a street, even—made. Ray was back behind her, and Mr. Hoffman's place was just ahead, on the right, the windows all dark. She thought about Mr. Hoffman's Theory of Realty, feeling the first dawn of understanding. Ray still lived right across town, and Ellen would inevitably cross her path at school. But they would never be close again.

"Mr. Hoffman's wife left him," she told her mother.

Her mother signaled, and they turned off of Sycamore and onto Forsythia, where the split levels like Mr. Hoffman's gave way to small ranch homes, shabbier as you got farther away from 9th. "How did you hear about that?" her mother said.

"I don't know," Ellen told her. "It's just going around."

They pulled into their driveway. "Well, folks aren't happy unless they've got bad news to spread, I guess." Her mother sighed. "Don't I know it."

"She's in Cincinnati."

Her mother nodded as if this made sense, as if Cincinnati were the destination for women who left their husbands. "Things hadn't been the same for them since Caleb died. We all knew that. But Greta—I shouldn't say this, but here I go: she can be a real handful."

Ellen remembered Mr. Hoffman, sunburned and angry, and the taste of that wine cooler. "I thought she was nice. She helped me with my makeup one day."

"A girl your age has no business wearing makeup, anyhow," her mother said. "If I'd known about that I would've thought twice about letting you go over there."

"Whatever," Ellen said.

"*Whatever*. I hate that word. That's your answer to everything."

The car's headlights hit the door to their garage and reflected back faintly, making her mother look old: jawline set but soft, wrinkles around her eyes more prominent than Ellen remembered them being. "Walt's a nice man. Women like her don't know a good thing when they've got it. They're always looking out for better."

"You think Mr. Hoffman's a good thing?"

"I think a girl could do a lot worse." Ellen saw the faraway look in her mother's eyes, could read the dream in them that her mother would never acknowledge and certainly never act on: she and Mr. Hoffman and a house with a pool, a life that had nothing to do with late nights spent sewing pockets into cheap blue jeans. And what else? Sex, sure. Something Ellen didn't know much about outside the science of it—the things she'd learned in seventh grade, when Ms. Burchett split up the girls and the boys and taught one half while the other got an extra thirty minutes in activities period—but it had to do with the way a shirt folded up to reveal a tanned forearm, the tangle of panties and bras in her dresser drawer, the noises Gloria and RoboCop were making in that back room, audible in the pauses between song tracks. Because sex, she figured, was just another way of saying *secret*: the secret lives of grown-ups. She looked at her mother and realized that she knew something about Mr. Hoffman that her mother did not, and she understood that the power between them was shifting—slowly and maybe imperceptibly now, but shifting nonetheless. And she didn't want it to. She craned her neck so that she could see through the window, trying to find a star to wish upon, a charm to bring her luck. But her view was blocked by a nearby streetlamp: the only point of light in a sky the size of infinity.

• RETROSPECTIVE •

1.

Libby learned of her ex-husband's move back to the old home-place the way such information was usually gathered in Roma, Kentucky: through contact with a barely tolerated acquaintance, in Super Wal-Mart, at the unhappy convergence of circumstance and Frozen Foods. Nita Greene, who was supposedly kin to Libby through her mother's side and several generations back, blocked Libby's path with her shopping cart, leaned in conspiratorially, and whispered, "You know about Stephen and that woman, don't you?" before Libby had time to realize she'd been cornered. Libby was holding a bag of broccoli florets, and she dropped them into her shopping cart almost guiltily.

"I'm sorry?"

"Stephen," Nita repeated, face flushed with—yes, Libby was sure of it—the pleasure of knowing that *she* had gotten to her first. "He and his new wife's building out on his people's property, where the two of you had that farmhouse. Bonnie Brentwood told me that the frame went up over the weekend."

"That a fact," Libby said, leaning on her cart a little.

"Sure enough," Nita said. Now she smiled sympathetically. "I know it's strange, hon, but I figured you ought to hear it from a friend before the gossip mill starts running."

Libby couldn't look at her. "That's good of you."

"Anytime," Nita said, and in another moment Libby was alone. The whole conversation had transpired so quickly that she couldn't be rightly sure it had happened, excepting the physical evidence: the lingering smell of Nita's lavender bouquet, her own white-knuckle grip on the blue plastic handle of her shopping cart.

Stephen was building on the homeplace.

She drove home from Wal-Mart in a daze of memory and vague bad feeling. It was the way she'd felt in the first year after her mother died: cleaning house, preparing dinner, going through the motions of a day, and realizing again—and again—that her mother was gone. That sense of reverberating loss. When she parked her car and unloaded her groceries, making that frustrating second trip to get all of the bags inside, she went to her bedroom and lay down on the bed, stunned. This, she believed, was Stephen's final act of betrayal, and also somehow the worst.

She forced herself up and into the kitchen after an hour spent staring at the ceiling, then prepared the meal she'd been looking forward to all day: a nicely marbled filet, sliced thick and cooked rare; a side of home fries. She ate with the familiar mix

of emotions that accompanied such an indulgence—deep satisfaction, guilt, distraction—in a manner that had also grown familiar to her through years and practice: seated on a bar stool at
her kitchen island, pulled up close to a 10-inch black-and-white
television. Libby wasn't any good at being single; her loneliness
dismayed and embarrassed her. She was a woman who had defined her worth through her abilities to please others, and eating
by herself was a ritual of the most painful sort. But she'd eaten
often in the kitchen as a young mother, retreating to its smells
and heat as a reprieve from the demands of her sons, and taking
her meals here was a comfort. It made her situation seem temporary—a matter of choice. On television, the six p.m. entertainment news program was doing a feature on "Oscar Fashions,"
and Libby learned that dark nail polish was back in vogue—
but only if the nails were worn short and neat—and that, if the
Golden Globes were any indication, the hair trend would be soft,
romantic, and artfully disheveled. Libby's own hair, at fifty, was
a yellow-brown that wanted to be gray, that could be perceived
as gray if the lighting were bad. She wore it most days pinned
back, half up and half down, with a Goody barrette. She kept a
spray of thick bangs to hide her high forehead.

   After eating, she went down to the basement with a flashlight
and a sweater, hunkered awkwardly beside the Rubbermaid tub
where she'd been storing the photos and mementos from her
other life, and spent two hours sorting, stopping every now and
then—too often—to fix her waning flashlight beam on some
picture, particularly those with the old farmhouse in the background. Seeing it again this way, a blurry impression behind the
smiling faces of Stephen and the boys and even herself, gave
Libby a chill. She had spent the five most difficult years of her

life in that two-bedroom shack—the first years of her marriage to Stephen—and she had spent the worst afternoon of her life there, too. She'd sworn never to go back. But here she was, wading into these memories again, hating Stephen all the more because his image, his smile, made her ache for him as much as for her old and better self. She threw all of the pictures from the homeplace back into the Rubbermaid tub, then all of the photos of Stephen except for two, and she weeded out the pictures of her sons—the ones that began after their move into town, the school photos and Christmas photos and studio shots of them as babies—and placed those in her stack, to keep.

Jaime and Sean were both grown and out of the house, living separate lives: Jaime a half-hour away in Bowling Green with his wife, a girl he'd met during college, and Sean in Louisville, playing minor league baseball and probably doing things that Libby didn't care to know about. Upon returning from the basement, Libby called them both and told them that they could come home and take whatever pictures and mementos they wanted; she would throw out the rest. Sean said, with exaggerated regret, that he didn't have any storage space. "Do what you need to do, Mama," he added gravely, as though he were granting her a difficult favor.

Jaime, however, was quiet for a moment, characteristically thoughtful. "You sound upset," he said. "Everything okay?"

"Well, you know," Libby said. "I hear he's building out at the homeplace. Threw me a little."

"It makes sense," Jaime said. "The land's just sitting there."

He didn't know what happened there so many years ago, and Libby fought a sudden urge, selfish and destructive, to blurt it out. "I just have a lot of memories attached to that place," she said instead. "Good ones and bad ones. And the good ones are about as difficult as the bad these days."

"I know what you mean," he said. "All right, then. I'll look through them. It might be fun."

He came down that weekend, leaving his wife, Ashley, in Bowling Green—a turn of events that pleased Libby more than she would ever tell him—and spent hours in the basement with a file box and a Sharpie, organizing and discarding, fastidious as always. Saturday night, over fried chicken and mashed potatoes, his favorite meal since childhood, Jaime told Libby that he'd kept about half: "The ones with me and Sean, plus a few others. Good riddance to the rest."

"You sure?"

He nodded.

She looked down at her plate, steeling herself, and made her old, halfhearted plea, honed now by time—six years—and repetition: "He's still your father. He was a good dad to you and Sean."

"That's bull and you know it."

"He didn't lay a hand on you," Libby said. "He coached all your sports. Spent time with you. He did better than most of my friends' husbands, and I can't take that away from him no matter what he's done since." She sighed. She couldn't.

"I'm tired, Mama," Jaime said. "I love you, but I'm tired of this martyr shit of yours. He was a bastard, okay? A grouch when we were kids and a cheater when we got old enough to know better. If he gave a damn about his family, he wouldn't have been so quick to throw it away for a piece of ass."

"Watch your mouth," Libby said, scraping their plates—bones in the trash, the rest in the garbage disposal. But she felt satisfied, and guilty for the satisfaction. She had promised herself that she would never play games with her and Stephen's children. Had she?

"You're going to have a kid of your own one of these days," she told him. "And you'll want it to know its granddaddy, even if you don't believe that now."

He rose and helped her load plates into the dishwasher, oddly quiet. "I don't know," he said finally. "I'll cross that bridge when I get to it."

She patted his arm. "You're a good boy," she said. "Go on now. Sit. I made a butter cake."

He didn't take much convincing. She fed him a slice with the chocolate sauce he loved—her mother's recipe—and they stayed up until almost midnight, watching a video and then *Saturday Night Live.* She fixed popcorn. And the next morning he was gone: back to Bowling Green and his wife, which was right and good—the way things ought to be once a son becomes a man— but no less painful. She wouldn't give up his visits for anything, but she wondered if they only made the balance of her life seem uglier and emptier in contrast. The Big Lonely, she thought some- times: a name that sounded like a Western. The Big Lonely was hours of television and sudden daydreams about men, strang- ers, whom she saw on the street or in the grocery—fantasies that were embarrassingly heatless and domestic, about holding hands in public or painting the new porch swing together. The Big Lonely meant eating microwave dinners or takeout from China Chef even though she loved to cook, because trying to prepare a meal for one seemed wasteful and pathetic. Getting sympathetic looks at the gynecologist's office where she worked as a receptionist; seeing the younger women with their rounded

bellies—*so young* some of them were, just babies themselves—
and aching with the memories from her own early motherhood,
the purity of her love, the security of her sons' devotion. It meant
looking in the mirror and not even registering what was there,
because she'd spent twenty years of her life depending on Stephen's judgment, Stephen's way of seeing her. This was her life.
This was what Stephen had left her.

When Jaime left, Libby took out the two photographs of Stephen that she hadn't been able to part with. The first was from
her wedding day: she and Stephen in the center, with both sets
of parents on either side of them. It was an eight-by-ten on heavy
paper, almost cardboard—common in those days. Color, but it
had the feel of black-and-white. Maybe because it was so dated:
Stephen's slicked-over hair, his mother's cat's eyeglasses, which
were beginning to seem retro even then. Her own mother's pill-
box hat. She'd kept the picture for reasons both practical and
sentimental. She didn't have many photographs of her parents,
who were both dead now, and this was a particularly good one.
Her mother had been a dour woman—loving and fair, but dour—
with a physical presence that bore testament to a lifetime of difficulty, even suffering, though Libby had only a vague sense of
the kind and degree. Her face had been stony and deep-lined, an
edifice that made her only lovely features—her light blue eyes,
which Libby had inherited—seem sad and woefully misplaced.
Like the chunks of quartz you sometimes found lodged deep in a
piece of mud-colored sandstone. In this photograph, though, her
mother was almost pretty, and that was reason enough for holding on to it. But Libby also wanted to remember what was very
likely the last perfect day of her life, when she'd wanted so very
little and what she wanted—a home and children, the everyday

joys of marriage—had seemed not just likely, but guaranteed.
She needed to remember that feeling, even if doing so made her
throat close tight and her chest hurt. You couldn't re-create that
kind of hopefulness, that naïveté. When it was lost, it was gone
for good.

The second picture was from her honeymoon. She and Stephen had driven to Asheville, North Carolina, to go hiking and
to visit the Biltmore estate. It was a good trip. The landscape had
been familiar but occasionally exotic; on the highway between
Asheville and Chimney Rock, where they'd gotten a motel room
for cheap, the hillsides were covered in a thick layer of kudzu, a
tangle of greenery that made everything look soft and uniform.
It dangled from the phone lines overhead, climbed the bumpers
of old cars—like something from a horror movie, but beautiful
at the same time. Libby couldn't have explained why. They drove
into the nearby hills, land bordering the eastern Appalachians,
and parked whenever they saw a trail marker that looked promising. They took photos of waterfalls and startling vistas. They
took some pictures of each other in front of the waterfalls and
the vistas, and when they met another hiker on the trail, they
occasionally posed together, faces serious, because the business
of marriage was serious. Libby had kept none of these pictures,
though the memories of making them were as clear as the photos
themselves. She supposed that they were in the garbage can out
front now, unless Jaime had lied about what he'd thrown away.

The one she kept was of Stephen, at the Biltmore estate. She
didn't remember taking it, though she supposed she must have;
otherwise, she would have been standing beside him. He was
at the entrance to the house, next to one of the stone lions that
flanked the front steps. He had an arm propped on the statue,

one leg crossed behind the other, and he was shading his eyes with a raised hand, squinting in a way that gave him a look of deep concentration, or contemplation. The photo was small, taken with the old 30–30 she'd received as a high school graduation gift, and the exposure gave the image a yellow tone. When she saw the picture for the first time, a few days after returning from their honeymoon and dropping the film canister off at the drug store, she'd laughed and told Stephen that he looked like an explorer, like he was on safari. Close, she thought now, but not exactly right.

A few years ago, looking at coffee table books on the discount shelf at Barnes & Noble, she'd come across an Old Hollywood retrospective: a beautiful volume, heavier than the family Bible she'd inherited. She'd thought about buying it, imagining it in her living room, weighty and sophisticated, an elegant touch among nicked furniture and stained upholstery and the dozens of cheap figurines her sons had given her as small children. In the end she'd only flipped through it, aghast at the thirty-dollar price sticker, and traced her finger across images from a long-gone era: Marlon Brando, handsome and muscular in a white T-shirt; the old stock photo of Marilyn Monroe with her dress billowing up around her hips; Jimmy Stewart, Greta Garbo, Charlie Chaplin, Vivien Leigh, Joan Crawford, hundreds of others. One photo caught her attention as she flipped through the pages, and she went back to it in a hurry, heart fluttering. It was John Barrymore, an actor she knew vaguely, and he was on a honeymoon in the Galápagos Islands with his much-younger wife. The photo was nothing like the one of Stephen, really—Barrymore and the woman were on the beach, guns jutting from their hips, and they were sitting on a dead alligator. "John and Dolores on the Biana

River, posing with their kill," the caption said. But there was something of the same spirit in the image: the singular maleness of it—perhaps real and perhaps staged—and the timelessness of the pose. Had men been picturing themselves this way even before they had cameras to do the work for them? Libby thought so. She pitied the dead alligator, sacrificed to some rich couple's whim. She pitied the young woman, who looked as much like a trophy as the animal.

She didn't know why she'd kept that second picture. Perhaps it was a reminder, or maybe a lesson: proof of Stephen's lesser nature. Or maybe she still loved him, and wouldn't that just beat all? If she'd needed rock-solid proof that he was through with her—beyond his recent marriage—then his move back to the homeplace was it. That weed-choked tract of land was everything that had been wrong about their marriage, and even after what happened there, Stephen had been resentful about moving into town, closer to Libby's parents and to the safety of streetlights and neighbors. He'd never stopped talking about "getting back to the country"—that was how he put it—and Libby had never had the constitution to even entertain such notions, no matter how sincerely Stephen had spoken of alarm systems and security lights and even guard dogs.

He had it his way, finally. He and that woman, the one Jaime had caught him with almost seven years ago now, when Stephen took a nighttime security job at Price Electric. He met her there, Libby had learned; the woman was working seconds in the winding room, and her smoke break overlapped with one of his evening rounds. The end came fast: Jaime, eighteen and two months away from starting college, waking her at one in the morning, crying and trying not to; Stephen's wordless exit a day later, old suitcase packed with work clothes and his shaving kit and nothing else. Once the affair was out in the open, he barely spoke to her, even when she begged him to explain himself, to say he loved her, to tell her where he would be, at least. This silent treatment hurt almost as bad as Jaime's account of what he'd witnessed—how he'd gone to the electric plant to surprise his father with a milk shake from the Bethel Dipper, feeling overwhelmed by the fact of his impending move to college, and found him kissing the woman outside in the open, where anyone could see them. Stephen was implicating her—blaming her, even—and he was the one who had transgressed. *He* was the one.

She was curious about Stephen's new house. She couldn't help herself.

2.

The old homeplace was small, poorly insulated: ramshackle, really. It was set back from the road a good piece, connected by a dirt drive, and with the exception of a small yard space that Stephen kept clear with a push mower, the surrounding acres were a tangle of weeds and briars. It was no place for small children to play, but Libby didn't have any other options. If her sons weren't out stretching their legs and collecting cockleburs and chigger bites—or hiking over to the ravine, swinging on vines and risking broken necks, despite Libby's warnings and the occasional spanking—they were underfoot while she tried to get the chores done. Her life had become a series of such compromises, of weighing one kind of bad against another. Buy the hamburger meat that they could afford and endure Stephen's grumbling? Or buy the skillet steaks they couldn't, wondering all night if his small smile and kiss were worth it? Walk a mile to the in-laws' place to use their telephone and put up with Stephen's mother's veiled criticisms? Or decide that Jaime didn't really need a dentist's appointment this month, that it could wait until Stephen was making runs from the Nashville hub again and would therefore be home more frequently? Her mother visited once a week, bringing by Coca-Colas for the boys and Little Debbie cakes for Libby, and the look on her face when she entered each time left Libby more and more heartbroken. She could see this place now as her mother did: tiny and dirty-looking, despite her daily scrubbings. The kind of home you saw welfare babies in, though she and Stephen had never once taken help from anyone, unless you counted those weekly treats of cakes and colas. And the house, of course. Whatever else you could say about it, the house was theirs, rent-free, because Stephen's folks no longer had any use for it. "Thank God for small blessings," as her mother would say. Or, "Don't look the gift horse in the mouth."

The year they finally moved away from the old homeplace was the most difficult of their marriage, of Libby's whole life. The boys were very small—Jaime five, Sean three—and Stephen was still driving trucks for Waltham, gone five or six days at a stretch and sleeping much of the time he was home. Libby blamed his crankiness on the trucking. She knew a little about his life away from her, some details Stephen had let slip when he had the energy for talking: how he spent sixteen hours or more in the cab some days, and the only way to make a deadline was to push through the exhaustion—with black beauties if you had them, with coffee and determination if you didn't. How the road food turned to poison in you sometimes, and you had to squat on the side of the interstate if the sickness caught you between exits, then wipe quickly with old Dairy Queen napkins. He told her that the hills over in east Tennessee were so bad that he'd worried for his life, not knowing if he'd be able to brake in time to avoid hitting the cars in front of him or losing his load. He'd had to use a runaway ramp once—this was in Maryland—and it took a wrecker and two days to get his rig out of the sand, repaired, and then back on the road again, costing him his per diem. He returned from that trip in a red fever, complaining about how he'd had to go without food for most of a week—living on tap water and Captain's Wafers and whatever else he could find free at fast food joints or in the waiting room of the service shop—just to make sure he could afford Sean's formula when he returned. He'd made it Libby's fault some way—the hills and his driving and the way the sun was shining in his eyes just so—and he'd only relented when she threatened to take the boys to her mother's place if he didn't calm down. He'd apologized, but the blame was out in the air between them, impossible to take back. These were the moments no one told you about a marriage: how proximity and time eventually added up to meanness. How two decent people could eventually bring out the worst in each other, simply because the odds were in favor of it.

Stephen was gone the day the stranger came knocking. Their sons were out back somewhere, just an occasional boyish whoop to remind Libby that they were alive and safe. He had left that morning for Cincinnati—Sin-Sin, he called it, when he was feeling playful—and he was going to be gone for at least a week this time, maybe even a few days more than that. Watching Stephen depart for work was always bittersweet. Despite herself, Libby felt lighter as soon as his pickup left their drive and turned onto Chandlers Chapel Road, a little trail of black exhaust following behind him. It wasn't that Stephen mistreated them. As she'd tell Jaime so many years later, he never once touched the boys in anger; she, in fact, always doled out what little spanking they received. And she'd never worried about her own safety, either. In fact, she regarded her husband with something much less potent than fear: unease, sometimes, and—on rare occasions—outright dislike. In his worst, weakest moments, he could be selfish and petty, and on a couple of occasions, he had been cruel. On a night not too long after Sean was born, she noticed him watching her as she was getting dinner together. His face was mild, interested even, and for a moment she wondered if he was admiring her, thinking about what they could get into later on, when the boys were tucked in. She'd stood straighter in her old, battered tennis shoes, the ones she wore for housework, and she'd even smiled at him a little over her shoulder. "Penny for your thoughts," she'd said, flirtatious, and he replied without missing a beat: "Your hips. You're so much wider than you used to be."

"Why would you say that?" she'd asked him, the disappointment sour and pungent-tasting, like the onions she was stirring around in her grandmother's old cast-iron skillet.

He'd shrugged, as if the answer were obvious. "Just noticed," he'd said, and then he'd gotten up to check on Sean, who was sleeping on a blanket on the floor of the family room. Libby had cried as she finished dinner, and when the food was on the table, she didn't eat any herself. Stephen didn't seem to notice.

When Stephen was gone, Libby didn't have to worry about those moments when he'd hurt her: casually and probably without malice, just because he didn't know any better. Or didn't try to. She felt better in her clothes, happier in her chores, more relaxed as she watched her sons tear off across the field full of

brambles and weeds and probably rattlesnakes that had somehow become her home. She allowed herself one Little Debbie
cake a day, and she'd eat it early in the morning, standing at
the kitchen window and watching the sun rise behind a distant
row of pine trees. She savored it—the chewy oatmeal cookie, the
sugary grit of the cream filling—and felt nothing, which was a
kind of blessing.

But Stephen was her husband, and whether the loneliness she
felt in his absence was love or habit, it was still loneliness: a deep
well of ache. She missed him most at night, because nights were
black out in the countryside: no security lights, no nearby houses
to break up her view of trees and farmland. In the summer, lying
in bed, she thought sometimes that the racket of crickets and
tree frogs would drive her mad, that if she didn't hear another
grown-up voice soon, she'd run out the back door and never return. She'd leave her sons sleeping—Jaime on his cousin's hand-
me-down big boy bed, Sean in a crib that was quickly becoming
too small—and tear off into the weeds and briars, howling at the
moon, or maybe just howling. This was no kind of life, she knew.
She was twenty-six years old, married, but most nights she slept
alone.

When the stranger came, Stephen was gone, her mother's visit
was still a few hours away, and the boys were out back somewhere. Libby was scrubbing the kitchen floor, down on hands and
knees with an old, hard brush, trying to make the black-flecked
tiles look passable. The knock on the door startled her so badly
that she dropped the brush, setting her heart to thumping. She
almost never had visitors this far out, only her mother. Traveling
salesmen, she suspected, usually took one look at her home—
the peeling wood siding, the crooked shutters and sagging front

porch—and assumed it was abandoned, or at the very least a lost cause. Not long after she and Stephen had married and moved in, a local Presbyterian preacher had stopped by with a box full of government cheese and peanut butter, and when he saw that Libby was pregnant, heavy and sweating with it, he'd offered to take her into town to fill out the WIC papers and to do some grocery shopping. "If you belong to a church, you're never alone," he'd said, pushing a small New Testament into her hands like she was some kind of South American missionary case and not a woman raised by decent town folks. She'd told him to take his charity and his sermon somewhere else, that she'd grown up going to New Haven Baptist and didn't need lessons on the Lord from the chant-leader at Podunk Presbyterian. She'd told him where he could put his box of government handouts, and she'd finished by saying that she was only in this house temporarily, until her husband got the post office job he'd put in for.

That was over five years ago now.

She thought about the preacher as she got up to answer her front door, thinking in a bitter way that he'd returned, finally; that after all this time, he'd dropped by again, box of groceries in hand, to say, "I told you so." But the man at her door wasn't a preacher, and he couldn't even be rightly called a man. He was a teenager, seventeen at most, one of those tall and gawky types with horsey front teeth and a lower jaw that couldn't seem to latch shut. He was wearing a sweat-stained John Deere baseball cap, and he yanked it off when he saw her—a poor impersonation of courtesy by a kid who probably hadn't even been taught to say "ma'am."

"Help you?" Libby said.

The kid jerked his head to the side, toward the highway. "Car went dead on me," he said. "Hoped there might be someone here who could give me a jump."

"Do you see a car here?" she replied, a little more sharply than she'd intended. He'd given her a good scare, and she realized now that the knock had been so startling because there hadn't been a car engine preceding it, or the crunch of gravel. Her heart was only now beginning to slow.

"Oh," he said, twisting that hat in his hands like he was Gomer Pyle. "You got a phone I could borrow, then?" He pronounced the word *borry,* making Libby angrier—an anger that she knew, even in its midst, was strange and unfair and probably larger than this sun-sleepy afternoon. An anger that had nothing to do with the poor, slow kid at her door.

"No, hon," she said, forcing herself to soften a bit. "My in-laws down the road a piece have one." She pointed. "About a mile ahead on your right, okay? Two-story house with a big oak tree and a tire swing out front."

The boy stood there, face slack. "I done walked a mile already," he said. "It sure is hot out."

"Nothing I can do about it," Libby told him. "It's not so far. I run down there and back all the time."

"Think you could let me have some water before I go?"

This request—this moment—was the thing she'd look back on later: the clue, the signal, the unacknowledged shadow of unease. She touched her midriff and craned her neck toward the kitchen, listening for the boys. A second passed, and then a sound: a high-pitched laugh, soft and far away. A slightly deeper voice echoed it.

"Stay out here," she told him. "On the porch. I'll bring you a glass."

He nodded, backing up a few steps, lifting his hand a little as if to say, *As you were:* a confident, perhaps even smug gesture, and it didn't match the rest of him. She closed the screen door, trying to smile a little, and thumbed the latch over so the wind wouldn't catch it. She went to the kitchen and pulled an old jelly jar out of the cabinet, thinking that she'd tell the boy to take it with him on the walk, that she had enough used jelly jars to last her a lifetime. She filled the glass at the tap, thought about dropping in an ice cube, then decided against it. This seemed like an important choice, a recognition of something, and her heart resumed its steady hammer. When she left the kitchen and found the boy in her living room—when she realized that he'd pushed his hand through a loose corner of the screen in her door, turning the latch so quietly that she hadn't heard him do it—she wasn't even surprised.

"You can just take this," she told him, holding the glass out in front of her, hoping he didn't notice the shake in her hand. "You hear me? You could just take this now and make your way down the road."

He did take it from her, and he sipped from it. "That right?" he said.

She nodded.

He kept staring, and what she saw in his eyes dismayed her. She didn't doubt that he'd come here because he was looking for a jump or a phone; and she'd bet her life that his car was around the corner and just out of sight, dead, exactly as he told her it was. But sometime between the knock and now, an idea had kindled, and he was too young and stupid to realize that actions like the one he was contemplating had consequences, that the excitement of this moment—the desire he was feeling, large and powerful and teenaged—could die out if he just gave it a few minutes. A few damned minutes, was all.

He put the glass of water down, carefully, on the little table by the front door: an antique, a gift from Libby's mother, and she had a second to mourn the ring of condensation his glass would leave. And then he was on top of her, stronger than his thin arms would have suggested, smarter than she could have known he'd be, because he paused, panting, and put a hand on her mouth and said, "Fast, then your babies won't hear," and she stopped putting up a struggle—or much of one—after that. She shut her eyes tight and counted to thirty, then to sixty, remembering to put *Mississippi* between each number. She could hear her boys, closer to the house now, and she lost count and started repeating in her head *Don't let them see this* and not too long after, the boy on top of her was done. Jerking up his jeans, breathing like he'd run a marathon. And then gone, door banging behind him. Libby pulled her own jeans up and closed as fast as she could and started crying, not knowing she was going to do it, not at any other time in her life the crying type. These were chest-deep cries, too, the kind that felt like strangling. She lay back down, rough-hewn wood boards hard and scratchy beneath her, and stared at the ceiling. A breeze drifted in her unlatched front door, cooling her face where the tears had streaked down, and Libby kept herself very still. The kitchen floors still needed finishing: that nagged at her. The boys needed to be checked on. They'd come running up in another few minutes, hungry, and if she wasn't pouring them each a glassful of the cherry Flav-R-Aid they loved and putting together cheese sandwiches or boiling hot dogs—if she was still lying on the floor with her face streaked—then she would've turned a corner with her sons, one she wasn't ready for yet.

She couldn't make herself move, though.

She was still on the floor when her mother drove up a half hour later, and it was her mother who sopped up the last of the mop water, who called the boys in and made their lunch, who helped Libby to the couch and cleaned her face with a damp washcloth. And when Libby said in a whisper, "I don't want Stephen to know," it was her mother who slapped her cheek, startling her, and grabbed Libby's chin.

"Bullshit," she hissed. "You hear me? If you don't tell him, I will."

"But Mama—"

Her mother shook her head, and Libby closed her eyes, not wanting to see what days like this one did to a face.

"You hear me, Libby?" her mother said, a voice from the void.

Libby nodded. She was no match against her mother's will.

They gathered the boys up in her mother's Buick Regal and drove down the road to her in-laws' place to use the phone.

"He was here," Stephen's mother kept saying. "Right in my house. Just as polite as he could be."

Libby's mother dialed the sheriff.

"You've got to be more careful about who you let in," Stephen's mother told Libby. "You got to be smarter about things. Especially with them boys to worry about."

Jaime and Sean were in the front yard on the tire swing. Laughing. Had they been laughing all morning?

"Stephen will be fit to be tied," his mother said, and Libby's mother slammed down the phone.

"Enough of you," she told her. "If your no-account son didn't have them living out here like a band of—of *heathens*; yes, you heard me right—then none of this would've happened."

"Why, I can't believe you'd—"

Libby wandered out of the house, leaving them to it. Sean saw her coming to the swing and grinned, monkeying his way up to the rope, straddling the tire. "See me, Mama?" he said.

"I see you good," she told him.

"And me," Jaime said from above her. He was in the tree, looking down. The sun hit the leaves behind his head, turning them gold. "Look how high I am."

She nodded, sleepy, and sat against the tree. The mothers were fighting inside. The ground was spongy beneath her. Somewhere not too far from here, the boy was probably still waiting by his car. She wondered, foggily, who would get to him first: his ride or the sheriff. She didn't know if it was the heat or the fact that she hadn't eaten yet today, but she felt disconnected from herself, almost drunk. Her son, scaling limbs over her head, might have been a strange, large bird. A firefighter. An angel.

Her mother came to the door a few minutes later. "I got ahold of Stephen," she said. "He's on his way home."

"Daddy's coming?" Jaime yelled. "All the way back from Sin-Sin?"

"All the way back," Libby said, feeling dread instead of relief.

Later that day, once she'd kept some food and water down and sat alone for a few minutes in the cool air of her mother's kitchen—a plain room, but friendly, and you could see the neighbor's house right outside the window—it seemed to Libby that she could just clean up and move on. Whenever Stephen made it home, she'd apologize, tell him to go back; no reason for him to lose a few days' pay. Because what this amounted to, in the end, was a rough five minutes or so in a dayful of minutes, in a lifetime of hours. The boy had been picked up by Sheriff Robeson, a good man, and Robeson had stood in this very room not an hour ago, sipping sweet tea, and he'd said—not to Libby or to her mother, but to Libby's father—"There's a couple of ways we can handle this. Quick and off the books. Or slow and proper. I'll do whatever you folks want me to."

"Quick," Libby's mother said, before her father could even open his mouth. Before Libby could process the choice she'd been given.

"Glenn?" the sheriff said.

Her father nodded.

"He's scared shitless," Robeson said. "Dumber than dirt, too. I've got him locked up now. I'll leave him there to think about it for a few more hours, then I'll drop in on him. If Stephen wants to come by when he gets to town, he can. Read me?"

"Yes," her mother said.

Now he looked at Libby. "You won't have any more trouble from him, sweetheart. I'll make sure of it. I think y'all are doing the right thing here."

"We thank you," Libby's father said.

"Nothing to thank," Robeson told him, and left.

Just five minutes, she thought now, waiting for Stephen. The amount of time it took to brush your teeth or to heat some water up on the stove. Already she was forgetting, it seemed to her: the boy's smell, like gasoline and musky man-sweat, the stench of filth and not merely exertion; the way his elbows had dug into her forearms; the occasional sting as his chin stubble grazed her forehead. She was losing these details, she felt sure.

A bad thing had happened to her, yes, but also a small thing. For her children's sake, she would do well to remember that.

About three hours after her mother's call, Stephen's truck pulled in outside. He must have been speeding to make it in that time, but that wasn't necessarily surprising—driving rigs had given him a lead foot, and he'd paid off plenty of speeding tickets as proof of it. He didn't say anything at first: just took a seat at the kitchen table, across from Libby, and looked her over. She couldn't make out what he was thinking. His face was calm.

Libby's mother came to the door. "Sheriff said you could come by the lockup if you wanted," she told him. "He won't let him go till he hears from you."

"Let him go?"

Her mother crossed her heavy, sun-spotted arms over her chest, and Libby wished that she had an ounce of her formidability. "We reckoned that the best way to handle this was amongst ourselves," she said. "And the sheriff agreed."

Stephen pulled a cotton handkerchief from his pants pocket and held it to his neck. "What's supposed to keep him from doing it again?"

"You," Libby said, and her mother looked surprised, but satisfied.

"Me." He looked from Libby to her mother. "I don't see how this became my fight. Send Glenn out there."

Her mother took another step into the kitchen and stopped herself. The lines in her face, mournful and perhaps even noble when she was calm, curled and stretched, transforming her into something terrifying and ancient-seeming, like an oracle. "This became your fight when you married my daughter. When you put her in that hovel. When you decided to have babies with her." She punctuated each sentence, jabbing her finger in the air at Stephen. "Now's your chance to step up and be a husband to her for once."

Stephen looked unruffled, but he turned to Libby and said, "Is this what you want?"

She wasn't sure. Before he'd gotten home, she'd thought about ways to dissuade him, to prove to him that what had happened was nothing to her: scary and humiliating, yes, but surmountable. As good as forgotten. She'd been prepared to make that argument, but she'd also expected for Stephen to be worried and maybe even raging, for him to need convincing. And what she saw in him now couldn't even rightly be called irritation.

"I think," she said, "that's up to you."

He sat for another moment, drumming his fingers on the veneered surface of the kitchen table. "All right, then," he said, and he was gone, leaving Libby and her mother to each other. Libby watched him drive away, watched the black trail of exhaust from his truck dissipate. She realized, once there was no trace of him, that he hadn't even asked her if she was okay. Hadn't even seemed to care.

She felt her mother's touch on her lower back—still familiar and warm, still the hand that she trusted more than anyone else's, despite the years and the varied disappointments. "He won't be gone long," her mother told her. "He'll be home before you know it."

Libby nodded.

Stephen came back an hour later with his right arm pulled to his chest. He passed Libby in her parents' den where she sat, pretending to watch TV, and went straight to the kitchen; she followed. She found him rummaging around in the lower cabinets, where her mother stored her pots and pans, and after a moment he stood, metal mixing bowl in his left hand. He dropped it into the sink with a clatter and started running water.

"What happened?" Libby said. "Are you okay?"

He took some ice cube trays out of the freezer, still using that left hand—his stupid hand, he called it—and closed the freezer door with his shoulder. Awkwardly, he started shaking ice cubes into the bowl of water, having to stop now and again to bang the tray against the countertop to loosen a stubborn cube. When this operation appeared to be complete, he shut off the faucet with two hard turns of the handle, picked up the bowl with his good hand, and walked over to the kitchen table, sloshing water onto the floor as he went. At the table he sat, then plunged his right hand into the bowl, face pained and relieved all at once. A tendril of gauzy red stained the water—thin and even delicate at first, dismissible; but the bowl was soon full of it, water now red and cheerful like the boys' cherry Flav-R-Aid.

"Stephen," Libby said softly.

His eyes were pinched shut. He was ignoring her.

"Stephen, let me see your hand."

He looked at her, then lifted his hand out of the water. Maybe it was the shock of the ice, but his skin was bright pink: a sick, infected color, punctuated here and there with blotches of white flesh. His knuckles were split in two places—she could see the separations in his skin from a few feet away, the raw meat like half-closed eyelids—and the whole hand was puffy and engorged.

"It's broke," he said. He tried to curl his fingers and moaned—a chilling sound, too primal for this sunlit kitchen—then put his hand back into the bowl. His face was wet: maybe with sweat, maybe with tears. Probably both.

"Hold on," Libby said. She went to the bathroom and grabbed the aspirin out of the medicine cabinet, then poured Stephen a glass of water from the tap. She pried the bottle open and shook out two pills; paused, considered, then shook out two more. Back in the kitchen, she held these to Stephen's mouth, and he let her place them on his tongue. Then she fed him some water, holding her hand under his chin to catch any dribble, just like she did with Sean.

"You need to go to the hospital," she said.

"No shit."

"I'll drive you."

He held up his good hand—*Not just yet*, it seemed to say—and put his forehead against the table.

Libby stroked his neck. His hair, in need of a cut, curled slightly at the nape: damp, dark with the dampness. The skin there was almost cold. "What happened?" she said.

"I'm not going to be able to work," Stephen told her. "Not for a while, anyhow. I've done busted up my shifting hand. I had to drive here the whole way in second."

"That doesn't matter," she said.

He laughed: forced, cheerless. "On the phone," he said. "Your mother. She was telling me that we need to move into town where it's safe, where she can keep a better eye on you and the boys. You tell her to say that?"

"Of course not," Libby told him.

"What is it you want, then?"

"I want you," Libby said. "I want you here, so we can be a

family. You know that Daddy could get you on at the plant. He still has friends there."

"Christ almighty," Stephen said. "I always told myself that's the last thing I'd end up doing. Do you know what you're asking of me?"

She looked at her hands.

"I'm not going to be able to work right now," he said again. "I guess you got me here. I guess you got what you wanted."

Libby started to cry, the second time that day. She hadn't been this unstable since the first weeks after Sean was born, and even then, dark as things could seem, she'd known that her tears were chemical as well as emotional, and that recognition had been a comfort.

"You think I planned this?" she said. "You think this was all just some kind of trick to get you home?"

"No," he said tiredly. He sounded sorry. "I don't think that about you, Lib."

"Well, there's that much, anyhow," she said, and for a while, they just sat. The refrigerator kicked on, vibrating the floor. *As the World Turns* played in the other room.

"I guess we ought to get me patched up," Stephen said finally. He lifted a hip and leaned in his chair so that he could pull his car keys out of his pants pocket. He pushed them across the table at her, the scrape of metal against laminate high and desperate in the quiet of the kitchen.

In the truck, Stephen was motionless, slumped against the passenger-side door, so Libby assumed that he'd passed out. She was so focused on driving—shifting gears, remembering to tap the drum brakes early and steadily so she wouldn't simply coast through a stoplight—that Stephen's last comment on the matter startled her, almost froze her in place.

"He was just a kid," he said: the thing that would haunt her, maybe both of them, for the rest of their marriage, a statement so mired in blame and disgust that Libby had no response to it. The hospital was just ahead, and she'd have to get the truck up a steep incline to pull into the emergency room bay. She felt the engine wanting to stall, so she downshifted, her husband's words persistent and insidious, like a virus. In the years to come, when she wasn't dreaming about the boy—and she did, she *did*; even when she seemed in the daytime to have forgotten, she remembered in her nightmares—she was reliving this moment in the truck.

She opened her mouth to ask Stephen what had happened—what he'd done—realizing that he'd never told her. But looking at him, seeing the guilt and pain on his face and not being able to distinguish between them, she discovered that she no longer wanted to know.

"Just a damn kid," he repeated.

3.

Once, about two years after that nightmare day, they were out riding. It was a Sunday afternoon and the boys were in the backseat of their new-used Olds wagon, making a mess of the Dilly bars they'd gotten at Dairy Queen. Stephen, who was driving, kept his milk shake between his legs and drank between shifting. Libby sipped on a Diet-Rite.

He liked these drives. "Let's go see the country," he'd say, and they would tear out on one of the highways that crossed Roma like wheel spokes: toward Olmstead, toward Elkton, no destination in mind, just the near-endless stretch of gorgeous, yellow-green tobacco and sweet corn—its mild muskiness, a summer smell—on either side of them. Stephen would tune the radio in to the Nashville New Classics station for as long as they could pick it up, because the boys, Jaime especially, loved singing along with the stuff that made Libby think of girlhood: Van Morrison, Lovin' Spoonful, Paul Anka, the Carpenters, whom Stephen claimed to despise. On this day, "Kentucky Woman" came on, the original Neil Diamond version, and Stephen started singing along like he had when they were dating, looking back and forth between Libby and the road: *"If she get to know you, she goin' to own you. . . ."*

There were moments like that between them, despite everything. The wind through the open window, blowing her long hair into tangles, and Stephen's hand on her knee as soon as they were rolling along in fifth gear. She put hers on top of his so that the scars were no longer visible, though she could feel the protrusion of one long-ago healed knuckle.

In another few minutes they came upon a farmhouse with a sign out front: PUPPIES. FREE.

"Stephen," she said. "We should stop here."

"Yeah?" He looked cautiously pleased.

Jaime, who had just finished first grade, started to hoot. "Puppies! Yeah, puppies!" And then Sean, who couldn't read yet but who looked up to his brother, chimed in: "Puppies, Daddy. C'mon, stop, Daddy."

Stephen looked over his shoulder at the boys, and they quieted. "We're just gonna look," he said, but Libby recognized the subtle note of excitement in his voice. Jaime went back to work on the last of his ice cream, a mime of solemnity that Sean mimicked.

They turned in to the long gravel drive and parked near the house, Stephen backing and positioning, as always, so that he could drive straight out on the return trip. "Wait here," he told Libby, and he trotted around the corner of the house, to the side door, and out of her sight. She shifted in her seat so she could see the boys, lifting her eyebrows and smiling at them, the secret shorthand she used whenever it seemed that Daddy would treat them all: when he pulled into Ponderosa instead of Wendy's on Saturday afternoons; when he came home from work with a VCR, rented, and some cassettes from Burgess Video—a Disney cartoon, then a horror movie or comedy to watch after the boys went to bed. She wasn't without dread when Stephen's impulse to give surfaced. There was always the threat of an hour spent cursing as he tried to figure out how to connect the Betamax to their TV, and a meal out could easily sour if the waitress didn't refill his sweet tea fast enough or if his steak was too pink in the center. But it was a faint dread, and Libby always felt a little like a traitor when her worries proved groundless, which was usually the case. Then she would remember that afternoon in her mother's sunny kitchen, the sight of Stephen's battered right hand, and everything that followed: his new job at the factory, which she knew he hated; the rental house in Chapman, where their windows looked out on a line of near-identical, ranch-style homes instead of the soft hills of briar and weeds that Stephen had inexplicably loved. She wondered what was harder: making sacrifices, or being the person to demand them. She was happier in town than she'd been out at the homeplace, but it was a transient happiness—happiness on loan, happiness with interest.

Stephen came out a few minutes later with an old man in bib overalls. They paused, and Stephen waved to her, a beckoning gesture.

She cranked the window down and stuck out her head. "Boys, too?" she yelled.

He gave an exaggerated nod.

"C'mon, kiddos," she said, and Jaime and Sean scurried out of the car in a hurry, hushed in their excitement.

"Got me a couple," the farmer was saying to Stephen as she approached, the two of them already starting toward a dilapidated barn out back. She was wearing her good shoes, a pair of navy blue leather pumps with sensibly low heels, and she had to goose-step through the foot-high sweet grass, already dreading the chigger bites—hadn't missed those a bit—that she'd find that night when she took her bath. Jaime and Sean ran off ahead, pushing each other a few times, yelling and laughing as they went. "Good, loving dogs," the farmer was adding. "Especially the mother of these pups. I ain't never had a better hunting dog. She's steady as they come, got a real sweet temperament, too."

"You know what the father was?" Stephen said.

"Hard to tell for sure when they're this small," the farmer said. "But the folks down the road have a yellow Lab they let loose most of the time, and I'm pretty sure he's the one. When she went into heat I tried to keep the barn door shut and barred, but that ain't much deterrent if an old boy's stirred up enough." He elbowed Stephen and grinned. "Know what I mean?"

Stephen glanced back at Libby: apologetic or something else, she wasn't sure. "Yeah," he said.

They got to the barn, and the farmer led them to an old horse stall. The mother, a beagle with dark stains running from her eyes to her snout, lifted her head when they approached. She was lying in a dark corner, and the puppies—seven or eight of them, hard to tell—were a few feet away, climbing atop one another, rolling on their backs, soft round bellies exposed. The mother considered the new visitors for a moment and then dropped her head again, bone-tired and disinterested.

"Cute little bastards," the farmer said. "I'll keep one or two of them, I reckon. Labs are a nice breed."

"Can I pick one up?" Jaime asked Libby.

"And me? And me?" Sean echoed.

"I don't know," she said, looking at the old man. "Is it safe this early?"

The farmer nodded. "They're already weaned." He went into the stall and scooped a puppy from the top of the pile, handling it with a gentle sort of carelessness that Libby supposed was the product of working with animals every day. He went to Jaime. "Let her sit on your wrist," he said, demonstrating, "and cuddle her with your other hand. Thisaway."

Jaime took the dog and did as he was told, then looked at Libby with big and grateful eyes. He leaned over and kissed the puppy's nose, a show of tenderness that touched her but didn't surprise her. He was a good boy. A good son.

"She's warm," he said softly.

"Now me," Sean said, whisper-yelling, and the farmer gave him a puppy too. They held their dogs, better behaved than Libby could remember, almost reverent. She knew that the feeding and walking responsibilities would fall on her shoulders—as she was all too aware, she was a woman among boys—but that seemed okay right then. Because this was something that she could give Stephen: a little bit of what he'd left behind. She watched him watching their sons, noticing his nervousness when Sean shifted the puppy to his other arm, his contained delight when the other puppy started licking Jaime's chin.

She would have taken his hand if they were standing closer together.

"What do you think?" the farmer said.

"They're precious," Libby told him. She hunched down and stroked the back of one of the puppies on the floor, this one the runt of the litter. It was an even buff color with white on its muzzle, like a beard. She picked it up, marveling, as her son had, at its extraordinary warmth—so much heat in such a small body; so much life still to burn. "Stephen," she said. "Look at this one."

"Oh yeah," he said, taking it. "Looks funny. Like a little bandit."

"That'd be a good name for him," the farmer offered.

The boys stopped stroking their puppies and looked at the runt in Stephen's hands, and Libby saw the change in their faces from hopeful to sure. She was feeling it herself: certain that this was the dog, *their* dog.

"Nothing wrong with a runt," the farmer said. "He'd make a good town dog."

"Why do you say that?" Stephen said.

The old man shrugged. "Smaller, you know. Not so likely to wander off."

"How did you know we were from town?"

The old man shrugged again.

Stephen sighed and put down the puppy. He looked from Libby to the boys and back, as if seeing them for the first time, and rubbed his mouth. "I guess we're wasting your time. We gotta be getting home."

Sean started to cry. "Why? Why can't we have it?"

Jaime put his own dog down, gingerly, his face sad but not devastated—not surprised at all, it seemed to Libby. And she realized then that Jaime knew something about Stephen that she didn't, that he had an insight into his father's capacity for pettiness that she herself had dismissed. Or had not allowed herself to recognize.

Stephen shook the farmer's hand. "I work with some folks who might be interested. I'll let them know you're out here."

"You sure you don't want to bring the little'un home? I think your boys took to him."

"No sir," Stephen said—more roughly this time—and the old man nodded. "Sean, put that pup down."

Sean shook his head, tears streaming down his face, and clutched the dog.

"Put that dog down or I'll whip your ass. I'm not putting up with any tantrums."

He did as he was told this time, moaning and hiccuping like his heart was going to break. He ran outside, his wail high-pitched and grating, even to Libby's ears. She could picture him out there, rolling around in a thick of weeds, thrashing his arms and legs and getting dirt stains on his good pair of slacks. She'd have to check his head for ticks when they got home. "I'm sorry," she said to the old man. "He's a handful."

"Most of them are," the farmer said.

Stephen and Jaime went on to the car, so similar in their silence. Libby loved the boys equally, but she'd always seen Jaime as hers, as the child who most reflected her own soul. Sean, like Stephen, was lighter-haired and nearly as tall as Jaime already; he shared his father's interest in basketball and baseball, he shared his father's moods: the turns from jolly to morose, the strange combination of neediness and distance. But Stephen and Jaime were walking to the wagon now, almost in step, and Libby was struck by how they seemed to oddly mirror one another: Jaime shorter and dark-haired—not chubby, but already having to wear the Sears and Roebuck Huskies with the roomier bottom—like a noontime shadow next to his tall, lean father. She felt that she was losing him, losing them both.

Behind her, Sean screamed: a loud, controlled wail, carefully timed. As always, Stephen had left him to her.

She crossed the yard, feeling the knee-high weeds make grabs at her hose, feeling her patience pulled tight and worn thin. She found Sean close to the cornfield, almost nesting in the patch of grass he'd hollowed out with his thrashing. His pants were stained a greenish-yellow at the knees. When their eyes met, his cries stopped and his face went slack and polite: his *Good day, ma'am* face, his goddamned *Care for a spot of tea?* face. Libby didn't take pride in much—her life choices or her body or her decorating tastes or her cooking abilities; any of it—but she was smug in her abilities to mother, was proud that she'd never spanked her children with a desire to hurt or frighten. But the look on Sean's face was too much. She grabbed him by his armpit and yanked him to his feet, turned him so that he was facing the cornfield, and started smacking his bottom, angling her strikes with a precision born of instinct, knowing just how to make it sting, to set that little ass of his on fire. She watched the corn quiver in a low breeze and stopped only when her son's crying lost that infuriating note of calculation. When she heard his pain and nothing else.

She looked at her hand. It was sore, bright red.

"Dammit, Sean," she said. "You know I hate spanking you." It felt, for the first time, like a lie.

He was crying again, silently this time. His nostrils were clotted with mucus, and she wiped his face with the hem of his shirt, then brushed his bangs over to one side and kissed his forehead. He slumped against her chest, locking his arms around her neck, and she stroked his back.

"I just wanted it," he whispered into her ear, breath wet and hot.

"I know," she said. She picked him up though he was much too big to be carried—he rested on her hip, butt bone sharp and painful, heels of his shoes hooked into the small of her back—and walked slowly to the car.

That night, once the boys were cleaned up and put to bed, Libby bathed quickly at the sink using a washcloth and some soapy water: "a Mexican shower," Stephen always called it, but it was the only kind she had time for most days. Then she slipped into her long nightgown—quickly, because she hated the sight of what motherhood had done to her figure. Sean had been born by cesarean, and the scar ran down her middle from belly button to pubic hair: hard and elastic, like a rubber band, crossed with a web of thin, gossamer stretch marks. She wondered if the boy, the stranger from the homeplace, had noticed this wreckage.

"Shut the light off," Stephen said when she climbed into bed.

She turned the knob on her bedside lamp.

Stephen didn't take the nightgown off when he had sex with her a few moments later—just bunched it up around her hips, so that she was as aware of the uncomfortable ridge of cloth beneath her as she was her husband's efforts. When he finished, they took turns in the bathroom: first Stephen—the flush, the running water, the creak of the medicine cabinet, all so familiar to Libby that they might have been choreographed—and then her. She washed again, dampening and reusing the same cloth from earlier, and then she checked the trash to make sure Stephen had covered the condom so that the boys wouldn't see it the next morning. He hadn't. He hardly ever remembered to.

When she returned to bed, Stephen kissed her—closed-lipped, on the mouth—and rolled to his side, facing the window.

"What was that about today?" she said softly. "Those dogs."

He shrugged, the muscles in his back clenching and releasing. "Thought it might be fun to have a look. I didn't know the boys were going to throw such a hissy fit."

She could see that he meant for this to end the conversation—he'd pulled the blanket up over his ear—but Libby cleared her throat and adjusted her gown, deliberately jostling the bed. She tried another comment, careful, negotiating his pet peeves and weaknesses the way she moved through her house during a power outage: knowing the landscape but still hesitant, all too aware that a bold step forward could send her crashing. "I could swear that you were ready to bring that little one home with us," she said finally. "You took to each other."

He shifted to his back. "I mean, I had a moment when I wondered. But town's no place for a dog. We don't even have a fenced-in backyard." He paused. "I don't know if I can be responsible for another helpless thing, Libby. That's the long and short of it."

"He could've been a house dog."

"Enough, Libby." He looked at her. "You want the house smelling? Feel like picking dog turds out of the carpet? All right, then. Drop it."

"You knew what you were doing," she told him. Certain, now, and afraid to say so, sure, but also so convinced of this fact that even his anger—never violent but always wounding, sometimes spiteful enough to make her believe a slap would have been better—even that couldn't deter her. "You put us through that just to make a point."

"What point is that?"

"That I ruined your life," Libby said. "That I dragged you to town and took your little bit of freedom away."

He laughed. "That's real good, hon. You've been watching too many soap operas."

"I don't watch soap operas," she said. "I don't sit around this house all day. I raise your sons and I try to give you a good home. I do the best I know how to."

"Well, so do I," Stephen said.

She listened for the boys down the hall, hoping one would cry out—Sean, whom she could count on to have a bad dream after a spanking, or Jaime, asking in his grateful way for a glass of water. But they were silent for once.

"You think that day was my fault." She said this quietly, almost hoping that he wouldn't hear her. Not wanting to know what his response would be.

"If you believe that," he said, "you don't know me at all."

She lay flat on her back, body rigid, not sure if she should apologize or go sleep on the couch. She didn't know what to believe anymore. She didn't know what to say.

Stephen ended up making the decision for her. He stood, grabbed his pillow and the throw blanket at the foot of the bed. He waited for a moment at their bedroom door, and Libby thought that he was going to tell her something, that he was only trying to find the right words.

In the end, he just walked away.

4.

Six months after Jaime's last overnight stay—the weekend when he'd come to sort through the old photos, and twenty years' worth of memories had been cast out on Libby's front curb—he called Libby to tell her about the baby.

"I've been wanting to tell you for a month now," he said, and Libby's grip on the handset tightened. She waited for some emotion to kick in, like the jubilation she saw at the office when a woman emerged from Dr. Tait's office, the news she'd received clear on her face: *You're pregnant.* Or, more fittingly, the joy of the person rising to meet that woman in the waiting area: the husband, the best friend, the mother. The happy ones, she'd noticed, always had someone waiting for them. But she didn't feel jubilation, and she couldn't rightly identify what it was she was experiencing at that moment.

"Sweetheart," she said. "That's fantastic."

She heard his shaky inhale. "Thanks. I mean, I'm still getting used to the idea. We weren't trying to get pregnant, but we weren't trying not to, either."

"Things will work out," she said, and wondered if this was the only real lie she'd ever told him. She had never been the kind of mother to offer her sons empty reassurances or sentiments, and she knew all too well that things *didn't* have to work out. But warning him wouldn't do any good. "You've got a good heart. That's the most important thing."

"And Ashley," Jaime said, sounding younger and hungrier for her approval than she'd heard him in a long time. "Ashley will be a good mom."

"Ashley, too."

She went to her bedroom, where the two photos she'd kept—the one of her wedding day and the one of Stephen at the Biltmore estate—were stored in her dresser drawer, under a pouch of cedar chips and some worn gloves. She picked up Stephen's picture while Jaime talked about his plans for the baby's room and for preschools and the time Ashley was going to take off from her job: details that had nothing to do with raising a child when it came down to brass tacks, but she supposed that he'd learn better with time. While Jaime rambled, she studied the photo, startled by how young Stephen looked in it. She'd seen him twice since learning of his move back to the homeplace: once at Wal-Mart, once at the post office. Both times they'd offered each other awkward acknowledgments, then made quick escapes. Roma was too small to avoid someone indefinitely, of course, but she and Stephen had managed surprisingly well since the day he walked out: they shared a pew at Jaime's wedding, crossed paths at some of Sean's ball games, occasionally saw each other at the grocery. But little else. Some people, she'd noticed, went on and on looking like they always had, and then boom: they were old. Like Robert Redford. Sometime between their last strained conversation and recently, Stephen had turned that corner from middle age to—well—something else. His shoulders were stooped, and he had a paunch, probably from drinking beer. His blond hair was thinning. He would never again be the man she'd married, or even the man who'd left her and the boys. It seemed there should be some happiness to be drawn from such a realization, but instead Libby was struck with finality. She had no claims on him anymore.

"—but you were right, is what I'm trying to say."

"What?"

"I'm going to call him tonight," Jaime said, and Libby understood. No recap necessary.

"That's the best thing," she told him, and wanted to take it back immediately. Jaime had called her a martyr before—*I'm tired of this martyr shit of yours*, that's what he'd said—but *pathetic* would have been closer to home. She was tired of trying to do the right thing. You could work hard all your life and think that you were managing to be a decent person, and all you got in the end was taken advantage of. All you got was grief. Stephen had cheated on her and divorced her, and now he had a new wife, young enough to tend to him once he could no longer tend to himself. Why did Stephen need his own children? He had married himself an insurance policy.

"I love you, Mom," Jaime was saying. Libby could hear his wife, Ashley, calling in the background. A good girl—good for Jaime, anyway—but headstrong, and Libby hated phoning over to their house for fear that she'd be the one to pick up. Her voice, never less than polite, was always edged with something flintier: *He's your son, not your husband. Get your own life. Let us be.* Before she'd seen her ex-husband's new wife in person, Libby had pictured her as an older version of Ashley: broader-hipped and not so pretty, but wearing that same combination of sympathy and disgust on her face. Libby didn't want to know what this said about her, the ease of the comparison.

"I love you, too," she said finally. "I'm proud of you. You and Ashley both."

When she hung up, she realized that she'd already resolved to get a look at Stephen's new home, which almost surely had to be complete—and perhaps even occupied. She was motivated by nothing nobler than curiosity, and she admitted to herself that the curiosity was perhaps a sour kind: the sort that expected much and hoped for little. Stephen didn't deserve a relationship with Jaime's baby, and he didn't deserve happiness on that plot of land she so hated—or any happiness at all.

The last time Libby had been to the homeplace was ten years ago, at least—Jaime had just gotten his driver's license, so that seemed right. She, Stephen, and the boys had driven out there to strip the old house clean, because Stephen's folks had decided to tear it down, finally. No one had lived there since Stephen and Libby moved out, and Libby doubted that Stephen's folks even went to check on it very often. She was right, of course. They'd found a rat's nest in the kitchen cabinets, a dead raccoon in the bedroom that she and Stephen had shared. The boards had smelled damp and moldy, and the window glass—what hadn't been busted out by storms or joyriders—was caked thick with filth. It had looked like a haunted house, which was appropriate, because that was what it had felt like, too. The only thing that had kept Libby from grabbing Stephen's keys and tearing off back to town was the knowledge that the old shack would be destroyed, that she could even have a hand in that destruction.

Stephen's father had a flatbed and a tractor, and they'd started dismantling early, before the sun had even risen. The appliances came out first—a refrigerator that looked like an artifact from another age, the wood-burning stove Libby had hated so much—then the cabinetry, the bathroom vanity, a shoddy built-in bookshelf. They'd torn up the stained asbestos kitchen tile, some scraggly carpet that had been laid down in the bedroom. Stephen had salvaged the plank floor from the living room, making a neat pile in the driveway. He hadn't seemed to remember what happened to Libby on that floor. Or else he hadn't acted like he did. He'd chatted with the boys as they worked: talked about growing up at the house, asked them what they remembered about their own time there. They'd swapped stories about swinging across the ravine, about catching tadpoles in the creek bed. Stephen had rested at one point on the front porch, hand propped against one of the pillars holding the roof aloft, and gazed at the house like it was an old, loyal friend.

Finally, they'd gone at the structure with sledgehammers. What they couldn't cart off to the dump they'd set on fire. By midnight the house had been completely dismantled: just a block foundation and a pile of ashes to prove it ever existed. And Libby had been naive enough to think, *It's over,* and *I'll never have to see this place again.* To think that she'd exorcised some old ghosts, once and for all.

And now she was back, parked just down the highway from that plot of land that she'd hated almost from the first moment she set foot on it. Downhill and around a turn in the road, just out of sight from the south- and east-facing windows. She didn't know if she wanted to see Stephen—she felt almost certain that she did not—but she wanted a look at that house of his. She was hungry for clues about his new life, even though she knew she'd probably return home with as much jealousy and regret as satisfaction. This seemed even more likely when Libby realized, shutting off the engine, that this was where the boy, the stranger, had parked; she knew because the sheriff had told her later on, explaining that he'd found the car pulled off on the shoulder close to where Brett Riley's horse fence ran out. Battery dead as a doornail, just like the boy had told her it was. The car had been impounded when he hadn't been able to produce a clean title, then junked. Libby wouldn't be surprised if that money had gone right into Sheriff Robeson's pocket, but she didn't hold it against him; he'd stood up for her when she'd needed a man to stand up for her. He'd done it not just because it was his job to, but because it was the right thing.

Libby left her car, walked a few paces toward the homeplace, then looked behind her. Just a car—*her* car—parked on a road that was almost sticky with a fresh black layer of hot-top. Not a memory, and certainly nothing that should have been stirring this much feeling up inside of her: an anxiety, a low terror so familiar it was as if she'd dreamed this very moment the night before. Maybe she had. She didn't believe in omens or fate, and she didn't believe in the magic of her girlhood: soulmates and lucky charms and wished-upon stars, a hundred little superstitions that had seemed not only possible, but *necessary*—because what was a life without them? She'd lost those notions long back, in the little house in the middle of nowhere. If The Big Lonely had sounded to her like a Western, a Jimmy Stewart movie, then this other sounded like a fairy tale: the dark kind, like Hansel and Gretel. A lonely house. A lonely girl. One day a stranger comes knocking, and everything changes, everything goes straight to hell. No happily ever after for Libby.

She hated herself for thinking like this. For being like this.

She didn't believe in ghosts and she wasn't certain she believed in God, but she couldn't deny this moment and what it was doing to her. She wasn't just walking back to the old homeplace, she was walking back in time, and when she rounded the corner and those trees that formed a wind-block, she would see herself: a twenty-six-year-old girl in blue jeans and a Roma High School T-shirt, standing in the backyard and calling her boys in to lunch. Too smart to appreciate the hand she'd been dealt. Too stupid to know how to fix it.

Boys! Come eat!

And then Libby rounded that last turn, and her first glimpse of Stephen's place arrested her. This wasn't the homeplace, it was a *home:* two stories with a garage, a paved drive, a sidewalk lined in flower beds. The design was simple and squared off—nothing fancy—but the walls had been sided in a shingle style that looked woodsy and cozy, and the window trims were painted in a clean brick red, a color Libby had admired on other homes. She could see a hummingbird feeder dangling from a tree branch. A garden hose coiled neatly around a spindle, hugging the side of the house like those snails her boys had always picked at as little ones. She saw a Kubota tractor, a bit larger than a riding mower, parked just outside the garage as if it had been used recently; and indeed, the yard was clipped close almost to the wood line out back, not manicured, but clean and pleasant. Plenty of space to put up a swing set—the quality wood kind and not those flimsy metal things that toppled over. Plenty of room for children. Would her grandchild someday play in that yard? The thought was almost unbearable.

She was standing at the turn in the road, admiring Stephen's house, when she heard the cheery, frantic jingle of what would soon become clear were dog tags; the animal was on top of her, pushing her to the cement, before she could even associate the sound with her sudden and terrific loss of breath. It had knocked the wind clear out of her.

The ache in her back was immediate and strong, but not excruciating. Nothing broken. She opened her eyes, wheezing, and saw the dog looking down at her. Its eyes were gold-rimmed and ancient-seeming, like a lion's, and it was huge, black—a German shepherd, maybe—one of those dogs so surreally large that they drew comparisons to horses. It was panting, exposing a set of impressively clean and sharp eyeteeth, but she supposed that it would have gone to work on her already if it was the biting kind. She pulled herself to a sit and the dog backed away a few steps: a polite gesture, she thought, rather than a nervous one. It sat at the side of the road, dignified as a statesman. She could smell its breath from this distance: sour, grassy, but not exactly unpleasant. This was a dog that matched its house. They both belonged to a simple and ordered world, and Libby realized with an ache that Stephen had been right all along. Could this have been her life if she'd only waited for it?

"Moses!" The call was tinny and distant, but Libby immediately recognized the voice as Stephen's. "Moses, *daun!*"

The dog, this Moses, lay down, forepaws extended toward Libby. He seemed calm, strangely intelligent, like he was thinking about speaking but only trying to find the right words first. She couldn't remember when she'd been this close to such a big dog; he seemed like an optical illusion.

"Moses," Stephen was calling again as he approached. He was running, and when he saw Libby sitting in the gravel of the shoulder, he stopped. For a second he leaned over with his hands on his knees, breathing heavily, and then he pulled to a stand all at once, the expression on his face impossible to interpret. His chest was still moving, choppy with short breaths, but she could see him trying to calm himself, to regain composure. He took one last exaggerated breath, swallowed, and extended his hand. "*Auf*, Moses." The dog stood. "*Hier.*" And the dog came to him.

"Libby." His voice was not so different from the one he'd used to address his dog. He put out his hand. "Let me help you up."

She allowed it, then put a few feet between them, brushing the road grit from her bottom. She felt humiliated. Caught. Once, when she was a teenager, her crush, Randy Barber, had turned his head just in time to see her staring at him. He'd frowned, then laughed: *Take a picture,* he'd said, that old standard. *It'll last longer.*

"Nice dog," she said now.

Stephen stroked the animal's back, which reached almost to his waist. "He still has a lot of puppy in him. You never see a body out this way on foot, or at least not much. It threw him."

"It threw *me,*" Libby said.

"Shepherds are police dogs." He said this proudly. "His impulse is going to be to protect his territory. Disable, then assess the situation. That's what the trainer told me. He didn't hurt you, did he?"

"I guess not," she said. "He knocked the wind out of me."

He touched the dog's head absently, more nervous than affectionate. "What are you doing out here, anyway?" He shaded his eyes and looked down the road: first one way, then the other. "How the hell did you get here?"

She was blushing now—she could feel it. "I parked around the turn," she told him.

"Oh." He looked that way and nodded, as if this answer made sense. "Sure."

"I guess I was coming to see you," she told him, not knowing for sure if it was a lie. "I mean, maybe. Shit. I hadn't decided yet."

"Here I am," Stephen told her.

"Yeah," Libby said.

He cleared his throat, kicked at some loose gravel. His shoes were leather, polished: nice.

"Christ, Stephen," Libby said finally. "Did you win the lottery or something?"

Now he reddened, looking over his shoulder and back, then shrugged. His hands were stuffed into the pockets of his blue jeans, a tight fit, and his fists caught as he lifted his shoulders. "We're doing all right. I took over the head security position at A&L's when Jim Lawson retired last fall. And Lottie's kitchen manager now at Shoney's."

"Good for her," Libby said.

His eyebrows drew together, an expression so ghastly familiar that it gave Libby a chill. She hadn't seen that look in a while. "It is, actually," he said. "So don't start in on me."

Libby sighed and thought about walking away. It had been so easy to forget this part of their marriage: the suspicion and bad feeling and hard words.

"I didn't mean anything by it," she said.

Stephen scratched his neck, glanced at the house, shrugged. "Do you want to come up? I don't guess there's any good reason for standing here in the road."

The offer was tempting. She knew the accommodations a person made to be half of a couple, the thousands of tiny ways you gave in or simply gave up, only to realize in the end that you'd both sacrificed yourselves to a life neither desired. She remembered how quickly she'd lost interest in sewing after settling down with Stephen, even though she'd had a real talent for it, because he didn't see the sense in spending good money on fabric and thread when you could buy something already put together for you at the new Wal-Mart; and how he'd hated the ruffled curtains she'd made for her hope chest during her engagement, said they looked like something Scarlett O'Hara would wear under her hoop skirt; and how he didn't like her reading romance novels at night when he was watching his programs, because it seemed to him that a woman ought to share her husband's interests, especially when that husband was gone for days at a stretch. And on and on. But Libby had made her own demands, and it startled her to think just how many: she'd guilt-tripped him into giving up his Saturday poker game at the American Legion, saying it was a shame to fritter away good money—even nickels and pennies—when he had two little boys to feed. She'd refused to put his favorite childhood rocker in their living room back at the homeplace, and Libby could not even rightly recall *why* now, except that the thing was old and a bit splintered, and she thought it made the place look white-trash. As if the rocker alone could accomplish that. In the end, she'd made Stephen give up everything—his house, this piece of land, his work—and she still felt justified, but she felt guilty, too. Because Stephen should have been motivated to give all of that up after the horrible thing that had happened to her, should have done it out of love. And out of love, Libby shouldn't have let him.

They had been so young, she thought now.

"No," Libby said. "I can't really stay."

"I'll walk you to your car, then."

Libby nodded her assent, and Stephen made a clicking sound in the back of his throat. "Moses, *fuus.*" They started walking to Libby's car, dog trailing.

"Jaime just called me," Stephen said.

"Yeah. I thought he might."

"Is that what brought you here?"

"Probably," Libby said, wondering if it was fair for her to pin a complicated set of motivations to what had amounted to little more than curiosity and a bit of meanness. "It's been on my mind," she added, and that was true enough.

The stroll downhill was easy, the air warm. Libby liked having Stephen beside her, matching her stride. She missed it. She missed the thoughtful look he got sometimes, when he was putting the words together in his head before saying them out loud. Like now. So few people thought about what they might say before saying it, but Libby had been lucky enough to know two who did: Stephen, at least some of the time, and her mother. Every time.

"I got the impression you had something to do with it," he told her. "Him calling, I mean. And I thank you. I don't know that I deserve it, but I'll take it. I've done a lot of things wrong in my life, but I love my sons."

"Jaime knows that."

"I guess he does." They had reached the car. "I mean, I realize where I came up short. You know? Do you believe me?"

"You didn't come up short," Libby said, wondering why it was so much easier to forgive a person—to see the good in him—when he was ready to claim fault. "I asked a lot of you. I demanded it. Mother demanded it."

"I always had a choice in the matter," he said, but Libby covered her face and shook her head, breathless, feeling for the first time the full weight of her debt to him. In the twenty-four years since that day, Libby had felt guilt and she'd even felt gratitude, but she'd never gotten past the resentment of having had to force his hand. She'd never once acknowledged, to him or to herself, the magnitude of what he'd done for her sake.

"Stephen," she said. "Stephen, I'm sorry."

"Don't say that," he told her, his voice thick, but she kept repeating it, and she might have gone on that way until he forgave her, until he touched her, if he hadn't finally said in that old, sharp tone of disgust, "Goddammit, Libby."

She stopped, shamed and angry.

"I never told you," he said.

"Never told me what?"

"About what happened that afternoon you got attacked."

He was just a kid, Stephen had said after it happened: words that she still carried around. The things the boy had done, the things she'd tried to do to stop him—they didn't matter. In the end, he'd been a teenager who didn't know any better. And she'd wished the worst on him. Then and later, when distance gave her time to reflect, to be creative, the fantasy she had most often was of grabbing a knife in those precious seconds away from him in the kitchen; instead of giving him water, she would have given him what he had coming, would have done it over and over until there was nothing left to rise up and hurt her. But thinking that way was bittersweet, because it could never be true, so she imagined sometimes what could have happened to him since that afternoon. She knew a few things for sure—that he dropped out of high school and moved down to Tennessee, maybe to work at a factory. This according to Sheriff Robeson. That his people, the Shivelys, still lived out Lewisburg way. "Bunch of no-accounts," Robeson had said, telling her that they festered up over there like a rash, like a crop of toadstools, like anything that thrives in filth and decay and wet heat. And that was it. So imagining the interim was easy: run-ins with the police, prison time, all the things that could happen to a man in prison. Car accidents. Disfigurements. A thousand tortures, a thousand hard fates. She liked the idea of it all, though she wasn't so good at picturing the particulars. In fact, just imagining what Stephen had done to him—the force it must have taken to rupture his hand the way he did—was enough to make her feel cold.

"Nothing happened," Stephen said now.

She looked at him, not understanding. She looked at his dog, a creature of far too much reserve and composure to be a mere animal.

"Libby, I'm telling you: I didn't do anything to him."

She felt light-headed and leaned against her car.

"Your hand," she said. She'd taken him to the emergency room, seen the X-rays. She'd filled out the insurance claim forms, for Christ's sake.

Stephen put the hand out in front of him, opening it and closing it in that habit he'd had during the months that it was healing. The doctor at the hospital had given him a crude exerciser: two pieces of interlocking plastic with finger holds, strapped together with rubber bands. He would work with it after dinner at night, in his easy chair, while the evening news played on TV. Clench and release. Tendons on his forearms standing at attention, then disappearing back into flesh. He'd complained of pain when the weather turned damp, saying to her as they lay in bed that it felt like a barbed ice cube was stuck between his knuckles. On those nights she'd fetched him aspirin. Water. She'd forged his signature on checks and documents when his hand was too stiff to grasp an ink pen.

"I went in there—Robeson let me in there and left, you see—and I was ready to do what had to be done. What you and your mother wanted me to do. And then I see him, and he's this punk of a teenager with a dirt ring around his neck and buckteeth, and I think he might have even pumped my gas for me once or twice. He looked like this fellow I'd seen working out at Swifty's."

"That shouldn't have made a goddamn difference," Libby said, surprised by the shake in her voice.

"No," he said. "Probably not. But I couldn't do it."

Libby opened her handbag, searched for her car keys, too rattled to make her hands behave as she fumbled past a hairbrush, a pack of Certs. She could hear the keys jingling, but she couldn't see them. Her bag spilled from her stupid hands, its contents fanning out across the highway. Her keys winked at her from the ground, silver-white in the low afternoon sun. She stared at them. She couldn't find the energy for anything else.

"I'm so sorry," Stephen said. "I was sorry then, too. That's what happened to my hand. I threatened this kid—told him if he didn't get out of town, if he showed his face to you again, I'd kill him. He believed me. He was nothing, Libby; he was a goddamn rube. He almost pissed his pants when I walked in the door. So I got in his face, twisted his ear a little until he moaned. I made him promise. And he did. He kept it."

She took a few steps finally, leaned down, snagged her keys. She could leave the rest of it lying here, she realized. The thought of missing a tube of lipstick later seemed absurd. "I've got to go," she whispered.

"Just a minute, please," he said, touching her shoulder. She cringed and he backed away, but she didn't open her car door. She didn't meet his eyes, either.

"It was impossible to be a man," he said. "I just wish I could make you understand that. I could have beat the kid within an inch of his life, easy. I was scared going over there, but I wasn't scared when I saw him. Not even close. And that's why I couldn't do it."

"That doesn't make any sense," Libby said.

Stephen threw up a hand in frustration.

"He was a kid who'd done bad, and he knew it. What was left? What could I do that would have made a difference? I did what I thought was right, but I paid for it, too. I got outside the jail and slammed my fist into the wall. And then I did it again. I wasn't trying to fool you. I was just frustrated. Because I was wrong either way. Damned if I did it, damned if I didn't."

"Then the choice should have been easy," she told him. "Be damned, and stand by your wife."

He wiped his face. "That's what I tried to do. For the rest of the marriage, Libby. And I failed at that, too."

"Well, I guess that's that," she said. She opened her car door.

"I'm sorry," Stephen repeated. "Maybe it would have been better if I never said anything. Maybe you deserved that from me."

It saddened her to hear it put that way—his uncertainty about what she deserved and didn't—and it saddened her more to think that his secret had perhaps cost them their marriage, flawed as it was. Sliding behind the wheel, connecting her seat belt, she imagined, in brief, another version of her life: one in which she'd returned to this plot of land, walked those old board floors that Stephen had scavenged from the farmhouse she'd so hated. They'd be sanded and stained, and perhaps Jaime's baby would have wheeled his trike across them as he and Sean had done. Perhaps she could have traded one set of associations for another.

None of that was likely, though. And Libby wasn't sure what was worse: the thought that they'd had a chance and ruined it, or that they were too young and foolish to understand that they were doomed from the start.

"I'll see you, Stephen," she managed, and he said something similar back, and then she put the car in drive and pressed the gas pedal. She made a U-turn in the road and took off, leaving Stephen and the contents of her bag behind her, like artifacts from another era.

Before the road curved and her view became obscured, she caught a glimpse of Stephen in her rearview mirror. She wasn't sure what she expected: perhaps his tall silhouette with the sun bright behind him, hand on the dog's head the way he'd once leaned on that stone lion at the Biltmore. That picture of singular maleness, staged for her benefit. But her glimpse—and it couldn't have been more than a flash in her mirror, and maybe she'd only imagined it, anyhow—was of Stephen on his knees, holding open her handbag, gathering its contents. His hands touching her things, the lipsticks and aspirin and other domestic notions. Sunlight not framing him but falling weakly on his slumped back, and even that weight too much to bear. The home awaiting Libby was empty, and the grandchild who awaited her would belong to Jaime and his wife and perhaps even to Stephen before it would belong to her. She knew all of these things. She'd known loneliness and desperation, and she now knew what it felt like to lose her life's one small certainty: that the stranger, the boy, had paid for what he'd done. But she could also take this image home with her, this picture of Stephen on his knees. She would file it away until those days came when she needed it most. It would last longer that way.

• PROOF OF GOD •

When Simon turned sixteen, his father gave him his old car: a red '88 Corvette, just four years off the showroom floor. Corvettes, his father insisted, were the only American vehicle worth a goddamn anymore, and made in Bowling Green, Kentucky, at that. Good for the local economy. Also, as a businessman and a local leader—*a pillar,* he'd say sometimes, if he was shitfaced—looking like a success was important. "I'm a walking advertisement," he'd tell Simon's mother, who'd pretend she hadn't heard the same bellowed proclamation a dozen times already. "Folks see me living high and know I must sell the good stuff."

Good stuff it wasn't. Jefferson Wells owned a small chain of furniture stores with locations in Kentucky and several surrounding states, and what he dealt in could only be called furniture by the most generous of observers: chipboard entertainment centers with plastic veneers meant to mimic the look of wood grain; kitchen chairs with metal legs that would start to bow upon too many sittings. The name of the chain—Wells Brothers Furniture Company—was also crap. Simon's father didn't have a brother. He just thought the name sounded old-fashioned, established, and so he put it on all of his stores in heavy Old West lettering. He told Simon that he might change the name to Wells and Son if Simon minded his p's and q's and got through a business degree at Western, and back then Simon had considered that more of a threat than an offer. He wanted to help the old man sell junk like he wanted a hole in the head.

A few weeks after Simon's sixteenth birthday, some guys from his high school trashed the Corvette. He'd been driving it to school every day, feeling good: folks at Bowling Green High School paid attention when he walked down the hall now; heads turned. One day, a couple of seniors, football players, asked him if he wanted to go down the road to G. D. Ritzy's with them after final bell, and Simon agreed, too dazed to do much more than nod and croak out a "yes." *This is how things change for a person,* he'd thought, walking out BGHS's big double doors with two of the most popular guys at school on either side of him, like bodyguards. He wished his father could see him. They rode in the Corvette with the windows down and the radio blaring Aerosmith; he wouldn't remember the song later, not for sure, but it was one of the ones with Alicia Silverstone in the video, who was, Kevin Britt proclaimed in the car that day, "hotter than sin."

They ate burgers and string fries, drank giant chocolate milk shakes in a dining room decorated with photos of '50s and '60s rock stars. Simon paid. The two older boys talked about Friday's game and about Sheila Foster's enormous tits. "Just wanna get my face between them," Ray Hunter said, putting his hands out in front of him in a honking motion, shaking his face vigorously side to side, so that his considerable jowls trembled. They all laughed. When the food was eaten, Simon dropped Kevin and Ray off back at school, next to Kevin's Pontiac Grand Am—a real clunker—and they raised hands to one another, made promises to do Ritzy's again next week. Simon's heart didn't slow until he pulled off Scottsville Road and down his family's long, paved drive. He'd never been good at making friends. Being with those boys had been a joy and a torture all at once.

The next morning, his father woke him at six a.m. by flipping on the light switch. "Get up," he said, and Simon did. He knew not to make his father say something twice.

Simon found him outside. The sun was just an ember several hills over, and fog clung to the cow pasture like sweat. His car was where he parked it, but it looked like a murder victim, destroyed and decomposing. Unrecognizable.

"Explain this," his father said.

Simon took a few steps forward, then circled the car. None of the glass was broken, or even the headlights, but there were deep gashes in the paint on the doors, the hood, and the trunk. He'd discover later that the culprits had also pulled the old sugar-in-the-gas-tank trick, but what hurt the most—what embarrassed him to the point of nausea—was the graffiti slashed across the hood and trailing down both sides of the car: FAG, over and over again, like a curse. On the trunk, just for variety: RICH FAG. He returned to his father's side.

"Who did this?" his father said.

Simon shook his head.

His father slapped him, a hard blow that almost knocked him off balance. "Jesus Christ," he said. "If this doesn't beat all. Can't you have anything nice?"

"It's not my fault," Simon said.

His father rubbed his lips and stared at the graffiti—that one word over and over, in purple paint, in white. BGHS school colors. He closed his eyes.

"They're just jealous, is all," Simon told him. He looked at that word, the big one on the hood. FAG. The letters were sturdy and authoritative. "They don't like seeing somebody have something they can't."

That seemed to relax his father a little, as Simon had hoped it would. "Well, that goes along with the territory, I guess," he said. "Goddamn shame, though. I ain't growing a fucking money tree back there." He thumbed toward their property, fifty acres of farmland and woods with a small stream coursing through its center.

"No, sir," Simon said.

"You may have to hitch a ride with your mother again for a while."

Simon looked at the ground, rubbing his sore cheek. "Okay."

They went back inside, where Simon's mother was just putting breakfast on the table: bacon and fried eggs, home fries, sliced cantaloupe and tomato sprinkled in salt. Jefferson Wells liked to eat a roadhouse breakfast every day of the week—called cereal "bird food"—and suffered the occasional pain in his left arm that terrified Simon but also delighted him a little. They ate and didn't speak, and Simon's mother chattered cheerily between them, a monologue that required neither response nor acknowledgment. Nobody ever listened to her. When the meal was done, she cleared the dishes and started loading the dishwasher, humming to herself. Later in his life, when she was the only person he could count on to love him—when he realized that she was probably the only person who had ever loved him, period—he'd try to remember details about her, fond memories, things they shared and laughed about. There were devastatingly few. But he'd think about how she liked to sing as she cleaned or cooked, and he understood that she must have had some personality outside the bland housekeeper role she occupied as his father's wife, because her repertoire was diverse and ever-changing, old-fashioned and current: the Rolling Stones and R.E.M., Frank Sinatra, Johnny Cash. She'd loved Simon and Garfunkel, and Simon was already a grown man when he realized that he was almost certainly Paul Simon's namesake—a fact his mother never confirmed and his father would have been furious to discover. One afternoon, when he was still a little kid too young to start school, she'd sung the "Bookends Theme" over and over as she hemmed pants, her voice plain, pleasant: a mother's voice.

On this morning, though, she merely hummed, an empty, cheerful tune meant to soothe his father and reassure them all. Simon felt his father staring at him.

"You aren't—" He paused, mashing a fried egg with his fork, the loose yolk running into his pile of home fries, neon and viscous. "You didn't"—he cleared his throat—"do anything to encourage this, did you?"

Simon knew to shake his head right away. But he thought about it. He was old enough to know what *fag* meant, just like the boys who'd vandalized the car knew. He wasn't sure that he understood what *being* a fag meant, though—if it should be as clear to him as hunger, if it meant that he had to feel only some things and never others—because all of that was mixed up and confused, what could excite or arouse him. None of it made sense.

What made the least sense to him was how yesterday had provoked this. He'd only taken those boys to the place they'd wanted to go, bought them some food, eaten with them, laughed with them. He hadn't touched them or said anything risky. He'd hardly spoken at all. That they were able to pin him with this word, to see something in him that he hadn't gotten sorted out for himself yet, that he hadn't even known he was transmitting— well, it was humiliating. But it also made him afraid. He felt like a wounded animal in a house with a predator.

"Okay, then," his father said, face wary. "See that you don't."

Simon met Marty in one of his classes at WKU: his second go at College Algebra, actually. He wasn't bad at math—wasn't bad at anything he applied himself toward—but college had been good to him, and as long as his father was willing to pay for it, he was willing to take the scenic route to a degree. At twenty-three, then, he was still eighteen credits short of graduating, and he'd be lucky to finish school with a 2.5 GPA. Like it mattered. His father would give him some token position at one of the stores whenever he finished, and Simon thought that they were both eager to postpone that day as long as possible.

Life, for the first time he could remember, was fine. He had a small apartment off College Drive, a generous food allowance, a nice car—another Corvette, black, his high school gradua- tion gift. Not a hand-me-down this time, either. He took twelve hours every semester, the full-time minimum, and always mixed in with his general ed classes something easy and interesting, like Intro to Drawing or Intro to Philosophy. The philosophy class was his favorite, the only class he scored an A in. He'd loved learning about Descartes, with his wild ideas about the world outside yourself, how everything you believe is real could just be the work of some evil genius or puppetmaster. He'd liked Descartes's proof of God, too, though Simon himself had an idea that God was a fairy tale, that dead was dead. God must exist, this Descartes guy thought, because imperfect beings are incapable of imagining perfection. Bullshit, really. But Simon thought about his father sometimes—about how it felt to try to be the son his father wanted him to be, and how that effort made him love and hate the man all the more fiercely—and couldn't help but wonder.

Marty was a freshman. He was a cool guy—good-looking in an accidental, unaware sort of way, easygoing, witty—the kind of person who wouldn't have had anything to do with Simon a few years before but now gave him some respect because he was old enough to buy the beer and flush enough to pay for it more times than not. Gullible enough too, Simon realized. But who cared? The money was his dad's, the good times just as good. And despite all of that, he felt a real connection to Marty, felt that what they had was legitimate. A friendship. He knew that Marty's mother was Mexican and barely spoke a lick of English, that Marty had been teased by other kids when he was little, called a spic and a wetback. "Words their daddies taught them," Marty had said, and Simon commiserated, though his own father's arsenal of derogatory terms and ethnic slurs was just short of breathtaking.

They started hanging out nights and on weekends. Marty had a dorm room free on minority scholarship, but he'd crash at Simon's place most nights after hours of drinking, or smoking pot if they could arrange it. Marty always had those connections. They stayed up till dawn two or three nights a week, sipped beers—Natural Lights when they felt cheap and sloppy, Anchor Steam, Marty's favorite, when they had a bottle of whiskey on hand. They'd try to remember the saying about mixing the two—"Liquor before beer, nothing to fear; beer before liquor, you've never been sicker"—but got the order screwed up half the time and usually ended up doing beer and shots all at once and getting sick anyway. They'd drink and play music; or drink and sit on the front porch of Simon's building, watching the traffic; or drink and walk down to Mickey O'Shea's on Cherry Street, where you could often catch a decent band for cheap on Fridays. Sometimes they'd get in the kitchen together and chef up a ridiculous meal that somehow ended up tasting all right, like the time when all they had was saltines and banana peppers and spicy mustard. They could be together and just *be*, that was the thing. No fake conversation, no showing off or showing up. Simon had never been good with other people, so for something like this to come along—well, it felt fated. Felt like a gift, a reward for suffering so much misery and bullshit in high school.

One morning, on a Thursday—late, though, nearly lunchtime—Simon woke to the smell of cooking meat, the sizzling sounds of breakfast. He'd missed his morning class, Business Ethics, five times now, and he'd be lucky if the prof didn't fail him. Marty was in the kitchen, standing over the stove. He was holding a big chunk of beef with a fork, and he laid it down carefully in the skillet, making the oil pop.

"What's cooking?" Simon said.

"Supper." Marty let the meat sit for just a few seconds, then he rotated it.

"Early for supper." Simon watched the meat cook, his stomach clenching around the alcohol he'd put away last night before crashing: six beers and the four shots of Jose Cuervo he downed for Marty's benefit. He hated tequila.

"We aren't eating it now, dumbass." Marty pulled the meat out of the skillet and set it on a pile of paper towels beside the sink. "I'm doing a roast. It won't be ready until four or five."

Simon went to the fridge and pulled out one of the bottled waters he kept stocked because Marty liked them. He sipped, goose bumps making a trail between his shoulder blades. *You know you're hungover,* he thought, *when even water tastes like poison.* "Maybe I'll have an appetite by then."

"Oh, you'll eat it," Marty said. "This is my mother's roast." He pulled ingredients out of a grocery bag on the counter: several spice containers and a package of bouillon cubes, red-skinned potatoes, a bag of baby carrots, one large white onion, and a bottle of red wine. "You've got nothing in this kitchen, man. I even had to buy a corkscrew." He pulled that out of the bag, too, and waved it at Simon: a cheap one, the kind that looked like a pocketknife.

"I'm not much of a wine drinker," Simon said.

"Thought you rich folks drank this shit every night."

"Dad's more of a beer man."

"Well, you're classy now," Marty said.

Marty started rinsing the potatoes, peeling the onion. Simon had a Crock-Pot, though he'd never once used it—his mother had bought it for him, along with a dozen other household items that had always been in his childhood home but seemed ridiculous in his apartment: a silverware tray; the fuzzy toilet seat cover and matching floor mat; coasters, designed to protect furniture much nicer than the junk sold by Jefferson Wells; a "While You Were Out" phone tablet. Marty piled ingredients into the Crock-Pot, topping the mess off with half of the bottle of wine. "This is good stuff," he said, taking a sip from the bottle. "Thought I'd splurge." He offered the wine to Simon, who waved it off.

"Suit yourself," Marty said. He turned the Crock-Pot's dial over to medium and set the lid on the top. "You're gonna love me in about four or five hours, friend."

Simon looked down at his water bottle. Shocked by that word, *love,* rising so suddenly and casually between them, he admitted the inevitable to himself: he already did.

The rest of the afternoon, they sat in the living room watching a movie on A&E, *Superman,* the smell of roast filling the apartment: rich, earthy. *Love,* Simon kept thinking, panicked, daring himself with the word the way he'd once climbed trees or taken spills on his skateboard. He knew that love came in all kinds of forms and degrees, even though he'd never been on the receiving end of much of it. His father loved him, he knew, in his way: a selfish sort of love, and limited. A love that asked for more than it could return. And his mother loved him, but she was a weak, ineffectual woman, and so her love, too, was weak and ineffectual.

He thought back to that day almost seven years ago when those football players had vandalized his car, branded it: FAG. When you were alone—a loner—you could put a memory like that and all of the insecurities that went along with it somewhere deep within yourself; and you could build walls around it; and you could pretend it didn't exist, at least most of the time. Other people complicated that. Marty made it impossible. Simon didn't know what he was, what loving Marty might make him, but he sat on the couch with him all afternoon, their arms just a foot or so away from touching, and his heart stuttered in his chest, his face and neck burned. In the movie, Superman was flying around the Earth in reverse, fast laps meant to make time spin back so that he could save Lois Lane.

"Hey, there's a party tonight," Marty said. "At the Sig Ep house. Keg passes are five bucks. You interested?"

"You know I'm not into that shit."

Marty sighed and shook his head, and Simon sensed his frustration—a frustration that Marty had managed to keep in check most of the three months they'd been hanging out but still let surface on occasion. "Let me tell you something, man. Something nobody else is gonna care enough to say to you. This ain't a fucking life, what you're doing. This is pathetic."

"You're here, too," Simon said. He wondered, not for the first time, why.

"That's the problem." Marty turned the TV off, shifting on the couch so that he was facing Simon. "It's easy to sit around and drink, and I've been letting you drag me down with you. But that's done. Let's go, all right? What do you say? Besides, I'm making you dinner."

"All right," Simon said. He looked at Marty's profile—the dark eyes and hair, skin the color of pie crust, the too-big, crooked nose. And he understood two things: that he wouldn't be able to go on much longer being with Marty this way, pretending brotherhood when he wanted something more; and that Marty surely, almost certainly, didn't feel the same way in return.

•   •   •

Simon paid the keg fee for them both at the door. He would have done it anyway—that was how he and Marty usually worked—but he felt especially obligated since Marty had made dinner and bought all of the ingredients, including the fourteen-dollar bottle of wine. And Marty hadn't exaggerated: the roast was incredible. They'd both eaten long and well, until Simon's stomach went from drunk-sick to food-sick. He would associate that feeling of fullness bordering on illness with Marty long after. But at the party, as they started to wander around the Sig Ep house, he only thought of his father, who complained about indigestion a couple of evenings a week. *Best thing a man can do,* he'd tell Simon, mouth smiling but not his eyes, *is pour a beer on top of it.*

Simon decided to do just that. He took a plastic cup from the guy manning the door—a pathetic thing, really, not much bigger than a Dixie cup—and got into the keg line, which was at least fifteen deep.

Marty handed him his cup. "Fill me up, would you, buddy? I'm going to go mingle a little."

Simon wasn't surprised. He nodded.

"Don't run off." Marty smiled—all those white, straight teeth, with one crooked eyetooth to make him approachable—and raised a finger. "This is the night everything changes for you, friend."

Simon laughed and turned toward the keg. The line was moving. "Get out of here."

He hated parties. Hated the music—the mix of hip-hop and Nashville country, whose only shared characteristic, as far as Simon could tell, was their god-awfulness. Hated the look of a fraternity house—how a once-decent building could be transformed into a stinking hole that somehow still attracted the good-looking girls. Green, threadbare carpet, stained here and there with beer or urine or puke that had only been soaked up, not properly cleaned. Pictures of the fraternity members, framed by year, matted loosely and hanging askew over a fireplace. Maybe he hated the girls the most—not all girls, just the ones who showed up to places like this one with their fake tans and oily mascara, their belly button piercings and side fat. The girls who got in free, cut to the front of the keg line without hearing boo from anyone, then complained all night about the taste of beer the whole time they were getting drunk off of it. Those girls.

So he noticed the girl in line ahead of him, the one with the brownish-blonde hair—dishwater blonde, his mother would've called it—who waited her turn instead of cutting ahead, which she easily could have done. She didn't look any different from the rest of them; she had streaky highlights and heavy eyeliner, wore a bright yellow T-shirt that hit her mid-stomach and blue jeans cut low enough that you could see the sharp angles of her hip bones jutting out over the waistband. But she *seemed* different. Quieter, not so desperate to be on exhibit. Across the room, two drunk girls—they barely looked old enough for college—were touching each other's faces and giggling, while a handful of frat boys tried to goad them into kissing.

"These keg parties suck," Simon said, waving his little cup. He felt mortified as soon as the words came out of his mouth—what the hell had possessed him to talk to this girl?—but she laughed, kindly, and shook her head up and down with enough exaggeration that Simon could tell she had been drinking.

"You got that right," she said. Her voice had the pronounced lilt of a local, oddly comforting. The line moved again and she took a step forward, awkwardly, with her body half-turned toward him. He could sense her uncertainty, so similar to his own, and he could tell that she wanted to keep talking—was relieved to hear a friendly voice—but was unsure about his intentions, whether he'd meant to engage her or had just tossed out a random observation for anyone within earshot. It touched him.

"Simon," he said, and he stuck his hand out. He was intoxicated by his own confidence.

"Fish," she said, shaking it, and she blushed right away. "Well, Felicia's really my name. But my nickname is Fish."

"Who calls you that?" Simon said. He regretted it immediately, because the question came out disbelieving instead of charming, like he suspected she'd given herself the name. And the look on her face—the cute blush turning to scarlet, the line appearing suddenly and decisively between her eyebrows—told him that she had done exactly that. Reinvented herself.

"My friends," she said. "My friends here call me that."

"I like it," Simon told her.

"Sure," she said. Sarcastically, Simon thought. She looked ready to turn around—they were almost to the keg now—when Marty returned, sipping from a bottle of Corona.

"Where did you get that?" Simon said.

Marty took another swig, a lime wedge sliding up the neck and down again. "Some guys," he said, shrugging. He noticed Fish. "Who is this?" he said, looking at her and not Simon.

"Felicia," she told him. Her cheeks were pink again, the smile back on her face. Simon could see the shift in their attention away from him and toward each other—monumental, it felt, disastrous, like the landscape around him was changing, the ground under his feet disappearing, sliding out from beneath him.

Then she left the line, and the keg was in front of him. He stared at the spout.

"Move it," someone yelled from behind.

"Whoa," the guy manning the keg said, putting his hand out like a goddamned police officer. "What's this two-cup shit?"

"I paid for two glasses," Simon said.

"All right," the guy said, so self-important that Simon wanted to punch him. "This time, okay. Next time, maybe not."

Simon put his cup under the spout, flipped the nozzle, and watched the beer trickle out, slowly filling his tiny glass. He filled Marty's, too, and when he turned, the inevitable: Marty and Felicia were gone. He got out of the line and found an empty corner to stand in.

"Two-fistin' it," a guy said, stumbling past him. He gave Simon a shaky thumbs-up. "Right on."

Simon looked down: his cup, Marty's cup. He sipped from one, then the other. In no time, the beer was gone. The young girls were kissing now as a group of boys cheered them on. Their movements were exaggerated, grotesque: heads swaying back and forth more than seemed necessary or even sexy, tongues flicking out at each other between kisses. He held the empty plastic cups in his hands and looked at the keg line, which was deeper than ever. Fucking ridiculous. And Marty, nowhere to be seen. He tossed the cups behind a recliner and left.

He stopped by Greenwood Liquors on his way back to the apartment, bought a bottle of Bushmills, and woke up to Marty's voice: "Hot, man."

Simon was sweating. He thrashed under the covers, feeling close to suffocating. His alarm blinked a single-number time,

5 or 6 a.m., he couldn't make it out, and he saw the empty Bushmills bottle on his nightstand.

"What?" he rasped.

"She was fucking hot," Marty said. "Goddamn."

I'm going to die, Simon thought. He needed to vomit, but he wouldn't—couldn't. He was going to drown in his own chest, with the taste of old whiskey and red meat in his throat. He was going to die.

At some point—then or later, he didn't know—he was rolled over, so that his chin hung over the edge of the bed.

Daylight. He blinked, eyes gummy and itchy. When the world came back into focus, he saw red: a pasta pot on the floor, last night's dinner a churned mess inside of it. He closed his eyes, sure that he was going to puke again.

The only person who'd ever know the facts of what happened three nights later in Felicia's dorm room—the facts, though not actually the truths behind them—was Simon's father. Simon had known that his father would have the power and smarts to help him, but he'd also sensed, on a level he didn't even care to acknowledge, that his father would understand. Would forgive him and maybe even support him in a way he couldn't have done had Simon confessed to something else. Telling him the sequence of events ended up being the easy part. Simon could think of it all like some story he was making up, or the plot of a movie, and just cling to the chronology when no other connections sufficed: *We were bored, had nothing better going on. Marty told me that she was easy, that he could get me laid. We'd talked about maybe driving out on Windsor Road, where they're clearing land to*

build that new subdivision, and do a campfire or something.
Marty put his sleeping bag in the trunk of my car, and I threw
in a couple of blankets, and we just went.

The truths, though—those he kept to himself. He couldn't
explain to his father what it felt like to wake up Friday afternoon, after the party, and listen to Marty tease him about getting drunk and sick and how Simon was lucky that Marty was
home in time to roll his dumb, plastered ass over. What it felt
like to listen as Marty gave him every sick fucking detail about
his night with Felicia: "We went to her room, and Jesus, dude,
I didn't even have to play nice. She didn't put on CDs or burn
incense or any of that dumb shit girls do when they're trying to
talk themselves into it. She was out of her shirt before the door
closed all the way."

And he could never, never tell his father the next part of the
conversation—how his face must've given away some of what he
was feeling, because Marty looked at him strangely, and Simon
was sure that Marty had finally figured out how he felt about
him, that there was a side to their friendship he'd been ignorant
about all this time. So when Marty spoke—when he asked Simon, "Have you ever been laid, man?"—Simon was so shocked
that he shook his head *no*, which was the truth. He hadn't.

"Jesus," Marty had said. "Goddamn, I'm sorry. I've been a
jerk."

"It's no big deal." He turned on the TV, but Marty shut it off.

"No, it is a big deal." He put a hand on Simon's knee. "We're
gonna fix you up, though. You don't worry about it."

Simon felt like crying: his head howled, his stomach was rot-
ten, and he just plain *hurt*, inside out. He'd been lulled by the
contentment of the last few months, tricked into thinking that

his life could be different and better, and now he was in hell. "Please, just leave it alone."

Marty got quiet then, but Simon knew that the conversation wasn't over. So he felt no surprise when Marty approached him Monday afternoon, looking like he'd thought hard and reached a difficult decision. "Felicia," he said. "Felicia'll do it."

"Do what?" Of course he knew.

"She'll fuck you."

Simon tried to laugh. "What the hell? Did you ask her?"

Marty shook his head. "No, but if we go over there, she'll do it. We just gotta get her a little drunk first, but she won't need much convincing."

"You're crazy," Simon said.

"No, I owe you," Marty told him. "You've been good to me. Let me do this for you, okay? It ain't that big a deal. That's the first thing you need to realize. You've got this shit built up so big in your head that you're paralyzed."

"It's not really like that," Simon said.

Marty picked up his cell phone. "Trust me." He flipped the receiver open, scrolled through his number list, and looked at Simon, lifting his eyebrows. Not getting laid—that was one thing: Marty could understand that, could even commiserate. But not *wanting* to: that was something else. Simon nodded.

"This time tomorrow," Marty said, smiling, "you'll be a stud."

Marty tried calling her around four, but her roommate told him she was out running or something, he'd tell his father early the next morning, weeping, on the edge of hysterics. This was later, after, and the streetlights on the way to his father's house had all been on their yellow caution sequence, as if none of the regular rules applied at such an ungodly hour. *Then she had to meet some guys about a group project, wouldn't be back till late. Marty said that we should just wait and surprise her later on. So we went down to the corner store and got some beers, then hung out at the house for a while.*

They bought tequila, too, and a bottle of peppermint schnapps that was on the bargain rack, plus some of those watermelon-flavored shots that cost two dollars apiece and came packaged like test tubes. They drank. Simon didn't want to. Since Friday morning he'd been in horrible shape—throwing up every couple of hours, feeling a kind of trembling ache that reminded him of the flu but was hideously worse, like a gunshot compared to a bee sting. Friday night he was just about convinced that he needed to be in the hospital—he almost certainly had alcohol poisoning—but he couldn't bring himself to go, knowing that his father would find out and push him with a million different questions and scoldings. So he'd lain in bed and suffered, and by Saturday night he was able to choke down a bowl of Campbell's Chicken & Stars without getting sick. Sunday he was still dizzy and weak, but he felt close to normal otherwise. Except for the depression. He'd been sad in his life lots of times, but this was different. This was nothingness: a total vacuum of hope. He'd awakened in the middle of the night at one point—Friday or Saturday; they blended together—and thought about killing himself. The idea was a relief but little more, and if he could have reached out and pressed a button and had it done, he would have. He didn't have the motivation to do anything more than that.

He drank Monday night because he felt weighed down by in-evitability, and he didn't know another way to disconnect from what was about to happen. He wasn't going to be able to have sex with that girl, he was sure—not with Marty watching or pre-tending to sleep on the other side of the campfire, maybe not at all. Even if he could, though, what would doing it accomplish? Marty wanted this for him—had gone out of his way to arrange it—and that hurt more than an outright rejection would have.

"What are you thinking right now?" Marty asked. Night had fallen, and they sat on the porch of Simon's apartment house, passing the bottle of schnapps back and forth. The blankets and sleeping bag were in the trunk. A Durex Ultra Thin condom, one of Marty's, was in his pocket.

"I don't know," Simon said.

"That's okay." Marty rocked his lawn chair back, tipped the bottle into his mouth at the same time. "I was a mess my first time. I was fourteen and she was sixteen, lived one street over in my neighborhood. She was my sister's friend."

Despite himself, Simon felt a cold excitement. He sat very still, the blood pulsing in his temples and his groin, making his body, still feverish from his illness, thrum like a giant, beating heart.

"We'd been building up to it, you know. Second-base shit, but I didn't know what the hell I was doing, of course. I was just grab-bing her tits and trying to kiss her and grope her like they do in the movies." He laughed, and a car passed by on the street ahead of them. "So when we finally got around to fucking, she pretty much took over. It was wild. And I wanted her all the time after that. It was like the first time you—I don't know—eat a steak or smoke pot. It's so good you don't know why you waited so long to try it."

"You didn't wait that long," Simon said.

"Nah." Simon could hear the pride in that one syllable. "I've never been too patient." Marty flipped his phone open and looked at the time. "It's eleven, friend. She should be home by now. You ready to cruise?"

"As I'll ever be," Simon said, his skin burning.

Marty's fingers grazed his arm in the dark. "Just chill out, okay? You're gonna love this."

Simon closed his eyes and focused on the sensation of Marty's fingers. "Okay," he whispered. This would be over in a few hours, no matter what happened. He clung to that.

Felicia's room was on the seventh floor. Keough Hall was female-only, and male guests weren't allowed up after eleven on weeknights, but Felicia had shown Marty a back way you could access through the common laundry room. Simon was out of breath after two flights—the alcohol had hit him harder than usual, and he was light-headed—but they couldn't have used the elevator without getting spotted by the rent-a-cop at the front desk. "Almost there," Marty kept saying. He was small and fit—he'd walked onto the soccer team in August, then dropped out a month later—and he laughed the whole way up, never once needing to rest. "Save some energy, big guy."

By the seventh floor, Simon realized that his left ear was ringing. He took a deep breath.

"No more stairs," Marty said. "She's just down the hall."

"Give me a minute," Simon told him.

Marty waited, and when Simon was feeling better Marty

handed him the tequila bottle. "One to grow on," he said. "And go wash your face."

Simon took a long, shuddering drink, swallowing past the oily taste he hated. He handed the bottle back to Marty and went to the restroom, hoping he wouldn't run into anyone. The bathroom was empty. He bent over the nearest sink and splashed water on his face, ran it through his short hair, took slow drinks of it by sticking his mouth right into the flow. He didn't look in the mirror. He had his father's face: the heavy eyebrows and full lower lip, the broad nose that made him—made both of them— look slow and mean. He didn't need to see that face right now.

In the hallway, Marty was holding the tequila bottle, now empty. "No worries," Marty said, voice thick, like his tongue was too big for his mouth. "She'll have something."

She'll just say no, Simon thought. His relief was instantaneous. Why had he assumed she wouldn't? No booze, no chance.

"Ready, man?" Marty said.

Her door was heavy oak—decorated, like the other doors on this floor, with two construction-paper clowns with googly eyes: "Steph" in block letters on the left, "Fish" on the right. They'd forgotten about the roommate, he realized; there was no way this could go down the way Marty had envisioned it. Too many unconsidered factors. He knocked on Felicia's door himself, three hard raps. He smiled at Marty. And after a pause—a bar of light appearing on the floor in front of them—the door opened. Felicia stood there, the room behind her empty. Simon could see that she had been sleeping.

"Marty?" She smiled in a confused way, looking from Marty to Simon and back again, loose ponytail swinging. She had on a tank top—no bra—and light cotton pajama pants with a drawstring waist. The pants legs were long, and Simon could see her finely shaped toes sticking out from beneath the material, nails a glossy bright blue. "What are you guys doing here?"

"Can we come inside?" Marty said.

She hesitated. Only for a second, but her eyes met Simon's, and though she never stopped smiling—a confident, breezy college girl's smirk, the one she even knew to call upon in her half-wakefulness—he sensed her unease, and shared it.

"Okay," she said, and Simon also saw what Marty was too drunk to notice: the pretty blush on her cheeks, the naked hope. Whatever she'd told Marty about their night together—whatever she'd even told herself—she'd slept with him because she liked him and wanted him to like her back. She would do whatever Marty asked of her.

Marty gave her a quick kiss on the cheek and crossed the room in two good strides, plopping down on what had to be Felicia's bed. The space was small, with identical desks and metal wall lamps, cheap chests of drawers—they could have come from the Wells Brothers showroom—and closets with no doors. Felicia's bulletin board was covered, every inch, in photographs of bright, tanned girl faces, a collage interspersed here and there with cutouts of fish—some real photographs from magazines, some cartoons. There was a stuffed fish on her bed, too: fluffy and colorful, with a zippered pocket. Simon took a seat at the roommate's desk.

"So what are you guys doing?" she asked again.

Marty shrugged. He got up from the bed and started wandering around the dorm room, checking the fridge, pulling up the corner of the roommate's mattress. Then he grinned, grabbed the stuffed fish from the bed, and unzipped the front pocket, jamming his hand inside. He pulled out a little bag of weed and a package of rolling papers.

"Bingo," he said.

Felicia grabbed at the bag, and Marty yanked it out of her reach. "Come on, give it back," she said. "That's got to last me until I get home again, and I don't usually do it here anyhow. The smoke detectors are really sensitive."

"Let's take off, then," Marty said. "We thought about camping out over on Windsor, close to where that drive-in movie used to be."

"I don't know," Felicia said, plopping down on the bed and pulling her legs up under her, Indian-style. "I have class at nine."

Simon noticed Marty looking at him. "We'd have you back in plenty of time," he said.

She laughed. "Are you crazy? It's already midnight."

Marty sat down beside her and leaned close, pushing her hair over so that he could kiss her neck. Simon's chest tightened, his breath cut short and painful—but there was an impatience in this pain, too, a kind of reluctant desire that was more potent for being wrong, so clearly counter to everything Simon thought he'd discovered about himself. He watched, and Marty brushed his lips lightly against her skin, raised his chin, murmured something into the cup of her ear: Simon couldn't make out what. Marty moved his hand to her stomach, working his thumb under the fabric of her tank top; from across the small room, Simon could see her chest expand with a quick breath, stomach withdrawing from Marty's touch. She looked from Marty to Simon, eyebrows knitting together.

"Skip," Marty said, loud enough this time that Simon could hear.

She sighed in an exaggerated way, leaning away from him, back against her cinderblock wall. "I can't camp, guys. If I miss my psych class again, my grade's going to drop by a letter."

Simon felt his chest loosen, his forehead cool. His relief was so powerful that it flooded him like adrenaline, and maybe that's what it was: a high, the high of realizing he had a way out. He stood. "Let's go, Marty. She's right. It's late." He added: "We could camp for real this weekend. Maybe drive out to Dale Hollow or something."

"I'd be up for that," Felicia said.

"Goddamn." Marty waved his arms in an exasperated way. "Seems like the harder I try to have a good time, the harder people make it. You two belong with each other." He rose and started for the door, a show that Simon knew to take for what it was: just bravado. Marty was always making grand exits, grand pronouncements. Especially when he was drunk. Last month, when they were drinking at Mickey O'Shea's and listening to the Friday band—Hard Knox, they were called, a name that Marty had declared was "straight-up retarded"—he'd waited for a pause between songs, a lull after the clapping, to yell in the bar-quiet, "Christ, you suck!" Most guys doing that would have gotten their asses beat. Marty got some cheers, a high five, and a halfhearted retort from the lead singer: "Not cool, man. Grow up."

It was conviction, Simon decided. Even the conviction to be a drunk asshole got you farther than none at all.

"Wait," Felicia said now, rising before Marty could swing open her door. She picked up the bag of weed, dangled it between her thumb and forefinger. "Don't run off. I can't camp, okay? But you guys can hang out here for a little while."

Marty motioned to the ceiling. "What about the smoke detector?"

She waved him back into the room, to her bed. He relented, smiling, and once he was seated, Felicia began a series of operations that had the air of ritual, oft-repeated and perfected: she went to the windows and turned the handles, pushing them out and open; then she unplugged a box fan that was propped up on her roommate's dresser and moved it to the windowsill, replugging it and cranking it on its highest setting, air blowing outside. She grabbed an aerosol can of air freshener, sprayed a little near her door, and sat it on the floor by her bed where she could grab it in a hurry.

"That's worked in the past," she said finally. "I usually do this at my friend's apartment or at the park, but we should be okay here."

"You sure?" Simon said. That beautiful feeling of relief from before had dissipated. The air freshener, some generic floral scent, sat heavy in the air and metallic on his tongue: mockingly cheerful, nauseating.

Felicia nodded, already smoothing a rolling paper out on some kind of monster textbook, shaking out a neat mound of bud, working the joint between her fingers and thumb and sealing the edge with her saliva. She twisted the ends expertly, a useless sort of grace that Simon couldn't help but admire. His father looked this way when he was operating the standard shift on a car, his mother when she was peeling potatoes or taste-testing a pot of her vegetable soup. And Simon himself could handle a batting cage like a major leaguer, his swings as fast and uniform as crochet stitches.

Felicia leaned close to the fan, lighting the joint. She puffed it twice, the way rich men tasted cigars in the movies, and exhaled into the blades—the hum made staccato, the funny robot sound Simon remembered from his childhood.

"Don't hog," Marty said, taking the joint and Felicia's spot near the fan. Then Simon had his turn, and he got a bit of pleasure from the intimacy of sharing this with Marty, their lips on the same soft twist of paper, the same smoke in their chests. He finally exhaled, light-headed. This seemed like a potent enough batch, which didn't surprise him: rich girls always got their hands on the good stuff, paying too much for it and not even knowing the difference. They were scoring from friends of their parents, not rednecks and black kids. No visits to bum-fucked Egypt to buy from a pregnant teenager, no drives down to the housing projects, where you were more likely to get approached about a rock than a dime bag. And Felicia had money, he could tell. It wasn't a matter of how he'd seen her dressed, either—the labels and nonsense, the dainty diamond earrings—and it wasn't her room, which was no more impressive on Felicia's side than on her roommate's. The same Target bedclothes, rumpled and overdue for a wash. Similar posters and makeup cases, shower caddies and rubber flip-flops. Near-identical Nike tennis shoes lining the closet floors: an old pair with some wear still in them, a newer pair for going to class. *I've measured my life in tennis shoes,* Simon thought then, remembering some poem he'd read in lit class.

No, it was something else. She had the manner of a girl who'd been denied nothing, whose rebellions were safe because they were sanctioned and contained and easily remedied, even if the worst happened. Her parents would have been the type to say, "If you drink too much, give us a call. You won't get in trouble. If you're going to have sex, let us take you to the doctor. You won't get in trouble."

Three hits, a fourth, a fifth. He was feeling it.

"Really, though, this stuff is fascinating," Felicia was saying, hand on the giant textbook. "I'm thinking of changing majors."

"Fascinating," Marty echoed.

It went on like this for a while, and then there was a second joint, and Simon was feeling tired, blurry. He faded out for a moment, and when he found his focus again, Felicia was on the bed with Marty on top of her, pajamas down around her knees, Marty between her hips. Music was playing lowly, some female-wailing stuff that Simon didn't recognize or much care for, and Marty's quick breaths were easily audible above the brash acoustic guitar chords. His head bobbed above her. Her fingers curled loosely in his dark hair. As Simon watched, Marty leaned down and lifted her tank top over her head, and she curled her shoulders up to make it easier for him, breasts so small that they barely stirred with the motion.

Marty finished, lifted his head, and saw Simon watching them. Simon's terror was instant but dulled—out-of-body. He felt himself slowly turning to the window, focusing on it. He had been looking that way all along. He'd been sleeping.

"Hey," Marty said. "Your turn."

This was the part he'd try to explain to his father—how nobody ever just lost everything at once, or crashed, or went screaming over an edge. No, you nickel-and-dimed your way there, you took a step and felt the ground solid beneath you and then thought another was safe enough, or maybe somebody was pushing you the whole way, little pushes, the kind that felt more like reassurances than actual pressure.

He managed to get the rubber on, and Marty was pulling him over before Felicia fully registered the change, before she had a chance to replace her clothes or otherwise react. She grabbed at her sheet, not saying no, just making a low moaning sound that could have been fear but seemed less certain somehow: *unnnnnh*. Her breath quickened, yet still she didn't say anything. Simon waited for her to stop him, to ask what the hell was going on, but her eyes flitted from his to Marty's and back again, frightened but resigned, as if she knew that all of this had been decided beforehand and her vote was futile against the majority's.

He was inside her when she started to cry.

"No," she managed now. "Off. Get him off me, Marty, please, get him off me."

Simon felt Marty's hand on his lower back, intimate as a kiss would have been. "She's just wigging," he said. "Hurry up."

Simon did, no longer stimulated but sick to his stomach and moving against her, rubber tugging uncomfortably, dangling, but neither Felicia nor Marty seemed to know the difference. She was moaning again, a chilling sound, and Simon had decided that he just needed to stop, collapse on top of her—like Marty had done, with the final thrust, the hard exhalation—but out of nowhere her moans turned to shrieks, screams, and he and Marty were both trying to cover her mouth before they all got caught. He felt something pushed into his hand, the stuffed fish with the zippered pocket, and he held it to Felicia's mouth, Marty's hands pressed on top of his own, like men making a pact. "Felicia, come on, shut the fuck up," Marty was saying when Simon pulled back, tugging his jeans over his hips and zipping his fly closed. He'd yanked off the rubber and stuffed it into his pocket before Marty could see that he'd wasted it, still thinking that way despite his panic, because all of this seemed disconnected from the kinds of anguish he was used to feeling. They'd figure this situation out—calm Felicia down, talk her out of reporting them to the R.A. or the God-forbid campus police—but then he'd have the rest of his life to contend with, the awkwardness with Marty, and maybe Marty wouldn't want another thing to do with him. Felicia was thrashing, sheets working themselves into ropes beneath her, and her leg pistoned out, catching Simon square in the kneecap, pain quick and bright as a lightning flash.

Marty pulled back, removing the pillow, and she screamed. "Goddammit," he said, covering her mouth again, but she was bucking now, panicked, and Simon could see that Marty was going to lose hold of her. So Simon leaned down with him, holding his weight over her legs and midriff, heart rebounding in his chest like a boxer's speed bag. "Jesus," Marty grunted, trying to keep her head still under his hands. "Fish, get it together. I thought you were into it, you stupid—" She jerked, and he pushed the stuffed fish against her face. "Fuck." He looked at Simon, his own face pale, the flesh under his eyes, always dusky, now heavy as graphite. "She's having a fucking conniption," Marty said breathlessly. "Fuck, fuck, I don't know what to do, man."

The rest happened very quickly. Simon would have trouble making sense of it later, because he'd remember Marty saying, "Shhh, honey," and "Please, kid, we're just gonna leave," and "Calm down, calm down," but she must have already been still by that time, and how long? He didn't know. At some point he realized that there wasn't any more tension in her legs, no resistance against him, and he said to Marty, "Hey, is she okay?" and Marty didn't answer him. And Simon knew.

"Oh my God," Simon said. He was sitting on the end of the cheap twin bed, and he thought her leg was maybe still under his hip, but he was so numb all over that he couldn't be sure. It struck him that he should try slapping her cheeks or checking for a pulse; or CPR, maybe that was what they needed to do. They'd have to call 911, come up with some kind of story. Get an ambulance here. Put the whole thing into more capable hands. But that was all balanced by fear—for her safety, sure, but mostly for himself—an emotion so pure it was primal.

"Marty," Simon found himself saying, voice cracking. "Marty, what if she's dead?"

Marty threw the pillow on the bed and wiped his hand on his jeans. He stared at Felicia and then the door, holding a finger to his lips. Neither moved for a moment, waiting, the only sounds their hard breathing and the fast hum of the box fan.

"We've got to do something," Simon said finally. "Right? Right?"

"Yeah," Marty muttered. He was crying, visibly desperate, and Simon ached because there wasn't an acceptable way for him to give comfort right now, or to take it. He ached, too, because this was Marty's fault, all Marty's fault, and it wasn't fucking right for him to worry right now, for him to feel anything for a man whose concern for Simon only extended as far as Simon's ability and willingness to keep him drunk. It wasn't right. But Simon couldn't change it.

"What do we do?" he asked Marty.

Marty started searching the room like he had hours before—pulling out drawers, checking the closet shelf—and Simon stood and backed toward the door, not sure what to ask, what to think. All at once Marty stopped, bent down, and grabbed the can of air freshener that Felicia had left on the floor. Before Simon could object, he stalked over to Felicia's bed and sprayed her down with it, dousing her face and her crotch most heavily and using his free hand to wipe sweat off his forehead. The air was thick with the floral scent from before, pink-smelling and nauseating, and Simon wasn't surprised when Marty turned and retched into a wastebasket.

"Oh God, what the hell," Simon said, but he guessed he understood.

Marty came to him and shoved the can into his hand, and Simon looked at it stupidly. "English Rose Garden," it said. There was a picture.

"Now you," Marty told him, hand still on Simon's.

He did it as much for himself as for Marty. He knew this was true when the time came to make it final, and he didn't trust Marty not to bungle it. One of them would have to go get the car, which was parked a half-mile up the way on Cherry Street, and pull it around for the other; that was the only way they stood a fighting chance of clearing the campus before the fire alarm engaged. The other had to stay here and make sure the fire caught, that the sprinklers couldn't soak it too quickly, and Simon was already seeing how that could maybe be done. But they had to get on it.

He pressed the keys to his Corvette into Marty's hand. "Get the car," he said. "You remember where it is?"

Marty nodded, visibly relieved. "Yeah," he said. "Sure."

"Wait for me at the corner, okay? I'll be there as soon as I can." It occurred to him that Marty could take his keys and drive off, leaving Simon stranded, but he decided that he'd have to risk it.

"I'll be there," Marty said, and Simon hated the sudden bloom of hope on his face. Worse than that, he hated the tone of that *I'll be there,* as if this were a favor and not simply

Marty's part. The whole time they'd known each other, Marty had managed to live off of Simon's good graces and make it seem that Simon was the one owing. He was dismayed by his own stupidity.

But Marty chose then to grab Simon, to hug him, and Simon felt the press of Marty's wet cheek against his neck. Simon hadn't hugged a man before—couldn't remember the last time he'd touched his own father, and only then for a hard handshake, or to have his back pummeled when a piece of food went down his windpipe—but he knew that this contact went on longer than it should have. Marty whispered *Thank you,* still holding him, and Simon squeezed back fiercely, not wanting to let go but afraid not to be the first to pull back. So he did.

"I'll be there," Marty repeated, and in a second he was gone.

Simon pulled Felicia's desk chair into the middle of the room, grabbed the roommate's comforter, and worked as quickly as he could, bunching the material tight around the two sprinklers. He knotted loose spots with rolled-up towels, and the mass looked bloated and misshapen when he was finished, like a toad-stool growing out of the ceiling, or a malignant mole. His shoulders ached when he jumped down, and he thought, absurdly, of Michelangelo.

He emptied the can of air freshener, spraying the textbook that Felicia had used for rolling joints—already that seemed like weeks ago—and placing it on the bed next to her. He tossed the empty can there, too, figuring it would explode when things got hot enough, help finish the job. He stayed as far from the body as he could, and only years later could he acknowledge that this wasn't just nausea or guilt, an irrational fear of the dead—it was the fear that she *wasn't* dead, that he'd get near enough to see her chest rise, and then what would he do? Could he stop what had been put into motion? Did he want to?

He started the fire with Felicia's lighter, the one she'd passed around with the joint. And when the first blue-white flame burst forth, he ran, the flames fast and hot behind him, the fire more successful and quick than he realized it could be. He exited the room as quietly as he could, pulling the door tight with the faintest *snick,* and then he dashed across the hallway and toward the stairwell, praying that he could get there without a door opening, without crossing the path of some girl on her late-night bathroom break. Then he was in the stairwell and circling down, no longer trying to soften his footfalls but taking the steps two and three at a time, almost falling, regaining balance, picking up speed again. In a minute or two he'd reached ground level and was sprinting down the hallway and back through the laundry room's back entrance, into the night. He ran so hard that his thoughts stayed behind for a little while, and he was filled with a beautiful energy and exhilaration—like he could lap the Earth in reverse, spin time back, change everything.

Marty was waiting when he reached the corner, the Corvette's engine humming smoothly in the stillness. The car was in motion before Simon could slam his door closed.

Two hours later, he waited for his father's judgment.

"This Marty kid," he said. "Will he keep his mouth shut?"

"I don't know," Simon said. He'd dropped Marty off in front of his dormitory barely an hour ago. They'd passed fire trucks on the way, and Marty looked shocked when he saw them, as if he hadn't really believed that Simon would finish what he'd started.

As if the flashing lights and sirens were more proof than he could stomach.

"Well, that's out of your hands now," his father told him. "It might not matter if you keep your mouth shut and don't give anything away. You say nobody saw you? Tell the truth, now."

"Nobody," Simon said.

"That's good." His father rose, started to pace their living room. "That's good," he repeated, rubbing his face.

"I used a condom," Simon said.

"What did you do with it?"

"Put it in my pocket."

His father stopped. "Still there?"

Simon nodded.

"We'll burn it," his father said. "And your clothes, too, while we're at it." Simon stripped down to his boxers and waited as his father went to the kitchen for a garbage bag. His father returned and held the bag open wide. "Anything else?"

"The lighter's in my pocket with the rubber," Simon said. He tossed the bundle in all at once.

His father looked in the bag. "Christ, kid. What a fucking mess."

"I'm sorry, Dad." And he was, though this sorry was much bigger than his father, or himself. A sorry he couldn't really contemplate just yet, tired as he was, numb as he felt. But he'd feel it later, Simon was sure. For the rest of his life, he'd feel it.

"Well," his father said. "A little late for sorries." But he crossed the living room and kissed Simon's forehead, holding his face roughly with his big hands, then rested his chin on Simon's crown. "Your mother loves you," he said.

Simon knew what his father meant. "I know."

"Go to bed, son. I'll take care of it."

Simon did. He went upstairs to his childhood room—the one his mother kept dusted, just in case he decided to come home for a night or a weekend. He climbed into his bed and the sheets were fresh, because his mother changed them once a week whether the bed had been slept in or not. His body ached—from tonight and from the culmination of the last several nights—and the soft mattress was a blessing, as were the familiar shadows of his childhood room and the familiar beam of moonlight hitting the end of his bed. He felt safe here, which was ironic, because he'd *never* felt safe in this house, or loved.

In a few moments, as he was starting to doze, the light in the room changed, started to shift and rollick. Simon sat up and looked out the window: his father was back behind the house, building up a small fire. Flames were already glowing in the center of a neat teepee of wood, and when the last chunks were arranged to his father's satisfaction, he stood, backed away a few feet, and shot a stream of lighter fluid over to the pile. It erupted, beautiful and startling, and Simon's father began to empty the bag, giving each item time to char before adding the next one: the jeans first, then the boxers and shirt. He wadded the bag into a ball and threw that on last.

His father stood back to watch. The flames climbed higher, black smoke roiling at their apex, and as a breeze picked up outside, bits of ash drifted off on a current, down toward the cow pasture, where the new day's fog was already starting to collect. The fire was a neat solution, and Simon knew that his father loved a neat solution. He'd known he could depend on that. He watched as his father crossed his arms, surveying his work and his property—the acreage, the far-off stream—like a king who had seen battle, fared well, and returned home to enjoy his spoils.

His car was vandalized a second time five years later.

He'd been at Mickey O'Shea's all evening, alone. The trial was long enough ago—coming up on three years—that most people didn't recognize him. Most people—even the angry ones who'd protested the day he was acquitted, marching with signs outside the courtroom, a hundred different photos of Felicia plastered everywhere, inescapable—wanted to move on at some point, to forget that bad things happened. Simon wanted to forget. But he came to this bar anyway, a few times a month, and thought about Marty, who'd broken down in the middle of class the day after Felicia's death and ended up confessing to everything.

For all the good it did.

Simon left Mickey's at one a.m. and started down Cherry Street to the gravel lot where he always parked the Corvette, remembering all of the times he'd cut this same path with Marty, both of them shitfaced but not bellowing idiots, usually just deep into some conversation about a movie or their folks or whether or not God was real. Marty believed in God. "Got to," he'd told Simon one night. "What else is there?" And Simon, knowing he'd bothered Marty by suggesting that there wasn't anything else, that there was nothing, was happy that he could tell him about Descartes.

"Proof of God," Marty had said. "I like it."

"So do I," Simon had told him.

He was glad he'd given Marty that—a gift, he thought now, something to carry him through difficult times. Marty had made a deal in the year after Felicia's death, pleading guilty to rape and conspiracy to rape, plus manslaughter—a twenty-to-life sentence—in exchange for testifying against Simon in the big trial. Simon had done what his father had told him to do: *Stick to the alibi and don't waver, no matter what the police tell you, no matter what evidence they produce.* As it turned out, despite some bluffs during the interrogation, they had nothing: no witnesses, no DNA, only Marty's testimony, ever-changing. In the end, Marty managed only to implicate himself.

Simon approached his car in the dark.

He felt the crunch of broken glass beneath his hiking boots and knew what had happened before he saw it: every window of the Corvette smashed, the headlights and taillights busted, cracks pounded into the black fiberglass with what must have been a baseball bat, or perhaps even a mallet of some kind. No graffiti this time, but the message was just as plain as that long-ago FAG had been, just as accurate. He realized that whoever had done this could still be lurking somewhere nearby, holding the weapon, and he stood as still as possible, listening.

Nothing. There was nothing.

He pulled his cell phone out of his pocket and opened it, the small screen glowing like a distress signal in the middle of so much darkness. He dialed his father's number and waited, thinking, as he always did when despair wanted to settle on him, of Marty's touch that night: the heat in his wet cheek, the only proof Simon had ever needed, the only higher power.

• ACKNOWLEDGMENTS •

I owe first thanks to my parents, John and Ruth Goddard, for their goodness, their smarts, and their unfailing support. And then I owe thanks to all of the wonderful teachers who took over where my parents couldn't follow, first at University of Kentucky and later at Ohio State University: Lee K. Abbott, who never worried; Kim Edwards; Nikky Finney; Michelle Herman; and Lee Martin. I can never repay any of you; I can only try to pass your generosity and wisdom down to my own students. And then there's Erin McGraw, who will always be my teacher but has also become a beloved friend: a distinction I hardly deserve but am grateful for.

To the three wise women, Jolie Lewis, Danielle Lavaque-Manty, and Margot Singer: infinite love and gratitude. These stories are better for your insights, and I am better for your friendship. Special thanks, too, to Nancy Zafris, whose support has been ongoing and extraordinary.

I am still stunned by the good fortune of receiving a Rona Jaffe Foundation Writers' Award. Thanks to Beth McCabe, Robert Wishnew, and the Foundation. Thanks also to the Kentucky Foundation for Women and the Sewanee Writers' Conference for much-needed early support.

Gail Hochman, my agent, heroically endured my always-jangly nerves. In Sally Kim I found an editor of rare insight, generosity, and overall loveliness. I thank my lucky stars every day for both of you.

I want to thank, too, my students, friends, and colleagues at Denison University, Murray State University, the Sewanee Young Writers' Conference, and UNC Greensboro.

Last thanks—for-the-rest-of-my-life thanks—go to Brandon. You deserve more than this line. You deserve more than me. But I'm glad that you don't realize it.

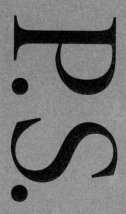

About the author

About the book

Read on

Insights,
Interviews
& More . . .

A Conversation with Holly Goddard Jones

by Nancy Zafris

Morgan M. Miller

This interview was previously published in The Kenyon Review, *January 2007 issue, as part of a series of conversations with authors, funded in part by a grant from the National Endowment for the Arts.*

NANCY ZAFRIS: It's a pleasure catching a talented young writer as she begins what is sure to be a stellar writing career.

HOLLY GODDARD JONES: Thanks so much.

NZ: The *Kenyon Review* story ("Life Expectancy," Winter 2007) is your second publication, I believe?

HGJ: "Life Expectancy" was what I think of as the second acceptance of my real writing life. Before the piece in *Southern Review*, there were two others: one in *Limestone*, which is published by the

English Department of University of Kentucky, and one in *American Literary Review*. Both were fine experiences, the first a result of a reading I gave in Lexington as an undergrad, the second—and this was the best feeling—plucked from *ALR*'s slush pile. I don't regret the publications because they were signs of encouragement at times when I needed encouragement, and because the editors both times were wonderful to work with. I don't think I'm that same writer, though, and those stories aren't part of the collection I completed in grad school.

NZ: Tell me a little bit about that collection.

HGJ: There are nine stories at this point, though I may need to cut one for length. I tend to write long, and many of my stories cover spans of years. I like seriousness and sweep and—to one of my professor's constant aggravation—exposition. When I talked about my "real" writing life, I was referring largely to my discovery that short fiction could be generous and soulful, in the manner of Andre Dubus, and not just a brief glimpse at some moment or idea. I think the collection reflects that interest. I wrote "Good Girl," the *Southern Review* story, at the beginning of my second year in graduate school. It was a leap forward for me. I learned something about the writer I wanted to be in the process of getting that story down, and I can look back at it ▶

> 66 When I talked about my 'real' writing life, I was referring largely to my discovery that short fiction could be generous and soulful, in the manner of Andre Dubus, and not just a brief glimpse at some moment or idea. 99

A Conversation with Holly Goddard Jones
(continued)

two years after completing the draft and think, Yeah, that's not bad. That's still me.

NZ: "Good Girl" is a fabulous story. When I read it in *Southern Review*, I was awestruck. It's a story that follows a retired widower, Jacob, in a tiny town. His son is in trouble with the law. What is it in that story that is the "writer you want to be"?

HGJ: Well, the generosity of vision is certainly part of that. I was told a few times that it could be a novel—frankly, I get that a lot about my stuff—but I knew that it wasn't a novel. I didn't need 250 pages to tell Jacob's story, so why force it? A short story can have something of a novel's breadth and richness, and it can also address heartbreak—frankly and painfully—in a way that maybe a novel isn't always meant to do. Let me qualify that. I'm not willing to spend years working on a book that doesn't have hope at its center, and as a reader, I don't tend to enjoy that sort of extended abuse, either. I think stories can go darker, or at least I'm willing to go darker in my stories.

NZ: That's very interesting. I've never thought of that before. I think you have something there. I wouldn't classify "Good Girl" as a dark, depressing story, however. Would you?

> ❝ I'm not willing to spend years working on a book that doesn't have hope at its center.... I think stories can go darker. ❞

HGJ: I think it's hopeful in the sense that Jacob is a truly decent man. He's flawed and he probably ends up making a bad choice at the story's end, but he does so thinking that it's his duty as a father to put his son first, no matter what that ends up costing him. And it does cost him, which is the depressing part. It hurt me to leave Jacob with so little at the end of that story because I cared about him. If "Good Girl" had expanded into a novel, maybe I wouldn't have had the fortitude to finish things that way, even though I'm fully convinced that any other ending would have been insincere.

NZ: "Life Expectancy," the *Kenyon Review* story, takes on a high school coach embroiled in an affair with one of his students. Both "Good Girl" and "Life Expectancy" seem written by someone much older, if I may for the moment equate age with wisdom. Where does someone in her twenties come by such maturity and empathy? Most writers your age seem to stick with writing about people similar to them.

HGJ: That's really kind of you. I feel sometimes like I have a better lock on the empathy part than the maturity part, so I'm grateful. If it's there, and it's authentic, I can't say for sure what inspires it. I suppose it could have something to do with the fact that ▶

A Conversation with Holly Goddard Jones
(*continued*)

I married young—I was nineteen—and went through most of my undergraduate years as a married woman, living on financial aid and trying to figure out how to do laundry at the same time I was figuring out how to be a wife. But actually, it makes more sense to me that my interests as a writer come from the same place—the upbringing and experiences and personal quirks—that made me decide, rightly and luckily, that getting married when I did would work for me.

NZ: Did you get feedback when you were younger—teachers commenting on your "insightfulness," for example?

HGJ: I remember my father telling me I was "tenderhearted" when I was a little girl, and that seems right. It's the tenderhearted part of me that wants to tell stories, and the characters who inspire that quality are folks like my dad—good people trying to figure out how to do the right thing in difficult circumstances.

NZ: Does that mean you're more at home with older characters?

HGJ: I'm interested in characters who have dignity and intelligence, even when they're making self-destructive choices. You can have dignity and intelligence in

66 It's the tenderhearted part of me that wants to tell stories. 99

a twenty-something narrator or even in a teenage narrator, and I write about those characters, too, but there's not the same sense of permanence. The stakes can't be as high. Part of Theo's tragedy in "Life Expectancy" is that he's beyond the point of a true fresh start. He set certain things into motion when he was younger—marriage and parenthood, his career—and those things can't be undone, even if he's unhappy.

NZ: So are stories about younger characters fated to have less consequence?

HGJ: No, certainly not. It's a different sort of consequence, though. My younger characters are often forced into an unwelcome understanding about the adult world—a preview of that permanence I mentioned before. I'm fumbling my way through a novel right now, and recently I was writing some exposition from the point of view of a teenage girl who realizes that her mother's boyfriend is being kinder to her, in giving her money for a school trip, than she and her mother deserve from him. And I felt heartbroken for that man, that minor character who will probably never make another appearance in the book, because I knew something about his goodness and his sadness. ▶

A Conversation with Holly Goddard Jones
(*continued*)

NZ: You write a lot and you talk a lot about goodness and good characters. I'm sensing Erin McGraw's influence on you. She was one of your professors, right? I love her narratives because she's one of the few writers whose riveting and usually very funny stories ask such an intelligent question—what does it mean to be good, to lead a good life?

HGJ: I adore Erin. Yes, she was one of my professors at OSU, and she is as wise and sharp as her fiction, which is saying a lot. A person might be tempted to think that her dialogue is too brilliant and snappy to belong in a strictly realistic fictional world, but if you've ever been engaged in a conversation with her, you know that's not the case.

NZ: That's absolutely true. My son adores having a conversation with her because she can get him laughing so.

HGJ: Oh, same here. She's been an enormous influence, a mentor, and also a very good friend. I hope she wouldn't mind my putting it that way.

NZ: Let's call her right now and ask. Sorry, not a very good line. Erin would have come up with something much better. So, Holly, stories in the *Southern Review* and the *Kenyon Review* . . . that's pretty impressive. I know other young writers out there must be reading this and going CONNECTIONS! Let's deal with that. Did you go right through the slush pile?

HGJ: With "Good Girl," I was going to the slush pile with a recommendation from one of my professors. I'd workshopped the story at OSU, and she was supportive of it. She told me where to send it, and she told me to use her name. I'm not sure what the process was once the story got to the *Southern Review* office, though. "Life Expectancy" did bypass the slush pile, as you of course know, because I was lucky enough to take a workshop you offered in Columbus.

NZ: Gee, those people living in Columbus, Ohio, get all the breaks. It's not fair.

HGJ: Oh, yes. It's the hub of all things literary. In all seriousness, though, that was a great opportunity. I went into it after you'd rejected another one of my stories, so I had no clue what to expect.

NZ: Please, don't tell me it was that *Southern Review* story.

HGJ: No, it was the one about the boy whose father takes him to see a peep show. ▶

A Conversation with Holly Goddard Jones
(continued)

NZ: Oh, I remember. Yes, that was nice story. But there was something about the way you structured it that seemed kind of academic, all the images in place or something.

HGJ: I actually got a lot of grief about the structure of that story in workshop, so I thought at the time that I was resisting some of the conventions of condensing the chronology, having a traditional boom-boom-boom story arc. I think that image thing you refer to was my way of trying to justify the other, less "academic" elements, like the leaps forward in time. It was a good lesson. I've done a lot of revising to that story since then, and—maybe doggedly on my part—it's still one of my favorites in the collection.

NZ: When I saw that you were in the weekend workshop, I immediately identified you with that story because of your unusual name, Jones. Good, though, good for you. I'm glad you're sticking with the story. Never shy away from revision. I'll be anxious to read the final version.

HGJ: Thanks. I hope you get the chance to.

NZ: There were a lot of good writers in that weekend workshop.

HGJ: Definitely.

NZ: And all of them living in Columbus! Why don't they ever submit? There were more than a couple stories that with a little rethinking and revision could get into *The Kenyon Review* or the equivalent.

HGJ: I have no idea! I just consider myself lucky that you liked the story enough to have me formally submit it.

NZ: We're so delighted to have your story. I hope people take note. Don't you have another story coming out this fall?

HGJ: Yes, a rather long story called "An Upright Man," in *Epoch*. Michael Koch, the editor, read "Good Girl" in the *Southern Review*. He solicited a submission, which I was all too happy to provide, because I think *Epoch*'s a terrific journal. Each acceptance has been an enormous honor. [Editor's note: The day after completing this interview, *Gettysburg Review* accepted another story of Holly's.]

NZ: That's great. That's how it should work. First thing, though, you've got to have a great story. So getting down to the actual story level, how do you think getting an MFA has helped you?

HGJ: There are so many ways, and I can't say enough in praise of the program at ▶

A Conversation with Holly Goddard Jones
(continued)

Ohio State. I didn't know what an MFA was until a couple of months before I started applying to schools, and even then, I didn't really think there was much I could formally learn about creative writing. I'd taken workshops as an undergraduate, and there wasn't a lot of emphasis on craft at that level. It was all about conversation and inspiration and support—wonderful, of course—but I didn't know what exposition was, for instance, or the many complexities of point of view. So one of the first things I learned in grad school was a vocabulary. It was empowering. I learned how to revise my work, which was critical, because I'd despised the revision process before. I think you can get good drafts down using pure instinct, but it takes a more conscious knowledge of craft to be any good at revising, and I'd lacked that before.

NZ: So inspiration and talent gives birth to the story and knowledge of craft takes over in the revision?

HGJ: That seems to have been my process, anyway. I know that revision became a lot easier and pleasurable for me when I was able to consciously consider issues of structure or point of view.

NZ: Speaking of craft issues, I'm curious: Do you write more often in first person or third person?

66 I think you can get good drafts down using pure instinct, but it takes a more conscious knowledge of craft to be any good at revising. 99

HGJ: Third. I wrote quite often in first person when I was an undergraduate, and as soon as I started to understand my style and interests more, I became wary of it. For a while, suspicious of it. I've since backed away from that stronger reaction, and the story coming out in *Epoch* is narrated in first person. Even so, I've had to figure out the circumstances in which I'm willing to write a first-person story.

NZ: You mean if you need an unreliable narrator or something like that?

HGJ: Not exactly. I guess it goes back to that whole issue of who I am as a writer, the kind of story I want to tell, the characters who inspire me. For one thing, I think my narrator has to be at least as intelligent as I am, which perhaps isn't saying much, but that's all I've got to go on. No little kids, no empty-headed rednecks. That latter, especially, is what soured me on first-person stories. I write about home, which for me is working-class southern Kentucky, and I have a lot of respect for that place, for the people. I think it's a little too easy to find a voice that doesn't really exist—the rube-with-a-heart-of-gold, for instance—and to exploit that for something fake and degrading. First person can be a window into that, though it's certainly not the only window. ▶

A Conversation with Holly Goddard Jones
(continued)

NZ: There's immediacy with first person, certainly, but third person can be immediate as well.

HGJ: I've found that third person is the point of view that lets me have it all: intimacy, distance, the spectrum of understanding in between. There's so much versatility. Most of the stories in my collection are told in a deeply embedded third person point of view, which allowed me to grasp a character's mental state without sacrificing a more sophisticated authorial voice. What's so rich about that approach is that you can occasionally adopt the point-of-view character's language—just a turn of phrase or a precise way of seeing something—and it's like a direct injection of that character, a spiritual possession.

NZ: Exactly. As a Kentuckian, you must appreciate how Flannery O'Connor does that. She injects their Southernness in a phrase, then backs off. In "A Good Man Is Hard to Find," the Misfit says to the grandmother, " 'I pre-chate that, lady.' " That little word—"pre-chate"—that's all she needed.

HGJ: Oh, it's brilliant. And she does that shift to the vernacular in the narrative as well as in the dialogue: "She wanted to visit some of her connections," for

> Third person is the point of view that lets me have it all: intimacy, distance, the spectrum of understanding in between.

instance. That story moves very subtly between a narrative perspective that's clearly more intelligent than the grandmother, but also at times seems to be adopting her sensibility, relating things to the reader in the way the grandmother might. I love that move. I love when I'm able to pull off something like that. For my novel, though, I'm growing more and more certain that I need a narrative perspective that's capable of greater range and distance, so I'm thinking a lot about omniscience these days. Wondering what sorts of rules I can write for myself.

NZ: Now that you're out of school, I guess you can make up your own rules. How was the MFA program for you in terms of atmosphere? Some people feel crushed socially. Others thrive.

HGJ: I felt the support and the agony, both. I adore my professors, but those relationships were earned, worked on. I wasn't very good at making myself vulnerable when I came to grad school, so it took me a while to understand that the professors wanted to hear from me outside of workshop, to see my interest and excitement. I was afraid to be too forward with my peers, too, and it took a full year for me to participate in the community that extended beyond workshop. It was immaturity, and ▶

A Conversation with Holly Goddard Jones
(*continued*)

I'm still learning. But I have these friendships now, and I'm very protective of them. One of my best adult friendships came out of graduate school, and that's significant because I thought for a long time that I wasn't any good at that. Maybe I'm not, but she puts up with me anyway, and we're able to share the hopes and anxieties of trying to be writers. We both get it. That, and she's a very wise reader with a sensibility that's similar to mine but not troublingly so, which means that she's always able to surprise me with the right kinds of questions and suggestions. Every writer should have someone like that in her life.

NZ: Do you think getting an MFA has any disadvantages?

HGJ: That's an interesting question. The experience was so positive for me, finally—despite that difficult first year, and plenty of difficult moments in the second two years—that my perspective is probably slanted. Some people say there's an "MFA story," but my professors were so different as writers and teachers that I'd be hard-pressed to come away from OSU with a sense that one aesthetic was being advocated. Certain wisdom gets circulated, of course—mostly structural principles—but you get to a point where you know the conventions, you learn to recognize them, and you take them or

> ❝ You get to the point where you know the conventions, you learn to recognize them, and you take them or leave them. ❞

leave them. Maybe others would disagree. I don't think that the credential could really hurt you, though of course it might not help you, and I said from the start that I wasn't going to take out loans to finance grad school. Looking back, I still wouldn't.

NZ: You also mentioned some of the social pressures.

HGJ: Oh yes, that's part of it. I've known people who felt dissatisfied with the grad school experience. It's not uncommon. They feel like they didn't get enough support or like their work was misunderstood. The workshop environment inevitably generates bad feeling, because your ego is at stake, and people have different ways of offering criticism, some less tactfully than one would hope. It all feels very dramatic when you're in the middle of it, and I certainly had my low days. I can imagine a very different outcome for myself if I hadn't received the right kinds of validation at the right times. It's easy to lose sight of what brought you to the MFA in the first place.

NZ: What about networking?

HGJ: Well, it's probably necessary—and smart—and I've benefited from certain kinds of networking. I'm wary of it, ▶

A Conversation with Holly Goddard Jones
(continued)

though, but maybe that's because I'm bad at it.

NZ: Bad at it? You, Holly? This from the woman who holed up in an Austin hotel during the three days of AWP? I'm sure that if you had left the room, you could have networked beautifully.

HGJ: That's exactly what I mean. I wasn't a complete hermit, but yes, I have a difficult time in environments like that. I enjoy the AWP book fair— getting good deals on a stack of journals, picking up a souvenir back-scratcher, you know. But there's a lot of networking, too, and some of it seems so misguided that it's painful. As a grad student, I took a turn manning our department's journal booth for an hour or so, and I had several conversations with writers who were clearly trying to make a connection, plant their names into my subconscious, whatever. And I wanted to say, "Look, you've got the wrong person! I don't have any power or influence!" Or course I couldn't say that. Even if I did have that power, though, I doubt that my judgment would be influenced by such a superficial meeting that has nothing to do with the work itself.

NZ: What kinds of networking have worked for you, then?

HGJ: It's easy for me to sign up for a workshop like the one you offered in Columbus, because it's structured, it has a purpose, because I stand to learn something. I can put my work into the mix, and if I'm not charming—and that's pretty much going to be a given with me—it's not a total bust. I went to the Sewanee Writers' Conference this summer, too, and that was an amazing experience. I met my literary agent there. Again, though, it was very structured, and I functioned best in the parts of day that didn't involve standing around with a canapé and a mixed drink, though certainly I enjoyed the canapés and the mixed drinks. Grad school worked for me because I was able to form bonds with professors who believed in my work and were willing to act on my behalf, and that seemed OK too, because that's what the teacher-student relationship is all about, and because I liked my professors very much. If I'm ever in a position to help my students that way, I'll pass the favors along. That said, I'm not good at that whole "face time" dynamic I talked about before. I don't see the value, the pay-off, in making myself uncomfortable, just to have an awkward one-minute exchange with someone I hardly know. I've done it, and I've realized the futility as soon as I walked away from the person. I don't have the right temperament for that kind ▶

A Conversation with Holly Goddard Jones
(continued)

of interaction. I fret, I dwell. I beat myself up for saying something stupid. So I try to avoid it.

NZ: Those are very wise remarks, Holly. I'm glad you've learned to play to your strengths. One last topic: You've graduated and now you're teaching at Denison University in Granville, Ohio. How's being on the other end affecting your writing?

HGJ: I had to teach one course a quarter through my second two years of graduate school, so I went into the job thinking I had a grasp on how much work was ahead of me: multiply effort times three. I knew it would be hard and draining. I knew that the commute would become a nuisance after a while. I've been surprised, though, by how much teaching takes out of me emotionally. It's not really an issue of "time for writing," because I can always carve out an hour or more a day to spend with my own projects. Logistically, it's more than possible. I take teaching personally, though, which means that I'm always dealing with a lot a disappointment but also a lot of joy. I come home some days thinking, That's it. That's all I've got to give. Of course, I'm wrong. I say that not to set myself up as extraordinarily generous with my students, because I don't think I'm at all extraordinary in that regard. I do believe, though, that some teachers are better at disconnecting their sense of self from their perceived success in the classroom, and I haven't yet figured out how to do that. But that's OK, maybe, because I appreciate the successes all the more for the frustrations. If it came easily to me, I'd suspect that I wasn't working hard enough.

NZ: Let's at least end on one of your successes.

HGJ: I was watching my freshman seminar students give presentations a couple of weeks ago, and I had a moment in class that was sort of beautiful and surprising. They seemed very earnest up there, doing their PowerPoint on rhetorical analysis. Very young and full of good. It was instantaneous: this realization of how much I cared, how much I wanted them all to succeed, in my class but also in life. I couldn't write an epiphany like that into a story because it would seem trite, probably, but I felt it, and it was powerful.

NZ: That sounds a lot like writing— those moments of sudden understanding.

HGJ: My approach to writing is actually pretty similar to my approach to teaching. I figure that it's the passion that makes the lows so low for me, the ▶

> " It was instantaneous: this realization of how much I cared, how much I wanted them all to succeed, in my class but also in life. I couldn't write an epiphany like that into a story because it would seem trite. "

A Conversation with Holly Goddard Jones
(continued)

highs so high. I see it, perhaps incorrectly, as proof of my commitment. I lead a pretty balanced life, the kind of life that would make terrible fiction. I have a great husband who makes me laugh. I have a dog that everyone hears way too much about. I run on a treadmill four times a week. I get along with my folks. The writing's where I go to imagine the loss of those things. It sounds morbid, but it's my way of reminding myself of what matters.

NZ: Thanks, Holly. It's been a pleasure talking with someone so talented and thoughtful.

HGJ: Thank you, Nancy. I'm grateful for the opportunity. ∽

Nancy Zafris, the former fiction editor of The Kenyon Review, *is now the series editor for the Flannery O'Connor Award for Short Fiction. The recipient of many awards, she is the author of three books:* Lucky Strike, The Metal Shredders, *and* The People I Know. *Her website is nancyzafris.net.*

Writing Kentucky

MY KENTUCKY was never the land of thoroughbred horses and mint juleps; neither was it a place where hollow-cheeked hillbillies gathered on the porches of shotgun houses to sip moonshine. There were gentle hills but not mountains, dilapidated farmhouses but plenty of cookie-cutter subdivisions too, and the folks I knew were generally more concerned about the fate of UK's basketball team than a bunch of racing horses owned by rich people.

Those other Kentuckys exist in some form or another, I'm sure—I can vouch now for the mint juleps, at least—but the land of my childhood was neither as romantic as the best stereotypes nor as hopeless as the worst. Western Kentucky isn't properly Southern *or* Midwestern, and it sure isn't Appalachian, though I sometimes run across Bobbie Ann Mason's name in Appalachian anthologies. If I could easily label it and be done, I probably wouldn't have set my entire book there. I certainly wouldn't have felt compelled to anchor these stories in a single, fictional Kentucky town, Roma, that I could populate with as many factories, barbecue joints, and festivals celebrating tobacco as I liked. Those are landmarks of my Kentucky, certainly, but so is Nashville, Tennessee, which figures large in this book as The City, the place to go if you want to be somewhere else. ▶

> " Western Kentucky isn't properly Southern *or* Midwestern, and it sure isn't Appalachian. "

Writing Kentucky *(continued)*

The border between southern Kentucky and Tennessee, like most borders, doesn't mean much unless it's Sunday and you need something alcoholic, or if you're paying sales tax; otherwise, we have towns, accents, and traditions that straddle the state line, even some nicknames: Tenntucky, Tuckasee.

The Kentucky in the pages of *Girl Trouble* is often, but not always, the Kentucky I know from experience. I've never seen a laptop computer in the joint upon which Gary's Pit Bar-B-Q is loosely based, but the spirit of that image is right, as is the character's sentiment, observing the business women "eating thick-piled pork barbecue sandwiches between spurts of typing on their laptops," that "his hometown could move on in some ways and stay the same where it counted." Despite the darkness of these stories, I've rendered the characters with as much empathy and depth as I know how to, so that there's great beauty alongside the ugliness. These characters contemplate the wisdom of Descartes *and* Johnny Cash. There's no reason why they shouldn't be able to.

My own home life was full of such juxtapositions. My parents, a factory worker and homemaker, were (and are) both avid readers, and their books were always scattered around the house, spread open on the edge of the bathtub or on the armrest of my father's recliner,

66 Despite the darkness of these stories, I've rendered the characters with as much empathy and depth as I know how to, so that there's great beauty alongside the ugliness. 99

so that I could dip in and out whenever I liked. I sampled my father's Westerns, horror novels, and true crime books, my mother's mysteries, and these are the kinds of stories I loved before I found my way into reading and writing "serious" literature. We did most of our reading (and eating, for that matter) with the TV on—the TV was a constant—and that meant, for good or ill, that reading wasn't sacred in the Goddard household. It was as comfortable as a casserole, as entertaining as an episode of *Roseanne*. We made a weekly pilgrimage to the library the way some families go to Blockbuster.

But there was no doubt that my parents felt, for all of their nonchalance toward the act of reading, an authentic love of learning. When I would ask my father the meaning of a word, he would send me to the dictionary, which he kept under the end table beside his recliner. "Look it up," he told me, but he wasn't passing the buck; he was interested, and if I begged off or decided "it doesn't matter," he'd find the word himself and recite the definition, which I suspect he already knew, to me. He believed in the authority of a dictionary over his own explanation, and he believed in seeking out, working for, what you wanted to know. I thought often of my father when I engaged problems of intellect in *Girl Trouble*, when it seemed occasionally to me that I could get a lot of mileage out ▶

of an exaggerated regional voice or otherwise exploit my country setting. By that same token, I know I run the risk of falling into the opposite trap, the trap of idealizing—and characters like that Plato-quoting truck driver in "Allegory of a Cave" would support such a reading. Perhaps not, though. When I came home from my first college anthropology course thrilled by an essay called "Body Ritual Among the Nacirema," prepared to blow my father's mind, it took him about two lines to figure out the trick. "This is about Americans," he said in his usual dry way. I was deflated. But not surprised.

I know I run the risk of being labeled a "regional" writer and I'm not sure how I feel about that. I've been told, too, that I'm not regional enough. After reading from "Life Expectancy" at a tour to promote *New Stories from the South 2007*, an audience member approached me to complain that I hadn't written about "the landscape," which is a fair critique. You'll see a bit of landscape in *Girl Trouble*—the view from Pilot Rock, the "tangle of weeds and briars" outside Libby's door in "Retrospective"— but I don't do it generally, or I don't do it out of a need to pay sentimental homage. I like interior landscapes more, the terrain of a complex character psychology, and I hope that I honor where I'm from by acknowledging the hearts and intellects of my Kentuckians

❝ I hope that I honor where I'm from by acknowledging the hearts and intellects of my Kentuckians before I wax poetic about a red barn at sunset. ❞

before I wax poetic about a red barn at sunset.

The Kentucky I know best can't be found in a wall calendar. It's the rusted antenna jutting up over an aluminum-sided ranch house, a gravel driveway with dandelions springing up in the thin spots, a red reflector marking the edge of that driveway, leaning on its metal stem like a dirty lollypop. It's my mother's cornbread: three ingredients, one of them lard, baked to miraculousness in a cast-iron skillet. I write this with the knowledge, exciting but bittersweet, that I'll be leaving Kentucky again in a few months to embark on a new job and life in North Carolina. I'll continue to live here in my fiction, though, as I work on a novel set on the same dark and bloody ground of Roma. It's a land too rich in goodness and sadness and infuriating contradiction to ever be exhaustible, and that's why I love it, and that's why it will always be home. ∾

Kentucky: A West-East Literary Tour in Quotes

"Now that Leroy has come home to stay, he notices how much the town has changed. Subdivisions are spreading across western Kentucky like an oil slick. The sign at the edge of town says 'Pop: 11,500'—only seven hundred more than it said twenty years before. Leroy can't figure out who is living in all the new houses. The farmers who used to gather around the courthouse square on Saturday afternoons to play checkers and spit tobacco juice have gone. It has been years since Leroy has thought about the farmers, and they have disappeared without his noticing."

—Bobbie Ann Mason, "Shiloh"

❝ I read 'Shiloh' as a freshman in college, and it was a revelation to me. You can write quiet stories about regular people from western Kentucky? There's an audience for that? ❞

No list of Kentucky quotes—at least, no list of mine—would be complete without something from Bobbie Ann Mason. I read "Shiloh" as a freshman in college, and it was a revelation to me. You can write quiet stories about regular people from western Kentucky? There's an audience for that? I've taught this story several times, and my students and I often marvel that the lines above are as true now as they were in the early '80s, when the story was published. What I've always loved about Mason is how well she captures a Kentucky that's caught between the old and the new, the tobacco field and the parking lot.

"I'm living in rural Kentucky and teaching my ass off. Why am I the one trying to cheer you up?"
—Ann Patchett,
Truth & Beauty: A Friendship

❝ Is Kentucky Southern? Midwestern? Some indefinable hodgepodge? ❞

Patchett spent a semester early in her career at Murray State University, where I taught fiction writing for two years. Murray, Kentucky, she said in this memoir, was "a dry county with a Wal-Mart, a Dairy Queen, and one excellent doughnut shop." That's still about right, though the doughnut shop is gone. Here she's talking on the phone to her friend Lucy Grealy, the subject of the memoir.

"Alone, I wait for the bus, trying not to notice that everything around me is dying the mildew death, the great cracked concrete standstill that is the case in the Midwest, a land that doesn't know whether to stay or grow, a realm that calls it quits after a Wal-Mart, a Red Lobster, and a winning basketball team, an undecided, unambitious region that ultimately ends up a halfway house for humanity, full of pointless towns and hindered sons. A god needs to drop a bomb here to improve it."
—Joey Goebel, *The Anomalies*

Goebel's novel is set in his native western Kentucky, so I find the label of Midwestern interesting. I can't get a firm consensus on this one: Is Kentucky ▶

Southern? Midwestern? Some indefinable hodgepodge?

"But any place was better than Odair County, Kentucky. She'd hated how everyone there oozed out their words, and how humble everyone pretended to be, and how all anyone ever cared about was watching basketball and waiting for the next Kentucky Derby."
—ZZ Packer, "Our Lady of Peace"

This, I think, represents one kind of conventional take. The narrator calls Kentucky "lackluster" at the beginning of the story, a critique that has always stung me, even lodged as it is in a particular character's viewpoint. The idea of "escaping" Kentucky—or at least my Kentucky hometown—resonates, though.

"And not until years and years later, when I too had become a Kentuckian again, did it come to me that in the Penington Club that night, in my own small and, I trust, ineffectual way, I had aided and abetted a ravishing of innocence: the Californication of Kentucky."
—Ed McClanahan,
"A Misdemeanor Against Nature"

This is from Famous People I Have Known, *McClanahan's hilarious memoir-*

in-essays about, in part at least, how a Kentucky boy finds himself becoming a California New Ager. The quote above is the end of a typical story: hippie walks into a bar, gets accosted by a good old boy, and must silver-tongue his way out of a beating. Only McClanahan makes a surprising connection with his would-be tormenters. Ed McClanahan visited my very first fiction workshop during my undergraduate days at University of Kentucky, so I count him among the Famous People I Have Briefly Met.

"Still, returning to Kentucky is coming home for Ben. Already he feels the change, a new lightness, this shedding of another skin that might or might not be his. He grew up here, after all, came of age in the Appalachian foothills. Family members going back four generations are buried in graveyards around Burkitt County. Their claims on the place make it his too."

—Jim Tomlinson, "Overburden"

Jim's a friend, and he's also represents a certain breed of Kentucky writer: the outsider who became an insider, the native de facto. "Overburden," from Jim's new collection Nothing Like an Ocean, *considers the effects of mountaintop removal in eastern Kentucky.* ▶

" I wonder if there's a living writer who appreciates Kentucky more than Silas House. His books are love songs to Appalachia, honest and affirmative and honorable. "

"When Alma saw the signs announcing that they were about to enter Cumberland Gap Tunnel, her stomach was heavy with homesickness. She fast-forwarded the tape to play a Bill Monroe instrumental called 'Scotland.' It was a full-throttle mess of wild, twirling fiddles, clicking Dobros, and plucking mandolins. They entered the tunnel, and when they burst out the other side in their own home state, the song had reached its fever pitch."

—Silas House, *Clay's Quilt*

I wonder if there's a living writer who appreciates Kentucky more than Silas House. His books are love songs to Appalachia, honest and affirmative and honorable; his characters need home like oxygen, and they're not patronized by their author because of it. ◡

Don't miss the next book by your favorite author. Sign up now for AuthorTracker by visiting www.AuthorTracker.com.